STEPHEN GAVE CARA'S HAND A REASSURING SQUEEZE AS THEY WAITED THEIR TURN TO ASCEND THE GRAND STAIRCASE TO THE ASSEMBLY ROOMS.

"You look beautiful, Cara, truly you do," he said softly, his gaze holding hers. "I am very proud of you."

She studied him for a long moment before her lips curved in a rueful smile. "In my time, your lordship," she drawled, her thick lashes fluttering at him flirtatiously, "a chauvinistic remark like that would earn you a swift kick in the backside. But as I am in your time, I shall thank you instead. I am pleased to think my appearance brings you pleasure."

Stephen wondered how she would respond if she were to learn precisely how much her appearance pleasured him, but he merely inclined his head with mock-gravity. "I have said it before, Mrs. Marsdale, but it would seem it bears repeating," he drawled, raising her gloved hand to his lips for a swift kiss. "I am most heartily grateful we are not in your time."

WATCH FOR THESE ZEBRA REGENCIES

LADY STEPHANIE   (0-8217-5341-X, $4.50)
by Jeanne Savery

Lady Stephanie Morris has only one true love: the family estate she has managed ever since her mother died. But then Lord Anthony Rider arrives on her estate, claiming he has plans for both the land and the woman. Stephanie soon realizes she's fallen in love with a man whose sensual caresses will plunge her into a world of peril and intrigue . . . a man as dangerous as he is irresistible.

BRIGHTON BEAUTY   (0-8217-5340-1, $4.50)
by Marilyn Clay

Chelsea Grant, pretty and poor, naively takes school friend Alayna Marchmont's place and spends a month in the country. The devastating man had sailed from Honduras to claim his promised bride, Miss Marchmont. An affair of the heart may lead to disaster . . . unless a resourceful Brighton beauty finds a way to stop a masquerade and keep a lord's love.

LORD DIABLO'S DEMISE   (0-8217-5338-X, $4.50)
by Meg-Lynn Roberts

The sinfully handsome Lord Harry Glendower was a gambler and the black sheep of his family. About to be forced into a marriage of convenience, the devilish fellow engineered his own demise, never having dreamed that faking his death would lead him to the heavenly refuge of spirited heiress Gwyn Morgan, the daughter of a physician.

A PERILOUS ATTRACTION   (0-8217-5339-8, $4.50)
by Dawn Aldridge Poore

Alissa Morgan is stunned when a frantic passenger thrusts her baby into Alissa's arms and flees, having heard rumors that a notorious highwayman posed a threat to their coach. Handsome stranger Hugh Sebastian secretly possesses the treasured necklace the highwayman seeks and volunteers to pose as Alissa's husband to save her reputation. With a lost baby and missing necklace in their care, the couple embarks on a journey into peril—and passion.

Available wherever paperbacks are sold, or order direct from the Publisher. Send cover price plus 50¢ per copy for mailing and handling to Penguin USA, P.O. Box 999, c/o Dept. 17109, Bergenfield, NJ 07621. Residents of New York and Tennessee must include sales tax. DO NOT SEND CASH.

Time's
Tapestry

Joan Overfield

ZEBRA BOOKS
KENSINGTON PUBLISHING CORP.

ZEBRA BOOKS are published by

Kensington Publishing Corp.
850 Third Avenue
New York, NY 10022

Zebra and the Z logo Reg. U.S. Pat. & TM Off.

First Printing: August, 1996
10 9 8 7 6 5 4 3 2 1

Printed in the United States of America

This book is dedicated to the memory of Marie Vanslate—one of the greatest ladies it has ever been my pleasure to know. I will never forget you.

> *"Hereafter she walks in a loving grace,*
> *In fields of flowers and gowns of lace.*
> *Hereafter she dwells on the gentle plain*
> *Of tranquil beauty, and lack of pain.*
> *Hereafter we will miss her joy, her laughter.*
> *But we know we shall soon see her; hereafter."*

Joan Overfield

One

London, England, 1996

"Bloody damn man!" Cara Marsdale slammed the front door of her flat as hard as she could. The violent action rattled the framed pictures on her wall; but it did little to soothe the foul temper simmering inside of her. Using Eric Thompson's head as a soccer ball, on the other hand, would prove the perfect panacea, and she allowed herself the luxury of contemplating the image before locking the door.

Not that tonight's fiasco was entirely Eric's fault, she admitted, scowling as she draped her jacket and scarf over the coat rack. She'd known he was a self-important stuffed shirt, but she'd thought there was some hope for him. She supposed she should have known better. She'd thought the same thing of Paul, and only look at the hash she'd made of their brief marriage. The thought was depressing, and her already sour mood turned decidedly acrid. It was a pity she wasn't Catholic, she decided, her sherry-colored eyes sparkling with silent laughter. Becoming a nun seemed a better prospect all the time.

She poured herself a glass of wine and was settling back with the latest Stephen King novel when her phone rang. She glanced at the clock, her spirits lifting when she saw it was well after eleven o'clock. A call this late could only mean murder, she thought, reaching out to snatch up the phone.

"Inspector Marsdale," she said briskly, tucking a strand of black hair behind her ear while turning her mind to how quickly she could get to the scene. She had her own car, so she wouldn't have to wait until a unit was made available to fetch her.

"Good evening, Inspector Marsdale," her sister-in-law's cultured tones sounded in Cara's ears, diluting the adrenaline pumping through her. "Am I disturbing you?"

"Miranda!" Cara resolutely ignored her brief twinge of disappointment and settled back against her divan. "How's the mother of my favorite nephew?"

"The mother of your only nephew, you mean," Miranda Bramwell replied with an indulgent chuckle, "and I am exhausted. Marcus has only just gone off to sleep after fussing the entire day. He has a touch of the colic, I am afraid."

Cara twined the phone's curly cord around her finger. "Is he all right?" she asked worriedly, wishing she knew more about such things. Babies and their little ills had never interested her, but her nephew's birth six months' earlier had changed that. Lately she'd found herself stopping in front of baby displays at the shops, staring at tiny pink and blue rompers and wondering.

"He's fine, although I'm not quite as certain his father will survive," Miranda's rueful voice softened the observation. "I managed to convince him we needn't ring the doctor every time Marcus sneezes, but it was a very near thing."

The thought of her usually unflappable brother hanging over a baby cot and fussing like a mother hen brought an uncomfortable lump to Cara's throat. In the past she would have teased Alec unmercifully, but now she understood his anxiety. Had she known Marcus was ill, she'd have done the same.

They chatted another few minutes before Miranda got around to the reason for the late-night call. "I was wondering, are you still having your flat painted next weekend?"

Cara pulled a face at the question. "Don't remind me," she grumbled with an aggrieved sigh. "You wouldn't believe what I've gone through having this done. Redecorating Buckingham Palace would have been easier."

"Alec and I did offer to help you," Miranda said soothingly, although Cara could detect a hint of laughter in the other woman's gentle voice. Her sister-in-law was still very much the Regency lady she'd first met well over a year ago, but Cara was delighted to see she was developing a wry sense of humor. Living with her obstinate, single-minded brother, Cara didn't doubt but that it came in handy when Alec was at his autocratic worst.

"I know, and I appreciate the offer," she said, answering Miranda with a self-deprecating chuckle. "But that would mean *I'd* have to help, and paint fumes give me a pounding headache. That's why I was putting up at your place; to give the smell time to dissipate." She paused as a sudden thought struck her.

"Listen, if there's some problem with my staying there I don't mind checking into a hotel," she said hurriedly. "That's what I was going to do in the first place, and—"

"Don't be absurd, of course you will stay here," Miranda interrupted, her voice firm. "I was only going to say that as it happens we are going out of town next weekend, and so it is just as well you will be available to watch the house for us."

Cara's interest was piqued. Since Miranda had come forward in time last year Alec had been trying to get her to travel outside of London, but with very little success. If he'd convinced her to leave the city, Cara was willing to do whatever she could to help. "Sounds fun," she said, taking another sip of wine and settling back against the divan. "Where are you going?"

"France," Miranda spoke the word with the disdain of someone who still regarded France as an enemy country. "To someplace Alec calls EuroDisney. He claims it is a carnival of sorts built around a mouse. Is that true?"

Cara laughed at the skepticism in Miranda's voice. "That's as good a description as any. Will you be taking the baby with you, or am I going to be granted the privilege of his company?"

"Neither. Your parents have been after us to leave him with them, and Alec has convinced me to agree. And I suppose he is right; they'll see so little of Marcus once they move to Canada."

The mention of her parents' imminent move to Alberta made Cara's spirits droop. While she was delighted they were finally putting some fun in their lives, part of her was already missing them; a confession she'd sooner die than admit. She was almost twenty-eight, she reminded herself sternly, and she could hardly expect Mummy and Daddy to make their lives revolve about her.

"They'll spoil the little blighter rotten," she warned, hiding her unhappiness behind a flippant laugh. "They'll buy him loads of toys and cuddle him every time he so much as whimpers."

"I know, Alec has already said as much," Miranda gave another chuckle. "But I console myself with the knowledge that they didn't do so badly by the pair of you."

"Not so badly by me, at least," Cara interjected impishly, knowing it was expected. "Alec is as spoilt as a prince."

"I shall tell him you said that," Miranda replied and then rang off, but not before reminding Cara that she was expected for dinner the following evening.

After hanging up Cara tried reading, but for once Stephen King failed to catch her up in the terrifying worlds he created. With her parents moving to Canada and Alec settling sedately into married life she would be more alone than ever before, and in the privacy of her own flat she was honest enough to admit the prospect terrified her.

If she and Paul had managed to make a go of it, they might have had a family by now. Their last bitter quarrel had been over the issue of family planning, and his adamant refusal to try for a child.

"It's not as if you mean to be a stay-at-home mum," he'd jeered, eyeing her with icy disdain. "You're never here as it is, and I see no reason to have a kid if you're only going to leave it with babyminders all day. That's what my mum did to me, and I want more for my son."

There were other problems, of course, but in the end it was the realization he wouldn't even consider a family unless she gave up her career that finally convinced her their marriage was a waste of time. They'd separated a few months later, and it had hurt more than she thought possible when she realized that everyone, her own parents included, assumed she had been the one who had balked at the thought of children. Their suspicions seemed borne out a few months later when Paul's new fiancee announced she was expecting his child.

The incident left her aching, and determined not to make the same mistake again. She liked men; adored them, really, but she would never again marry one. There were some women who simply weren't cut out for hearth and home, and the sooner she faced that fact, the happier she would be. Her work and her brother's growing family would be enough to keep her happy, she decided, picking up her discarded book and settling back against the divan's plump pillows. She would dedicate herself to that, and to devil with everything else. Who needed love anyway? She was better off without it.

"You want to *what?*" Detective Chief Inspector Hamilton's voice rose several octaves as he glowered at Cara. "Inspector Marsdale, have you lost your mind?"

Cara gritted her teeth, holding back a flip reply with effort. She'd known Hamilton would oppose her recommendation, but she hadn't thought he would be this much of an ass about it. "I'm afraid I don't understand your objections, guv'nor," she said, forcing herself to keep her tone respectful. "I've worked the prostie beat hundreds of times since joining the force."

"Yes, while you were in uniform," Hamilton huffed, shuffling the papers on his desk. "But you're a member of my squad now, and I'm not about to put one of my men . . . er . . . detectives on the streets to solve a crime. A crime which doesn't even fall under this department's jurisdiction, if I may remind you," he added, frowning at her like a disapproving father.

Cara made another grab for her temper. "Sir," she began carefully, "there's a lunatic out there carving up women, and the fact he hasn't killed one has more to do with chance than intent. The last victim almost died en route to hospital."

Hamilton's expression grew more stern. "I saw the report, Inspector," he said coolly. "You aren't the only one to read flash reports; much as it may please you to think otherwise."

To hell with tact, Cara decided, placing her palms on Hamilton's desk and leaning toward him. "Then you know this man has all the indicators of a serial killer," she said bluntly, holding his gaze with her own. "He's escalated from assault to armed rape within six months' time. Do you really want this department to sit back on their thumbs doing nothing until he starts dumping bodies on the steps of St. Paul's?" Despite her effort to remain in control, her voice rose with fury.

Hamilton drew back in indignation. "There's no need to take that tone with me, Inspector," he said stiffly. "I'm well aware of this department's obligations to the citizens of this city, and I can assure you we will do everything we can to assist in this matter should we be asked to do so."

"But—"

"I should also like to know why you are so interested in this case," Hamilton interrupted. "I've not been informed Sex Crimes has requested our assistance."

Cara gave the paper weight on Hamilton's desk a longing look, and then decided it wasn't worth her job to bash it against his head. She knew that if the thought of her going undercover played havoc with his blood pressure, then what she was about to say would doubtlessly send him into cardiac arrest.

"The request didn't come from the SCU," she said, deciding the old adage in for a penny, in for a pound, never rang truer. "It came from Vikki Norris, a snitch from my days in Vice. Her flatmate, Miriam Wilkes, was the offender's third victim."

As she expected, Hamilton turned an alarming shade of red. "A prostitute rang you?"

"A *citizen* rang me, as is her right," Cara corrected, taking great pleasure in putting the older man in his place. "Or are you saying that because a woman earns her living on her back she's not entitled to police assistance?"

"I was merely wondering why this woman should ring you," Hamilton replied, ignoring the challenge in her voice. "CID has assigned the case a full task force, after all."

Yes, comprised mostly of men, who, however sympathetic they

might be, could never begin to understand these girls the way she did, Cara thought, although she was too wise to say as much. "Look," she said quietly, deciding for one final attempt at reason, "I'm not asking to be sent in as bait, I'm asking to be sent in to talk to these girls. If they think I'm one of them, I could get them to tell me things they'd never tell a copper. I'm not guaranteeing success," she added when she sensed he was weakening, "but at least I could try. We need to catch this man, before he slices another woman's face to ribbons."

There was an agonizing silence before Hamilton finally spoke. "Very well," he said, picking up a pen from his desk. "I'll discuss this with Geoffries in Sex Crimes, and if he's agreeable, I'll arrange for your temporary transfer. You may go now."

"Thank you, sir, I appreciate this," Cara said, although the words all but choked her. Alec was right, she mused, mentally shaking her head as she started toward the door. The bigger an ass a man was, the higher he was likely to rise in the Force. Hamilton would probably end as the police commissioner.

Cara was almost to the door when he called out to her. She turned and gave him a forced smile. "Yes, guv'nor?"

"I meant to ask, how's the Brigg's case coming? The husband is an old schoolchum, and he's been ringing me about the case."

Cara thought of the well-dressed suspect she and her partner had charged that morning. He'd been red-faced and screaming for his solicitor even while they were cautioning him.

"We made an arrest this morning," she replied, fighting back a smile.

"Did you?" Hamilton looked pleased. "That ought to relieve poor Alfred. He's been terribly concerned. Who was it?"

Cara gave up the battle. "It was the husband, sir," she said, a wide grin spreading across her face. "He'll probably get twenty years."

"You should have seen his expression," Cara chortled, as she repeated the story over dinner. "He looked like he was about to choke on his precious school tie!"

"I don't see why he should be surprised," Cara's brother, Alec Bramwell, replied, shrugging as he reached for another roll. "It's usually the husband, isn't it?"

"Usually," Cara agreed, her mirth fading at the thought of the sobering statistics. "But you know Hamilton. He's such a bloody fool he wouldn't recognize a fact if it bit him on the——"

"Cara!" Alec interrupted, giving the chubby-cheeked baby perched in his highchair a pointed look.

Cara accepted the reprimand with a good-natured laugh, leaning over to tickle her nephew's knee. "I was going to say nose," she said, turning back to Alec with a smile. "But even if I weren't, there's no reason to scold me. Marcus is only six months old. I doubt he knows the difference between a proper word and an improper one."

"That's not what the magazines say," a gentle voice corrected as Miranda, Alec's wife, emerged from the kitchen, a platter of fruit in her hands. "According to them Marcus has a full understanding of a variety of words, and he can differentiate between the good and bad ones. Can't you, my darling?" She pressed a kiss to the baby's glossy black curls.

"And she should know," Alec added, his gold-flecked eyes warm as he studied his wife. "She's bought enough of those wretched magazines to open up her own news shop."

"Merely because I wish to educate myself on the art of raising a child in the twentieth century," Miranda answered, setting a plate of grapes and peaches in front of Alec. "Now stop plaguing me and eat your dessert."

Alec eyed the fruit with resignation. "Can't I have some cheese?" He asked, scowling as he popped a grape into his mouth.

"No, the magazines say it is important for a man your age to monitor his fat intake," Miranda scolded, setting down plates for Cara and herself. "Cheese is filled with fat, you know," she informed Cara as she slid on to her chair. "I was quite appalled to learn of it. No wonder the men of my time suffered so from gout and other ills. They were poisoning themselves with all that rich food they ate."

Cara leaned forward, eager as always to learn more of the world Miranda had left behind when she'd been brought forward through time. "What about your husband? Was he fat as well?"

"Her *first* husband, you mean," Alec retorted, his expression darkening at the mention of the man Miranda had married some one hundred and eighty-five years ago. "I'm as fit as I was the day I signed on as an SAS recruit."

"Yes, and I mean to see you stay that way." Miranda teased her glowering husband before turning to Cara. "But to answer your question, Stephen wasn't in the least overweight. He was quite muscular as I recall."

Tempted as Cara was to press for more information, one glance at Alec's stormy expression changed her mind. She knew how much her brother adored his wife, and knew he still hadn't recovered from his fear of losing her to the unpredictable time spell that had transported her from the genteel world of Regency London to the raucous present. Thinking of the time spell made her frown, and she cast the ceiling an apprehensive look.

"Speaking of Stephen, have you decided what to do about the room?" she asked, repressing a shudder at the memory of the painful affect the room had on her the one time she'd ventured inside. "You're going to wall it back up, aren't you?"

Miranda and Alec exchanged a private look before Alec answered. "We haven't decided," he said, his tone wary. "It's been over a year since Miranda's been back, and it hasn't shown any signs of reactivating. We're hoping the spell or whatever it was has faded. On the other hand . . ." His glance slid to his son playing happily with his steamed carrots.

"On the other hand it's best not to take chances," Cara agreed, relieved the room and its awesome power would soon be safely behind layers of plaster and wood. "Do you think you'll have it done by next weekend? I can't say I relish the thought of waking up to find whoever cast the spell in the first place has come forward looking for a bit of fun."

Alec shook his head. "There's no time. With the EOC meeting in London, the entire counter-terrorism unit is on high alert for possible attacks. In fact, if the bloody thing wasn't ending on Tuesday, I'd have had to put off our holiday for another week."

"I shouldn't have minded," Miranda assured him with a quick smile. "I've no desire to see either France or a dancing mouse."

Alec leaned over and pressed a quick kiss on his wife's lips. "You'll love it once we're there," he promised, giving her another kiss before turning to waggle his finger at Cara. "And as for you, I want your word you'll stay out of there, do you hear me? I don't want to come home and discover you've transported yourself back to bloody Camelot."

The thought of entering the pentagon-shaped room with its ancient symbols of power scrawled on the floor and walls turned Cara's blood to ice. "Don't worry, brother dearest," she assured him fervently. "I'd rather face a review board than step one foot over the threshold of that room. I've no intention of going anywhere near it, I promise you."

"Good," Alec gave a decisive nod. "We've mucked about with time quite enough, if you want my opinion, and the last thing we need is to send you careening through the time-space continuum. God only knows the havoc you'd wreak."

Cara poked out her tongue at him. "I shouldn't worry about the fat my brother consumes going to his waist if I were you," she informed Miranda with a smirk. "It's already settled safely in his head."

The next week Cara was too busy to give her conversation with Alec and Miranda other than a passing thought. The Forensic Psychologist assigned to the rapist case agreed with her that their prime suspect was a serial-killer in the making, and she was transferred to the task force. After presenting herself to her new DCI she went into the Debriefing Room where the other inspectors were gathered. One look at their closed, hostile faces and she bit her tongue in grim resignation. So it was going to be like that, was it? she thought, taking her seat at the end of the table.

"Nice of you to join us, Marsdale, now you can show us poor

sods how real inspectors deal with serial offenders." The opening salvo was fired by Kenneth Hughes, an aging detective Cara remembered from her days in uniform. He was small-minded and territorial, and deeply resentful against anyone with more brains and drive than he; which covered most of the department.

"That's all right, luv, glad to be of service," Cara answered cheerfully, and because she knew it would embarrass him and amuse the others, she gave his beefy hand a maternal pat. "Now, let's begin, shall we? What do we know of the last victim?"

There was a brief pause, and Cara could hear the others shifting restlessly on their chairs. She held her breath, knowing the next few minutes would set the tone for the rest of the investigation. She'd already come in with two penalties against her; she was a female *and* an outsider brought in against their wishes, and she knew she'd have to scramble like mad if she had any hopes of winning their cooperation. Finally one of the younger inspectors picked up the file in front of him and flicked it open.

"The victim's name is Mary York, a twenty-five year old prostitute working the leather trade in Soho. She was found laying near a dustbin in back of one of the clubs."

"Was the discovery chance, or was a call received?" Cara asked, although she already knew the answer. She also knew the others expected her to ask for the information, and the little game she was forced to play angered her.

"A call was placed to one of the hospitals," another man answered, also picking up his folder. "The same as the others."

"So either he wants the victims found in time or he's bragging about what he's done," Cara said, nodding. "All right. What about the other victims? Were they leather girls as well?"

There was another pause, and she glanced up to catch them exchanging mortified looks. "Do you mean no one's asked?" she demanded, appalled such an obvious clue may have been overlooked.

"Of course we asked," one of the men, Donnor, Cara recalled, answered with a scowl. "But it took us two bloody days to think of it. *You* tumbled to it at once. I guess that's why you're in

Homicide, and the rest of us are rotting away in CID." This last was added with a deliberate sneer.

Cara could sense their hostility escalating, and bit back a furious curse. Humor them, she told herself, lowering her hands to hide the fact she'd curled them into tight fists.

"Or it could be because I spent three months undercover learning the intricacies of the trade," she said, giving a reminiscent laugh. "You wouldn't believe how specialized the ladies are. They're more organized than the bleeding unions."

As she hoped her wry comment made the others burst out laughing, and in that moment she knew she had them. She spent the rest of the morning pulling information together, and working out a viable plan with the two officers who would be serving as her back-up. Although she wasn't setting herself up as bait that was a probability they had to consider; especially as she was disguising herself as the target he seemed to prefer most.

"I'll never understand you men," she groused, glancing down at her notes. "Who would want to have sex with someone who looks as if they just escaped from a Martian insane asylum?"

"It's the thrill of the thing," Bristan answered, looking thoughtful. "Something on the exotic side can make for a nice change of pace. Men like that."

"Well, you'd never catch a woman getting all hot and bothered over someone with green hair and more make-up than Marcel Marceau," she retorted firmly. "Give us Richard Gere naked and laying on satin sheets, and we'd be in heaven."

"I know my wife would," the second officer, Johns, agreed, grinning. "But she likes a bit of the unexpected as well."

"Good, does she have a leather bustier and a skirt she can lend me?" Cara asked, turning her mind to the practicalities of the assignment. "Punk S and M isn't my usual style, and I'm not certain even Vice has the disguise I'm going to need."

"So buy what you need and submit the vouchers to Admin," Johns suggested, his grin widening. "Just let me go with you when you do. I'd kill to see their expressions when you submit receipts from The House of Leather."

The next night as Cara stood in front of the mirror in Alec and Miranda's bedroom, she decided the penny counters in Admin would doubtlessly swoon once they got her bill. The cost of tarting oneself up in studs and leather was staggering, and she thought she understood why so many of the women who bought the clothes were prostitutes. It was the only way to pay for the bloody outfits.

She turned to one side, scarce recognizing herself in the bizarre creature she saw reflected there. Her face was smeared with paint and glitter, accentuating her high cheekbones and full, pouting mouth. Her eyelashes and eyelids held so much makeup she could scarce lift them, and a paste-on ring sparkled in her nostril. She supposed she could have had the thing pierced, but there was a limit to how far she was prepared to go to do her duty.

Her lean body was strapped into a leather vest and a thigh-high skirt, and her legs were encased in fishnet nylons and a pair of boots with spiked heels that had cost a week's salary. The vest wasn't so bad, she decided, running her hand down her waist. It was uncomfortable as hell, but in it she almost had cleavage; a life's ambition, she admitted, grinning to herself.

"Cara," Miranda walked briskly into the room, her head down as she studied the list in her hand, "I just remembered I put some meat in the fridge to thaw, and I want you to—oh my heavens!" Whatever she was about to say ended in a shriek of horror as she glanced up and saw Cara.

"Like it?" Cara laughed at her sister-in-law's expression. "It's my new look."

"Alec! Get in here now!" Miranda called out in response, her face paling as she continued studying Cara. "You can not mean to leave the house like that," she pleaded, her tone making it obvious she had sincere reservations as to Cara's morals and sanity. "You look like—like—" words failed her, and she fluttered her hands helplessly.

"A trollop from the other side of the galaxy?" Cara suggested brightly, enjoying herself to the hilt. She was willing to believe that nothing in the past Miranda had seen could have prepared her for a punk prostitute.

"Like something out of those dreadful novels you are always reading," Miranda corrected, relief on her face as Alec burst into the room.

"What the—oh," he skidded to a halt, his fierce expression fading into amusement when he saw Cara. "A little early for Carnival, aren't you?" he drawled, placing a comforting arm about his wife's shoulders.

"Alec, this is no joking matter," Miranda raised her face to him, her green eyes filled with panic. "Your sister means to go out looking like that. You can not let her do such a thing. Whatever would people think?"

"Whatever they like, I suppose," Alec soothed, although there was worry on his face as well as he studied Cara. "Are you certain about this?" he asked. "You look precisely like the last three victims."

"That's the idea," Cara turned back to her reflection. "And don't worry, I'm not only going in wired and with back-up, but I'll be armed as well. I'll be fine, I promise."

"Well, that's something, I suppose," Alec said, looking far from convinced. "But a gun won't do you any good if the bastard gets too close."

Cara slid a small black box out of the leather thong strapped to her upper thigh. "That's what this is for," she said, showing it to Alec. "If I can't handle him with my tai qwan do, a zap from this ought to do it."

Alec's brows met in an immediate scowl. "What the hell are you doing with a tazer?"

Cara slid the stun gun back into place. "Protecting myself," she said, giving her bright green wig a final swipe with the teasing comb. "There, what do you think?"

"That it's a good thing Mum and Dad picked Marcus up this afternoon," Alec replied feelingly. "If Dad saw you like this, he'd lock you in that damned room so fast, your head would spin."

The thought of the room made Cara shiver, a reaction she was quick to hide from her brother's discerning eye. "Then we won't tell him, will we?" she said, swinging around to fix him with a warning glance. "Just think of the things I could tell him about you, if I was of a mind."

Miranda stepped between them. "You shouldn't be so hard on your brother, Cara," she reproved in her gentle manner. "He is only trying to help you, and—" she broke off and frowned. "What sort of things?"

"Nothing a wife would find objectionable," Cara assured her with a laugh. "But you know how unforgiving parents can be."

Miranda looked skeptical, but allowed the matter to drop. Ten minutes later she and Alec left, leaving Cara to finish donning her disguise. When she was done she stepped back from the mirror, eyeing her reflection with professional interest. In addition to her leather vest and skirt she had a row of bracelets marching up one arm, while a pair of dangling earrings hung almost to her shoulders. Rings glittered on every finger, and she had so many necklaces draped about her neck it was a wonder she could even lift her head. She looked a perfect tart, she decided with a frown, but something was still missing.

She turned toward the photos of the rape victims, studying each one in turn as she looked for whatever it was she was missing. She was going through them a second time when she saw a familiar symbol dangling from one of the victim's ear. A pentagram. She looked through the other photographs, her lips tightening when she saw that every victim was wearing some kind of satanic emblem.

Terrific, she thought, scowling as she tossed the photo back on the bed. The presence of the pentagrams hadn't been mentioned in any of the reports, which either meant it was considered a coincidence by the other investigators, or no one else had caught the connection. She'd been a cop too long to believe six victims assaulted while wearing the same symbol could be coincidental, and that could mean the rapist was choosing his victims because they were wearing the pentagrams. The realization made her heart race with excitement, and she cast the clock a quick glance.

It was almost four-thirty, and Johns and Bristan were supposed to pick her up at a quarter of five. She had fifteen minutes to ring the shops catering to the occult, and hope one of them was close enough for her to stop by. Or she could ring her friend Jeanine and ask her if—her thoughts slammed to a halt as a sudden image of Alec placing a necklace in the drawer of his desk burst into her mind.

No, she shook her head; she was crazy to even think of it. The pentagram Miranda had been wearing when she'd come forward in time was the key that activated the secret room, and wearing it made one vulnerable to the room's power. But the room no longer held any power, her logical mind reminded her. According to Alec it hadn't so much as glowed in over a year, and even if it was active, she should be safe enough so long as she didn't wear the bloody necklace in the house.

It might work, she decided, nibbling her lip nervously. She could put it on in the car, and take it off before she returned. How dangerous could it be? She vacillated back and forth, torn between the need to do her duty and her fear of the room. When the doorbell rang several minutes later, she was no closer to a decision. Furious with herself for her indecisiveness she turned away from the mirror, scooping up her purse and weapon. She was about to leave when her gaze fell on the photographs.

Six women savagely attacked, she thought, her hands tightening about her weapon. Did she want to be responsible for the seventh? The doorbell rang again, and when she turned to leave the room, there was no doubt left in Cara's mind.

"Well, that was ten hours shot to hell," Bristan grumbled, rolling his shoulders to work out the kinks. "I might as well have stayed at home watching the soccer matches."

"I don't know why you're complaining," Cara shot back, wincing as she wiggled her toes out of the boots. "You're not the one who had to fight off the dregs of society."

"That's true," Johns's dark eyes gleamed with laughter as he shot Cara a grin. "Too bad we're not working Vice, Marsdale, we could have made a dozen collars before tea break."

"Which only proves my point that men are depraved beasts," Cara shot back, although she was privately pleased her disguise had worked so well. Unfortunately she'd been too busy turning down clients to have more than a brief conversation with the other women working out of the smoke-filled club. She had learned, however, that three of the victims shared the same client, and she'd already passed the information on to the other members of the task force. A description of the suspect would be quietly passed to the other prostitutes, and she could only hope their desperation wouldn't overcome their common sense.

"Are we on for tomorrow night?" Bristan asked, pulling up in front of Alec's house on Curzon Street. "My wife's mother is coming for dinner, so I've no objections if you want to have another go at it."

"We might as well," Cara said, working her finger under her wig to scratch her scalp. The damned thing itched like the devil, and she couldn't wait to get it off. "But let's try another club. I don't care if I ever see the Beat It as long as I live."

"I don't know, it had its charms," Johns quipped, getting out to hold the door open for Cara. "Maybe I'll bring my wife there for our anniversary."

"Maybe I'll tell her you said that so she can start divorce proceedings," Cara retorted, albeit with a friendly smile. "Good night, luvs. I'll see you tomorrow."

Her feet were aching so much Cara barely made it up the stairs and into the house. She was tempted to take off her boots the moment she stepped inside the narrow hall but that meant she'd have to sit down, and she knew that if she did that she wouldn't get up again. Cursing at the pain she limped up the stairs, her thoughts centered on getting out of her clothes and into a hot bath. Maybe she'd even start a new book, she thought, smiling with anticipation. She didn't have to be at work until afternoon, and so she could read all night if she wanted.

She was almost at the door of the guest bedroom when the skin at the nape of her neck began tingling. Without pausing to question the warning her instincts were screaming she spun around, bracing herself for a possible attack. Nothing. What the hell . . . she wondered, and then she saw the eerie glow spilling into the hallway from the secret room.

Alec had knocked down the rest of the wall some months after Miranda had returned from her trip into the past, planning, or so he said, to use the space to expand the rooms on the other side of the hidden chamber. Carpet now covered the floor and the symbols had been plastered over, but for some odd reason she could see them shining as bright as if they were newly-painted. Even the pentagram on the floor was visible, and the sight drew her step by dragging step into the room.

The power hummed and sang around her, sounding like the roar of a musical sea, and she thought it quite the most compelling sound she had ever heard. It reminded her of the stories she had heard of the Lorelei, and in that moment she thought she could understand how ancient sailors had allowed themselves to be lured to their deaths on the treacherous rocks. She'd almost reached the center of the room when she remembered the pentagram about her neck.

She stopped, blinking her eyes and shaking her head in an effort to clear her mind. The pentagram was dangerous, she remembered, sweating as she tried to focus her thoughts. She had to get it off, or she would die, she thought, lifting her hand toward her throat. It took every ounce of strength she possessed, and her fingers were shaking as they closed around the pentagram. The metal was warm, almost hot to the touch, and she could feel it vibrating in time with the hum emanating from the walls. The room exploded in a sudden burst of light, and her last thought as the pain overwhelmed her was that if she died before catching the rapist, the bastard would go free. The realization filled her with desolation and defeat, and she gave a cry of fury as she vanished in a blinding flash of white and green light.

Two

London, 1813

"I am sorry, Aidan," Stephen Hallforth, the Earl of Harrington, spoke firmly, his dark blue eyes wary as he studied the black-haired man sitting opposite him. "But my answer is the same as it has always been. I will not sell."

Sir Aidan Quarry remained silent for a moment, the expression on his lean face enigmatic as always. "I see," he said at last, raising his snifter of brandy and partaking of a thoughtful sip. "May I ask why? It's not as if the place holds any particularly pleasant memories for you."

The laconic observation almost made Stephen laugh. Trust Aidan to touch upon that which other men never dared mention, he thought, his lips twisting in a bitter smile. Or at least they refrained from mentioning it to his face. Behind his back he was well aware of the shocked gasps and whispers that still followed him whenever he entered a ballroom.

"All the more reason I should stay," he said, meeting Aidan's gaze with hauteur. "I won't be driven from my home, Quarry; not even by you."

There was another pause, and then Aidan gave a put-upon sigh. "I was unaware offering to purchase a man's home constituted driving him from it," he observed, a glimmer of silent laughter dancing in his silver-colored eyes. "And if the rumors making the rounds hold even a particle of truth, it's not even a home you shall be using overly much once the Season ends. I have heard Lady Felicity cares little for town ways."

The mention of the very respectable lady he had been studiously courting for the past few months drove the smile from Stephen's lips. In the last year he had done all he could to repair the considerable damage done to his reputation after being branded first a murderer and then a cuckold, and his pride was still as raw as an open wound. The realization others were speculating as to whether or not he would offer for the Earl of Berksham's daughter horrified him, and he shuddered to think how the rigidly-proper earl would react should he learn of it.

"The lady's likes or dislikes have little to do with my decision not to sell," he informed Aidan in an icy voice. "And I will thank you not to mention the matter again."

Aidan studied him for a long moment, and then slowly inclined his head. "As you wish, my lord," he said, his manner coolly correct. "I had not meant to impose upon our friendship, I assure you. I shall speak no more if it."

Stephen thrust a hand through his light brown hair, feeling more than a little ashamed of his conduct. He'd known Aidan since their salad days at Oxford, and the baronet was one of the few people who had stood by him during last year's debacle. He hated the thought of offending such a friend, and he hastily set out to make amends.

"You aren't imposing, Aidan," he said with a heavy sigh, "and I did not mean to be so snappish. It is just that after last year I am somewhat sore at the thought of providing the gossips with further *on-dits*."

"An understandable reaction, considering what you endured," Aidan replied, accepting Stephen's apology without comment. "I still can not credit the magistrates believed one word of the lies Proctor was spouting. He must have lined their pockets with a pretty amount of gold to have earned their cooperation."

Stephen didn't reply, the mention of his former wife's stepfather filling him with fury. It had been Elias Proctor who first proposed he marry Miranda and then turn her fortune over to him. He even offered him fifty thousand pounds, enough money to settle the punishing debts Stephen had inherited along with his father's title, and he'd been desperate enough to agree. Then Miranda had disappeared on their wedding night; stolen away by a power Stephen didn't completely believe in or understand, and his nightmarish existence began.

Even now, all these months later, if he closed his eyes he could still smell the stench of the cell where he had been shackled. He could hear the moans and screams of his fellow prisoners, and the awful sound of the carts hauling the condemned to Tyburn Hill. He could feel the heavy weight of the manacles cutting into his flesh, and he could see the expressions on the faces of the lords in Parliament as they sat waiting to pronounce the sentence of death upon him. Had it not been for Miranda's miraculous return he would have hung; he was certain of it. Indeed, she even claimed such was the case, showing him a book from the future detailing his trial and execution.

"Speaking of Proctor, did you know he was back in London?" If Aidan noticed Stephen's silence he was too much of a gentleman to comment upon it. "I saw him at White's yesterday morning, attempting to gain entry. He was denied, needless to say."

The image of the blustering, self-important Proctor being given his *congé* by the club's priggish major domo did much to improve Stephen's mood. "I suppose I should be amazed he has dared show his face in Society again," he drawled. "But the truth is I am not in the least surprised. The man has brass enough for a legion of encroaching Cits. Did he make a scene?"

"About what one would expect from a man of his ilk," Aidan replied with a shrug. "He bullied and threatened, and when that failed he turned his hand to bribery. It was when that failed as well that matters turned ugly. Your name was mentioned," he added, casting Stephen a warning look.

Stephen stiffened at once. "My name? What was said?"

"Proctor accused you of having him blacklisted. He also called you a liar and a cheat, and said that if he sees you again he means to tell you so to your face."

"I am a liar?" Stephen exclaimed in furious disbelief. "That bastard dares cast stones at me after perjuring himself in the witness box?"

Aidan gave another shrug. "As you said, he has brass enough for a legion, and he seems to bear you a deep enmity. I should watch my back, were I you. There is a man who would dearly love to stick a knife in it."

Stephen gave a disgusted snort. "It would be better for Proctor to watch his own back," he muttered, taking a sip of brandy. "Only I won't bother sticking a blade there; I'll slit his damned throat instead."

"Such violent sentiments, Harrington, you shall put me off my feed altogether." A low voice sounded behind Stephen, and he glanced over his shoulder to see Gilbert Holloway, another old friend, standing there.

"Gil!" he exclaimed, setting his glass down and rising to offer the other man his hand. "When did you return to town?"

"Yesterday evening," Gilbert replied with an easy laugh. "I stopped by your house, and was told you had already gone out for the evening. I tried White's but when I didn't find you there I decided to try Brook's, and here you are." He turned a friendly smile upon Aidan. "Hello, Quarry, nice to see you again. I trust you are well?"

"Quite well, Holloway, I thank you," Aidan's greeting was noticeably cooler than Stephen's had been. "And you?"

"All the better for having spent a month rusticating at my great-uncle's estate in Chichester," Gilbert admitted with an easy laugh. "I actually think the old boy is considering naming me as his heir, rather than my dear cousin. What a shame he can't leave me the title, too. I would outrank you." He cast a teasing glance at Aidan.

"Titles are meaningless amongst friends," Aidan replied, the smile on his lips not quite reaching his eyes. "But allow me to be the first to congratulate you should you accede to the title. You will make an excellent viscount, I am sure."

"Thank you, I think," Gilbert replied, inclining his head mockingly. "I shall do my best to follow the example set by my illustrious friends."

An attentive footman brought a glass of brandy for the new arrival, and the three sat sharing a companionable drink. Still Stephen was not overly surprised when Aidan rose to take his leave a few minutes later.

"A previous engagement," he apologized, bowing first to Gilbert and then to Stephen. "I trust I shall see you at the Fulbrights' later this evening?" he asked, addressing the comment to Stephen.

"Yes, I promised Lady Felicity I would be stopping by to claim a dance," he said, hoping Gilbert would not take offense at Aidan's behavior. "I will look for you there."

Aidan gave a curt nod and then departed, his elegant figure disappearing quickly in the crowds gathered by the door. Stephen watched him go, and then turned to Gilbert.

"I wish the two of you would at least try to get along," he said reprovingly. "It pains me that my two oldest friends should be at daggers drawn."

"If our daggers are drawn, the fault is more your dear Aidan's than mine," Gilbert answered with a laugh. "Quarry still hasn't forgiven me for accidentally setting fire to one of his dusty old books while we were still at Oxford."

Stephen vividly recalled the incident in question and bent a stern frown upon his friend. "It wasn't an accident."

"I was merely trying to spare him from being sent down for possessing questionable reading material," Gilbert defended his actions with a shrug. "You should have seen the nonsense those books contained, Harrington; all about mysticism and magic and the devil only knows what else. The dons would have swooned with horror should they have clapped eyes on it, I promise you."

The mention of magic made Stephen think of the secret room in his house; a house Aidan was so anxious to purchase. Could he know of the room and desire its strange powers? he wondered, and then dismissed the idea as ludicrous. Of course Aidan knew nothing of the room, he assured himself. How could he?

Stephen and Gilbert shared another glass of brandy before Stephen reluctantly took his leave. As Gilbert had arrived in town unexpectedly he hadn't received an invitation to the Fulbrights' ball, and he refused Stephen's offer to bring him.

"I'm not a viscount, Harrington," he said with a rueful smile. "And young men without position or fortune aren't so welcome as eligible earls and handsome barons. Besides, I have other plans for the evening."

Judging from the wolfish expression on his friend's face Stephen took that to mean Gilbert had arranged a tryst with his inamorata, and set out for the Fulbrights' on his own. The ball was well underway when he arrived, and he was able to slip in without being announced. He was still uncertain enough of his reception to dread the ceremony of having his name called out by a liveried servant.

It took him several minutes to make his way through the crowd, and he was glancing about him for some sight of Lady Felicity when he felt the light touch of a hand on his elbow. He turned and found the object of his search standing beside him.

"Good evening, my lord," Lady Felicity Barring said, her usually pale face suffused with color. "Have you only just arrived? I did not hear your name announced."

"As I am so shockingly late I thought to keep my arrival as unobtrusive as possible," Stephen replied, taking her gloved hand and raising it to his lips for a brief kiss. His gaze moved beyond her and came to rest on the plainly-dressed woman standing behind her.

"Miss Blackwell," he said, giving her a polite bow. "I trust your cousin hasn't been plagued with any disreputable persons while I was not here to guard her? If so you must give me their names so that I might call them to accounts."

"There is no reason to exert yourself, my lord," Miss Blackwell assured him, the graveness of her tone belied by the mischief dancing in her light green eyes. "I have been perfecting my basilisk-like glare, and I sent no less than a dozen fortune-hunters and rakes in flight. Did I not, Cousin?" She turned to Felicity for confirmation of her story.

Lady Felicity's lips curved in the sweet smile that had first caught Stephen's notice. "I fear a dozen to be a slight exaggeration, Jane," she said gently. "There were only six or so of the creatures, and I am certain it was the thought of approaching Mama and asking her permission to dance with me that sent them packing."

Having already stormed that particular fortress Stephen could well sympathize with the other men's plight, although he was far too intelligent to say so. The Countess of Berksham was even more terrifyingly puritanical than her husband, and he was determined to do all that he could to win her permission to pay his address to her daughter. If the Berkshams accepted his suit, he knew it would mean he had succeeded in restoring his good name. *If* they accepted, he added grimly. So far the countess, while not discouraging him, had yet to accept his invitations to come to tea at his home.

As if privy to his thoughts, Lady Felicity said, "I wished to ask, sir, if you were going to be at home tomorrow afternoon? Mama and I are going to be out paying calls, and she mentioned she was thinking of calling upon you. If-if you do not mind, that is," she added, lowering her gaze in pretty embarrassment.

He had plans to join a friend at Mabton's, but he canceled them without a moment's hesitation. "I should be delighted," he assured her, hoping he did not appear overly eager. "Shall we say four o'clock, then?"

Her hazel eyes flashed up to his face and then she lowered them again. "I shall speak with Mama, but I am sure that will be fine," she said, and then quickly turned the conversation to another topic.

The next few hours passed pleasantly enough for Stephen. He danced the two dances he was allowed with Lady Felicity, and was even able to coax Miss Blackwell out on to the floor for a country reel. He rather liked the blunt companion with her sparkling eyes and cutting tongue, and he thought that if he and Lady

Felicity did marry he would invite Miss Blackwell to make her home with them. His business in Parliament would take him away from Harrington a great deal of the time, and he didn't relish the notion of leaving his wife to rusticate all alone in the country. Not that he thought she would betray him, but after his experience with Miranda he was unwilling to take any chances.

After leaving the Fulbrights' he stopped briefly at another ball, doing his duty with the wallflowers and speaking with several of his friends. He carefully avoided the lively widows and those married ladies who were infamous for their lovers, determined to keep his reputation as spotless as possible. He wasn't about to risk scandal now, just as all his hopes and dreams were about to be realized.

Those hopes and dreams were much on his mind when he returned to his house on Curzon Street several hours later. The house had been built shortly before the Great Fire, and his former bride had it redone as a present for him prior to their marriage. After her disappearance and all the madness that followed, he often wondered what might have happened had she bought him a coach and four instead.

It was while the house was being remodeled that the secret room had been uncovered. The room contained a powerful spell that had sent Miranda hurtling through time one hundred and eighty-four years into the future, and sweeping him into a hell from which he was only now extricating himself. He had promised Miranda to wall the room closed once she had returned to the future, but so far he hadn't done anything about it.

Part of the reason was that he was reluctant to close up the room in the event Miranda should need to return. But the greater reason was that the room with its mysterious forces fascinated him; a confession he would sooner die than admit. He often went into the room and just stood there, dreaming of the strange world he had glimpsed in the magical box Miranda had shown him. He even sometimes fancied what it would be like to travel to that world and see for himself the miracles she had described. Carriages without horses, mechanical devices that communicated with one another across thousands of miles, even, he thought with dazed wonder, a man on the moon.

A sleepy-eyed footman was there to take his hat and gloves, and after asking after the rest of the household Stephen sent the lad off to bed. He liked the sensation of being alone in the house, and he helped himself to some brandy before starting up the narrow stairs. He hadn't take more than a few sips when he reached the top of the stairs, and as was his custom, cast a glance at the secret room. The door was open.

He stared at it in amazement, scarce believing a member of his staff would dare enter the room against his orders. It must have been the new maid, he decided, his lips thinning in anger. Mrs. Finch had said she was proving difficult. He moved closer, debating whether to close the door or go inside when he saw the pale, glowing light spilling out into the hall. The snifter of brandy fell from his fingers and he dashed into the room, his heart almost stopping when he saw the figure laying in the center of the oddly-shaped star.

It was a woman, he realized, his pulses racing as he edged nearer. Or at least, he mused, staring down at the green hair and outlandish clothing, he *thought* it was a woman. At this point he was unwilling to swear if the creature was even human. Certainly she resembled no female he had ever seen. Then he noticed the soft swell of breasts rising and falling in uneven breaths, and swallowed uncomfortably. She was human, all right, and very, very feminine.

His mind reassured on that score, he knelt beside the woman and turned her gently on her back. Beneath the layers of garish paint that would have put a Covent Garden Abbess to shame, he detected traces of an exotic beauty in the slash of cheekbones and lush, full lips. He was wondering who she might be and from what time she had come when she gave a low moan, her head moving fitfully on the dusty floor. Concern banished his curiosity, and he leaned over her.

"Are you injured, ma'am?" he asked, resting his hand on her shoulder. "Do you require—" his words ended in a choked gasp as pain exploded in a sensitive portion of his anatomy. He clutched himself, his vision graying as he slumped over to one side.

"Get off me, you lout!" the woman snapped, adding to his discomfort by giving his shins a vicious kick. She rolled to her knees and then to her feet, swaying slightly as she assumed a pugilistic pose. Stephen gaped at her, too stunned and in too much pain to offer any comment.

"Who the bloody hell are you?" The creature demanded, scowling down at him. "How did you get into my brother's house? And before you say anything," she added before he could speak, "I'm cautioning you that I am a police officer, and anything you say will be held in evidence against you."

A police officer . . . the expression rolled around in Stephen's head. That was the occupation Miranda's lover held in the future. It was like being a Runner, if memory served, and was a position of some authority. He frowned as he remembered something else as well; the face of a woman scowling out at him from the magic box, threatening him with dire consequences if he did not allow Miranda to return to the future . . .

"Miranda!" He managed to get the word past his clenched teeth, although it was both painful and difficult.

He saw the confusion then the hesitation on the woman's face. "What about Miranda?" she asked warily, although she still kept her hands in front of her in a battle-ready stance.

Stephen took another painful breath, lifting himself on to one elbow and eyeing the woman with as much dignity as he could muster. "Did she not return to the future?" he asked coolly, resisting the temptation to check himself to make sure he hadn't been done a permanent injury. "When she vanished once again, I was certain that was what she had done."

The woman's head snapped back at his words. She studied him thoroughly, lowering her hands as she took in his black velvet evening jacket, starched cravat, and cream-colored satin breeches. She next glanced about her, uttering a word Stephen never thought to hear from a lady's lips as she turned in a slow circle. When she next met his gaze, her expression was oddly resigned. "I've done it, haven't I?" she asked, sighing as she pinched the bridge of her nose.

"Done what?" Stephen discovered that if he did so very carefully, he could move, and he rose unsteadily to his feet.

"I've come back in time."

The stark statement brought Stephen's head snapping up, and he studied her in astonishment. It was one thing to suspect a truth so incredible it defied logic, he realized, but it was another to have those suspicions confirmed quite so bluntly. He took a deep breath, allowing his pulse to stead before speaking.

"Yes, it would seem you have," he said, his voice calm despite the dozen different emotions rioting in his head. "Might I ask from where and when? Are you from the future my wife . . . Miss Winthrop," he corrected, "showed me in the magic box?"

The woman gave a weak nod. "Yes, I'm her sister-in-law, Cara Marsdale," she said, her bracelets jangling as she raised a hand to brush back a strand of bilious green hair from her cheek.

Another jolt of panic shot through Stephen, and he took a hasty step toward her. "Then she is all right?" he pressed. "She was able to return to your time without injury?"

To his amazement rather than retreating, or more lowering still, felling him with another blow, Miss Marsdale took a step forward, her expression gentling as she laid her hand on his arm. "She is fine," she said softly, eyes the shimmering amber of Spanish sherry meeting his with compassion. "She and my brother have been married for almost a year now. They've a little boy, Marcus." Her painted lips curved in a loving smile. "He's a proper little terror."

The news his former wife had borne a child by another man rocked Stephen's composure. "I see," he said, feeling oddly bereft. He'd known she was with child when she returned to the future, but he'd managed to put the matter from his mind. Now he would carry with him the ghostly image of a child; a son who might have been his had time and fate not conspired against him.

Thinking of time made him remember the threat Miss Marsdale had made all those months ago, and he gave her a suspicious frown. "But I do not understand. If Miranda has returned to your time, then why have you come back to mine?"

She was silent a long moment, and he was beginning to think she did not mean to answer. Then she gave a heavy sigh, a look of disgust flashing across her painted features.

"Because I was careless," she admitted with a scowl. "If I ever manage to make it back to my own time Alec will—" her voice broke off and her face went blank. Stephen leapt forward and caught her just as she crumpled to the floor.

He lowered her gently to the ground, calling out for a servant as he did so. Perhaps he should summon a physician, he worried, studying her delicate features with mounting concern. Although how he would explain her appearance, he knew not. And to think that only this evening he was congratulating himself at having salvaged something of his reputation, he mused, his mouth twisting in an ironic smile. 'Twould seem pride indeed came before a very painful fall.

He called out for a servant a second time, and was about to go rouse the household when Miss Marsdale stirred restlessly, her thick lashes fluttering as she gazed up at him in confusion. Fearing a repeat of her earlier assault, he moved swiftly out of harm's way. "How are you feeling?" he asked, eyeing her anxiously. "I could send for a doctor, if you like."

"No, that won't be necessary," she assured him, and then gave a heavy sigh. "I fainted, didn't I?" At Stephen's nod, she closed her eyes again.

"Miranda warned me being zapped about in time was rather like having an entire rugby team fall on you," she said, looking disgruntled. "I suppose I ought to have listened."

Stephen wondered what a rugby team might be, but before he could ask, a footman, still struggling into his livery, came scurrying into the room.

"Yes, my lord? May I be of—" the lad's voice broke off, his eyes widening in horror at the sight of Miss Marsdale. "Cor!" he exclaimed, pointing a shaking finger at her. "Wot's that?"

"Fetch Mrs. Finch," Stephen snapped, interposing himself between Miss Marsdale and the gawking servant. "Tell her she is to meet me in my aunt's bedchamber at once."

The footman swallowed uneasily, doing his best to peer over Stephen's shoulder. "But your lordship—"

"Do it." Stephen interrupted, his cold tone making it obvious he would brook no insubordination. "And if I learn you have breathed a word of this to anyone, I shall see that you never hold a position again. Is that understood?"

"Y-yes, my lord," the lad stammered, paling at the threat. He then turned and fled, stumbling in his haste to carry out Stephen's instructions.

Stephen watched him go, accepting fatalistically that he would count himself lucky if he could keep the matter secret for even a few days. When Miranda disappeared on their wedding night, it was common knowledge all over London before the *ton* was even sitting down to breakfast. He sighed, and turned to find Miss Marsdale watching him with amused interest.

"Yes, my lord, no, my lord," she mimicked, shaking her head. "Now I know I'm back in time. If you talked to a member of staff like that in *my* day, they'd likely tell you to go to hell."

Stephen tried not to wince at her bold manner of speaking. "Then I am profoundly grateful we are not in your day," he said, studying her with mounting concern. Even through the layers of hideous paint he thought she looked dangerously wan, and he feared she would swoon again. He stared at her for another few seconds, weighing the possible dangers of how she might react against performing what he considered to be his duty. As always, his sense of duty won. He reached down and gathered her in his arms before she could protest.

"Hey! What do you think you're doing?" she demanded, twisting indignantly in an effort to free herself. "Put me down, you beast! I can walk, I'm not a bloody invalid!"

Stephen easily controlled her struggles, carrying her out of the room and across the hall in silence. He slept at the other end of the hall, but he had ordered the bedchamber opposite the hidden chamber kept in readiness should his aunt pay him one of her sporadic visits. He shouldered the door open, turning a deaf ear to Miss Marsdale's increasingly pungent language. She would need to learn to mind her tongue if she meant to stay in this time, he thought, laying her gently on the bed.

"See that you stay there," he told her, pinning her with a stern glare. "I will be back in a moment." And then he turned and walked out, ignoring the sizzling epithets she hurled at him.

He dashed down the steps, fetching a candle and flint from the hall table before hurrying back into the room. He was fully expecting to be met with even more colorful insults and possibly even a physical assault, but when he returned she was already asleep, her painted face buried in the bed's velvet counterpane.

He edged closer to the bed, his gaze fixed on the glossy brown curls laying damply against her head. A mound of green hair lay on the floor, and he was relieved to note the thing was a wig. Although why she should wish to wear such a monstrosity, he could not imagine. Her own hair was really quite lovely, he decided, reaching down to brush back a curl from her face.

He was gazing down at her when the door to the room burst open, and Mrs. Finch came scurrying in. She was wearing an old-fashioned nightrail, covered by a grey shawl and her graying hair was poking out every which way from beneath a crooked mob cap. He turned away from the bed, temporarily blocking her view.

"Good evening, Mrs. Finch," he said, bowing politely. "My apologies for disturbing your rest. But as you can see," he stepped back, giving the stunned woman her first glimpse of their guest, "we have something of a problem."

Three

The first thought to penetrate the mists filling Cara's head was that she would never drink again. Her body hurt. Her head hurt. Even her hair hurt, and the worst of it was she couldn't remember taking a single drink. It must have been ouzo, she decided, snuggling deeper beneath the covers. The last time she'd felt this muzzy-headed was after tangling with a bottle of the fiery liqueur at a taverna in Queensway. She, Alec, and Miranda had gone there to celebrate her promotion to the Homicide Squad, and—her thoughts slammed to a halt. Miranda, she mused, her brows gathering in a frown. Something about Miranda . . .

"Bloody hell!" The exclamation burst from her lips and she bolted up in the bed, only to collapse back against the pillows a second later as the wrath of God came slamming down on her head.

"That should teach you not to make any unwise moves," a cultured voice observed moments before a cool cloth was pressed against her forehead. "I shouldn't advise doing it again."

"Now you tell me," Cara muttered, peeling open one eye to study the man sitting at her bedside. She took in his appearance in stoic silence, and then closed her eye again. So much for hoping this was all some kind of bizarre nightmare, she thought, with icy fatalism. She was back in time. The enormity of it was overwhelming, and for a moment she was tempted to burst into tears. But only for a moment. Reaching deep inside for the control acquired on London's deadly streets, she opened her eyes and met the Earl of Harrington's wary gaze.

"Lord Hallforth, I presume?" she asked, striving for the cockiness that had always been her shield.

A dark blond eyebrow arched in disapproving hauteur. "I am properly called Lord Harrington," he informed her, his dark blue eyes as icy as his coolly precise tones. "Hallforth is my family name. It is a distinction you had best learn should you be forced to remain in this time."

"There's a cheering thought," she grumbled, trying to think beyond the fear and confusion she was feeling. As a police officer she'd known fear before, but she'd learned to ignore such emotions in order to stay alive. Not for the first time she thanked God for her decision to follow Alec into the Metropolitan Police Force. Had she been nothing more than a barrister's wife, like her mother wanted, she'd be a screaming maniac by now.

"What year is it?" she asked, forcing herself to think rationally. The more she knew of her situation, she told herself, the sooner she could decide what to do.

"It is 1813," Lord Harrington replied, studying her with that same measuring watchfulness. "It has been a little over a year since I was accused of my wife's murder."

Cara heard the cold anger in his voice, and gave him a measuring look of her own. "You can't blame Miranda for that," she retorted, angrily defending her sister-in-law. "Getting transported forward in time was no more her idea than being zapped back here was mine."

There was a strained silence before he responded. "Yes, I recall your mentioning your presence was something of a mistake," he drawled, folding his arms across his chest and holding her gaze. "But my question is, is it a mistake you can rectify, or am I to be blessed with your company for an indeterminate period of time?"

The condescending remark made Cara's eyes narrow. She was trying to be calm, given the extraordinary circumstances, but his high and mighty attitude was starting to get to her. "How am I supposed to know?" she snapped, making a desperate grab at her temper. "But you can be very sure that if *I* have anything to say in the matter, I'll be out of here the moment the bloody room begins to glow. And that's another thing," she added, as the thought occurred to her. "Why hasn't the room been walled shut? I thought Miranda said you promised to see to it."

The earl's lean jaw clenched at the reprimand. "Considering the uncomfortable position such an action would have placed you in, I fail to see why you are complaining," he said stiffly. "However, if it will help to satisfy your vulgar curiosity, I was reluctant to enclose the room should Miranda ever need it to return to her own time."

His reply shocked Cara, and she gaped at him in astonishment. Miranda had once told her Stephen was possessed of a deep sense of duty, but she hadn't realized his concept of duty extended to a wife living one hundred and eighty-three years in the future. Yet, looking at him now, she wondered why she should be surprised. If ever a man looked like the rigid, honor-bound hero straight out of a novel, it was the man sitting opposite her.

His thick, straight hair was a shade caught somewhere between brown and blond, and it was brushed back from a face that was almost absurdly handsome. High cheekbones and a strong chin were a counterbalance to a sharp, aquiline nose, and a mouth that managed to look sexy and stern at the same time. He was dressed much as he had been last night in a velvet jacket, white shirt, and breeches, but this time his lower legs were encased in gleaming black leather boots. Hessians, she remembered, staring at them in blank wonder. They were called Hessians, and they were supposed to be polished with the froth of champagne. She raised her gaze to find him watching her with dubious concern.

"Do you polish them with champagne?" The words popped out before Cara could stop them.

He blinked in confusion. "I beg your pardon?"

"Your boots," she said, fighting the urge to blush. "Do you polish them with champagne? That's what the books said you did."

"What books?" He seemed more perplexed than ever.

Cara hesitated, uncertain how much she could tell him without jeopardizing the future. A future that could be irrevocably altered with one incautious word, she realized, tightening her fingers around the velvet counterpane. "Books about this time," she replied, keeping her answers deliberately vague. "I remember reading something about it shortly after meeting Miranda."

He leaned back in his chair, the expression on his face making it obvious he was far from convinced. "I see," he answered obliquely. "How very interesting."

Cara wasn't at all sure what to make of that, but before she could think of a suitably pithy reply the earl rose to his feet.

"I daresay you must be feeling rather hungry," he said, straightening his cuffs with an expert flick of his wrists. "I shall send Mrs. Finch in to attend you, but first we must think of some way to explain you. Have you any suggestions?"

Cara bit her lip as she considered the matter. She'd always been a brilliant strategist, and was well-regarded by her superiors for her ability to think her way out of any situation. If she could talk her way out of a terrorist's house in the east end, she told herself sternly, then she should be able to talk her way out of this. All she had to do was think . . .

"What have you told the servants?" she asked, trying to remember everything Miranda had told her of the unique relationship that existed between servant and master during this time.

"Nothing," the earl's expression grew grim. "My housekeeper, Mrs. Finch, is the only servant I have allowed close to you, and I know she may be counted on to mind her tongue. Unfortunately one of the footmen caught a glimpse of you, and I fear he is not as trustworthy. The story will doubtlessly be all over London by day's end, and when it becomes known you passed the night beneath my roof, both our reputations are certain to suffer."

Cara recalled joking with Miranda about the rigid propriety of the period, but now she could see it was no laughing matter. "Couldn't you tell everyone I was a cousin from Canada or something?" she asked, thinking quickly. "Just say I arrived late at night without warning, and you had no choice but to let me stay. How scandalous could that be?"

"More scandalous than you may realize," he replied, his brows meeting in thought. "But it is better than nothing, and certainly it will help explain your lack of social skills should you be unable to return to your own time."

His cutting observation made Cara's lips thin, and she cast him a resentful glare. "You're so kind, your grace," she muttered, her temper returning with her strength. "I'll try to remember not to drink from my soup bowl and lick my fingers."

Rather than being offended, he gave her another of those superior looks. "Only a duke is referred to as 'your grace,' " he informed her, inclining his head. "An important distinction you had best take pains to learn unless you wish to be taken for a complete savage." And with that he turned and left, leaving Cara glaring after him.

"Bloody damn arrogant bastard," she said, taking great relish in speaking the words out loud. She knew he was right, and that if she remained trapped in this time there was a great deal she would need to learn. She also knew she'd have to put a lock on her tongue when she was in public, and the admission made her tug the covers over her head.

She lay there for several minutes, trying to work up the energy to climb out of the bed. She was just about to make the attempt when the door to her room opened, and an older woman in a somber black dress came bustling in.

"Good morning, Miss Marsdale," she said, her manner as briskly efficient as a jail matron's. "I am Mrs. Finch, his lordship's housekeeper, and he has charged me most sternly to see to you myself. Naturally I would not dream of disappointing him," she added, eyeing Cara with obvious disapproval.

"Naturally," Cara echoed, trying to reconcile her twentieth century independence with nineteenth century mores.

"His lordship has told me of your unfortunate accident," Mrs. Finch continued, lowering herself on to the chair the earl had recently vacated. "It is small wonder you were in such a state when you arrived."

"Uh . . . yes, our carriage overturned, and I was knocked on the head," Cara improvised, imitating Miranda's precise way of speaking. "It was quite terrifying, and I was certain I should be killed at any moment."

Mrs. Finch's bushy brows met in a puzzled frown. "The carriage overturned?" she echoed. "I thought Lord Harrington said you were set upon by footpads."

"Oh, yes, and so we were," Cara said, without missing a beat. "The villains tossed up a barricade practically beneath our horses' hooves, and that is what forced us off the road."

Evidently she was convincing because Mrs. Finch leaned forward to give her a maternal pat. "Poor lamb, how perfectly awful for you," she said, her voice filled with sympathy. "And then to have your outer garments taken from you as well. . . ." She shuddered and leaned back in her chair. "If you ask me, 'tis a mercy you can not recall *precisely* what happened. Heaven only knows what terrible memories you might have."

From that Cara concluded the housekeeper was trying to determine if she had been sexually assaulted. She wasn't certain how Regency society treated rape victims, but she doubted it was any kinder than the way they were treated in her time.

The woman began stuffing pillows beneath Cara's head, raising her carefully to a sitting position. "His lordship wished me to tell you he has removed to his club," she said, tucking the sheets beneath Cara's chin. "He did promise to stop by later this morning to see how you were faring, but naturally he can not remain. It would be most—"

"Improper," Cara concluded with a bitter sigh, recalling the earl's earlier words. "God, I think I'm going to be sick."

A look of alarm flashed across the woman's face, and seconds later a porcelain basin was thrust beneath Cara's nose. She stared at it for a few seconds and then gave a wry chuckle. "I'm fine, Mrs. Finch," she said, offering the older woman an apologetic smile. "I was only joking."

The housekeeper tilted her head to one side, studying Cara with professional skepticism. "If you are certain, Miss Marsdale," she said, looking far from convinced. "But if you do not mind my saying so, you are still looking rather feeble."

"No, really, I'm fine," Cara assured her, then gave a confused frown. "Why are you calling me Miss Marsdale?"

"Do you mean to say that is not your name?" Mrs. Finch asked, looking more baffled than ever. "I am certain that is what Lord Harrington called you. Although I suppose I may have mistaken him. I was in such a taking when I first saw you, I vow I almost swooned myself!"

Recalling how she was dressed when she got zapped back in time, Cara could well imagine what the housekeeper's reaction must have been. "Oh, no, Marsdale is my name, all right," she answered hastily. "But it is my married name. I'm a widow." This last was a bit of divine inspiration, as she remembered Miranda's horror upon learning she was a divorcée.

"A widow?" Mrs. Finch gasped, clasping her hands together and gazing at Cara in pity. "Poor dear! And you little more than a child yourself. How simply ghastly for you!"

Cara made a non-committal noise, wishing the housekeeper would go polish the silver, or whatever it was servants did, and leave her to suffer in peace. Her head was throbbing, and adding to her discomfort was a physical need that was growing more pressing with each passing second. She shifted uncomfortably several times before surrendering to the inevitable.

"I was wondering, Mrs. Finch, if this house has . . . er . . . all of the modern conveniences?" she asked, hoping she didn't sound as asinine as she felt. "I am especially hoping you have one of those water closets I have been hearing about."

Mrs. Finch beamed with pride. "A necessary?" she asked. "Why, I should say that we have, Mrs. Marsdale! But," she added, before Cara's relief could soar, "you are far too weak to go downstairs now. Just use the chamber utensil my dear, and we shall see to it for you."

"Terrific," Cara muttered, and was more relieved than she

would admit when the older woman finally departed, leaving her to deal with her needs in private. It was awkward and embarrassing, but Cara consoled herself that it need only be for a little while. If the bloody room was acting up again, she reasoned she should be able to return home with little or no problem at all.

After resting Cara rose somewhat shakily from the bed and weaved her way across the room to the window. In her day the window was covered with blinds, and she had to admit the rose silk sheers and darker rose velvet drapes were far more attractive. Perhaps she'd mention it to Miranda, she thought, drawing a deep breath before jerking open the drapes to gaze down on Curzon Street.

The street was a bit wider than she remembered, and there were different buildings situated across the way, but the scene was still remarkably similar to the Curzon Street of her day. Traffic was as heavy as ever, even if it was composed entirely of horse-drawn vehicles, and the narrow sidewalks were jammed with people all rushing about in a frenzied bustle. She heard a loud jangle and glanced down as a pretty young girl came strolling past, driving several dirty and disinterested-looking cows in front of her.

"Sweet milk!" The girl called out in a clarion tone. "Buy your sweet milk from Bessie!"

The door to the house across the street opened and a maid came dashing out, a bucket in her hand. Cara stared at her, remembering a particularly gruesome film she'd been shown while still in grammar school. The film had been about the spread of diseases in the past, and as she recalled, unprocessed milk was blamed for most of the ills. The thought was decidedly sobering. She was turning away when Mrs. Finch and an army of servants came hurrying into the room.

"I thought you would be liking a bath, ma'am," the housekeeper said, motioning three maids carrying buckets of steaming water forward. "You'll feel better, I'm sure, once you've changed into some *proper* clothes."

Her emphasis on the word made Cara glance down, and she

was shocked to discover her leather bustier and miniskirt had been replaced by a peach silk peignoir. The discovery both relieved and alarmed her. Wearing the peignoir spared her having to explain her scandalous attire to the gawking servants, but the thought someone had stripped her without her being aware of it was profoundly disturbing. Especially since she wasn't certain who that someone had been, she thought, an image of the earl flashing in her mind.

While the maids were filling the copper tub that had also been brought into the room, Mrs. Finch began helping Cara out of her filmy nightgown, ignoring her protests with stern indifference.

"There is no need to be so priggish, Mrs. Marsdale," the older woman scolded, pulling the silk robe from Cara's shoulders. " 'Tisn't as if I haven't done this before. Who do you think helped you out of those heathenish rags you were wearing when his lordship brought you home?"

"I realize that," Cara said, doing her best not to blush when the gown was removed as well. "It's just I'm not accustomed to servants waiting on me, and I really prefer doing this myself."

"No need for that when I've three maids sitting idle," Mrs. Finch said, shoving her gently toward the copper bath. "Enough dawdling, now. That water will be cold as ice if you don't stop prattling. Into the tub with you."

Cara was intelligent enough to recognize a lost cause when she saw one, and surrendered with only a grumble of complaint. She'd never considered herself particularly modest, but she found the process of being bathed beyond humiliating. It was worse than being strip-searched, she thought, recalling the time she'd been arrested as part of an undercover operation. If she remained stuck in this time for more than a day or two she'd have to make it plain she didn't need to be waited on hand and foot.

After being bathed Cara was helped into another night gown and bundled back into bed. Once more her protests were ignored, leaving her feeling both resentful and frustrated.

"You've missed your calling," she informed Mrs. Finch as the housekeeper placed a tray over her lap. "You'd have made a first-class top sergeant."

"*Humph,* as if I'd waste my time instructing a group of thick-headed men," the housekeeper retorted, slicing a boiled egg and pushing it toward Cara. "Now, mind you eat every bite. His lordship will be that mad if he finds you've not eaten."

From that Cara deduced the earl would be returning shortly, and breathed a silent sigh of relief. He was the only one in this time who knew who and what she was, and she realized she had a dozen questions she wanted to ask him. She gave herself a few moments to marshal her thoughts, and then slanted Mrs. Finch a hopeful look.

"Will it be possible for me to see his lordship?" she asked, adopting a diffident tone. "I know he can't come in here," she added, anticipating the housekeeper's protest, "but couldn't I meet him in another room? The downstairs parlor, perhaps?"

Mrs. Finch frowned. "I am not certain that would be at all the thing," she said, reluctantly. "Lord Harrington did not say, but I fear he believes that the fewer who know of your presence, the better. You must know your arriving here late at night and dressed so strangely is certain to cause the most unpleasant speculation," she added, bending a chiding frown on Cara.

Cara's lips tightened at the none-too-gentle hint. She kept forgetting how uptight and prudish this time was; especially when it came to anything smacking of sex. She took a sip of tea, forcing herself to think coolly.

From what she recalled of her conversations with Miranda she knew women of this time were expected to walk a razor-thin line, and much as it might gall her, so long as she remained trapped here, she would be expected to walk that very same line. It would be rather like operating under deep cover, she mused, remembering the times when her very life had depended on her assuming a persona different than her own. The sudden thought made her swear beneath her breath.

That was it! she realized in shock. Unless she could find a way back to her own time, she would have to stop thinking of this world in terms of her own experience. If she wanted to be taken for a Regency lady, then she would have to learn to act and think like a Regency lady. And she'd have to speak like one, too, she realized, wishing now she'd paid more attention when her class had studied Jane Austen. It looked as if Mrs. Hardwicke, her literature teacher, was right, she mused, a rueful smile touching her mouth. She *would* need that stuff one day

"I realize it would be most awkward if others should learn of my situation, Mrs. Finch," she said, trying her best to sound like a proper lady. "And I truly appreciate the care you and his lordship have taken to guard my reputation, but I really must speak with him. If the earl doesn't wish me to go downstairs, perhaps I could meet him in another room on this floor?"

There was a long pause before Mrs. Finch spoke. "I daresay that could be arranged," she said, her lips pursed in thought. "The countess's sitting room hasn't been used since last year, but it is still acceptable. And if I or one of the other servants remains close by, I can see no reason why anyone should find the slightest degree of fault in your receiving his lordship there. But of course, you must change first. You can not receive him dressed like *that*," she indicated the peignoir with a jerky nod.

Cara glanced down at the offending gown. "Of course, Mrs. Finch," she said, swallowing her pride with gritted teeth. "Whatever you think proper. I shall place myself completely in your hands."

The housekeeper simpered with pride. "That's probably wisest, Mrs. Marsdale. I once served as an abigail for the Countess of Mountjoy, and I have made a point of following the fashions. Fortunately his lordship ordered a trunk of her ladyship's clothing kept in readiness should she return, so we shan't have to send for a modiste. That is where we obtained the nightgown, you know," she added in a confiding whisper.

Cara thought of her sister-in-law's delicate build and winced. She was a good four inches taller than Miranda, and ten pounds heavier, and the thought of being stuffed into one of the thin, gauzy gowns so popular during this time appealed about as much as a visit to the dentist.

"I am certain whatever you choose will be fine, Mrs. Finch," she said, accepting she had no recourse but to cooperate. "But if you don't mind, I should prefer to meet Lord Harrington in private. We have . . . certain matters to discuss."

"But Mrs. Marsdale, that would not be—"

"Proper," Cara finished, deciding she was beginning to loathe that particular word. "I know, but what I have to say is for the earl's ears alone, and I don't want anyone overhearing; not even you, much as I trust you."

From the pleased expression on Mrs. Finch's face, it was obvious Cara's grudging admission had turned the tide in her favor. "Well, I suppose it might be permissible," she said at last, "but for a few minutes only, mind. His lordship is very particular when it comes to matters of honor, and he will not be at all pleased if the proprieties are not most sternly observed."

This came as no surprise to Cara. Despite the fact the earl was one of the most handsome and virile men she'd ever met, he was as prissy and tight-assed as her old chief inspector. If this was her time, nothing would have given her greater pleasure that to tell his snotty lordship to go to hell. Unfortunately, this wasn't her time.

This was the earl's time, and until she could access the time portal, she had no choice but to play the part of a sweet, submissive female, and pray she could make it through without killing him. If she ever made it back to her own time, she decided glumly, she'd never complain about going undercover again. Compared to putting up with an arrogant aristocrat and a society that kept its women shackled in the chains of respectability, posing as a punk prostitute was a walk in the park.

Four

It was approaching three in the afternoon before Stephen was able to settle into his temporary lodgings. With Parliament in session respectable rooms were at a premium, and it required a great deal of charm and a hefty bribe to convince the club's manager to part with the remaining set of rooms. If the good man wondered why Stephen, who owned a perfectly good house not ten blocks to the north, should require bachelor quarters, he was too well-trained to give voice to these thoughts. Although the gold coins Stephen slipped in his pockets doubtlessly had more to do with his discretion, than a simple reluctance to gossip about his betters.

While his valet was arranging his belongings Stephen retired to the club's excellent dining room to take his mid-day meal. He was just finishing his sweet when Aidan joined him at his table.

"I must say I'm surprised to find you here," he drawled, his gray gaze resting on Stephen's face. "I was certain you would be at Gentleman Jackson's watching the Marquess of Glenbury thrash his wife's latest cicisbeo."

The mocking words made Stephen scowl. "Why the devil should you think that?" he demanded, vividly recalling the humiliation he had suffered when Miranda publicly admitted to having taken a lover. "Since when have I ever shown a preference for indulging in such idiotic behavior?"

"Never," Aidan admitted, nodding when the footman offered him a cup of tea. "But since that is where our mutual friend, Holloway, is to be found, I assumed you would be with him."

"Well, you assumed wrong," Stephen retorted, glowering at his friend. "I have better things to do than watch Glenbury making a fool of himself over that immoral marchioness of his."

"Haven't we all," Aidan agreed, inclining his head coolly. "Speaking of which, I was thinking of attending a debate at the City Philosophical Society in about an hour. Care to join me?"

Stephen was sorely tempted by Aidan's offer. He enjoyed the intellectual discussions to be found at the city's premier scientific society, but thanks to his uninvited guest, he didn't have the time. It was a pity he couldn't bring the unruly chit with him, he mused, hiding a smile. She would doubtlessly set the staid Society on its collective ear were she to admit to being a visitor from the distant future.

"It is kind of you to invite me," he told Aidan, shaking his head with regret. "But unfortunately I cannot. A distant relation of mine deposited herself on my doorstep last night, and I am trying to decide what the deuce to do with her."

Aidan raised a jet-black eyebrow in mock-amazement. "Indeed?" he drawled, looking intrigued. "What relation might this mystery lady be? I thought you were the last of your line."

"Of my father's line, yes," Stephen said, cringing at the thought of lying to such an old and valued acquaintance, "but Miss Marsdale is descended from a relation of my mother who immigrated to Canada some years ago. Apparently her father has died, and she has come to England to seek out her family."

"Is she pretty?"

The question caught Stephen unawares. He had been so preoccupied with where and when Miss Marsdale came from, he hadn't given her appearance much thought. But at Aidan's words he found it appallingly easy to conjure up the image of an exotic face with stunning topaz-colored eyes, and soft, inviting lips curved in a smile that invited even as it annoyed. He shook off the wayward direction of his thoughts and forced himself to think in a rational manner.

"I suppose she might be counted as passingly pretty," he conceded grudgingly. "But she has the manners of a heathen. And as for her language . . ." he gave a visible shudder. "She has a vocabulary that would even make the Duke of Clarence swoon with horror, and she doesn't hesitate airing it, I assure you."

To his surprise Aidan gave a soft chuckle. "You make her sound irresistible," he said, a wicked grin touching his mouth. "But I can see why she would present you with such a decided dilemma; especially if you mean to trot her out in Society. Are you?" He cast Stephen an inquisitive look.

"Good God, no!" Stephen exclaimed, the thought of the havoc Miss Marsdale could wreak if given free rein making him blanch. "I would be well and truly finished in Society if the *ton* clapped eyes on that hellion. And besides," he added, as the hopeful thought occurred, "she may not be remaining overly long."

"Especially if you have anything to say about it, *n'cest pas?*" Aidan said with another chuckle. "Well, what will you do with her in the meantime? Not keeping her locked in the attic like a mad aunt, are you?"

Aidan's teasing comment almost made Stephen smile. "No, tempting though that thought might be," he said, envisioning what Miss Marsdale's likely response to such an action might be. "She is currently settled in one of my best bedchambers, which means *I* am putting up here. The foolish chit arrived without baggage or a chaperon to lend her countenance, if you can imagine."

Aidan looked much struck by this. "Are you sure she is related to you?" he asked after a thoughtful pause. "This could be a trick to compromise you into marrying her."

"I have already considered and rejected that possibility," Stephen said, feeling another stab of guilt. "But she had letters from my mother to prove her identity, and she looks enough like my maternal grandmother to be her twin. I am satisfied she is who she claims."

"Mmm." Aidan responded cryptically. "What will you do if you decide to keep her? I can't see you remaining here indefinitely." He cast a speaking glance about the club's elegant dining room.

"That is what I was mulling over when you joined me," Stephen admitted, feeling a great sense of relief at discussing his problem with someone as intelligent as Aidan. "In the event Miss Marsdale stays something will have to be done with her, but I'm damned if I can think of a single thing. Any suggestions?"

"You could always do what our class does with its poor relations and find her a position as a governess or companion," Aidan replied after another long silence. "Or if you are feeling particularly generous, you could set her up in a small house, like you did with that cousin of yours . . . what was her name?"

"Mrs. Minerva Greenborough," Stephen said, straightening at the mention of the elderly relation he had all but forgotten. "And she isn't a cousin, she's my great-aunt."

"There you are," Aidan nodded wisely. "In the event your Miss Marsdale proves particularly tenacious you can pack her off to act as your great-aunt's companion. And if she refuses to do that, may the devil take her. No one can fault you for not having done your best by her, at least."

Stephen did not reply, caught in the coils of a scheme so bizarre it horrified him to have thought of it. His great aunt Minn was the widow of a respected member of Parliament, and well-connected enough to be considered above reproach. Moreover she was the biggest gudgeon to ever draw breath, and he knew she would happily believe and support whatever Banbury tale he cared to spin. It might work, he told himself, shifting restlessly. It *had* to work . . .

"Stephen? Are you all right?" Aidan's worried voice cut into Stephen's spinning thoughts, and he looked up to find the baron studying him with marked concern. He shook his head as if to clear it, and gave Aidan a strained smile.

"I am sorry, Aidan," he apologized coolly. "What did you say? I fear I was not attending."

Aidan's expression became amused. "So I gathered," he drawled. "You were looking so pensive I thought I should have to dash a blunt object over your head to get your attention. I was asking what you intended doing about your prospective bride."

"Lady Felicity?" Stephen frowned in confusion, failing to understand what his friend was getting at. "What has she to do with Miss Marsdale?"

"Perhaps nothing, perhaps everything," Aidan said, shrugging with indifference. "But certainly they will meet; especially if the earl agrees to let you court his daughter. In fact, seeing you take responsibility for a lady who in truth has no claims upon your generosity can only serve to show you in the best possible light to his lordship. The old tyrant is known for being hide-bound when it comes to matters of duty. He is almost as obsessed on the matter as you are," he added this last with a teasing grin.

Instead of replying in kind Stephen shot to his feet, a look of utter horror spreading across his face. "Oh my God, Felicity!" he gasped, pushing away from the table. "I completely forgot! She and her mother are coming to my house for tea!"

"When?" Aidan asked, his expression abruptly serious.

Stephen grabbed the watch fob dangling from his waistcoat, and studied it grimly. "Five minutes ago," he said, closing the watch's engraved lid and returning it to his pocket. "Even if I manage to catch a hack, I am going to be shockingly late."

"There is no reason for you to wait for a rig," Aidan said, rising to his feet. "My curricle is just outside, and I would be delighted to take you wherever you need to go."

Stephen was torn between the desperate need to get home as quickly as possible, and the fear of what might happen should Aidan encounter Miss Marsdale. He was about to refuse, when common sense intervened. Of course Aidan wouldn't meet Miss Marsdale, he chided himself sternly. The poor woman was still suffering from the effects of her journey through time, and even if she was not, it was doubtful she would be hen-witted enough to leave the sanctuary of the upper floors. So long as Aidan didn't take it into his head to go exploring, it should be safe enough.

"Could you?" he asked, already signaling the footman for his hat and gloves. "I own it would save me a considerable amount of pain. Lady Berksham is fiendishly devoted to her schedule, and she would cut me dead if I set her back so much as a second."

"I should be delighted," Aidan assured him, his eyes beginning to twinkle. "And in any case, it will give me the chance to meet your newly-discovered cousin. I have always wanted to meet a native of our North American colony. Is it as wild and dangerous a place as they say?"

"If Miss Marsdale's conduct is any indication, it is," Stephen grumbled, trying to think of some plausible reason why his old friend and his unlikely visitor should not meet. "But I am afraid she isn't yet up to receiving visitors. The journey from Canada was somewhat . . . arduous," he finished lamely.

"Some other time, then," Aidan accepted the explanation good-naturedly. "Although, if you have no objections, I should still like to come in for a few minutes. I am anxious to see how you explain your cousin to her ladyship," he added as they hurried out to the street where a glistening black curricle was waiting.

The thought of the daunting task laying before him sent Stephen's spirits plummeting to the soles of his polished Hessians. "So am I," he muttered, wondering what the devil he could say to explain the unexplainable. "So am I."

"Excuse me, Mrs. Marsdale, but I was wondering if I might have a word with you?" Mrs. Finch hovered in the doorway of the sitting room, her hands twisted together in obvious agitation.

"Certainly, Mrs. Finch, what is it?" Cara responded politely, wondering what could have put the austere housekeeper in such a flap. Maybe one of the maids had found her mini skirt and bustier and was trying to seduce a footman, she thought, grinning at the possibility.

"You must know I would never presume to go against his lordship's express wishes unless I thought it was of the utmost importance," Mrs. Finch rushed on, inching into the room. "Indeed, I should never dream of such a thing, but when her ladyship told me his lordship was expecting them I had no notion what to do. The butler has placed them in the Drawing Room, but I am sure they must be growing restive by now. Her ladyship is a high stickler for the proprieties, and—"

Cara held up her hand. "Hold it," she interrupted, her head whirling at the torrent of words. "What her ladyship are you talking about?"

"The Countess of Berksham," Mrs. Finch clarified, looking more agitated than ever. "She and her daughter, Lady Felicity, have come to call upon Lord Harrington, at his invitation, mind, and he is not here to greet them. He is at his club, but I can not tell them that without offending them beyond all measure," she paused, drawing a deep breath and studying Cara hopefully.

"We . . . that is, I was hoping you might see fit to act as their hostess until his lordship arrives," she said, offering Cara a cajoling smile. "You *are* his cousin, after all, and it would be perfectly respectable, I promise you."

At first Cara was too stunned to respond. Common sense told her she would have to be out of her bloody mind to leave the sitting room, and that the fewer people she encountered in this time, the better. She also reminded herself such an action was certain to send the earl into a fit of apoplexy, and he would probably toss her out into the streets. Not a pleasant state of affairs, if she recalled her history correctly. In fact, she'd probably have to use the leather skirt and bustier to keep from starving.

On the other hand, she decided, her heart racing with excitement, how could she turn down the opportunity to meet a genuine Regency countess who was a high stickler for proprieties? She envisioned Bette Davis with a feathered turban and a lorgnette and knew she had to go downstairs. What the hell, she mused, rising to her feet. In for a penny, in for a pound.

"Very well, Mrs. Finch," she said, slipping easily into her disguise of a woman of this time, "if you are certain it would be permissible, I should be happy to be of assistance."

"Oh, thank you, Mrs. Marsdale," the elderly houskeeper looked so relieved Cara was afraid she would burst into tears. "That is very good of you, I must say."

"Not at all," Cara replied, a new concern suddenly occurring to her. As a rule she didn't give a tinker's curse what she wore, but from the little she'd read and her experiences with Miranda, she knew such was not the case in this time. A real Regency lady would have sooner died than appear in a gown that wasn't perfectly suited for the occasion, and she gave the low-necked gown she was wearing a pensive look.

"Will my gown suit, do you think?" she asked worriedly. "Or should I change into something else?"

Mrs. Finch studied the short-sleeved dress of blue silk for several seconds before reaching a decision. "It is a trifle informal for receiving guests," she announced with obvious expertise, "but with a bit of fixing up, it will do. A shawl and some ear bobs should help you look more the thing."

Cara brightened at the mention of a shawl. She'd been freezing her bum off in the thin gown, and had been thinking of throwing another scoop of coal on the fire when Mrs. Finch had arrived.

Ten minutes later she was making her way down the staircase, clinging to the banister for support. To her annoyance she discovered that in addition to being horribly drafty, the, silk gown was a positive menace. The wispy material clung to her ankles, making it impossible to walk without feeling as if she was about to end up on her face, and the shoes Mrs. Finch had procured for her were about as substantial as a pair of ballet slippers. She kept expecting her feet to slide out from beneath her, and when she reached the bottom of the steps without killing herself, she sent a silent prayer of thanks heavenward.

An elderly man was standing in front of the door that in her time led to Alec's office, and when he saw Cara, he inclined his head with a studied pomposity that had her biting back a grin.

"I am Hargraves, Mrs. Marsdale," he intoned, his solemn tones reminding her of Charles Laughton in *Mutiny on the Bounty.* "I am his lordship's butler. I apologize for not greeting you when you arrived last evening. I trust you were able to find your rooms without incident?"

From his supercilious voice and the way he was staring down his beaked nose at her, Cara knew he was trying none-too-subtly to let her know he didn't trust her for one moment. Since decking him was out of the question, she tried to imagine how Miranda would deal with such gall.

"That is quite all right, Hargraves," she told him, raising her chin with cool hauteur. "Just see it doesn't happen again. You can be replaced, you know," and she brushed her way past him before he could respond.

There were three women sitting in front of the fire, and even as Cara was taking in their appearance, the oldest woman turned to glower at her, her lips pursed in a thin line of peevish displeasure.

"Well, 'tis about time *someone* has seen fit to check on our welfare," she said in a waspish voice that reminded Cara of a jail matron she once knew. "Are you the housekeeper here? If so, I take leave to tell you that you run a very poor household. We might have perished from the lack of attention the staff has paid us."

God, she was wonderful! Cara thought, beaming at her in delight; she even made the queen sound like a wimp! She allowed herself a few seconds to enjoy the experience, and then fell immediately into her role.

"My apologies, my lady, if the servants have failed to attend to your needs," she said, performing what she hoped was an acceptable curtsy. "I shall see to it at once." She hurried back to the door and jerked it open without warning, and wasn't the least bit surprised when Hargraves all but tumbled into the room. She gave him a frosty look, and then said,

"Hargraves, bring our guests some refreshments as soon as it can be arranged. For some reason I can not fathom, the matter has yet to be attended to."

Hargraves rose to his full height, his thin face rigid with mortification. "As you wish, Mrs. Marsdale," he said, bowing so deeply Cara wondered why he didn't break in half. When he straightened, she was surprised to see grudging respect in his dark eyes. "Will there be anything else?"

"When his lordship arrives, please inform him that his guests

are here, and that we are waiting for him in the drawing room."
Cara had survived too many squad room skirmishes to gloat over
her victory. She had an ally now, but he would turn quickly into
an enemy if she made the mistake of humiliating him in front of
others.

"Very well, Mrs. Marsdale," he said, and then bowed his way
out of the room, closing the door behind him. Cara turned back
to find the three women studying her with varying degrees of
skepticism and interest.

Cara took a few moments to organize her thoughts, and then
hurried back to join them. "I suppose I ought to explain," she
began, offering them a hesitant smile. "My name is Mrs. Cara
Marsdale, and I am distantly related to Lord Harrington on my
father's side of the family. I arrived in England last evening from
Canada, and was almost immediately set upon by footpads. I was
knocked unconscious in the attack, but the authorities found his
lordship's address in my pocket and notified him of what happened. He came at once, and was good enough to bring me here.
I-I can not bear to think of what might have become of me had
it not been for his kindness," she added, throwing in a shudder
for dramatic effect.

Lady Berksham looked like a pekingese sniffing a suspicious
piece of food. "And pray, how did his lordship's address come
to be in your possession?" she asked, her nose twitching in disapproval.

Sanctimonious old cow! Cara thought, her expression of cha-
grin and humility never changing. "As I said, Lady Berksham,
we are distantly related, and I was hoping to visit him while I
was in the city. I don't know how things are here, but in Canada,
family is everything. To be in the same city as a relation, and not
even attempt to visit them would be unthinkable. Did-did I do
something wrong?" and she forced herself to make her voice
quiver.

To her relief, the countess's rigid expression thawed somewhat.
"No," she conceded gruffly, "I suppose you did not. But what

do you mean Lord Harrington brought you here? Never say you passed the night beneath his roof without a chaperon?"

Cara couldn't help herself. She clapped her hand over her heart, her eyes going wide in mock-horror. "Certainly not, my lady!" she exclaimed, acting the outraged virgin for all she was worth. "That would have been most improper! Once his lordship was certain I was receiving the best of care, he went to his club to spend the night."

There was a strained silence, and then the countess sat back in her chair. "Precisely the sort of behavior one might hope for in a gentleman of Harrington's rank," she said with a satisfied nod. "I will own that after last year's unpleasantness I had my doubts, but if what you say is so, his treatment of you shows his lordship is all that is proper. And," here she cast Cara an approving look, "your behavior does you credit as well, Mrs. Marsdale. It is good that you are so mindful of the proprieties."

Cara fought the urge to gag, and lowered her eyes demurely. "Your ladyship is very kind," she simpered, wondering if she should curtsy again. "Being a stranger in the country, I'm afraid I haven't any idea how to conduct myself, and I am terrified of committing some dreadful error."

"Well, you needn't trouble yourself any further on that score, Mrs. Marsdale," the pretty blonde Cara had mentally tagged as Lady Felicity rose in a graceful rustle of silk and hurried forward to take her hand. "Mama, Jane, and I would be happy to instruct you on how to go on. Wouldn't we, Mama?" And to Cara's surprise she turned an admonishing glance on the old biddy.

"I am sure I am always ready to lend assistance to a stranger," the countess acknowledged in a stiff manner, and then turned a sharp-eyed look on Cara. "But what are your plans, Mrs. Marsdale, if you do not mind my asking?" she asked, her eyebrows arching. "Will you be staying in London?"

The arrival of the maid carrying a laden tea tray distracted the others, giving Cara a much needed breather. She supposed it was naive of her to think a tough customer like the countess could be won over so easily. She'd have to do some pretty fast tap-dancing if she was going to succeed in convincing her audience she was who and what she was purporting herself to be.

Judging by the way the maid set the tray on a table next to Clara, she gathered she was supposed to act as the hostess. Sending a silent thank-you to her mother for insisting she learn the proper way to prepare and serve tea when she'd been a rebellious teenager, she began dispensing tea to her guests; adding milk and lemon at their direction. When everyone had been served, she prepared a cup for herself and then sat back to sip it. God, she thought, wincing at the taste, she'd kill for a Pepsi about now.

"I am afraid my plans are rather undecided, Lady Berksham," she began, raising her eyes to meet the countess's suspicious gaze. "His lordship has been kind enough to offer me shelter, but I can't presume upon his generosity forever. My original plan was to come to England and seek employment as a governess, and once I am recovered, that is precisely what I shall do."

Her bald declaration was met with a variety of reactions. Lady Berksham looked baffled, Lady Felicity looked concerned, and the brunette with green eyes, who, Cara assumed, was "Jane," appeared intrigued. To her surprise, the brunette was the first to speak.

"A friend of mine is headmistress of an excellent academy for young ladies in Hertfordshire," she said, in a frank manner that took Cara pleasantly by surprise. "If you like, I can write her asking if there are any positions available."

Since the woman she was pretending to be would have leapt at such an offer, Cara gave her a grateful look. "Would you?" she asked shyly. "I would be eternally in your debt."

"I shouldn't be too indebted, Mrs. Marsdale, until you've had to deal with the little devils," Jane said with a roll of her slender shoulders. "I attempted it for one term, and almost went mad. That was when I decided I was better suited to being a companion. Have you had much experience of children?"

"I . . . no," Cara said, deciding her character would be as ignorant of teaching as she was everything else. "My husband and I were never blessed with children of our own, and it has only been since his death that I have had to make my own way. That is why I decided to return to England," she confessed, pleased with her own deviousness. "Life on the frontier can be terribly hard on a woman who is all alone."

"So one may imagine," Lady Berksham seemed to have recovered her wits and was once more taking charge of the conversation. "But I shouldn't worry overly-much about obtaining a position were I you, my dear. Naturally the earl would never allow you to seek employment."

Cara almost dropped her cup. "What?"

"It simply would not do," Lady Berksham said slowly, as if addressing a particularly dense child. "He is the Earl of Harrington, after all, and it would cause a most dreadful scandal if it ever became known he had turned his back on a member of his family; especially a female. It would touch heavily upon his honor, and to be frank, Mrs. Marsdale, that could prove most uncomfortable to all parties concerned."

Cara was speechless with incredulity. Miranda had told her what this time had been like for women; she'd read books and seen films, but until this moment she realized she hadn't a clue what it had been really like. She said the first thing to pop into her head. "I'd bloody well like to see him try and stop me!"

A horrified silence followed, and just as she was about to grovel in apology something made her glance toward the door. Lord Harrington was standing there, his deep blue eyes glacial as he studied her. Nor was he alone. Standing just behind him was a startlingly handsome man with jet-black hair and smoke-gray eyes, who was regarding her with obvious amusement.

The earl was the first to recover. He folded his arms across his chest, meeting her dismayed glance with icy aplomb. "Indeed, *Mrs*. Marsdale?" he drawled, emphasizing her title mockingly. "And pray what is it, precisely, that I am to try and stop you from doing?"

Five

Stephen could not believe the evidence of his own senses any more than he could believe the depth of his bad luck. When Hargraves had told him his cousin was taking tea with the Berkshams he'd wanted to howl in frustration, but Aidan's presence prevented him from indulging in such displays. Instead he consoled himself with the knowledge that not even a hell-cat like Miss . . . Mrs. Marsdale, he corrected grimly, had proven herself to be, would risk exposing the fact she was a visitor from another time to the countess. That optimistic thought had no sooner formed than he walked in to hear her issuing her ill-bred challenge. Had it not been for his terror of tempting fate, he would have wondered what could possibly go wrong next.

"Well, Cousin?" he taunted, hiding his trepidation behind a facade of mocking indifference. "I am waiting for your answer. What is it you wish to do that you feel I will be compelled to oppose? I am most curious."

I'll bet you are, you stuffy, over-bearing twit. Cara contained her embarrassment and anger by roundly cursing Stephen. She knew she'd strayed way over the line with her stupid remark, but she was certain she could have salvaged the situation with her dignity still intact if he hadn't chosen that particular moment to arrive. Now she'd probably have to swoon or something to get out of the mess she had inadvertently made.

"Your cousin was but expressing surprise you would oppose her seeking employment, my lord." Rescue came from Jane, who had risen from her place beside Lady Felicity to sit beside Cara. "Will you?"

Stephen opened his mouth to say he didn't give a brass farthing if the absurd creature took to riding bareback at Astley's Amphitheatre when Lady Berksham forestalled him.

"Of course he shall oppose it, Miss Blackwell," she said, bending a censorious look on her daughter's companion. "It is as I have already said, Lord Harrington is a gentleman, and naturally he would never countenance a female relation of his making her own way in the world. Is that not so, my lord?"

"And Mrs. Marsdale," she turned to Cara before Stephen could find his voice. "I would be remiss in my duties did I not tell you that however things may be done in Canada, in England, *ladies* do not use such strong language in Polite Company. I trust we shan't be treated to another display of such shocking vulgarity?"

Cara thought of the language that was a matter of course in her day and lowered her head in mock-shame. "Yes, my lady," she said meekly. "And thank you for correcting me. I should hate to make such a mistake in front of others."

"Quite right, my dear," the countess replied, inclining her head with gracious approval. "Your manners want but the slightest bit of polishing, and then I am sure you should do quite well on the Marriage Mart."

"The Marriage Mart?" Cara and Stephen echoed the words in unison and with equal degrees of horror.

"Well, certainly," Lady Berksham answered coolly. "It is the best solution for us all. Just leave it to me, and I shall arrange everything. A widower, I think, one with children who will appreciate the attributes of a more mature bride."

Stephen felt himself paling, and for one humiliating moment feared he would become ill. Never in his wildest nightmares could he have envisioned such a contretemps, and he could think of no way to stop events from progressing. He turned to Mrs. Marsdale, only to find her looking every bit as green.

"I . . . your ladyship is too kind," Cara stammered, trying her damnedest to extricate herself from the ridiculous situation. "But

I . . . uh . . . I'm still in mourning. Yes!" she brightened as inspiration dawned. "Yes, I'm still in mourning for my poor husband, and I couldn't think of entering into Society just now. The proprieties, you know," and she gave a tragic sigh.

Lady Berksham also sighed. "I did not mean to imply I should be marrying you off within the hour, Mrs. Marsdale," she said in a vinegary tone. "When did your husband die?"

Cara was too upset to remember what would have been considered a proper mourning period in this time. "Eleven months ago," she said, naming the first date to leap into her head.

"A bit too soon for you to be completely casting off your widow's weeds, but not too soon as to invite unfavorable comment," the countess decided. "Of what did your husband die? Something respectable, I trust? The fever, perhaps, or better still, did he fall in gallant defense of his country? This dreadful war has created a veritable army of widows, I vow."

"Yes!" Cara exclaimed, mentally raising her hands in surrender. It was a pity the countess didn't live in her day, or she'd have recruited her for the Yard in a heartbeat, she thought sourly. She'd never undergone a more thorough interrogation.

"He was killed by the Americans," she added, hoping she was getting her wars right. "They attempted to invade us last year, and my husband marched off to stop them. He never came back."

"I must say I'm not surprised," the older woman said with a sniff. "My lord always said it was a mistake granting the louts their independence; only look at how they repay us for our kindness. Ah well," she rose to her feet, "a war widow from the colonies will make an interesting addition to Almack's. I shall arrange a voucher at once."

"But—"

"Naturally you cannot waltz," Lady Berksham added, nodding to her daughter and Jane who rose dutifully to their feet. "It is one thing to partake of a few genteel entertainments while still in mourning, but quite another to disport yourself on the dance floor with every widower and caper merchant who approaches you. I shall leave it to Lord Harrington to explain the difference to you. In the meanwhile, my lord, might I suggest you arrange a chaperon for your cousin so that you may return to your own home? The sooner she is seen to be under your aegis, the better her chances of making an acceptable alliance."

"I was about to send for my great-aunt, Mrs. Minerva Greenborough, to serve in that capacity," Stephen answered, feeling as helpless as a leaf caught in a whirlwind.

"Minn?" Lady Berksham paused, her brow wrinkling in thought. "Good heavens, I'd forgotten she was still about. A bit of a featherbrain, as I recollect, but of unapproachable birth, for all that. Yes, she will do quite well to chaperon Mrs. Marsdale. An excellent choice, Harrington, I congratulate you."

"Thank you, my lady," Stephen bowed gravely, aware of a sudden urge to laugh, although for the life of him he couldn't fathom why. "It is kind of you to say so."

"Not at all," the countess granted him a vague smile. "Now, we really must be on our way as we have already stayed longer than is permissible, Mrs. Marsdale," she nodded briskly at Cara. "I shall call upon you next week and take you shopping. Your wardrobe as well as your manners will want refurbishing, I can see," and then she departed, dragging her daughter and Miss Blackwell with her.

The three people remaining in the drawing room watched them go in silence, and then Aidan turned to Cara.

"I do believe those are the most words I have ever heard Lady Berksham exchange with anyone," he commented, giving Cara a low bow. "You are to be congratulated, Mrs. Marsdale, it would appear you have completely won over her ladyship; not an easy task, as I am sure Stephen would tell you."

Cara watched him warily, hearing the mockery in his cultured voice. Having already had her powers of restraint pushed to the limits by the countess she was strongly tempted to tell him to go bugger himself; instead she gave him a frosty look.

"It would appear you have the advantage of me, sir," she said, easily mimicking Lady Berksham's imperious manner. "I do not believe I know your name."

Stephen's jaw almost dropped at her performance. Had he not seen her outlandish appearance when she first materialized in the secret room, he would have sworn she was as proper a lady as one could ever hope to meet. This evidence of her mercurial nature troubled him, and he made a mental note to keep a judicious eye on her. It was obvious she was not to be trusted.

"My pardon, Cousin, for being so behind-handed in my manners," he said, moving forward to slip his arm about her shoulder. "Allow me to present you to my very good friend, Sir Aidan Quarry. Aidan, this lovely creature is my cousin, Mrs. Cara Marsdale, newly-arrived in our country from the wilds of Canada."

"Mrs. Marsdale," Aidan gave another sweeping bow. "It is an honor to meet you." He straightened, his silver-colored eyes impaling her with an incisive look. "Precisely where in the wilds of Canada are you from, if I may ask? Montreal, perhaps?"

Why hadn't she paid attention in geography class? Cara wondered, frantically trying to remember a city that would have existed in the early 1800's. "Toronto is the nearest city of any importance," she said, all but slumping with relief when she pulled the name out of thin air. "I'm sure you wouldn't have heard of the village closest to our farm."

"Ah, you are from our eastern province, then," Sir Aidan said, nodding. "You must tell me what it is like. I have always wanted to visit Quebec."

Shaky as was her memory of Canadian geography, Cara did know Toronto was in Ontario, not Quebec. She was also willing to bet Quarry knew this as well, and realized he was trying to trap her. "I fear you have mistaken the matter, sir," she informed him gently, deciding her best bet was to treat him like a clod who didn't know any better. "Toronto is in Ontario, which is located to the west of Quebec; nearer to the frontier."

"An," he inclined his head with formal politeness. "My mistake, ma'am. Geography was never my strongest suit."

"Chemistry was more your forte, as I recall," Stephen interjected, deciding he'd had enough of watching his friend and Mrs. Marsdale fencing with one another. He gave Aidan an apologetic look before adding, "Will you be staying for tea, or must you be on your way? I believe you mentioned you were expected at the City Philosophical Society?"

As he'd hoped, Aidan accepted his *congé* without turning a hair. "Yes, I was about to take my leave," he said, giving Mrs. Marsdale a charming smile. "Good day to you, Mrs. Marsdale, I look forward to seeing you again."

"Sir," Cara inclined her head as she had seen Miranda do. "It was a pleasure to meet you."

He raised his eyebrows. "Was it?" he drawled, and then left before Cara could think of a snappy comeback.

A charged silence followed, and Cara knew she was about to be given a dressing down by her straitlaced host. Instead of waiting to be chastised like a misbehaving brat, she fell back on one of the first lessons she'd learned as a constable; when in danger of attack, strike first, and strike hard.

"Before you say another word, I think you should know it wasn't my idea to act as bloody Lady Bountiful," she said, folding her arms across her chest and glaring at him. "Mrs. Finch seemed to think it was my duty as your cousin to greet your guests, and she wouldn't take no for an answer. I was only trying to help."

Since Hargraves had already told him more or less the same thing, Stephen wasn't in the least surprised by her heated defense. Not that he intended letting her escape retribution so easily, however, he decided, determined to get something of his own back. He'd suffered sweet hell expecting her to say or do some horrifyingly outrageous thing, and he wanted to be certain the incident was not repeated.

"That may as be, Mrs. Marsdale," he informed her loftily, "but in future, I should appreciate your *trying* a trifle harder. Things could have become most awkward had you inadvertently revealed your true origins."

Cara dropped her arms, her eyes narrowing in indignation. "What do you take me for?" she demanded furiously. "I know a bloody sight more about time-travel than you do, mate, and I know better than to let anyone know the truth! It would be like violating the Prime Directive."

"The Prime Directive?" The term was unfamiliar to Stephen, although upon reflection he rather liked the sound of it. It implied a degree of inflexibility and honor he found intriguing.

"About not interfering with the customs and futures of other planets," Cara said, waving her hand impatiently. "But what I meant was—"

"Other planets?" Stephen interrupted. "Do you mean to say that in the future you are from, man has ascended to the stars?"

His incredulous expression stopped Cara, melting her anger and leaving her oddly tired. She stared at him, feeling the weight of every day of the one hundred and eighty-three years that separated her world from his. "No," she said quietly, wondering precisely how much she would tell him in the event she stayed. "It's just an expression from—from a play." She stumbled over the explanation, deciding that if she couldn't tell him about space flight, she certainly wasn't going to attempt to explain television programs to him.

"Oh." He looked disappointed.

She smiled slightly, then abruptly sobered. "I know I shouldn't have come downstairs," she said, meeting his gaze with cool dignity. "But short of telling Mrs. Finch the truth, I couldn't think of a graceful way to say no."

Her unexpected apology rocked Stephen back on his heels. He was prepared to do battle over her audacious behavior, now it seemed there would be no need. He wasn't certain if he was relieved or disappointed. He shook off the troubling notion, and offered her a conciliatory smile of his own.

"I would suppose that given the facts you behaved as you thought best," he conceded with a slight inclination of his head. "And I must say it went well. Aidan wasn't teasing when he said you were to be congratulated for your success with Lady Berksham. The countess is well-known for her icy reticence."

Cara thought of the bossy old woman who had dominated the conversation and bit back a chuckle. "Well, you couldn't prove it by me," she said ruefully. "I thought the old bird would never shut up. Maybe the secret to getting her to talk is to let her take over; she rather relishes being in control."

"So I noted," Stephen said, thinking a mother-in-law who enjoyed handling the reins sounded more than a trifle alarming. Not that it mattered, he decided with a heavy sigh. If the earl gave his permission for him to marry Lady Felicity, he would marry her regardless of how interfering her mother might be.

There was another long silence as the two stared at each other, and finally Cara gave a nervous shrug.

"Well, it looks like playtime's over," she said, aware of a flat sense of disappointment. "I guess I should be going back upstairs. Goodbye," and she turned toward the door.

"Mrs. Marsdale, wait."

She paused in surprise and flashed him a curious look. "Yes?"

"I am about to leave for Hampton Heath to fetch my great-aunt," Stephen said, condemning himself for a fool even as he made his offer. "Would you care to accompany me?"

Cara's heart leapt in excitement. "Leave the house?" she asked, hardly believing what she was hearing. She'd have sworn he would have walled her up in the secret room sooner than let her poke her nose out the door.

He cocked his eyebrows at her. "Are you saying the possibility never entered your head?"

She didn't bother denying the charge. "Maybe, if I couldn't access the room right away," she said, pleasure overwhelming her usual sense of caution. "But if you're offering now, I'm certainly not going to say no. When do we leave?"

"As soon as you are properly attired," he said, striding across the room to the rope pull. "It wouldn't do for you to make your first public appearance dressed so casually."

Cara opened her mouth in automatic protest, then quickly closed it. Being properly attired was just part of the disguise, she decided, and it was no different than the wild outfit she'd been wearing when she'd been zapped back in time. If she could tear around her London tarted up in punk make-up and black leather, then she could well do it dressed in a long dress and a cape. After all, she reasoned, how hard could it be?

Less than an hour later Cara and Stephen were in a carriage rumbling across London's teeming streets. Ignoring Stephen's admonishments that gawking was not good *ton,* Cara kept her nose pressed to the carriage's smudged window pane; trying to take in everything all at once. Some of what she saw was reassuringly familiar, while other sights were strange and somewhat horrifying. She found the spectacle of the gallows, set near the edge of what would be Oxford Street, particularly appalling, and she didn't hesitate sharing her disgust with Stephen.

"If you find the concept distressing, Mrs. Marsdale," he replied, his face set in grim lines, "consider how the poor prisoner must feel knowing his last moments on this earth will serve only to provide coarse amusement for his fellow man. Not a tantalizing prospect, I can assure you."

Cara turned to him, recalling too late that had Miranda not returned in time to prevent Stephen from being convicted of her murder, he would have ended his life at the end of a rope. She reached across the tight confines of the enclosed carriage and placed a gloved hand on his arm.

"I'm sorry," she said, meeting his turbulent gaze. "I'd forgotten you were put on trial last year. It must have been awful for you."

Stephen's lips twisted in a bitter smile. "Awful, Mrs, Marsdale, doesn't even begin to describe it," he said, recalling the fear and bleak horror that had been his constant companions in those terrible days. This was the first time he'd been near Tyburn Hill since being exonerated, and he felt a fatalistic tingling at the back of his neck. Anxious to shrug off the troubling sensation, he quickly turned the conversation to another topic.

"You must tell me your impressions of the city, ma'am," he said, shifting away from her. "Is it much changed in your day?"

She stared at him a long moment before replying. "In some

ways," she replied, understanding his need to distance himself from memories too terrible to bear. "The traffic's as bad, and God knows it's just about as noisy. Most of the area around here was destroyed in the Blitz, though, so there aren't many buildings left you'd recognize."

Stephen gave her an interested look. "The Blitz?"

Cara clamped her lips shut belatedly, furious with herself for revealing more of the future than she considered safe. From her years of watching the telly and her conversations with Alec she knew the dangers of mucking with time, and she wasn't about to risk apocalyptic repercussions by speaking out of turn. Aware he was waiting for an answer, she flashed him a quick smile.

"Sorry," she said, rolling her shoulders in an apologetic shrug. "I'm afraid I can't tell you any more than that."

He looked both astonished and insulted. "Whyever not?"

She hesitated, trying to find the words to explain. "Remember what I told you about the Prime Directive?" she asked, and at his wary nod, continued, "Telling you specific details of the future would violate that directive. It could alter what should be, and that could have implications I don't even want to contemplate. I'll gladly tell you certain things of what life is like in my day, but I can't discuss anything dealing with history. All right?" She studied him anxiously.

Stephen leaned back in his seat, surprised as much by what she said, as by the intensity with which she said it. He still found the concept of travelling between one time and another beyond comprehension, but upon reflection he realized that if such travel was possible, there must be some sort of rules in place governing it. Given that, he could not dispute the logic behind her stout refusal to tell him of the future.

"Very well," he said coolly, "I agree that you should refrain from telling me anything which you feel would be dangerous. But I would be most interested in learning more of the amazing things Miranda showed me in the magic box. Would that be permissible?"

Cara remembered the camcorder and tape Miranda had carried

back with her, and began cautiously discussing the wonders of the twentieth century with Stephen. His intelligence and enthusiasm surprised her, and she found herself losing her wariness as the carriage rumbled its way out of London.

Hampton Heath, a suburb of the city in her day, was a picturesque village lined with quaint cottages and elegant homes of rose-colored bricks and mullioned windows. Stephen ordered the carriage to stop in front of the smaller houses, his manner somber as he turned to Cara.

"I should warn you that Aunt Minn is a bit of an eccentric," he said slowly. "She is the dearest soul alive, but she has always been a bit vague. I think it would be best if you let me do the majority of the talking, and then follow my lead."

"Certainly, if you think it best," Cara agreed, tugging at the gloves covering her hands. Like the gown and pelisse they were about one size too small, and she prayed she wouldn't split the finely-grained leather.

A sullen maid admitted them into the house, and a few moments later they were escorted into a sitting room where a tiny woman in an ancient gown of black silk was sitting in front of the fire. She glanced up at their arrival, her face lighting with pleasure when she recognized Stephen.

"Stephen. Dear boy, whatever are you doing here?" she exclaimed, rising awkwardly to her feet. "Come and give your Auntie Minn a kiss."

"Hello, Aunt Minn," Stephen did as he was bid, bending from his considerable height to press a kiss on the woman's lined cheek. "How are you feeling this fine day?"

"In fighting trim, as my papa used to say," the older woman replied with a light laugh, her faded blue eyes focusing on Cara. "But who is this charming young lady? Have you brought your betrothed to meet your poor old aunt?"

"No, Aunt," Stephen replied hastily, gesturing Cara to join them. "This is Mrs. Cara Marsdale, she is Cousin Reginald's daughter. You remember Cousin Reginald, don't you?"

As Stephen hoped, the good lady bristled at this hint her memory was not all that it should be. "I should say that I do!" she replied, pokering up with indignation. "My mind ain't so dicked as that. Er . . . precisely which cousin was he?"

"The one who immigrated to Canada shortly before my parents were wed," Stephen said, elaborating on the old family scandal he could scarce recall. "He was a bit of a cardsharp, it was said, and there was something about his involvement with an actress—"

"Yes, well, there is no need to go into all of that right now," Minn interrupted, sending Stephen a warning glance and jerking her head in Cara's direction. "I am sure it was nothing more than a young man's folly, and all greatly exaggerated over the years. Hello, my dear," she held out her hand to Cara, "it is a pleasure to meet you. You have your father's looks about you, I must say."

"Mrs. Greensborough," Cara accepted her hand and managed an awkward curtsy. "It is kind of you to receive me."

"Nonsense, child," Minn replied, patting Cara's hand with brisk kindness, "you are family, after all, of course you shall be welcomed in my home. And you must call me Aunt Minn, as Stephen does. Your papa and I were the dearest of friends in our childhood days. How is he, by the by?"

Cara shot Stephen a panicked look, uncertain how to respond.

"Cousin Reginald died some years ago, Aunt Minn," Stephen replied smoothly. "You will recall, I showed you the letter."

"Oh, yes, I'd forgotten," Minn said, looking apologetic. "That is the problem of obtaining one's dotage, I fear. So many of one's friends and family pass on, it is quite impossible to remember who has died and who has not. But tell me of yourself, my dear. How do you come to be in London? Are you and your husband visiting Stephen for the Season?"

"Cousin Cara is a widow, Aunt, that is why she has come to England. She wishes to become acquainted with her father's family," Stephen answered, not missing a beat. "She arrived late last night, and I put her up at my house before going to my club. That's why we have come to see you. I am hoping you will see fit to accompany us back to London and act as Cara's chaperon."

Minn's eyes widened in astonishment. "Come to London for the Season?" she gasped, clasping her thin hands together. "Oh, my dears, I should be delighted!"

"Are you certain?" Cara felt she should say something. "It is a great imposition, I realize, but——"

"Oh, no, no, it is no imposition whatsoever!" Minn assured her, all but dancing in her excitement. "And even if it was, it shouldn't make the slightest whit of difference. I am a Harrington, and a Harrington always does their duty. Is that not so, Stephen?" And she cast Stephen a bright smile.

Stephen returned it slowly, thinking of the heavy cost he had paid and would doubtlessly still pay for proving the veracity of his aunt's proud boast. "Yes, Aunt Minn," he said in heavy tones. "A Harrington always does his duty."

"There, you see?" Minn gave Cara a quick hug. "Now, if you will pardon me, I must see to my packing. It will take but a few minutes, I promise you!" And she dashed from the room, eager as a young girl to set out for a ride with her favorite beau.

Six

To no one's surprise Aunt Minn's estimation proved optimistic, and it was over an hour before they were able to set out for London. Beside herself with excitement the older woman kept up a constant stream of chatter, bombarding Cara with questions and opinions as they journeyed back into the city.

"Cara is a lovely name, dearest, Italian, is it not? And such beautiful eyes you have! You will be counted as a diamond of the first water, I am sure. It is a pity your hair is cut so dreadfully; the first order of business will be to hire an abigail who is talented with the curling tongs.

"And you'll need a new wardrobe, of course. Nothing *too* stylish, as you are in mourning, but I daresay a modiste will be able to come up with something suitable. I shall certainly consult Lady Berksham on the matter, since she has graciously consented to sponsor you. Such a kind lady, the countess, and so proper, it is well she has given you the nod."

Cara listened in fascinated silence; stunned to think so much could have happened in less than twenty-four hours. This time yesterday she was searching for a violent rapist, and today she was preparing to be presented to a society that hadn't existed in close to two hundred years. Not even Stephen King could have dreamed up a scenario as bizarre as this, she decided, holding back a smile. It was simply too fantastic.

The household was expecting them, and everything had been arranged according to Stephen's orders. As a child of middle-class parents Cara was alternately appalled and astonished by the luxuries Stephen could command by merely lifting an eyebrow. She was placed in a room which in her day was part of the house next door, and she decided the first order of business would be to do some serious reconnoitering. There was a lot she felt she needed to know, and an undetermined amount of time in which to learn it.

While the maids were seeing to Mrs. Greensborough's comfort, she slipped out of her room and began exploring her surroundings. She counted the servants, making note of the security and sneering at what she found. A ten-year-old with a hat pin would yawn at the locks, she thought, wondering if Stephen would let her harden the place for him. From her conversations with Miranda she knew burglary was as much a problem in this time as it was in hers.

She continued roaming through the house, using her expertise to determine various points of entrance and exit that might prove tempting to a thief. She also checked out the room which from Miranda's descriptions had been her bridal chamber. The door was closed but not locked, and Cara was unable to resist the impulse to poke her head inside for a quick look. The room was small as were most of the rooms in the house, and decorated in fragile shades of rose and softest blue. A delicately-carved bed topped with a cream silk canopy was set opposite the fireplace, and against her will she felt drawn to it.

What had it been like for Miranda; a virginal bride waiting for a man she didn't really know to come and make love to her? she mused, tracing her finger down the rosewood post. Was she terrified? Resigned? Or was she shyly eager, excited by the thought of a man as handsome and compelling as Stephen touching her? Cara was the first to admit she was hardly an expert on the subject, but instincts she hadn't known she possessed told her that Stephen would be an attentive, thorough lover. He—

"What are you doing in here?"

The sound of a voice directly behind her jolted Cara and she spun around, her knees flexed and her hands held out in front of her. Stephen stood there, the expression on his face coolly superior as he studied her.

"Is this how men and women greet one another in your century?" he asked, his voice taking on the smoothly cultured tone that set her teeth on edge. "If so, I fear for the continuation of the species."

Cara lowered her hands to her sides and glared at him. "In my century a man would know better than to sneak up on a woman; especially a police officer, not unless he wanted to risk having his teeth kicked in," she grumbled, feeling slightly foolish.

"Something I shall try to remember should I ever find myself transported to your world," he said, his eyes never leaving her face. "But you haven't answered my question. Why are you here? Is the room Mrs. Finch selected for you not to your liking?"

"The room is fine, I was just doing a bit of exploring," she said, defending her actions with a scowl. "The house is larger than it is in my time."

"Is it?" Stephen was faintly amused by her sulky expression. "But the secret room is still there?"

She nodded, her hand going to the medallion she was wearing beneath the lacy scarf tucked into the neckline of her gown. "Alec found it after moving back into the house. It must have been walled up after Miranda disappeared; at least, that's what happened before," and she frowned at a sudden thought.

"Before what?" Stephen asked, watching the shifting of her mercurial expression and wondering if all women in 1996 were as prickly and as appealing as was she.

"I need to see the room," Cara said decisively, brushing past him. "I just thought of something." She hurried out of the room, leaving Stephen no choice but to follow. It was only when they reached the door to the secret room that he reached out a hand to stay her.

"Is it safe for you to enter?" he asked, gazing down at her. "I recall Miranda mentioning there was a danger the room could function incorrectly and sweep a person into the wrong time."

"That's a possibility, I suppose," Cara agreed, trying not to let her fear show. "But it hasn't happened so far. We think the room has some sort of homing device incorporated into it, and automatically returns the person to the point of origin."

The words meant nothing to Stephen and he dismissed them impatiently. "I am certain you must be anxious to return to your own time," he said, closing his hands over her shoulders, "and at the risk of sounding inhospitable, I admit I shan't be sorry to see you go. But," he added, when she opened her mouth in protest, "that doesn't mean I shall allow you to risk yourself needlessly. Tell me why you wish to go inside."

Cara glared at him, furious because much as she felt like telling him to sod off, she understood his need to protect her. She was a cop, and protecting people was second nature to her. She took a mental step back from the sharp edge of anger, and raised her head to meet his gaze.

"In the future we found or will find several items hidden in the wall," she said, speaking calmly. "For Miranda to make her way back and save you from the gallows, those items need to be there. I just wanted to see if they were safe."

He didn't so much as blink. "What sort of items?"

Cara frowned, trying to remember. "Some journals, jewelry, a knife, and several sacks of coins dating back to the Elizabethan era," she said, listing each one carefully. "But the journals are what are most important. They contain the spell that activates the time-travel mechanism."

Stephen looked at the hidden room and then down at her. "Where in the wall have these items been hidden?" he asked, reaching a decision.

Cara understood he meant to go in and check himself, and had to bite her lip to hold back her words of protest. Who went in wasn't worth debating, she told herself, trying to be logical. What was important was determining if the items were where they were supposed to be.

"In the very back, at the point where the back wall and the curved wall on the right side of the room meet," she said, refusing to acknowledge the secret feeling of relief coursing through her when she realized she wouldn't yet have to face the awesome power humming behind the painted plaster just yet. "There's a recess built into the wall, and if you feel around you'll find a lever to open it."

He nodded, visualizing the area she was describing. "Do you wish me to remove anything?"

She remembered what had happened when Alec had poked about in the thing and shook her head. "No, it might activate something. Just check to make sure everything's there and report back."

The note of command in her voice made him raise an eyebrow, but he said nothing. Instead he moved her gently to one side, opening a door Cara hadn't even seen until that moment. He gave her a final, silent look of warning and then slipped inside, closing the door behind him.

She stared at the hidden door, and swore inventively beneath her breath. The earl had missed his calling, she thought, moving forward to press her ear against the door. With his arrogance and knack for taking over, he should be in whatever passed for the Special Air Services in this benighted time. God knew he was every bit as provoking as Alec and his grim friends.

Much to her annoyance she couldn't hear a thing, and she was considering giving the door a discreet shove when she realized she wasn't alone. She whirled around to find Hargraves standing behind her, his bushy eyebrows lifted in disdain.

"Is there something you wish, madam?" he asked, his tone fairly dripping with condescending pleasure.

To her everlasting fury Cara felt an embarrassed flush steal across her cheeks. "No, Hargraves," she replied, drawing herself up with what pride she could muster. "Everything's fine, thank you. I was just waiting for his lordship."

Hargraves's beaked nose twitched, reminding Cara of a cat at a mouse hole. "Indeed?"

Cara was about to tell him where he could put his superior attitude when the door opened and Stephen stepped out into the hall. There was a strained expression on his face, but it vanished the moment he saw Hargraves standing behind Cara.

"Is there some difficulty, Hargraves?" he asked, addressing the butler with the unmistakable edge of authority in his voice.

"I was about to ask Mrs. Marsdale if she will be joining Mrs. Greensborough for tea, my lord," Hargraves responded with one of his deep bows. "Mrs. Finch was enquiring."

"Tell Mrs. Finch we shall take our tea in the sitting room," Stephen answered, stepping forward to take Cara's arm. "There is something of great importance I must discuss with my cousin."

Hargraves's gaze flicked from his master to Cara. "As you wish, sir," he said, his expression resigned as he gave another bow. "Will there be anything else?"

"No, Hargraves, you may go." Stephen dismissed the butler with a graceful nod before dragging Cara down the hall to the sitting room. The moment they were inside he closed the door, his expression grave as he turned to her.

"I was able to find the jewels and other artifacts you told me of," he began, sounding very much like a constable giving a report. "But there was no sign of the journals, or indeed of any books in the hidden vault."

Cara dropped on to the nearest chair. *"What?"*

Stephen repeated his message, adding that he had even searched for a second hidden compartment, but to no avail. The books were nowhere to be found.

"But they have to be there," Cara exclaimed when he finished speaking. "We find them in the future!"

"That may as be," Stephen replied, feeling every bit as baffled as she sounded, "but they aren't there now."

Cara sat in silence, trying to absorb the implications of what Stephen had told her. Something must have happened when she'd been zapped back to upset the time-space continuum, she decided unhappily. The question was, what? Had history itself been changed, and if so, how? Was whatever followed destiny or a ghastly mistake that could have horrific repercussions?

Or, she brooded, her mind racing off in the opposite direction, was her coming back meant to be? Maybe she'd been sent back to find the journals and place them in the vault so Alec would find then one hundred and eighty-three years in the future. Stephen was still alive and kicking which meant he hadn't hung for Miranda's murder, and that must mean the bloody things were still found. Or did it? Cara shook her head, bewildered and defeated at the enormity of trying to unravel the Gordian knot of time and fate.

Stephen watched her closely, wondering what dark thoughts could be responsible for the anguished expression in her gold-colored eyes. She had said the journals contained the formula to operate the time spell, and he surmised that without it, she was well and truly trapped in this time. He was still trying to decide how he felt about that when a maid appeared with the tea tray. He waited until she had deposited her burden and he and Mrs. Marsdale were alone again before speaking.

"I think it might be best if you had a cup of tea," he said, consciously adopting a soothing tone. It was obvious from the alabaster cast to her skin that she was near to swooning, he thought, wondering if he ought to send for Aunt Minn.

The delicate creature he was so concerned about glared up at him, her dark brows meeting in a scowl. "Tea, hell," she grumbled, pushing herself to her feet. "I want a bloody drink." Without waiting for a reply she stalked across the room to the decanter and poured a generous amount of brandy and downed it before turning back to face him.

"All right," she said, her voice decisive, "the first order of business is to decide what we do next. I think it's obvious I'm not going anywhere for the time being, so it would probably be best if we stick with the cover we've already established. If we pull out now, it could blow everything. Agreed?"

Stephen picked through her incomprehensible chatter and found just enough words to make some sense. "Agreed," he said, impressed once more by her almost masculine sense of logic.

"Good." She gave a jerky nod. "Since everyone accepts I'm from Canada I won't have to worry about every little move I

make, and that will leave me free to concentrate on more important matters. I'll leave it up to you to decide how deep my cover's
going to be, but I'm warning you," here she shot him another
scowl, "I'm not going to learn to faint. I don't care how lady-like
it's supposed to be, I'm not going to do it."

Her recalcitrant comment made Stephen smile. "If that is your
wish," he said "But you'll never be counted a true lady if you
can't affect the occasional swoon."

"Then it's a good thing I'm not supposed to be a true lady,
isn't it?" she retorted, looking pleased by the fact. "And don't
try telling me Miranda went about swooning all over the place,
either, because I don't believe it. She'd never act so asinine."

The mention of his former wife made Stephen sober. Mrs.
Marsdale was right to say Miranda never engaged in such missish
behavior, he brooded, recalling the exquisite manners that had
first brought her to his notice. A man grown, he had little use
for the silly, giggling chits who comprised that year's crop of
debs, and Miranda's serenity and gentle beauty had been sweetly
enticing. To say nothing of her fortune, he added with a bitter
flash of honesty. That had been the most attractive thing of all
to a man but two steps from the ignominy of debtor's prison.

"Stephen?" He felt a tentative touch on his arm and glanced
up to find Mrs. Marsdale studying him with concern. "What's
wrong?"

Stephen gazed deep into her remarkably-colored eyes, seeing
such a wealth of compassion and understanding that for a moment he was tempted to tell her everything. But he had kept his
own counsel for too long to trust so completely, and after a moment he glanced away.

"I was but wondering how best to handle the coming Season,"
he said, moving back from her and forcing himself to contemplate
the situation with the same cold deduction as had she. "Your
appearance will cause talk enough, but I shudder to contemplate
what your disappearance might mean."

"My disappearance?" She cocked her head to one side.

He took a moment to organize his thoughts before replying.

"I have been thinking, and I have decided it would be best if you not attempt to return to your own time just yet; even if such an attempt was possible," he said, watching her closely. "You have met too many people to simply vanish without a trace, and to be bluntly honest, madam, I do not care to be accused of murdering another female. Neither my sanity nor my honor could survive a second incarceration."

Cara's eyes widened, her preoccupation with time and space temporarily forgotten. He was right, she realized, angry with herself for not having considered the possibility. Naturally there'd be questions if she disappeared, and because of the scandal involving Miranda, those questions would be decidedly pointed. As a homicide inspector, she knew *she'd* be damned leery if two different women disappeared around the same suspect.

"You're right," she said, giving him a sheepish look. "If I zapped out again, I expect the magistrates would lock you up first, and ask questions later. I—" she broke off, a sudden memory poking viciously at her cognizance.

"What is it?"

She bit her lip, debating how to tell him about the original trial that had resulted in his execution. Since Miranda's return had altered the outcome she supposed it was no longer relevant, and learning one of his friends had betrayed him would only cause him further pain.

"Nothing," she said, scraping up a smile. "I was about to say that since I'm going to be staying a bit I'd prefer it if you called me Cara. I detest being called Mrs. Marsdale in that oh-so-polite way of yours. It's almost as bad as being called 'madam' by some snot-nosed clerk at the shop."

Stephen sensed there was more she was not telling him, but short of employing violence, he couldn't see any way he could force her to tell him. "Cara," he said, not admitting even to himself how sweet the name tasted on his tongue. "I shall be happy to address you so when we are private, but when others are about I fear we shall have to be more formal. I shall call you Cousin, or even Mrs. Marsdale, much as it pains you, and you shall address me as either Cousin, my lord, or by my title. Calling me by my given name would be considered fast. Agreed?"

Since it sounded sensible Cara nodded her head. "Agreed . . . Harrington," she said, wrinkling her nose. "But I'm warning you I'll only call you 'my lord' under penalty of death. Women's Liberation might not come for another century or so, but I'm damned if I'll kowtow to some clown just because he has a title."

Stephen scowled at her, disliking being called a clown; even in jest. "What the devil is Women's Liberation?" he asked, fair certain he would not care for the answer.

Her cat-in-the-cream smirk added to his certainty. "An idea whose time will come," she said sweetly. "And when it comes, *Cousin,* you'd best watch your back."

"No, no, my dear," Mrs. Greensborough's gentle voice was edged with reproach as she shook her head at Cara. "A duke is properly addressed as your grace, and a viscount is to be called my lord. Really, it is all very simple."

"To you, perhaps, but I still don't see why I have to know all of this. How many dukes will I be tripping over anyway?" Cara grumbled, feeling both stupid and resentful as she struggled to master the intricacies of Regency protocol. They'd been at it all morning, and she was no better informed now than when they started. No wonder the Americans revolted, she thought sourly. Waging war was far easier than trying to differentiate between a marquis and a baronet.

"More than one may suppose," Aunt Minn said with a sigh. "Dukes are rather like spots on one's face, you see; forever popping up to plague one when one least expects it. Now, in terms of formal address, who takes precedence; the daughter or the second son of an earl?"

Cara spent a few moments to wonder how a haughty duke would like being compared to a pimple before replying. "The daughter," she replied, mentally tallying one for the ladies' side.

"She is always called Lady Whatever while he's just plain mister."

"An honorable, if you please," the older woman corrected with a sniff, "and there is nothing plain about it. My dear father was an honorable, and he carried the distinction with pride. Titles may mean nothing in Canada, child, but here they are of the utmost importance. I trust you will remember that," and she gave Cara such a chiding look that she actually felt guilty.

"Yes, Aunt Minn," she said, ducking her head and feeling like a school girl being scolded by the head mistress. The sensation was one she'd been used to during her rebellious teenage years when she'd been the bane of the preparatory school her parents had sent her to out of sheer desperation.

Thinking of her parents brought a sharp pain to her heart, and she wondered if she'd been reported missing yet. It was now over three days since she had passed through time, and as she recalled, time passed at a different pace here than in the future. For all she knew only a few hours may have lapsed since she'd entered the hidden room, which meant it could be several more hours before anyone realized she'd gone missing. Alec and Miranda wouldn't be home for days, and likely it would be her partners who would be the first ones to notice she wasn't where she was supposed to be.

Given the nature of the duty she'd been on at the time of her disappearance there would be an immediate investigation, and she knew the Yard would throw all of their considerable resources into finding her. She winced when she pictured Interpol tracking down Alec and Miranda, and the looks on their faces when they were told she was missing. Would they realize what had happened? she wondered. Or would they think she was dead . . . or worse? She prayed it wasn't the latter, because she wasn't certain how Alec would face the pain of losing someone else he loved. He all but went crazy after his fiancee, Jane, was killed in a bombing.

"The modiste is coming this afternoon," Aunt Minn continued, not seeming to notice Cara's brooding silence. "And you are not to send her scurrying with your sharp remarks as you did yesterday. That was exceedingly unkind of you, Cara."

Cara remembered the incident well. The modiste, a plump woman with the nasty habit of using her pins to punish anyone who disagreed with her, had been trying to convince her to purchase a god-awful gown of puce silk with a neckline so low she doubted even Madonna would have the gall to wear it. She tried diplomacy, she tried imitating Lady Berksham's icy superiority, and when that failed she fell back on her best weapon, sarcasm, and told the dressmaker she'd seen a couple of prostitutes on the wharf who would probably appreciate her skills. The woman had fled in tears, and Aunt Minn had come in a few minutes later to shake her head and scold her.

"I'm not used to London fashions, Aunt," Cara replied, deciding it was close enough to the truth to suit. "In Canada we aren't nearly so . . . ah . . . daring."

"Yes, but you aren't in the colonies now, are you?" Aunt Minn asked rhetorically. "You are in London, about to make your bows, and your toilette must be of the first stare else it will cause endless talk. You don't want the *ton* gossiping about your cousin, do you? Not after he has been kindness itself to you?"

Even knowing the wily old woman was manipulating her couldn't keep Cara from squirming. "Of course not," she muttered, "I just don't see why they should care. My father wasn't even an honorable . . . was he?" Panicked, she couldn't remember.

"No," Aunt Minn said, much to Cara's relief, "but his father was, and your great-uncle was an earl. It will be expected that you will be fired off with all the ceremony due a debutante; even at your advanced age, and to do otherwise would be to invite the most unpleasant tattle. And believe me, after last year, the last thing poor Harrington needs is more gossip."

Cara's ears pricked up at this. She'd been dying to learn more details of Stephen's arrest and trial, but so far she hadn't worked up the nerve to ask him directly. She was also reluctant to ask the servants, afraid they'd go running to that damned Hargraves and tell him she was snooping. She shot Aunt Minn a calculating look, trying to decide the best way of getting information from her. Interrogating informants had been one of her strengths while still a WPC, and after taking a few moments to formulate her questions she sat up in her chair and assumed her most innocent expression.

"Why, Aunt Minn, whatever do you mean?" she asked, deciding that if she'd come from the wilds of Canada as she claimed, it was unlikely she would have even heard of the trial. "Never say Cousin Stephen was involved in a scandal!"

Her shocked exclamation was all it took for the tale to come tumbling out of the older woman. "It was dreadful," she began, scooting her chair closer to Cara's and lowering her voice to a confidential whisper. "His bride disappeared on her wedding night, and they said he killed her!"

"Really?" Cara concentrated on keeping her expression properly horrified. "But why should they suspect him of murder? Cousin Stephen is clearly a gentleman."

"Indeed he is!" Aunt Minn agreed, nodding her head vigorously. "One of the finest gentleman I have ever known, and so I told that fool of a magistrate who had him arrested, but he would not listen. He even refused to let me give testimony on Stephen's behalf once the trial started; said it wasn't relevant." And she gave a loud sniff.

Cara stiffened at this bit of news. In the future she had read the book Miranda had found detailing the trial, and she remembered how the many inaccuracies in jurisprudence had troubled her. Her ex-husband had been appointed Queen's Counsel, and while helping him prepare she'd learned more about the tenants of British Law than she'd ever cared to know. And among the things she'd learned was that even in this time when no one had heard of the concept of suspect's rights, character witnesses were routinely allowed to speak at trials; especially those involving capital offenses. And yet Stephen, a powerful peer, had been denied this basic right, she brooded, recalling her suspicions he had been framed. But the question was who had framed him? And more importantly, why?

"Poor Stephen was beside himself as you may well imagine," Aunt Minn continued in her gossipy way. "For any man to be accused of such a crime is distressing, but for a man of your cousin's pride and sense of honor, it was unbearable. The evidence presented against him was overwhelming, and had the Jezebel he'd so unadvisedly married not returned from Ireland to prevent it, I am certain he would have hung."

Cara bristled instantly in Miranda's defense. "I don't see why you have to call her names," she said indignantly. "She came back, didn't she? She could have just let him hang."

"That is so," Aunt Minn allowed with visible reluctance, "but you do not know the reason *why* she left in the first place. It was so she could be with her lover; a fact she admitted before Parliament, if you can believe such brass! Naturally Harrington had the marriage annulled the moment he was able, but there was still the most awful scandal. That is why you must be so very careful in your behavior, my dear. Your cousin is only now recovering from the slurs cast upon his name, and it would take little to undo everything he has worked so hard to accomplish."

Cara nodded dutifully, murmuring a promise to do nothing that would endanger her dear cousin's good name. But even as she was vowing to behave as piously as a nun, she was already planning on how to follow up on what she'd learned. It wasn't much, admittedly, but as an inspector she'd learned that the best way of building a case was bit by agonizing bit.

If Stephen had been framed, then the person or persons responsible were still out there. And if they were still out there, she mused, carrying the equation to its logical end, then they were still a danger to Stephen. A great deal of time and effort had gone in to having him charged, and she doubted whoever had gone to that trouble would be content to shrug their shoulders and walk merrily away. Whoever they were, wherever they were, they were probably watching and waiting for the opportunity to strike again. But this time Stephen had a weapon the others didn't have, she decided, unconsciously squaring her shoulders. He had her; a twentieth-century police officer, skilled in investigation, and she was determined to put all those skills to use in his defense should the need arise.

Not because she was particularly fond of the earl, but because there was something she disliked even more than his chauvinistic, imperial manner; injustice, and those who would subvert the law to their own ends. She had sworn an oath to uphold and defend the law, and uphold and defend it she would. And if Harrington knew what was good for him, he would bloody well stay out of her way.

Seven

Cara saw little of Stephen over the next several days as Aunt Minn and Lady Berksham put her through a training regime that would have made Alec's SAS sergeants weep with envy. Mornings were devoted to fittings and shopping, while afternoons were given over to lessons in deportment and etiquette. Cara felt like a dim-witted Eliza Dolittle being put through her paces, except that the cockney flower girl only had one Professor Higgins riding her case while she had two hard-nosed, sharp-eyed critics who found fault with everything she said or did.

"Your walk is still too masculine," Lady Berksham announced, studying Cara through a piece of glass she discovered was called a quizzing glass. "A lady must move through a room like a scented breeze, my dear, not blow through the house like a winter gale off the North Sea."

"Yes, my lady," Cara said through gritted teeth, clinging to her patience with effort. It was four in the afternoon, and she felt like she'd been on riot duty. Her head ached, her feet ached, and her back, strapped to a length of board, felt as if it would break. And to think she used to believe women of this time were weak, she mused, sending a mental apology to her sister-in-law. Evidently they had to possess the strength of Samson, the wisdom of Solomon, and the patience of Job, and that was before they even encountered any blasted males. God only knew what biblical aptitudes they would need then, she thought, moving her shoulders in a tired shrug. The ability to walk on water, doubtlessly.

"You are at a dinner party," Lady Berksham began in the tones of a senior officer grilling a raw constable, "and the hostess, *not* a person of the first consequence, introduces you to a gentleman of dubious morals and reputation. What do you do?"

Throw him into the punch bowl, Cara thought, even as she said, "Acknowledge the introduction, and then move away from him as quickly as propriety allows."

"And?" The gentle prod came from Aunt Minn.

"And I mention the incident to Lord Harrington so that he might have a word with the lady, and naturally I accept no further invitations from her," she concluded, resisting the urge to mimic sticking a finger down her throat in a gesture so common in the latter part of her century. Not that she needed to fake gagging, she thought with a grimace. Any more of this nonsense, and she'd be . . . what was the expression she heard the footman say the other day . . . ah yes, casting up her accounts.

"Very good, child," Lady Berksham was nodding her approval of Cara's delicate manners. "You need only a few more lessons, and you will be ready to be presented to the *ton*. But first you must work on your air of consequence. It will need refining if you are to be taken for a *femme du monde*."

"Yes, my lady," Cara murmured, making a note to include the word in the dictionary she was secretly composing. Learning the lingo was the first thing a detective did when going undercover, she told herself, smiling reminiscently as she remembered her horror and embarrassment when she'd first worked the prostitute beat as a decoy. She'd no idea there could be so many colorful euphemisms for sex acts.

"Well, what do you say, Mrs. Greensborough?" Lady Berksham was regarding Aunt Minn with indulgence. "Shall we take our little chit for an outing?"

"Oh, yes, Lady Berksham, the very thing!" Aunt Minn gushed, paying no attention to Cara's furious scowl. "And I have just the place in mind; the tea Lady Burlough is giving for her son. An invitation arrived yesterday morning, and I have been toying with the notion of attending."

Cara remembered the invitation as well, and stepped forward in alarm. "But that's today!" she protested, and then snapped her lips shut, disgusted with herself for being such a coward.

"Yes, and if we mean to make it there at a fashionable hour, we shall have to leave now," the countess said, rising to her feet and shaking out her skirts. "You may go as you are dressed, Mrs. Marsdale, although you may wish to remove your backboard first. I fear it spoils the line of your gown."

Less than an hour later Cara was seated in a spindly chair of striped silk, a cup of tea clasped in a shaking hand. Around her the hum of conversation rose and fell, but she sat silently, unable to think of a single word to say. Not that she was afraid, her pride insisted mutinously, she was just being cautious. One of the first lessons her training officer had taught her was that for a plain-clothed operative, silence was indeed golden. Not that he'd phrased it that way, she reflected with a half smile. As she recalled, his exact words were, "Keep your mouth closed, rookie, and you just might keep breathing."

The rustle of silk penetrated her thoughts, and she glanced up just as Lady Felicity settled in the chair beside her.

"I am so pleased to see you, Mrs. Marsdale," she said, her soft hazel gaze resting on Cara's face. "How are you enjoying your visit to our city?"

Cara glanced to the corner where several men in high-collared shirts, enormous cravats, and bright jackets were clustered around a trio of giggling girls dressed in gowns similar to the ones she and Lady Felicity were wearing. "Interesting," she said at last. "Very interesting."

"Mama is most pleased with the progress you have been making," Lady Felicity continued anxiously. "Indeed, she said you were a most intelligent young lady."

"Did she?" The confession both surprised and pleased Cara. She'd been certain the countess was one of those instructors who delighted in finding fault with their pupils, but it seemed she'd misjudged the old girl.

"I shouldn't look so honored, Mrs. Marsdale," Miss Blackwell drawled, dropping on the other chair and flashing Cara a teasing grin. "To her ladyship, intelligence in a female is almost as fatal a quality as plain-spokenness."

"Jane," Lady Felicity shook her head at her companion in gentle disapproval, "you know that is not so. You are hipped because mama scolded you for reading those political tracts."

"And for discussing them with you," Miss Blackwell said, rolling her shoulders. "But I still feel that if you're going to marry Lord Harrington, you should have some understanding of the political process. It is obvious his lordship takes his responsibilities to his party quite seriously, and as his wife, he will expect you to do the same."

Cara choked on the sip of tea she had just taken. Lady Felicity was going to marry Stephen? she thought, then wondered why she should be shocked. The younger woman was very pretty and seemed quite sweet, and Stephen was undoubtedly handsome and sexy. It wasn't surprising they should fall in love. Then she remembered the calm way Miranda had discussed marriage in this day, and turned to the blonde.

"I didn't know you and my cousin were engaged," she said, offering her a quick smile. "My congratulations, Lady Felicity."

The girl began to blush. "I fear my companion has spoken out of turn," she said, frowning at Miss Blackwell. "His lordship hasn't asked for my hand in marriage."

"Yet," Miss Blackwell supplied, ignoring her employer's reaction. "But it is only a matter of time before he does ask; and is accepted. I heard your papa telling your mother he had no objections to the match should the earl chose to press his suit."

"But how do you feel?" Cara asked Lady Felicity. "Do you love Steph—Lord Harrington?" she hastily corrected herself.

Lady Felicity's cheeks grew even rosier. "His lordship is very kind," she said, lowering her gaze to her clenched hands. "I do not know him well enough to have deeper feelings for him, but what I do know of him, I admire. He is a good, decent man."

Much as she agreed with the younger girl on that score, Cara was curious to learn more about why an obviously intelligent woman like Lady Felicity would willingly enter into the cold-blooded morass of an arranged marriage. "You will forgive me, but in Canada, we view these things differently," she said, choosing her words with care. "We tend to marry for love, and consider it the most important ingredient in any marriage. I find the notion of marrying a man one scarce knows . . . puzzling," she concluded, deciding that word fit as well as any.

Much to Cara's relief, Lady Felicity seemed more flustered than angry. "I am sure that given time I could learn to love his lordship," she said, shyly meeting Cara's gaze. "As I said, he is a good man, and one I know would never dishonor me or our vows. That is more than many females in my position can say," she added, her voice showing the first hint of bitterness.

That hint as well as the resignation in her manner intrigued Cara, but before she could question her further several gentlemen wandered over to join them. Two of the men were dandies, and she listened derisively as they bragged about their neckcloths and the cut of their jackets. When that topic had been exhausted they moved on to relating the latest gossip, and she was about to excuse herself when she heard one of the men say,

"There was another murder last night; did you hear about it? That makes the third one in less than a month. Disgraceful, I would call it."

"I quite agree with you," a second dandy, Mr. Dickson, said with a delicate shudder. "First there was that unpleasantness at Wapping Docks, and now this. Really, it quite makes one wonder where it will all end."

"Murder?" Cara repeated, trying not to sound too eager. She'd been too busy in the past few days to read the paper, but she decided to remedy the mistake the moment she got back home. Provided the ever-efficient Hargraves hadn't already disposed of the papers, she thought with a flash of annoyance.

"Yes, dreadful business, and not at all fit for a young lady's ears," a new arrival said, bending a disapproving frown on the other men. "You must forgive my friends, ma'am, for being so indiscreet as to mention the matter."

"But I am concerned," Cara protested, scowling up at the man. "If a maniac is at large, I think I should be told so that I might defend myself!"

"You needn't worry on that score," the man said blushing awkwardly. "The unfortunate victims were . . . er . . . soiled doves."

Prostitutes. Cara stiffened slightly, her thoughts racing to the mutilated hookers in her own time. She remembered her frustration and guilt at not being able to solve those cases, and wondered if she'd just been given a way of making amends to those women. Since she couldn't help them, she reasoned, then maybe she could help these victims.

"How very sad," she murmured, deciding to pursue the matter on her own. "I hope the authorities will find the man responsible and punish him accordingly."

"As do I," the man agreed with a sigh. "But I much doubt that will happen. The Runners do well enough when it comes to simple crimes like theft and house-breaking, but something like this cries out for more. What is wanted here is a professional police force; like they have in France."

Cara almost fell off her chair. "Professional police?" she echoed, wondering if she was in the presence of Sir Robert Peel; the man who founded the Metropolitan Police force in the 1820s.

"Yes," the man gave an eager nod. "Say what you will of the French, their methods of dealing with crime are extraordinary."

"Please, Mrs. Marsdale," one of the dandies interrupted with an affected yawn, "do not encourage McNeil, I beg of you. An organized police force is his *raison d'etre,* and he will prattle on about the matter forever if you let him."

Remembering her cover, Cara managed not to tell the mincing dandy where he could stuff it. Instead she turned her shoulder on him, giving him what Lady Berksham told her was the cut direct. "You present an interesting hypothesis, Mr. McNeil," she said, offering the dark-haired man an encouraging smile. "I would enjoy hearing more about it, if you don't mind."

Instead of agreeing, he shook his head. "I am afraid Bevil is correct, ma'am," he said, his brown gaze flicking to the others.

"And in any case, murder is hardly a suitable topic of conversation for ladies. I would not wish to give offense."

"But what about—"

"Mrs. Marsdale, I believe your aunt wishes you to attend her," Miss Blackwell interrupted, laying her hand on Cara's arm. "She has been signaling you with her fan."

Cara took the hint, and tried to be grateful Miss Blackwell had prevented her from making a fool out of herself. Murmuring an apology to the others she rose to her feet, and hurried to the corner where Aunt Minn and Lady Berksham were sitting.

"Are you enjoying yourself, ma'am?" she asked, automatically straightening the silk shawl on the older woman's shoulders. In the week she'd spent in her company she'd noticed her erstwhile aunt was incapable of remaining tidy for more than five minutes at a time. Just like Marcus, she thought, her heart aching at the thought of the nephew she might never see again.

"Oh indeed, my dear," Aunt Minn said, her eyes shining with pleasure. "I'd forgotten how delightful these little parties can be. We must have one of our own once you have been properly introduced to society."

Cara glanced around the elegant green and gold salon, counting well over twenty people crammed inside. Apparently her idea of little and Aunt Minn's idea of little were different, she decided, trying to imagine a crowd this size stuffed into the small rooms in the house on Curzon Street.

"Yes, Aunt Minn," she said, feeling decidedly claustrophobic at the thought. "I'm sure that will be fine."

"Of course it will." Minn gave her hand a distracted pat. "Now, you must tell me what you think of Mr. Elliott; the gray-haired gentleman standing by the window. He is a widower with an income of six hundred pounds per annum, and on the catch for a new wife, they say. Lady Berksham and I have been discussing whether or not he would suit."

Cara swallowed, sensing uncomfortably what was to come next. "Suit?" she asked, casting the plump man with the sullen face and hard eyes a worried look.

"For you, dearest," her hand was treated to another pat. "But do not worry. If you don't care for him, I am certain we can find someone else for you. After all, the Season is young. We have all the time in the world to find you a new husband."

All the time in the world, Cara thought, not certain whether to laugh or cry. *Oh, Aunt Minn, if only you knew.*

Tattersall's was doing its usual brisk business as Stephen walked into the portion of the Subscription Room set aside for members of the Jockey Club. He'd joined the prestigious club a few weeks ago; not daring to submit his name for admittance until he was certain the worst of the scandal was well behind him. The disgrace of applying and then being rejected was a risk he had not cared to take.

He nodded to a few casual acquaintances, accepting a glass of port from the liveried servant as he took his seat before the fireplace. He'd taken but a few sips when he heard someone call his name, and he glanced up to find Gilbert Holloway strolling toward him, a tankard of ale in his hand.

"I really must make more of an effort to keep *au courant,*" he drawled, coming to a halt in front of Stephen's chair. "I must be sadly behind times to have missed the great tragedy that has befallen our nation."

"What great tragedy?" Stephen demanded, hoping the old king hadn't died. That would make Prinny king; a circumstance Stephen could not bear to even contemplate.

"It is mid-day and you are not in Parliament," Gil explained, settling easily into one of the club's soft leather chairs. "What else can I think but that the entire edifice has crumbled into dust? Certainly nothing else could account for your presence here while the House is in session."

Stephen accepted the good-natured ribbing in the spirit with which it was intended. "You may scoff now," he said, leaning back in his chair to grin lazily at his friend. "But if your sickly cousin turns up his toes, you will be joining me there. You should begin studying the issues now, so that you will be better informed when you take your seat."

Gil opened his eyes wide in mock-horror. "A Viscount Quigley be informed on the issues?" he asked in shocked tones. "Come, Harrington, how can you say such a thing? You must know we chose to remain in blissful ignorance, voting whatever way our party leader tells us. It would not do to fly in the face of such a noble tradition; who knows what chaos might follow?"

Stephen threw back his head and laughed. He knew Gil's careless sense of humor offended many; Aidan, included, but he couldn't help but be amused. Being around Gil kept a man on his toes, and if he was sometimes a trifle cutting with his wit, he was just as sincere with his apologies afterward.

"You still haven't told me what you are doing at Tatts when you ought to be hissing the Prime Minister," Gil said, studying Stephen with narrowed eyes. "Never say you are actually going to purchase yourself some decent cattle? About time, I should say."

Gil had been trying to talk him into purchasing a coach and four since he and Miranda had become engaged, but Stephen had never done so. He'd been impoverished too long to squander money so foolishly, but of late he had been reconsidering the matter. And now that his aunt and Cara were staying with him, he thought it might be best to have a coach at their disposal.

"The thought had crossed my mind," he admitted, "but the reason I am here is to purchase a horse for my cousin. I mean to take her riding once my aunt and Lady Berksham have finished putting her through her paces."

Gil's lips curved in a mocking smile. "Ah yes, your mysterious cousin, I have been hearing much about her."

Stephen wasn't sure he cared for the thought of Cara being fodder for the rumor mongers, and he was definitely certain he didn't care for the sneering note in Gil's voice. He set his glass down, his eyes narrowing as he studied his friend.

"What is that supposed to mean?" he asked, keeping his voice neutral with an effort. "What have you been hearing about Cara?"

"Only that she seems to have appeared out of thin air," Gil said with a careless shrug. "You know how it is with the *ton;* there is nothing they relish more than a juicy bit of tattle. You mustn't be so priggish, old fellow. It's not as if they are gossiping about you."

Stephen's willingness to indulge Gil's acerbic wit vanished under a wave of cold anger. "No," he agreed in deadly tones, "but they are gossiping about my cousin, and any gossip that touches upon a member of my family touches upon me. I will not tolerate it, Holloway, do you hear me?"

An odd look crossed Gil's face, but it was gone so quickly Stephen could not put a name to it. "Now you are hipped," he said, giving one of his weary sighs. "You must know I am only teasing. You oughtn't be so quick to rise to the bait, my friend; it only encourages me."

The answer was so like Gil, Stephen's anger vanished. "I am sure it does, but I will thank you not to joke about my name or my honor," he said, bending a stern look on his friend. "After last year, you can understand my sensitivity on the matter."

Gil sobered abruptly. "I had forgotten about that," he said, setting down his tankard and frowning. "Christ, Stephen, I still can not believe the magistrates were foolish enough to charge you with Miranda's death. They must have been mad."

"Aidan hinted he thought they may have been bribed," Stephen said quietly. This was the first time he and Gil had discussed the trial, and he was relieved to know the other man accepted his innocence without question.

"It wouldn't be the first time a magistrate lined his pockets at someone else's expense," Gil commented, then shook his head. "If only I could have been here to help you. I wanted to, you must know that, but my uncle had taken dangerously ill and his solicitor insisted that I be present. But even then I wrote the courts offering testimony on your behalf, only to be told it wasn't necessary."

"Wasn't necessary?" Stephen repeated, remembering how the bookish man who had been his solicitor had scrambled to find someone willing to testify in his defense.

"You know how ponderously slow the courts move," Gil said, picking up his tankard. "By the time the old fools got around to responding to my offer, Miranda had already reappeared and the charges against you had been dismissed."

Stephen accepted the explanation in silence, although he still felt a prickling of unease. If the magistrates knew of Gil's offer to testify, he mused, why hadn't they shared that information with his solicitor? One of the reasons the case against him was so strong was that there was no one who could testify he could not have killed Miranda. If the magistrates knew of Gil's testimony but kept it to themselves, then the possibility they had been bribed became a certainty. The question was, what would he do about it? He was pondering the matter when Gil muttered a sudden curse beneath his breath.

"Talk of the devil," he said, nodding toward the doorway. "Look who just walked in."

Stephen obediently glanced up, his lips thinning at the sight of the plump, overly-dressed man who was bearing down on them; his face red with anger.

"Bloody hell," he said, unconsciously repeating one of the curses Cara was forever uttering. "What is he doing here?"

"He must have settled his gaming debts," Gil answered, and then fell silent as the man under discussion stalked up to them.

"I must have a word with the directors," he sneered, glaring at Stephen over his hooked nose. "Their standards must indeed be lax to admit an accused murderer to their club."

There were several shocked gasps followed by a heavy silence, and Stephen was acutely aware that every eye in the place was resting on him. He knew Proctor was only goading him, just as he knew that he would be the one most hurt by the ensuing gossip should he respond to that goading. He told himself his best response was an icy indifference, and his jaw tightened as he fought down the fury rising inside him.

"How strange you should say so, Mr. Proctor, when I was only this moment commenting on the same thing," Gil interjected, lifting his quizzing glass and regarding Proctor with an insolence there was no mistaking. "Harrington, I said, we must speak with the board of governors in charge of this place. The membership has gone to rack and ruin. They'll be letting just anyone in if we do not keep a sharp eye on them."

There were more gasps, and Proctor's face turned an alarming shade of purple. "Mind your own business, you know-nothing dandy," he bellowed, his hands balling into impotent fists. "No one was talking to you!"

"Indeed they are not," Gil responded silkily, his meaning all too clear in the cutting smile he offered. "This is a club for gentlemen, Proctor, so might I suggest you leave? You are sadly out of your element here."

Proctor's eyes all but bulged from his face, and there was murder in their depths when he turned to Stephen. "So that's how you mean to play it, eh?" he scoffed. "You're not man enough to stand up to me yourself, so you hide behind this man-milliner here. Well, it won't wash, you bastard. The courts may not hold you to fault, but I say to your face you are not but a cheat and a murderer! You killed my stepdaughter, and stole the fortune what should have been mine!"

Stephen rose slowly to his feet, a cold fury curling in his belly. "You go too far, Proctor," he warned, his voice tight with anger. "I am trying very hard to remember that you are years older than I, but if you say another word, you will leave no choice but to challenge you."

"You'd like that, wouldn't you?" Proctor responded with a contemptuous laugh. "You'd like nothing better than to put a bullet in old Elias Proctor and be done with him."

"I would like nothing of the sort," Stephen corrected, making a desperate grab for control. "But if you insult me or my family again, make no doubt I *will* seek satisfaction. Is that clear?"

Several footmen appeared, and the way they were bearing down on Proctor told its own story. He cast them a furious glare, before turning back to face Stephen. "All right, my fine lord," he snarled, "this round I give to you. But if you think this is the end of it, you're wrong. I want what's owed me, and I'll get it. One way or the other, I'll get it." And with that he turned and stormed out, leaving a roar of gossip in his wake.

Eight

Two days following the confrontation at The Jockey Club Stephen was in his study when Cara came storming in, her jaw set at a pugnacious angle.

"That's it," she announced, her amber eyes flashing fire as she stalked toward Stephen. "I've tried to fit in, I've tried not to draw any attention to myself, but this is the last straw! I'm not taking any more of this, do you hear me?"

Stephen's eyebrows rose at her fiery tones, but he gave away nothing of his thoughts as he set down his quill with studied care. "I would say the flower sellers in Covent Garden hear you, Cousin," he said, leaning back in his chair to study her. "Now, precisely what is it you refuse to take any longer?"

His calm, reasonable tone made Cara want to toss him over her shoulder, and for the briefest of moments she considered doing it. She knew how to control a throw so he wouldn't be seriously hurt, and it would be worth incurring his fury; if only to wipe that cool, superior look from his face. She contemplated the image for a few moments and then gave a disheartened sigh.

"Being a lady," she said, turning from him and walking over to the window. "You have to understand things are different in my time. I'm used to working out every day, and I can't take any more of this sitting on my hands and doing nothing. I feel like I'm in stir, and if I don't get out and do something, I'll go out of my mind!"

Stephen hid his shock at her impassioned words. He'd thought Cara had adapted rather well to his time. Indeed, there were times when he'd found it easy to forget the incredible truth of who and what she was, and he'd been lost in admiration of the cool control she exercised over her every word and action. Now it seemed he had been overly optimistic.

"I know you are accustomed to holding a position," he began heavily, hating that he should have to deprive her of the only thing she had ever asked of him. "But I fear I can not let you seek employment just yet. It would cause talk, and as well you know, that is something I would as lief avoid."

"Employment?" She swung around from the window, a confused look on her face. "What are you talking about?"

Now it was Stephen who was baffled. "You did say you wished to work in some capacity or another," he said slowly. "I was but explaining why that is not possible."

"Work . . . oh!" Understanding dawned, and Cara shook her head at him. "No, I didn't mean work out as in a job, I meant work out as in exercise. You know, like aerobics and free weights."

Stephen didn't know what those things might be, but he did understand enough of her conversation to comprehend she meant she wished to do something invigorating such as walking, or, he brightened at the thought, riding.

"I wanted to go running," Cara said, relieved he was listening, "but I'm smart enough to know that would never work here. I tried tai chi, but it's impossible to move in these bloody skirts, and doing it in the raw made me feel like an idiot. Do you know what I mean?" She cast him a hopeful look.

An image of Cara, delightfully naked, flashed in Stephen's mind, temporarily robbing him of the ability to speak . . . or think. "Indeed," he managed, drawing a deep breath to steady his galloping pulse. "I quite understand your dilemma."

"Good," Cara said, settling in one of the leather chairs facing his desk. "I was hoping you would. With your permission, I thought I'd have one of the rooms on the top floor turned into a gym. I wouldn't need anything fancy, mind. Just some mirrors and some mats on the floor so I won't hurt myself when I fall."

Stephen put a hand to the head that was beginning to throb. "You plan to fall?"

"I will if I do any tai qwan do," she said, warming to her plans. "I have a second degree brown belt, and I need to keep my skills toned so I don't lose them. Never know when they might come in handy, right?" She flashed him a gamine grin.

"Right," Stephen mumbled, feeling as hopelessly confused as he did when his tutor first began rattling Greek at him.

"In the meanwhile I thought I'd run up and down the back-stairs," Cara continued blithely. "It won't give me as good a workout as a stairmaster, but it's better than nothing, and at least it will get my heart rate up. What do you think?"

Stephen could think of nothing less productive than racing up and down flights of stairs, but if it would give Cara pleasure, he supposed there was no harm in it. "If that is what you wish to do, then you must by all means do so," he said, picking up a letter opener and examining it carefully. "But I have in mind an alternative which you may find interesting. Do you ride?"

Cara sat up. "Horses?"

He smiled at her enthusiastic tones. "Yes."

Cara bit her lip, torn between her eagerness to get out in the fresh air and her own innate honesty. She'd been on a horse a grand total of five times her entire life, and that had been several years ago. But, the thought slid slyly into her mind, she hadn't fallen off any of those times, and one of her dates who'd taken her told her she had a 'nice seat'.

"It's been awhile," she temporized, "but I do enjoy it. When could we go?"

Stephen thought of the pretty mare he'd purchased two days earlier; it was being stabled at the mews at the end of the street along with his own bay gelding. He glanced at the ornate clock on his mantel and back at Cara's eager face. "Shall we say thirty minutes?" he asked politely. "It will probably take you that long to change into your riding habit."

Cara's delight turned into dismay. "Riding habit?"

"Certainly," Stephen wouldn't have been human not to feel a

surge of amusement at her crest-fallen expression. "As you say, my time is different than yours, and I fear we require our ladies to wear habits when riding. But you needn't feel slighted," he added before she could sputter a protest, "we gentlemen must also be dressed in proper riding togs. Now hurry and change. I'll meet you in the entryway in half an hour."

"Sidesaddle," Cara grumbled, a ball of fear knotting in her stomach as she clung to the horse's mane. "I forgot women rode bloody sidesaddle."

Stephen studied her stiff figure worriedly, fearing she would topple from her mount at any moment. "Would you like to go back?" he asked, angry with himself for not taking better care of her. He hadn't stopped to think riding styles might be different in the future, and it was only when her mount had been led out and he saw her face that the possibility occurred to him. Now he felt foolish and more than a little concerned, knowing Cara's fierce pride would decree that she die before admitting she was not in complete control of herself and the situation.

As if sensing his thoughts, she sent him a resentful look. "Don't be stupid," she said, her hands tightening on the reins. "I'll be all right in a moment. This just takes some getting used to, is all."

Stephen clenched his jaw, fighting the urge to take command and insist they return to the stables. That might work with the ladies of his day, but he knew better than to employ such tactics with his houseguest. He could only keep them plodding along at a sedate pace, and pray she didn't come up a cropper. They rode down Curzon Street in the direction of Hyde Park, and for once traffic along the busy street was light. They'd gone less than a block before he risked addressing her.

"You look very lovely in that color," he commented, flicking an approving glance over her slender figure draped in black velvet. "Black becomes you."

"Well, I'm glad you like it," Cara shot back, struggling to find and keep her center of gravity. "It's the most uncomfortable thing I've ever ridden in. I know I can't wear breeches, but couldn't I at least wear culottes? These blasted skirts keep getting caught around my legs."

Stephen hadn't a clue what culottes might be, but he decided he didn't like the sounds of them. He also refrained from telling her that ladies did not refer to their nether regions in front of members of the opposite sex, and silently congratulated himself on his forbearance. "I fear the style is as you find it," he said, nodding to an acquaintance. "But if you are too uncomfortable, you need not ride again. We can always walk. It is an activity usually reserved for the country, but that doesn't mean we cannot set a new fashion."

Cara thought of the people she'd seen strolling indolently down the elegant streets in Mayfair, and shook her head. "No, thank you," she said, tightening her leg around the pommel and shifting her weight until she felt more secure. When she didn't tumble over backwards her confidence bumped up a cautious notch, and she settled back to enjoy the ride.

They rode in silence for several minutes, and Cara took the opportunity to steal several covert glances at Stephen. He sat in the saddle as if born there, his back soldier-straight, and the horse's reins held competently in his gloved hands. He was wearing a dark red riding jacket and a pair of buff-colored breeches tucked into a pair of gleaming black boots; a black beaver hat set firmly on his head. She'd seen men similarly dressed in her day, but she'd always thought they looked rather silly and effeminate; like poor, befuddled Bertie in those old Geeves and Wooster movies her mother watched on the BBC.

Only Stephen didn't look silly, and God knew he didn't look the slightest bit effeminate. He looked decidedly masculine, power and sensuality evident in the clean lines of his face, and in the depths of his navy-blue eyes. Her gaze drifted back to his gloved hands, and she wondered what it would be like to have those hands touching her with such easy mastery . . .

"Have a care!" Stephen's voice jolted her out of her daydream, and she started, almost toppling from her precarious perch. She wiggled a bit to regain her seat, and then shot him an embarrassed look.

"Sorry," she said, wrapping the reins more firmly about her wrists. "I'm afraid I was wool-gathering."

Stephen remembered the dreamy look on her face, and wondered what thoughts could be responsible for such a soft expression. She looked like a woman thinking of her lover, he decided, and then scowled in annoyance.

"So I noticed," he said tartly, his gaze snapping forward, "but might I suggest you pay closer attention to your mount? If I hadn't called out a warning, you should have tumbled out of the saddle and on to your face."

Since it was the truth Cara didn't feel it would be polite to tell him to sod off, but the words burned temptingly on her tongue. They continued down Curzon Street before turning on to Park Lane and the outskirts of Hyde Park. In the future this was one of the most congested parts of the city, and it was obvious from the tangle of carts and elegant carriages clogging the streets that was another thing that hadn't changed.

They rode on the edge of the park before coming to the expanse of turf called Rotten Row. Cara reined in her horse, surveying the scene with wistful eyes.

"What is it?" Stephen asked, holding his prancing gelding in check with a casual flick of the wrist. "Is something wrong?"

"No," Cara replied, annoyed to find herself fighting off tears. "I was just thinking about the last time I was in Hyde Park, that's all."

As Cara seldom spoke of the mysterious future, Stephen was instantly intrigued. "Do you mean Hyde Park exists in your time?" he asked nudging his mount closer. "Tell me about it."

Cara blinked back her tears. "I'm not sure it's as big as it is now," she confessed in a husky voice, "but it's still there. On sunny days parents still bring their children down to feed the swans on the Serpentine, lovers still steal into the bushes for a kiss, even this is there," she nodded at the loamy soil stretching out before them. "You can rent horses from the stables and go riding. Alec took Miranda there one afternoon, and I remember how she—" She broke off abruptly, recalling how her sister-in-law had cried softly afterward.

"How she what?" Stephen demanded, steeling himself as if for a blow. "She was my *wife,* curse it all," he added when Cara didn't answer. "I have the right to know."

"How she cried," Cara said at last, acknowledging his right with a troubled sigh. "She said it was almost like being home again, and the thought made her sad. It was just after she'd had Marcus, so it was probably just the post-partum blues," she added when she saw him flinch. "She's happy there, Stephen, you must believe that. She's where and when she belongs."

Stephen turned away, unable to speak for several seconds. "I cared for her, you know," he said awkwardly, feeling the need to explain himself to Cara. "I admit I did not love her, but I-I cared. When she disappeared, I thought I should go mad. I looked everywhere for her, terrified she'd been murdered like that other poor girl."

"What poor girl?" Cara was immediately side-tracked.

Stephen was staring off into space, lost in a memory so terrible he still woke at night drenched in sweat, a scream of horror on his lips. "She was blond, like Miranda," he said in a strained voice. "And young, God, she was so young, although it was difficult to tell so little remained of her. She looked as if she'd been butchered, and—" he shook his head. "I don't want to talk about it anymore."

Cara's thoughts flew to the murdered prostitutes. "Who was she?" she asked, her investigative skills clicking into action. "Was she a prostitute?"

Stephen's eyes burned like blue fire in his ashen face. "What the devil has that to do with anything?" he demanded in an angry tone. "Not even the most vile of strumpets deserved to die such a wretched death!"

"I realize that," she said gently, "but—"

"I just told you I didn't wish to discuss the matter," he interrupted, his stomach rolling at the memory of what he had seen. "Besides, the matter is hardly a fit topic for a lady. We will not mention it again."

Cara wanted to tell him she was a cop, not a lady, but the anguished look on his face stopped her. She'd dealt with enough traumatized witnesses to know that pressing him now would accomplish nothing. She'd have to wait and hope he'd open up to her and tell her what she needed to know. In the meanwhile she filed the information she'd learned, anxious to compare it to the information she was gathering on the other victims. All blond, she thought grimly, all prostitutes, and all carved up in a manner so brutal it made Jack the Ripper's work look tame.

As it was approaching three in the afternoon the park was rapidly filling with riders, and Stephen was greeted eagerly by most of them. He introduced her to each man in turn, but even though she nodded and smiled graciously in return, she dismissed most of them with a mental sniff. Stephen had just suggested they return home when a handsome black-haired man she recalled from her first day in London came galloping up to greet them.

"Harrington, it has been awhile since you honored us with your presence," Aidan greeted Stephen before turning to Cara. "Mrs. Marsdale," he drawled, doffing his hat with a low bow. "I see you are settling in to your new home quite comfortably. One hears your praises sung everywhere one goes."

Cara decided she didn't care for the man or his mocking tones. "Does one?" she countered, meeting his icy gray gaze with cool pride. "How fascinating."

Stephen could feel the distrust and dislike crackling between the two, and spoke before Cara could say something outrageous. "I didn't see you at Tattersall's the other day," he said, deliberately choosing a subject that would exclude Cara. "The Duke of Clarence was auctioning off part of his stable, and there were several grays on the block which would have interested you."

Aidan reached down to pat the neck of the magnificent gray stallion he was riding. "I was at a meeting of my scientific society," he replied, his gaze resting on Stephen's face. "But I'm glad you mentioned the auction. I heard some rather unpleasant gossip I should like to discuss with you."

Stephen bit back an impatient curse. He'd known that rumors about his acrimonious confrontation with Proctor were already flying about the city, and he supposed it was only a matter of time before they reached Aidan's sharp ears. Now he would have to listen to one of his old friend's frigid lectures on discretion, he thought, suppressing a resigned sigh.

Because he knew Cara wouldn't give him a moment's peace until she had the truth, he turned to her before speaking to Aidan. "I encountered Miranda's stepfather the other day, and I fear we exchanged several unpleasant words. Should anyone be ill-bred enough to mention the matter in your hearing, you are to say nothing. Is that understood?"

"Perfectly," Cara replied, wondering what else Stephen wasn't telling her. She could tell by the set line to his mouth that the matter was serious, and decided to pump Aunt Minn for the truth. The old girl might have the brains of a flea, but she was as good as a paid informant when it came to ferreting out information on the doings of Society.

Wary of the easy way she accepted his command, Stephen glanced at Aidan. "We are returning home," he said formally. "Perhaps you would care to join us? We can talk later."

Aidan fell in beside them, and as they returned to Curzon Street Cara took the opportunity to study the man she now viewed as an adversary. Like Stephen he was dressed for riding, but while Stephen favored brighter colors, Sir Aidan wore a pale blue coat and dark gray pantaloons, his jet-black hair brushed back from the austere planes of his face. She was woman enough to admit he was handsome in a cold sort of way, but there was something about him that triggered all of her alarms.

It was his eyes, she decided at last. The color and temperature of a bleak January sky, they watched everything about him with a cold detachment she found oddly unsettling and yet somehow familiar. Then it came to her; he had cop's eyes. She was absorbing this shock when she became aware he was returning her intense scrutiny, a sardonic smile curving his lips.

"Is something amiss with my toilette, Mrs. Marsdale?" he asked, arching an eyebrow in polite inquiry. "You look as if you do not quite approve of my appearance."

Cara flushed guiltily, aware Stephen was listening to their exchange with a frown of disapproval. Trying to think of some graceful way out, her gaze fell on one of the fobs dangling from his silver brocade waistcoat. She seized on it eagerly, managing a simpering smile as she met his gaze.

"I was but noticing your fob, sir," she murmured, indicating the silver charm with the end of her quirt. "It is most unusual. Is it your family's crest, perhaps?"

To her surprise a look of guarded fury stole into his eyes. "No, it is nothing," he said curtly, turning his head to gaze straight ahead. "Just an interesting design I saw and fancied."

His reaction intrigued Cara, and she gave the fob a second glance. It looked like a capital 'I' with a backward 'c' laid over it, and she tried to remember if she'd ever seen anything like it. It was a pity she wasn't back home, she mused, or she could turn it over to the lads in SO 7, and let them have at it. There was nothing Forensic Sciences liked more than a challenge, and then she remembered Flemming, the ghoulish technician who had helped decipher the journals they'd found in the hidden safe. *Hadn't he told Alec parts of the journal were written in a language he hadn't recognized?*

While she was brooding over that she also brooded over what to do about the missing journals themselves. She knew Stephen had told her he'd made a thorough search of the room, and she believed he'd done the best job he was capable of. But now she wondered if perhaps she shouldn't search as well. She was a trained police officer, and if she could find a stash of drugs hidden in the lining of a child's stuffed toy, then she should be able to find a witch's journal hidden somewhere in a magical room.

The thought of entering the room made her sweat, but she

didn't see that she had a choice. The journals had to be some-where in there; all she had to do was find them, hide them in the safe, and then get out of there. So long as she wasn't wearing the pentagram she should be safe enough from the room's power. Or would she? Her stomach tightened as she remembered the jolt of pain she'd experienced when she and Alec had gone into the room shortly before Miranda had gone back to prevent Stephen's death.

The rest of the ride was accomplished in silence, broken only when Stephen politely pointed out a person or a building he thought would be of interest to Cara. They rode up to the house, leaving it to the servants to see the horses stabled and cared for. Stephen helped her dismount, his hands resting briefly on her waist as he studied her troubled expression.

"You mustn't mind Aidan," he said in a soft voice, his gaze holding hers. "I know he can be a bit top-lofty at times, but no truer friend exists. I don't know what I would have done if it hadn't been for him. He was the only one to visit me in prison, and he stood by me when everyone else was placing bets to see if I would hang or take the honorable way out and kill myself."

Cara gave the elegant man standing at the curb and talking to the groom a thoughtful look. Strange as it was, she could believe he was the type to stand resolutely by a friend, and to hell with what anyone else might think. The thought warmed her, and she was relieved to know Stephen had someone who believed in his innocence with him during those dark and terrible days.

"I guess he's all right," she said, scowling slightly. "But you'd better tell him he'd best watch his tone around me, or I'll toss him on his backside."

He smiled slightly, his blue eyes dancing as if he was picturing the image of his outraged friend sitting in the dust. "That I should very much like to see," he said, giving the dark green feather adorning her riding hat a teasing flick with his finger. "But may I remind you that you are supposed to be a lady? And ladies don't go about assaulting gentlemen, regardless of the provocation."

Cara could smell the crisp fragrance of the cologne he was

wearing, and for the first time since her separation from Paul she was physically aware of a man's nearness. The realization unnerved her, and she shook it off; grinning and doing her best to match his light, teasing tone.

"Ah, but I'm a *Canadian* lady," she boasted, moving out of his half-embrace. "And we Canadian ladies are raised to take very good care of ourselves. You might warn your haughty friend."

Stephen merely chuckled, stepping back to give her a low bow. "I shall do that," he promised, eyes twinkling. "And while I am about it, perhaps I shall warn myself as well. After all, I have personal knowledge of your expertise, and it is not an experience I should care to repeat."

"Well?" Aidan folded his arms across his chest and regarded Stephen down the length of his nose. "I am waiting."

Stephen stared at him, and then shook his head with wry amusement. "Cara is right," he said, his eyes twinkling at Aidan's stern expression. "You are as arrogant as the devil."

Aidan's expression grew even sterner. "Is that what you and your cousin were talking about while you had your heads together? You ought to be glad it was I who was with you, and not someone else, else you might find yourself explaining the precise nature of your relationship with Mrs. Marsdale."

Stephen's amusement vanished as he took Aidan's meaning. "Blast you, Aidan, if you are hinting there is anything improper between Cara and myself, I—"

Aidan held up a hand, stopping him. "I am hinting at nothing of the kind," he returned coolly. "*I* know you, and I know you would face death by slow torture before doing anything to besmirch your precious honor. I am just saying that others who do not know you so well might be easily misled, and that it would be in your best interest to keep more of a distance between you and your charming cousin. There is already talk, you know."

Stephen blew out a heavy sigh, his anger collapsing as he

turned away. "I know," he said bleakly, "Gil has already warned me of it. I was expecting it; after last year, especially, but I can not think of any way to stop it. As Gil said, there's nothing Society enjoys more than gossip, and naturally as a stranger, Cara is certain to draw more than her share of interest. We'll just have to remain above it all, and hope the gossip-mongers will find something else to prattle about."

"The way Prinny's wife has been flaunting her lovers that is a foregone conclusion," Aidan said, walking over to the cellaret and pouring himself a drink with the ease of an old friend. "And I must say it is in Mrs. Marsdale's favor that Lady Berksham has made her approval of the chit so obvious. The countess is such a stickler for the proprieties anyone to whom she gives the nod is instantly accepted in the very best of homes. I hear she even obtained vouchers to Almacks for your cousin, is that true?"

Stephen nodded, recalling Cara's amusement when informed by Aunt Minn of the great honor that had been accorded her. "She is acting as Cara's sponsor, and she will be acting as a hostess for a ball I will be giving in Cara's honor next month."

Aidan took a sip of brandy, his gaze never leaving Stephen's face. "Speaking of her ladyship, am I to take it that you are continuing in your courtship of the Lady Felicity?"

Stephen glanced up in surprise. "Of course I am," he said, wondering what new maggot had crawled into Aidan's brain this time. "Why should I not?"

Aidan moved his shoulders in a negligent shrug. "No reason I can think of. I just thought perhaps you might wish to postpone it until you have decided what to do about your cousin. I am assuming you've abandoned your plans to find her a suitable position?"

It took Stephen a few seconds to recall what Aidan was talking about. When he did remember, he sent his old friend a dark scowl. "Finding her a position was more your idea than mine," he said, wincing at the thought of Cara trying to earn a living as a meek and mild companion. "As to any future plans, that will be entirely up to Cara. She may not stay in England."

Aidan looked startled by Stephen's admission. "Indeed?" he said, setting his brandy glass on the side table. "Will she return to Canada, then?"

Stephen thought of the power in the secret room and nodded. "That is her intention," he said, feeling like a traitor for deceiving his life-long friend. "To be honest, I have no idea how long she means to remain. She told me from the start her visit here was of an uncertain duration."

There was a long silence as Aidan continued studying Stephen. "And that didn't strike you as odd?"

"Not if you knew my Cousin Reginald, Cara's father," Stephen answered quickly, discovering a heretofore unknown gift of sophistry. "He was a rather ramshackle fellow, and as flighty as a will-o'-the-wisp. I assumed Cara had inherited the family failing. And naturally, as she had no way of knowing whether or not she would be accepted by the family, she was careful to keep the date of her departure open. You must have observed she is rather independent-minded," he added with an apologetic shrug.

A gleam of amusement shone in Aidan's gray eyes. "Do you mean, did I notice your cousin is a termagant without equal?" he drawled. "Yes, it did catch my notice. As did her threat to . . . how did she phrase it? . . . ah yes, toss me on my backside."

Stephen gaped at Aidan in astonishment. "You *heard* us?" he demanded in horror, trying desperately to remember if Cara had said anything about being a visitor from another time.

Aidan inclined his head in mocking assent. "You must remember I have a rather acute sense of hearing," he said, taking visible delight in Stephen's discomfiture. "But you needn't look so green, Harrington; neither you nor the lady revealed anything particularly shocking. Although," he added slyly, "I should very much like to know how you came to gain personal knowledge of your cousin's expertise in assaulting men. I am sure it must be a most fascinating tale."

Nine

Cara waited until she was certain Stephen was occupied with his guest before making her move. From her conversations with Mrs. Finch she knew Stephen had declared the secret room off-limits to the staff, so she knew she didn't need to worry about some over-zealous maid interrupting her search. Which meant she need only worry about the room itself interrupting her; a far more terrifying possibility, as far as she was concerned.

With that thought in mind she retrieved her stun gun from the drawer where she'd hidden it a few days after her arrival. The lack of a pocket in her gown proved an obstacle at first, but in the end she tucked it in the square-cut bodice of her gown. She didn't really think she'd need a weapon, but she was too well-trained to go into an unknown situation without being armed. She also made sure the pentagram was safely locked away in another drawer; not wanting to take the slightest chance with the room's capricious power. Lighting the candle at her bedside, she picked it up and crept stealthily down the hall to the secret room.

It took her a few minutes of fumbling before she managed to open the door, but at last it swung open, and she hurried inside before her nerve failed her. Her first glance around had her jaw dropping, and for a wild moment she wondered if she'd broken into the wrong room.

The floor was covered with an Aubusson carpet in cream and royal blue, while the walls were covered with silk damask in a softer shade of blue. A gilded mirror was hung on one wall and Cara stared at it in confusion, recalling a mirror of polished obsidian hanging there in the future. What was going on? she wondered, venturing further into the room. The room she was seeing now was nothing like the room Alec discovered, and the differences were as troubling as they were confusing.

She quickly found the hidden compartment, and opened it with no difficulty. A frantic search showed that Stephen was right, unfortunately, and she could find no trace of the journals. Nor were the journals the only missing items. The ceremonial dagger with its curving blade was missing, as with the ring with a pentagram carved in its center. The ring especially troubled her, as she remembered Alec had once triggered the room when he picked it up to examine it. Like the pendant it was evidently keyed to the room, and the fact it wasn't where it should be troubled her more than a little.

She stood in the center of the room, her hands on her hips, as she forced herself to consider the mystery logically. Clearly there were several possibilities to be considered, she decided, chewing her lip thoughtfully. The most obvious one was that someone else had been in the room since Miranda's disappearance and removed the items for some unknown reason. Idle curiosity? she wondered, or was there a more basic, more sinister motive?

She brooded over the matter for several seconds and then began searching for another safe; hoping against hope she would find the lost artifacts safely tucked away. She was disappointed but not surprised to come up empty-handed, and after half an hour of searching she finally admitted defeat. The journals weren't in the room, but that didn't mean they weren't hidden somewhere else in the house. She'd conduct a room-to-room search, she decided, starting toward the door. Stephen was certain to have a safe in his study, she'd start there.

Her fingers were curving around the door's handle when a sudden thought stopped her. The journals and other artifacts weren't the only things that were missing, she realized in stunned dismay. She'd been in the room for almost an hour, and she hadn't experienced any of the room's usual affects. There'd been no pain, no eerie glow, no humming awareness of a power about to be unleashed. She'd once told Alec the power in the room reminded her of the vibrations from a stereo, and if that was the case, then it was obvious someone or something had turned the stereo off; perhaps forever.

Trapped. The word exploded in Cara's chest with the impact of a bullet. She staggered back from the door, tears filling her eyes as she realized she'd been deluding herself. Oh, she'd pretended to adapt, pretended to accept she might never see her home and family again, but now she knew she'd never really believed it. No matter how she'd acted, always in the back of her mind had been the naive belief that she'd find her way back to the future. It was where she belonged, where she wanted to be, and now it was lost to her. Forever.

A low moan of pain slipped from her lips and she dropped to the floor, burying her face in her hands and giving in to the grief that was tearing her to pieces. Not even the break-up of her marriage hurt like this, and for a moment she wasn't sure she could take the agony of her loss. She cried for herself, for her family, and for all she once had known. All gone, she thought brokenly, rocking back and forth on her heels. All gone.

"Cara!" She heard Stephen's startled exclamation seconds before he knelt beside her. "What is it?" he asked anxiously, his arms closing about her. "Are you hurt?"

Tears made speech impossible but she managed to shake her head, not wanting to alarm him any more than she already had. Later she could be embarrassed for acting like such a ninny, but for the moment she needed to be held more than she needed her next breath. She turned and flung her arms about his neck, finding solace in his solid strength as she clung to him.

Her reaction stunned Stephen, and he held her even closer. He didn't know what odd impulse had made him pause to peek into the hidden room, but he was profoundly grateful he had done so. The image of Cara, crying and alone, was one that would haunt him for a long time to come.

"It's all right," he said softly, brushing his lips over her forehead and wondering if he should send for his aunt. "Nothing is going to harm you."

Cara still couldn't speak, the task of finding the words to express what she was feeling beyond her. She snuggled closer to him, her body trembling as she succumbed to the emotions she'd kept locked inside for far too long. She could feel Stephen's hands gently stroking her back, and hear the low, soothing sound of his deep voice. She wasn't certain what he said, she only knew she felt safe; an admission almost as upsetting as the realization she was never going home.

The one time she'd cried in Paul's arms after working her first homicide—a little girl beaten to death by a deranged neighbor—he'd told her she'd have to learn to buck up if she was going to be a decent constable. At the time she'd decided he was being no harder on her than she was being on herself, but now she wondered what might have happened if he'd held her as Stephen was holding her, offering her quiet comfort instead of condemnation.

Would the marriage still have ended in divorce, or would it have survived? She didn't know, but the question was enough to shake her out of her tears. She drew back, hastily averting her eyes and swiping ineffectually at her wet cheeks. When he handed her his handkerchief, she accepted with an embarrassed mumble of thanks.

"God, I hate crying," she said, ducking her head and vigorously blowing her nose. "It always makes my nose run."

He smiled, oddly touched by the quarrelsome note in her voice. She sounded like a cross child; an admission he was certain would earn him a grievous injury should he be so foolish as to utter it. Instead he reached out, cupping her chin and tilting her face up to his.

"Do you wish to tell me what these are about?" he asked, brushing a gentle finger over her flushed cheek. "Or how you come to be in a room I thought we both agreed you should avoid?"

Cara glared at him, resentment edging out her embarrassment. "I was only trying to help," she muttered, meeting his gaze with as much pride as she could muster. "I told you those journals were important, and I wanted a go at finding them."

"I see," he said, continuing to study her. "You did not trust my search, I take it?"

She gave an uncomfortable shrug. "I'm an inspector," she said, knowing she sounded defensive and hating it. "I figured I'd stand a better chance of finding them."

"But you didn't?"

"No, I didn't." It hurt to admit it, but Cara was too honest to lie. She even told him of her suspicions the items had been removed following Miranda's disappearance, and was surprised when he looked thoughtful.

"It is possible I suppose," he said, tilting his head to one side. "I was sadly distracted those first few weeks, and several people were in and out of the house all hours of the day. It's not inconceivable one of them could have come up here without my being aware of it, but—" he broke off abruptly, an odd look stealing into his blue eyes.

"What is it?" she asked, edging closer.

Stephen shook his head, appalled he could suspect Aidan for even a single moment. His friend had moved earth and heaven to help free him, he reminded himself angrily. How could he think him guilty of so contemptible a thing as theft?

"I was thinking that if the journals were taken, it was likely done after I was arrested," he said quickly, knowing if he didn't say something Cara would plague him until he answered. "The household was in shambles, and when it looked as if I would indeed be convicted, things became even more uncertain. And Proctor was running tame here, now that I think of it," he added, frowning at the sudden memory. "He even tried moving in, but my butler tossed him into the street."

The image of the elegant Hargraves body-checking some blustering man at the door appealed to Cara's sense of humor, and she sent Stephen a wry smile. "Good for him," she said, accepting his help as she struggled to her feet. "I always thought that slimy

stepfather of Miranda's bore watching. He was the one responsible for your being charged with her death, wasn't he?"

Stephen remembered the pitiful body pulled from the Thames
and identified by Proctor as being Miranda. "Indeed he was,"
he said, pushing the ugly memory from his mind, "but we were
talking about you, not me. You still haven't told me what upset
you." He studied her wan face worriedly before hazarding a
guess. "Has it anything to do with the missing journals?"

Considering how he'd found her, Cara could see no point in
denying the obvious. "I was missing my family, and facing the
fact I'll likely never see them again," she said, feeling the fresh
sting of tears as she baldly stated the truth. "Up until now I've
managed to delude myself into thinking I'd make it home one
day, but now I know that's probably not going to happen."

Stephen was greatly affected by the painful acceptance he detected in her soft voice. He tried to envision what it must feel
like to lose the only world you'd ever known, and then he realized
he *did* know. That was precisely how he'd felt when he heard the
prison door clanging shut behind him.

"I am sorry, Cara," he murmured, reaching out to brush a damp
curl back from her cheek. "I am so sorry."

His touch rocked Cara's composure, and she found herself
fighting tears once more. "It's Alec I'm most worried about,"
she confessed in a broken voice. "He almost went crazy when
his fiancee was killed in a bombing, and if it hadn't been for
Miranda I don't think he would have ever recovered. He'll blame
himself, and he'll leave no stone unturned trying to find me. He
might even try coming back; if he suspects what's happened."

Stephen thought of the hard-faced man he'd seen in the magic
box and felt a prickle of unease. He'd not want such a man coming
in search of him, he decided, then dismissed the possibility as
unlikely. If the journals remained missing in the future, his adversary would have no means to pursue him.

The sound of the clock in the hallway chiming the hour penetrated the fog of misery surrounding Cara; recalling her belatedly
to the present. She realized she was alone in a room with a man;

a situation which in this time was tantamount to scandal. She took a hasty step backward, and began awkwardly rearranging her hair. It had come down from its usual arrangement, and was hanging about her face in a curly tangle.

"I should be getting back to my room," she said, feeling flustered and annoyed at her new-found sensibilities. "I don't want one of the maids to see us walking out of here together, or we'll be compromised or some damned such thing."

Although he could see the merit of her reasoning, Stephen was reluctant to end their interlude. "Are you certain you're all right?" he asked, his gaze resting on her face. "You'll forgive me for being so blunt, but you look far from well. If you wish, I can tell Aunt Minn you have the headache. That should win you respite from tonight's festivities, if nothing else."

The offer was tempting, but Cara wouldn't let herself accept it. If she was truly stuck in this time, the sooner she got on with her new life, the better. On the other hand . . .

"Do you know where we're going?" she asked, trying to recall the plans Aunt Minn had discussed with her that morning.

"We're to meet the Berkshams at Lord Newbury's, and then we will all be going on to the Blakewells' ball."

Cara thought about an evening spent with the imperious countess and her pompous husband, and decided she had a headache after all. "I do feel rather wretched," she admitted, and in many ways it was the truth. "I think I'll . . . what's the expression . . . ah yes," she placed the back of her hand on her forehead and gave him a limpid look, "have a fit of the vapors."

Stephen's lips quirked at her performance. "It is as well you have decided to become a lady," he said, clenching his hands to keep from touching her. "I fear you would never make a success of it treading the boards."

Cara remembered her years undercover and glared at him. "Oh yeah?" she demanded belligerently.

"Yeah." Stephen replied, deciding he rather liked the clipped, abrasive word. "Now, go to your room and collapse as befits a proper lady. Only mind you're recovered by tomorrow."

"What's so important about tomorrow?" Cara demanded, her brow wrinkling as she mentally reviewed her calendar.

"You are being introduced at Almack's," he reminded her. "And only death is considered a proper excuse not to make one's bows in front of the Patronesses."

The image of a room filled with Lady Berkshams made Cara's precarious emotions take another sickening plunge. Paul had belonged to a number of snooty clubs, and she remembered their reaction to her all to well.

"A police inspector," they all said, painfully polite smiles pasted to their faces. "How simply fascinating." And then they'd turned their backs on her. Paul had been furious with her, and ordered her never to mention her job again.

"Cara?" Stephen saw a ghost of sorrow shimmering in her topaz-colored eyes and took another step forward. "Is anything wrong?"

Cara shook off the old memories and raised her head to meet his gaze. The concern and compassion she saw on his handsome face stirred her, tempting her to hand him all her doubts and fears and let him deal with them. And he'd do it, too, she thought, perversely angered by the knowledge. She'd managed fine without a man in the future, she decided, her chin jutting out with pride, and she'd damned well manage without one now.

"Everything's fine," she said, unconsciously straightening her shoulders as she faced him. "I'll see you tomorrow then," and she brushed past him without another word.

"Really, Stephen, I do wish you would stop that infernal pacing!" Mrs. Greensborough exclaimed, fixing Stephen with an aggrieved scowl. "You will wear a hole in the carpet at the rate you are going."

"I am sorry, Aunt Minn," Stephen apologized, his gaze stealing to the clock on the mantelpiece for the fifth time in as many minutes. "But if Cousin Cara does not hurry, I fear we shall be shockingly late. It is almost nine o' clock."

Aunt Minn's sigh let Stephen know what she thought of such implacable punctuality. "You are refining upon nothing," she informed him, unfurling her fan with a practiced flick of her wrist. "So long as we arrive before eleven, I assure you we have nothing to fear from the Patronesses. Now do sit down; you are beginning to give me the megrims."

Stephen's cheeks grew slightly red at the scold, and he settled on the edge of his chair. What the devil was keeping Cara? he wondered, his fingers drumming an impatient tattoo on his silk-clad knee. Had it been any other female he would have assumed she was keeping him cooling his heels so that she might make a proper entrance, but he knew Cara too well to suspect her of such missish behavior. Normally she was prompt to a fault, and her tardiness did not bode well.

Perhaps she was ill, he thought, his anxiety increasing. Or perhaps she was still overset at not finding the items she had been desperately seeking. She seemed truly devastated at the realization she might never see her family or loved ones again, and the memory of the torment in her amber-colored eyes made his jaw clench in pain.

There had to be something he could do to help her, he thought, frustration making him even more impatient. He could have the entire house searched, and in the event that proved fruitless, he might ask Aidan for assistance. His friend was something of an antiquarian, and if anyone knew anything about such matters, it would be him. Perhaps he would—

"I'm ready, and if either of you says a word, I'm not going." The grumbled comment sounded from the doorway, and he glanced up, his jaw dropping at the sight that met his astonished eyes.

He'd always thought his guest attractive, but gazing at her now he realized how paltry that description was. Draped in shimmering gold silk, her jet-black hair tumbling in riotous curls about her face, Cara was the most exciting woman he had ever seen. She looked like an exotic Egyptian princess come to life, he thought dazedly, staring at the swell of her breasts bared by the cut of the exquisite gown. The London bucks would take one look at her and go mad.

"Why are you looking at me like that?" she demanded, her eyes narrowing in suspicion. "It's the neckline, isn't it?" she added, clapping a protective hand over her chest. "I told that snobby modiste it was too low, but she wouldn't listen. I'll go upstairs and change—"

"I . . . no, your décolletage is more than modest," Stephen stammered, finding his tongue with effort. He could feel his blood heating with passion, and prayed she would not notice the effect she was having upon him.

"Are you certain?" She scowled down at her gown with obvious dissatisfaction. "I feel like I'm falling out of the bloody thing."

"Truly, Cara, I do not know whether to scold you for your appalling language, or reprimand you for your prudery," Aunt Minn's comment spared Stephen the necessity of a reply. "Your cousin has already assured you your appearance is pleasing; if you persist in questioning his judgment, I will begin to think you are dangling for compliments."

Cara's hand dropped to her side, and Stephen could see the older woman's remark stung her considerable pride. "I wasn't dangling for a compliment," she denied heatedly, her jaw clenching in temper. "But if I make the mistake of bending over in this blasted thing, I *will* be dangling in some man's face!"

"Cara!" Aunt Minn gasped, turning an alarming shade of white.

"Well, I will," Cara grumbled, sliding a sullen glare in Stephen's direction. "And you had the nerve to criticize my clothes when I first got here," she said, her tone resentful.

The memory of the low-cut leather corset was almost his undoing, but Stephen managed to banish it from his mind. "I can not recall being so ungentlemanly as to offer an unfavorable comment on your attire," he replied, rising swiftly to his feet. "But Aunt is right; if you continuing harping on your gown I will suspect you of being hopelessly vain. Now let us go, you have kept us waiting quite long enough."

As Stephen hoped, Cara maintained an injured silence during the short ride to Almack's; unbending occasionally to respond to Aunt Minn's litany of last minute instructions. Stephen listened quietly, trying to reconcile his strong sense of duty with an equally strong urge to tell the hack driver to turn around. He had a sudden sense of foreboding, and he was fair certain the evening was going to end in disaster. How could it not, he brooded, when every time he so much as glanced at Cara he was all but overcome with the need to make sweet, hot love to her.

The admission horrified him. Cara was his guest, dependent upon him for her very survival; whether she would admit it or nay. His passion did neither of them credit, and even though he had no intention of dishonoring himself by approaching her, it still troubled him that she could have such an affect upon him. He had always considered himself master of his emotions, and he could not like that he was unable to keep thoughts of her from creeping into his mind during the day, and slipping into his most secret dreams at night.

By the time their hack pulled up in front of the elegant establishment on King Street Stephen had himself under firm control once more. He even gave Cara's hand a reassuring squeeze as they waited their turn to ascend the grand staircase to the Assembly Rooms.

"You look beautiful, Cara, truly you do," he said softly, his gaze holding hers. "I am very proud of you."

She studied him for a long moment before her lips curved in a rueful smile. "In my time, your lordship," she drawled, her thick lashes fluttering at him flirtatiously, "a chauvinistic remark like that would earn you a swift kick in the backside. But as I am in your time, I shall thank you instead. I am pleased to think my appearance brings you pleasure."

Stephen wondered how she would respond if she were to learn precisely how much her appearance pleasured him, but he merely inclined his head with mock-gravity. "I have said it before, Mrs.

Marsdale, but it would seem it bears repeating," he drawled, raising her gloved hand to his lips for a swift kiss. "I am most heartily grateful we are not in your time."

To his relief the introductions to the Patronesses went amazingly well, although he knew this miracle was due in no small part to Countess Berksham who stood at Cara's side beaming at her like a proud parent. With such a nonesuch sponsoring her even the haughty Mrs. Burrell pronounced herself "charmed" to make Mrs. Marsdale's acquaintance, and Cara was soon swept away to be introduced to the *haut ton*. His duties done for the moment, Stephen retired to a corner to sip some of the disgusting brew that passed for refreshment in the Grand Assembly Room. He was considering tossing the wretched stuff in the nearest potted palm when Gilbert walked up to join him.

"Good heavens, Harrington, never say you are so foolish as to actually drink that stuff!" he exclaimed, his nose wrinkling in disgust. "You are only supposed to hold it, old fellow, and fetch it for the ladies when they ask it of you."

"Now you tell me," Stephen riposted, setting his cup on a nearby table. He then turned back to Gil, his eyebrows raised in curiosity. "And what brings you here, if I may be so bold as to ask? I thought you had foresworn the place."

"Necessity, I fear," Gilbert replied, his expression wry. "Uncle may not leave me a penny, so if I would find an heiress . . . Looks like I shall be following you into the ranks of *mariage de convenance,* although I shall try to do a better job of holding on to my bride," he added this last with a teasing laugh.

Stephen turned away, struggling to hold onto his temper. He knew Gil wasn't being purposefully malicious, but that did little to take the sting out of his words. For a moment he was strongly tempted to tell his old friend to go to the devil, but he could not bring himself to do. Being angry with Gil for his acid wit would be as useless being angry with Prinny for his girth, he decided. Neither man could help their affliction. Still, he felt compelled to say something, and gave his friend a cool look.

"It is a good thing we are such old friends," he said in a stiff tone, "else I would be tempted to teach you some manners."

"Oh, dear, I have offended you yet again," Gil said, looking ruefully penitent. "Pray pay me no mind, Harrington. I fear the prospect of the parson's mousetrap has made me as disagreeable as an old woman. You will not be calling me out, will you? You must know I am the most awful shot."

Stephen's lips twitched in a reluctant smile. "I know," he said at last, "and that is all that is saving you. I have no desire to blow a hole in a defenseless opponent."

Gil sketched an elaborate bow. "You have no idea how grateful I am that you are burdened with such notions of nobility, my lord," he replied, his dark eyes dancing with laughter. "Were our situations reversed, I would not suffer from any such scruples, I promise you. Now, be so good as to point me in the direction of the nearest available heiress, and I shall be off. Pity you have already laid claim to the Berksham chit, else I should be tempted to have a go at her myself. She looks like a biddable sort of bride."

Stephen frowned, not caring for Gil's slighting reference to Lady Felicity. Not for the first time he wondered how much of Gil's outlandish speech was show, and how much was genuinely meant. Did he think his friend serious in pursuing Felicity, he would warn him off without the slightest hesitation.

"The Parkers' girl is said to be quite wealthy," he replied, taking care to keep his disapproval from showing in his voice. "She's a bit of a feather-brain, but as I recall intelligence in females has never been a prerequisite with you."

"Heavens, no," Gil responded with an affected shudder. "May God and all his ministering angels preserve me from a needle-witted woman; they are the most dangerous creatures on the face of the earth. That is all that is keeping me from making an offer for that stunning cousin of yours, you know. That and the knowledge that you *would* blow a hole in me if I but flirted with her," he added, sliding Stephen a knowing grin. "Wouldn't you?"

Stephen did not need to think before replying. "I would put a bullet through your black heart," he said fiercely, and was startled by his own vehemence.

A ghost of some nebulous emotion shone in Gil's brown eyes and was gone. "Then it is just as well I have decided we will not suit, isn't it?" He asked silkily. "I should hate for us to be enemies, Harrington, although I would not have you think me a poor opponent. I should be most formidable, I promise you.

"Au revoir, my lord," he concluded before Stephen could respond. "I am off to make the acquaintance of the lovely Miss Parker. I am sure I shall find her most charming."

"Good evening, Mrs. Marsdale, how delightful to see you again," the dark-haired man with earnest brown eyes said, honoring Cara with a polite bow. "I hope I am not intruding upon your solitude?"

Cara glared up at the intruder, choking back the urge to tell him that was precisely what he was doing. Her feet were killing her, and the strain of trying to remember all the steps to the various dances was making her head pound with a vengeance. For two pence she'd tell the blasted twit to go dance with himself, but unfortunately the lessons in manners Lady Berksham and Aunt Minn had drilled into her had stuck, and she found she couldn't say the words. Not that she intended doing nothing, however, she decided, raising her chin and fixing the man with one of the countess's frozen stares.

"Have we been introduced, sir?" she asked in a chilly voice, her eyebrow lifted in an imitation of Stephen's haughty manner. "If we have, I fear I can not recall your name."

The man's cheeks turned brick-red, and he shifted uncertainly from one foot to another. "I should have known you would not remember me," he said, his tone as diffident as his expression. "I am Thomas McNeil. We were introduced at Lady Burlough's a week or so ago."

The man interested in organizing a police force! Cara remembered, her irritation vanishing at once. "Of course, I remember you now, Mr. McNeil!" she exclaimed, holding out her hand to him with an apologetic smile. "How are you?"

"I am well, ma'am, and relieved that you remembered me. For a moment I feared I would be making explanations to your rather alarming cousin," he said, bowing over her hand with an awkwardness she found endearing after the polished courtesy she'd received from the other guests. She wondered if he was going to ask her to dance, and decided her abused feet weren't up to the task. Thinking quickly, she withdrew her hand and patted the chair beside her.

"Won't you join me, sir?" she asked, praying she wasn't breaching some obscure point of etiquette. "I fear all the noise and the crowds have . . . uh . . . overwhelmed me."

He didn't seem to notice her hesitation, but settled on the chair she indicated. "I should be honored, ma'am," he said, a look of profound relief crossing his boyish features. "And I understand what you mean about the crowds. I daresay they must prove quite a change for a lady accustomed to the unspoiled wilderness of Canada. That is where you are from, is it not?"

"Yes, from a small farm outside of Toronto," Cara answered, hoping he was as ignorant of Canada as everyone else she had met. "Er . . . are you familiar with Toronto, Mr. McNeil?" she asked, mentally crossing her fingers.

"I am afraid I am not, although I do hear it is a lovely city," he replied with a sheepish grin.

"It will be, some day," Cara murmured, thinking of the pictures her parents had taken on their last visit to Canada. Then she remembered where she was, and gave a quick laugh. "That is to say, it is quite lovely to *our* eyes, but I'm sure it would seem quite primitive to one used to the amenities of London."

They chatted for several minutes before Cara was able to guide the conversation to the murders. "Tell me, Mr. McNeil," she said, striving to hide her excitement as she leaned toward him, "how are your efforts to organize a police force coming? Have you had any luck?"

"Not as much as I would like, unfortunately," he admitted,

shaking his head with a sigh. "People are fond of complaining about crime, but they seem singularly disinclined to do anything about it. You have no idea how disheartening it can be."

A secretive smile touched Cara's lips. "Oh, I think you might be surprised," she drawled, thinking once again how little things had changed in the past one hundred or so years. The Sunday before she'd been brought back in time the *Times* had carried an article saying very much the same thing. And as a police officer, she had known well the daily frustration of trying to stem the rising tide of violence.

"If it is any consolation, at least there haven't been any more of those dreadful murders we discussed the last time we met. Do you recall the ones I mean?" he added, blushing as if he feared offending her.

"The prostitutes, yes," Cara forced herself to answer calmly, even though her heart was racing with impatience. She'd been following the investigation in the papers, and she had several questions she was eager to ask. But slowly, she cautioned herself, remembering that in this time and place women were kept strictly away from such unpleasantries. Slowly.

"I have been following the matter in the papers," she continued, unfurling her fan in the graceful gesture Aunt Minn had taught her. "I saw your name mentioned several times, and I must say I was most impressed. Are-are you a Runner, sir?" she asked, giving him one of the melting looks she'd often seen women casting Alec when he had been a constable.

As she expected, he preened with obvious pride. "No, Mrs. Marsdale, I am not, although I will admit I would very much like to be. I am merely an observer, I suppose you would call me, acting on behalf of the magistrates. In the event the monster responsible for these outrages is caught, the crown will require a great deal of evidence. We don't wish a repeat of the scandal surrounding the Ratcliffe Highway Murders. Are you familiar with that case?" He asked, giving her a diffident look.

As it happened, Cara *was* familiar with the case. Two families, including an infant, had been killed in December of 1811, and although a suspect had been charged, he was never convicted. The case was still studied in beginning Law Enforcement classes, and as Cara recalled, popular opinion held the suspect had been framed and then killed to make it look as if he'd committed suicide.

"I've heard of it, yes," she replied, keeping her answer purposefully vague. "But are you saying there is some doubt as to the suspect's guilt or innocence? What does the physical evidence on the scene indicate?"

Mr. McNeil's brows knit in confusion. "Physical evidence?"

Cara could cheerfully have bitten off her own tongue. She hadn't meant to reveal so much, but she'd been so caught up in the discussion, she'd let her enthusiasm overcome her common sense. Knowing it would happen again if she pursued the matter, she bit her lip, trying to think of some plausible excuse that would explain her extraordinary knowledge. Then it came to her.

"Mr. McNeil," she began, lowering her voice and leaning toward him in a confiding manner, "might I tell you something I've never told another soul in England, not even my cousin?"

He looked alarmed and then flattered. "Certainly," Mrs. Marsdale," he said, his voice pitched low to match hers. "And you may rely upon my complete discretion, I promise you."

"Good." She patted his hand. "While I was growing up in Canada I spent a great deal of time with the local tribes, and they were kind enough to train me in the skills of what we might call detection. That is, the close observation of physical evidence. It helps them track game through the forest, you see."

"Indeed?" He looked both startled and intrigued by her confession. "Yes, I suppose I can see how that might work."

"Well," she cleared her throat nervously, "and as it happens, the same skills that help the Indians track deer also prove quite useful in solving all sorts of crimes . . . including murder. If one studies a scene where a crime has been committed, makes careful notations of what he observes, and applies deductive reasoning to the facts collected, he can use all of what he has learned to solve the crime."

Mr. McNeil jerked back as if she'd slapped him. "You do not mean to say so!" he exclaimed, looking stunned. "How singularly extraordinary!"

"Oh, yes," Cara could see she had him hooked, and began reeling him in. "The captain of our garrison often employed these deduction skills, and he was able to solve a great many crimes. I helped him."

"You?" His eyes widened so much Cara expected them to pop. "But-but you are a lady!"

"Yes," Cara had been expecting this objection and was already prepared. "As I said, the Indians had trained me most strenuously, and I proved to be quite proficient at analyzing the clues I was given. Although Captain Butler was at first reluctant to accept my help, he gradually came to rely upon my skills, and I was able to help him apprehend several dangerous criminals. That is what I wish to do now. I want to help you catch the man killing these poor women. Will you let me?"

Ten

"Thank you for the dance, my lord," Lady Felicity murmured, her hazel eyes sparkling with shy pleasure as she gazed up at Stephen. "It was very good of you to partner me in the reel when you must know I am hopeless at the steps. I only hope your poor toes shall recover."

Stephen remembered the moment when her slippered foot came down on his own, and bit back a chuckle. "Nonsense, my lady," he said, raising her hand to his lips for a quick kiss. "You are graceful as a swan, and it was an honor to be your partner. I daresay I was the envy of every man watching."

"Only if that man had aspirations to being a cripple," Lady Felicity replied, tucking a blond curl back into place. "But I thank you for your compliment. Last night I trod all over poor Lord Thurston's feet, and you would not believe the speed with which he escorted me back to Mama's side."

"If he could move with speed one may only assume you did him no lasting damage," Stephen riposted, hiding his shock that the countess had allowed her gently-bred daughter to dance with an aging roué like the marquess. Perhaps the countess's notions of propriety had undergone a drastic change, he mused, either that, or her ladyship was becoming more anxious to see Lady Felicity married off to a man of rank. Everyone knew the wealthy marquess was on the catch for a new wife.

"I saw you dancing with Mrs. Marsdale when we came in," Lady Felicity continued in her gentle voice. "She is very lovely, and so graceful! I vow I was quite green with envy."

Stephen's body tightened at the memory of holding Cara in his arms. They'd been dancing the Allemande—a more decorous version of the wanton waltz—and the feel of her lithe body brushing against his had made his heart race with desire. Even over the lilting music and the strain of concentrating on the complicated steps he'd been achingly aware of her every movement; of the heady sweetness of perfume, and the way her breasts rose and fell with each breath. He'd even been aware of the "bloody hell" she'd muttered when she'd missed a step, and he remembered chuckling in response.

In retrospect the memories shamed him, and he made a silent vow to avoid dancing with Cara unless absolutely necessary. He was only human, and to continue tempting himself like this was foolhardy at best. Perhaps he should consider moving back into his club, he thought, trying to decide if he could do so without risking further unpleasant speculation.

"Speaking of your cousin, where is she?" Felicity asked, glancing about her with polite curiosity, "I was hoping I might see her so that I could compliment her on her *toilette.*"

Stephen glanced dutifully about him, and wasn't unduly alarmed when he saw no sign of Cara. She'd doubtlessly wandered off into one of the other rooms, and he was about to suggest he and Felicity go in search of her when a flash of gold near the potted palms caught his eye. He looked again, his eyes narrowing when he recognized Cara sitting so close to some man their knees were almost touching.

"Ah, I see her, over there," he said, his calm voice giving no indication to the fury raging inside him. "But who is that gentleman with her? He looks familiar, but I can not quite recall his name."

"Oh, that is Mr. McNeil," Felicity replied, smiling as she recognized Cara's companion. "He is second cousin to the Duke of Langhew, and was recently elected as the member from Dorking. Mama says he is wealthy and quite well connected, and I have always thought him a very nice man although a trifle shy. It is kind of your cousin to sit with him."

Stephen muttered something appropriate in response, his temper easing as he now had a name and a history to put to the man with Cara. As Felicity said McNeil was a decent enough fellow, with connections good enough to grant him entrance to the most exclusive of homes. He was moderate in his politics, and an earnest party member who was causing some stir because of his desire to establish a professional police force.

Police force! His jaw tightening with anger. Well, at least that explained why Cara was locked in private conversation with him. He only hoped the foolish chit remembered to hold her tongue, else they would both end up in the suds. Tamping down the thought he offered his arm to Felicity, his face expressionless as they walked over to the secluded corner where Cara and Mr. McNeil were sitting.

"Help me? Mrs. Marsdale, you can not possibly be serious," Mr. McNeil said, looking properly horrified. "Your cousin would never allow such a thing!"

"This has nothing to do with Stephen—Lord Harrington," Cara corrected herself hastily, not in the least surprised by McNeil's response. "The skills I am offering are mine, not his, and in any case I might remind you that I am not his lordship's ward. I do as I see fit, and at the moment I see fit to catch this man before he kills another woman. It's my job, blast it!" she added, her caution evaporating as he continued gaping at her as if she'd grown a second head.

"Y-your j-job?" Mr. McNeil stammered, his hand shaking as he reached up to tug at his neat cravat. "I do not understand. Never say that *you* are a Runner?" And he looked so appalled Cara fully expected him to keel over in a swoon.

Just for that moment she was tempted to tell him precisely who and what she was, but she managed to swallow the impulse. "Of course not," she said, all but choking on her explanation. "I am a woman. I merely meant that as a Christian and a loyal subject of the king, it is my duty to do all that is in my power to help these poor, unfortunate women. My training could help you capture this villain, and all I am asking is for the opportunity to try. Can't you understand that?"

There was a sharp silence, and Cara could see a contemplative expression stealing across his face. She held her breath, hoping she'd made her point, and yet afraid to believe it. But with or without his help, she was determined to investigate the vicious murders. She had wasted enough time as it was, and as far as she was concerned, the next victim's death would be her fault.

She knew the suspect was a serial killer, and as that was more or less her specialty, she considered herself criminally negligent for not moving sooner. She'd already made the first tentative steps toward establishing a profile on the man, and all she needed now was just a little bit of help. It had to happen, she thought, refusing to acknowledge the desperation growing inside her. She'd already lost her family, and she was damned if she'd lose her soul as well. Being a cop was all she knew, and if she couldn't be that, she was as good as dead.

"Mrs. Marsdale," Mr. McNeil began at last, her expression somber, "I am moved by your concern for your wretched sisters, but I am afraid I can not allow—"

"Mrs. Marsdale, Mr. McNeil, good evening to you!" Lady Felicity exclaimed, a pretty smile of welcome on her lips as she walked up to them on Stephen's arm. "How lovely to see you both. I trust you are well?"

"Very well, my lady," Mr. McNeil had scrambled to his feet, and was bowing first to Felicity and then to Stephen, who was regarding him with an implacable look in his dark blue eyes.

"My lord," he said, inclining his head with grave courtesy. "I have been following your participation in the debates regarding support for Wellington, and it is an honor to meet you at last. I am Thomas McNeil."

"Mr. McNeil," Stephen's icy expression didn't thaw by a single degree. "I read the article you wrote regarding crime in the metropolis. It was most persuasive. If you wish to have another go at passing a bill implementing your suggestions, I should be happy to support you."

Mr. McNeil blinked owlishly and for a moment he seemed to be overcome. "I . . . that is very good of you, Lord Harrington," he said at last, venturing a tentative smile. "Thank you."

"Bill? What bill?" Cara interrupted, a sudden alarm sounding in her head. She knew as well as any English school kid that it was Sir Robert Peel's Metropolitan Police Improvement Bill that had led to the MPF being established in 1829. If McNeil had tried passing a similar bill sixteen years earlier, she fretted, surely there would have been some mention of it. Unless her being zapped back had unexpected repercussions, she amended, her stomach twisting in fear. First the missing artifacts and now this . . . what was going on?

"A bill I drafted last session proposing the establishment of a trained, permanent police force," McNeil said, turning to her with a rueful expression on his face. "Alas, my fellow members of the House of Commons did not share my concerns, and the bill suffered a quiet death. Would that you had been there, ma'am, to lend your persuasive arguments to mine. I am sure it would have passed at once."

Stephen stiffened, his blue gaze shifting to her. "You spoke of a police force with Mr. McNeil?" he asked, his quiet tone setting Cara's teeth on edge.

"Do you mean to say you know of your cousin's interest in such matters, my lord?" McNeil interposed, glancing at Stephen in confusion.

Stephen's glance returned to the younger man. "Know of it, yes," he said coolly. "Approve of it . . . ?" he allowed his voice to trail off before turning to Cara.

"Aunt Minn will be waiting to hear your report on your first visit," he said, fixing her with a pointed look. "And I am sure you must be anxious to give it to her. Shall we go?"

Ordinarily such bloody nerve would have had Cara telling the offender where to stuff it, but at the moment she was too rattled to argue. Mr. McNeil's revelation troubled her, and she wanted to get away so that she could consider the matter in private.

"As you say, Cousin," she replied, holding out her hand to Mr. McNeil with a cool smile. "Good night, sir. I enjoyed talking with you. I hope we shall see each other again. Your discourse is most interesting."

"As was yours, Mrs. Marsdale," he replied, sliding Stephen a look. "If your cousin does not object, I would like to take you for a drive in the park next Monday. I should like to take you sooner, but I shall be going out of town."

Sensing Stephen was about to refuse, Cara gave Mr. McNeil a bright smile. "Monday would be fine," she said firmly. "Shall we say four o'clock?"

Mr. McNeil looked uncertain, but at Stephen's curt nod he gave her a low bow. "Until Monday, ma'am," he agreed, inclining his head to Stephen and Lady Felicity before disappearing into the crowd of dancers.

Four hours later Cara was pacing the floor of her room; too upset to sleep. She kept thinking about Mr. McNeil's failed bill, and the more she thought of it, the more agitated she became. She knew that bill shouldn't exist, and the very fact it had even been proposed scared the hell out of her. As a child she'd been weaned on reruns of *Dr. Who,* and she knew all about the dangers of altering the past. That's why she was doing her best to fit into this damned time; because she didn't want to do anything to upset the gossamer balance between what was and what would be.

If only Alec were here, she thought wistfully, her heart aching as she thought of her brother. He was an overbearing pain in the arse most of the times, but when it came to bouncing ideas back and forth, there was no one better. She paused, her expression growing pensive as she thought of Stephen. He was also a royal pain, she mused, and God knew he was as overbearing and pompous as they came. But he was also one of the most intelligent men she'd encountered in this time, and however much he was inclined to lecture her, he'd never treated her with anything other than the utmost respect.

Her gaze strayed to the clock on the mantel. It was after two in the morning and although they'd been home for a little over an hour, she hadn't heard Stephen coming to bed. He'd taken a room on the second floor shortly after Aunt Minn moved in, and she'd grown accustomed to listening for him as he retired for the evening. Not that she was consciously waiting for him, she assured herself. It was just the cop in her; making sure everyone was in and safe for the night.

She gave the clock another glance, and then reached a decision. Pausing long enough to grab her robe off the bed she crept down the stairs to the Ground Floor where Stephen's study was located. There was a faint shaft of light spilling through the bottom of the door, and she pushed it open without bothering to knock.

Stephen was standing in front of the fireplace, his arm draped across the mantel as he stared down into the flames. At the sound of the door opening he glanced up, his face registering no emotion when he saw Cara standing there. He had removed his jacket, and she saw a white scrap of fabric dangling from his fingers. His hair looked more blond than usual in the glow from the fire, and it was tousled as if he'd been running his fingers through it. He looked more masculine and attractive than she had ever seen him, and even as she was making the silent admission, she was banishing it from her mind with an annoyed scowl.

"Good, you're up," she said, keeping her tone brisk as she shut the door behind her. "We need to talk."

He raised an eyebrow at her peremptory tone. "Can it not wait until tomorrow?" he asked, his dark blue gaze sweeping over her silk-clad body in a way that made her tingle. "It is rather late, and I fear you are not properly dressed."

"Oh, bugger the way I'm dressed," she said crossly, advancing toward him with a purposeful stride. "This is important."

He hesitated, and Cara had the strong impression he was about to argue the matter. Then he gave a negligent shrug, indicating a nearby chair with a wave of his hand. "As you wish, Mrs. Marsdale," he said, his use of her last name telling her of his displeasure more clearly than an angry curse would have done. "What is it you wish to say?"

She ignored the chair and the mocking note in his deep voice. "It's about Mr. McNeil," she began, pacing as she spoke. "What did this bill of his say?"

"I beg your pardon?" He looked non-plussed.

"His bill, the one dealing with crime," she said, turning to face him. "I need to know what it contained."

"Why?"

Cara shoved a strand of hair behind her ear. "What bloody difference does that make?" she grumbled, stalling for time to marshal her thoughts. "I just want to know."

Stephen continued studying her, his face as expressionless as it had been when she'd first walked through the door. "Why?"

"Oh, for God's sake!" she exclaimed, strongly tempted to toss him on his aristocratic behind. Unfortunately she couldn't do that, not after all he'd done to help her, and so she had to content herself with a burning look instead. When he ignored it, she gave a heavy sigh; accepting the inevitable.

"I want to know because it shouldn't be happening," she said wearily, struggling to put her nebulous terror into words.

He gave her a searching look. "What do you mean?" he asked, and Cara knew he wasn't being obstinate, but was simply trying to understand what she was saying.

She joined him in front of the fire, gazing down at the glowing embers as she spoke. "In 1829 Parliament passed—will pass—a bill establishing the Metropolitan Police Force," she said quietly. "That bill is the beginning of modern law enforcement, and it's vital that it happens when it's supposed to happen. If it's passed here, now, everything could change."

He folded his arms across his chest, his navy-blue eyes somber as he considered what she had just said. "But if the bill is destined, what possible difference could a dozen or so years make?" he asked in a thoughtful voice. "How could it be so important?"

Cara continued staring down at the flames. "When I was first married my husband and I went to a lecture on tapestries at the V and A," she said, remembering a day one hundred and eighty years into the future. "The curator spoke at great length about tapestries, explaining how they were woven. They had to be careful, he said, because if even one thread unraveled, the entire tapestry was ruined. One thread; that's all it would take, and a lifetime's work would be gone."

Stephen slipped his hand beneath Cara's chin, tilting her face up to his. "And you think this bill is such a thread?" he asked, his thumb brushing over her trembling mouth as his troubled gaze held hers.

She nodded. "Everything is such a thread," she said, confessing all her fears with a shaky sigh. "You . . . me . . . even those damned missing journals. They're all connected. I used to read Tennyson, his poem *Ulysses* is one of my favorites. In one stanza he says:

"I am a part of all that I have met.
Yet all experience is an arch
Wherethrough gleams that untravelled world
Whose margins fade forever and ever when I move."

Her lips twisted in a bitter smile.

"I always thought I knew what Tennyson was talking about, but now I know I didn't have the vaguest notion." And she glanced away, tears burning her eyes.

Stephen's fingers tightened on her jaw, staying her. He gazed down at her mouth, a hard, male hunger making his own lips thin. Cara gazed up into his face, seeing the reflection of the same desires she had been denying since first meeting him, and the knowledge both thrilled and frightened her. The only man she had ever been with was Paul, and he'd let her know in no uncertain terms what a disappointment she'd been as a sex partner. She had all the parts, he'd sneered, but she'd never been willing to put her badge down long enough to make proper use of them.

Stephen was twice the man Paul could ever hope to be, she realized, her heart beginning to thunder beneath the lace of her silk peignoir. If she couldn't please her rat of an ex-husband, what on earth made her think a man like Stephen could ever want her? Her teeth sank into her bottom lip, and for a moment her old insecurities threatened to swamp her. Then she felt his fingers flex once as if he was fighting the need to keep touching her, and that simple hesitation banished the last remaining doubts. She reached for him, her lashes fluttering closed as she buried her fingers in the golden-brown strands of his hair.

"Stephen . . ." she sighed, her tremulous voice giving way to a soft sigh of pleasure as his mouth descended on hers.

For all he was a gentleman Stephen's kiss was wild and passionate, overwhelming her with its fierce intensity. His lips parted hers expertly, demanding an intimacy she was only too happy to give. He brushed his tongue over hers in a teasing caress that made her burn.

"Cara," he moaned her name, his voice raw and shaking with need. "I've wanted you for so damned long."

His words filled her with heady feminine pride, making her own passion flare even brighter. She pressed closer, delighting in the feel of his strong arms crushing her to his lean body. Beneath the silk of his pantaloons she could feel his arousal, and the knowledge she could have such a powerful affect on him, made her go soft and warm with a deliciously aching desire.

In his arms she wasn't Inspector Marsdale, she was simply a woman, hungry and demanding; one who gave as much as she took and revelled in the giving. She stroked his neck, his face, her mouth avidly feasting on his while her hips brushed against his in a pagan rhythm that had them both gasping. Just as she was certain he was going to sweep her up and carry her to one of the big leather chairs he was jerking out of her embrace, his chest rising and falling as he dragged air into his lungs.

"We have to stop, Cara," he said, his voice so deep and guttural he scare recognized it. "If we don't, we shall be making love."

Her eyes were lambent as she met his burning gaze. "I know."

He stared at her for a long moment and then he squeezed his eyes shut, tipping back his head as he gave a strangled laugh. "So honest," he said at last, opening his eyes to study her. "I wonder if you have any concept how arousing it is to a man to have a woman look at him with such blunt desire."

She thought about that for a moment. "No."

He drew another deep breath. "I thought not," he said, reaching out a tentative hand to brush a strand of hair back from her face. "Cara, I want to make love to you more than I want to draw my next breath, but I cannot. We've had this discussion before, and I know it angers you to admit it, but the simple fact remains that you are in my care. If I make love to you I would feel as if I was taking some sort of advantage, and I would hate myself for it."

"But that's nonsense!" she argued, feeling flustered and thoroughly frustrated by his obstinacy. "I'm a grown woman, damn it! If you take advantage of me it's because I want you to take advantage!"

His lips twisted in a half-smile. "I am not going to say this won't happen again," he said, stunning her with his candor, "because I'm hoping very much that it will. I'll even admit it is likely we shall make love, but if it happens . . . *when* it happens, I don't wish it to be because we were too overcome by the moment to consider the ramifications."

She wondered what the masculine equivalent of a tease might be. "What ramifications?" she demanded, physical passion giving way to an urge to pop him in the nose.

To her surprise his expression sobered, and when he tilted her face up to his, his eyes were dark with unwavering integrity. "I am not a man who wears either his title or his honor lightly, Cara," he said softly. "I never have been. If we become lovers, everything changes. Do you accept that?"

Cara wasn't certain how to answer that. She assumed he meant that as lovers they would spend more time together, and that he would be even more demanding of her. The thought should have outraged her liberated sensibilities, but instead she found she was reluctantly intrigued.

"Yes," she said, bravely meeting his gaze, "I accept that."

"Good." He pressed a chaste kiss to her forehead before shoving her gently back. "Now, go back to your room before I forget all about my damned nobility and tumble you to the floor. I'm only human, you know."

She took a few steps before remembering one of the other reasons she had come in search of Stephen. "I want to know if you're going to object to my seeing Mr. McNeil," she said, turning to face him with as much dignity as she could muster. "He's terrified of you, and if he even suspects you disapprove, I'll probably never see him again."

Stephen didn't answer at first. "Why do you wish to see him?" he asked, and Cara couldn't tell if he was jealous or merely curious. "Is it because of this bill of his you are so concerned about?"

That seemed as good an explanation as any, and Cara gave a hasty nod. "I thought I would see if he would give me a copy to read," she said, brightening as the thought suddenly occurred. "Maybe I'm panicking over nothing, and the bills really aren't so similar. I'll know more once I get my hands on one."

"In that case I suppose it might be permissible if he should pay you a call," Stephen announced, inclining his head like an Oriental potentate conferring favor on a chosen concubine.

Cara glared at him. She might be madly in lust with the wretch, she fumed, but that didn't mean she intended acting like a submissive twit! "I wasn't asking you for permission, your lordship," she snapped, her hand resting on the doorhandle as she paused by the door.

He gave her a smug grin. "I know," he said, sounding so thoroughly pleased with himself she felt like screeching. She jerked the door open instead, his husky laughter ringing in her ears as she slammed the door behind her.

Eleven

GRUESOME MURDER! LATEST OUTRAGE MOST HORRIBLE OF ALL!!!

The headlines proclaiming another murder stared up at Cara as she took her seat at the breakfast table the following morning. Her brows puckered and she picked up the paper, hoping the accompanying article would prove less sensationalistic than the lurid headlines. She was quickly disappointed. It seemed hack writers existed in this era as well, she mused, her nose wrinkling at the graphic prose. And as in her own time, it was plain they were paid by the adjective.

"You shouldn't be reading that if it distresses you," Aunt Minn scolded, her expression stern as she regarded Cara. "You shouldn't be reading it at all, if you want my opinion. It is hardly fit reading for a gently-bred female."

"I have a right to know what is going on in my world, Aunt," Cara replied, noting that in this particular crime, unlike the others, the victim was found indoors, rather than in an alley. It could indicate a significant change in the perpetrator's M.O., or it could simply mean it was where he had located the victim. If she understood the phrase "abandoned woman," then this victim had also been a prostitute.

"That may as be," Aunt Minn continued with an aggrieved sniff, "but I still say it is *not* proper. I am sure your dear cousin would never approve."

"Of what would I not approve?" Stephen's deep voice sounded from the doorway, and Cara turned her head as he came strolling into the dining room. To her horror she could feel herself blushing, and she lowered her gaze to the paper.

If Stephen noticed her reaction, he was too much of a gentleman to say anything. She heard the rustle of cloth as he bent to press a kiss on Minn's lined cheek. "Good morning, Aunt Minn," he murmured, and when Cara reluctantly glanced up, he gave her a cool nod, "Cousin."

"Lord Harrington," she managed a polite nod, her heart hammering as she tried and failed to suppress the memory of last night's kiss. She had only to look at his brownish-gold hair to remember what it had felt like between her fingers, and as for his mouth . . . she took a hasty sip of coffee, almost burning her tongue. No, she would definitely not think about his mouth.

"You still haven't answered my question," Stephen said, directing his conversation to Minn as the footman moved forward to fill his cup with coffee. "What has Cara done now?"

"There has been another murder," Aunt Minn spoke quickly, correctly interpreting the scowl Cara could feel gathering on her face, "and Cara has been reading of it in the papers. I was only saying I was certain you would not wish her to know of such things, but you know how stubborn our dear girl can be." Here she cast Cara a fond look.

"Indeed I do," Stephen drawled, leaving Cara to wonder what he meant by *that*. "But I hardly think reading about something that will be common knowledge by night fall will place her in danger of becoming an antidote, Aunt. You refine on nothing."

Cara listened to the conversation with mounting indignation. "I am neither invisible nor a child," she informed the others in a stiff voice, "and I wish you'd stop discussing me as if I were. Now, may I please go back to reading the paper?"

Stephen's blue eyes glinted in amusement. "Please do," he said politely, and then turned to Minn and began discussing last night's triumphs and disasters at Almack's.

Cara glared at him for a brief moment, mentally calling him every colorful name she could think of before turning her attention back to the graphic description of the crime scene. Words smeared on the wall with blood, she noted, and the mattress the victim had been found lying on had also been slashed. Had it happened while the victim was being killed? she wondered, or was the killer venting a rage that hadn't been appeased even by a brutal murder? God, she hoped it wasn't that. If it was, it meant his condition was deteriorating, and that the murders would increase in frequency and violence. Not a pleasant thought, she decided, repressing a shudder of horror.

While Cara buried herself in the paper, Stephen welcomed the opportunity to study her covertly. She was wearing a day dress of dark lavender silk, a fichu of creamy lace tucked decorously in the rounded neckline of the gown. He stared at the fichu, a smile softening the corners of his mouth. For such a fiercely independent lady, she was surprisingly modest when it came to wearing the low-cut gowns that were the fashion of the day. He found the dichotomy enchanting, and wondered what other secrets she kept hidden beneath her prickly exterior.

He did know she was an innocent. Oh, he knew she'd been married, and had doubtlessly been intimate with her husband. But in all the ways that counted, she was as innocent as a virgin. It had been obvious in the way she had responded to his kiss, in the open delight she showed at pleasing him and being pleased. It was her shy satisfaction that had told him more than he'd wanted to know, and that was why he'd ended the kiss when he had.

God knew he hadn't wanted to, he mused, grimacing at the memory of the frustrated pain that had raked his fevered body. It had been like tearing the skin from his bones, but as he'd told Cara, he had too much honor to take advantage of a woman dependent upon him for protection. So long as Cara was his guest he would do his best to keep a respectful distance from her. Or at least, he mused, casting her another surreptitious glance, he would try.

As if feeling the weight of that gaze she glanced up, and for a moment he found himself lost in the golden depths of her amber-flecked eyes. A charged silence flashed between them, and he was interested to note she was the first to glance away. He allowed himself to savor the small victory before turning to his aunt, who was still chattering away in blithe oblivion.

". . . and so I told her," she said with a decisive nod. "Why, not even Prinny, who is surely one of the biggest dolts to ever draw breath, would attempt to gain entry to Almack's at so late an hour. But that is Proctor for you. I know you were . . . er . . . affianced to his stepdaughter, my lord, but there is no denying the man is not good *ton.*"

One of the many colorful epithets he'd heard Cara muttering flashed into Stephen's mind as he realized his aunt had been talking about Elias Proctor. Considering the acrimonious nature of their last encounter, he wanted to be kept well-apprised of the man's every movement. He was debating whether he should wait until he got to his club to hear the gossip or ask his aunt to repeat herself, when Cara suddenly spoke.

"Elias Proctor?" she queried, giving Aunt Minn a curious look. "Isn't he Miranda's stepfather?"

Judging from the way his aunt started guiltily, Stephen assumed she had been gossiping with Cara. "Er . . . yes, so he is," she said, twisting her napkin in her nervous fingers. "Have-have you met the man, my dear?"

Cara shook her head. "No, and I can't say as I want to," she said, making no attempt to hide her disgust. "The man's a thief and a liar."

"Cara!" Aunt Minn clasped a hand to her bosom.

"What?" Cara demanded, scowling at the older woman. "You were just sitting there gloating over the fact he'd been kicked out of Almack's. Why are you acting so shocked now?"

"Offering an opinion as to the advisability of a man's actions is a far different thing than casting aspersions on his character," Aunt Minn said stiffly, her face red with mortification. "Such things are simply not done."

Cara gave a careless shrug and reached for her coffee cup. "It's the truth, isn't it?" she asked rhetorically. "Stephen told me the man lied in the witness box, and that he almost swung because of it. That makes him a liar in anyone's books. And as for the other, I also heard he was stealing his stepdaughter's inheritance, and would have taken it all if Stephen had been convicted. Why shouldn't I behave as if he's anything other than a complete puke?"

"A-a puke?" Aunt Minn stammered, her hand fluttering to her breast. "Oh dear."

Stephen decided it was time to regain control of the conversation, and stepped coolly into the fray. "Your eloquent defense on my behalf is greatly appreciated, Cousin," he said, giving her a warning glance, "but in future I would request that you not mount that defense quite so spiritedly. Whatever you may think of Proctor, such thoughts are best left kept to yourself."

She tossed back her head with the defiance he was coming to adore, and gave him a freezing stare. "As you wish, your lordship," she said, and he could hear the challenge fairly crackling in the mocking emphasis she placed on his title.

Stephen wisely ignored the challenge, giving his aunt his full attention. "And what are your plans for the day, ma'am?" he queried, applying himself to his meal. "Will you go shopping?"

"I had thought to," Aunt Minn eagerly accepted the change in the conversation. "There are some lovely silks that have just come in from the Orient, and I mean to lay claim to my share of them before they are all gone. And later I thought to call upon Lady Berksham. She said she has something of great import to discuss with me." And she gave Stephen a coquettish smile.

Stephen did not respond, although he had a fair idea what it was the countess wished to discuss with his aunt. Undoubtedly she, like her husband, was anxious to learn the precise nature of his intentions toward Lady Felicity. The earl had taken him aside a few days ago, bluntly telling him that should he offer for Felicity, his offer would be accepted. As he recalled he'd thanked the older man profusely, and then had fled from the club as if all the fiends in hell were nipping at his heels.

What the devil was wrong with him? he brooded, setting down his fork with a heavy sigh. A few short weeks ago such news would have been all he could have hoped for, and he would have been offering his hand and name to Felicity in a heartbeat. Now . . . his gaze flicked to Cara. Now he didn't know. He just didn't know.

Cara spent the rest of breakfast pouring over the papers and making plans. She'd had one of the footmen fetch her a pen, ink and paper from the study, and while the others ate and carried on desultory conversations, she made careful notes. With the information she'd already gathered she had the beginnings of a theory regarding the killer and his motives, but she needed more. She needed to see the crime scene. Unfortunately that entailed overcoming some very large obstacles, and for that she knew she would need Stephen's help. The problem was how she could obtain his help without incurring his considerable wrath. In the end, assistance came from an unexpected quarter.

"And how will you be spending your day, my dear?" Aunt Minn asked, lingering over her tea. "I would ask you to join me at the mantuamakers, but I know how little you care for shopping."

Cara could have kissed the tiny woman. "That's so," she agreed, although she was careful to hide her relief. "And as for how I plan to spend my day, I was hoping I could convince Lord Harrington to show me Covent Garden."

"Covent Garden?" Aunt Minn exclaimed, looking puzzled. "Heavens, child, why would you be wanting to go there? There's nothing to be seen during the day but onions and cabbages."

"I like cabbages," Cara lied, aware Stephen was watching her with narrow-eyed suspicion. "Besides, I've been hearing how very large Covent Garden is since I got here, and I'm anxious to see it for myself. Will you take me, Cousin?" And she gave him a sweet smile, fluttering her lashes for all she was worth.

His lips twitched, but his expression remained aloof. "I might," he said, his tone betraying nothing. "We shall discuss it later in my study."

His words made Cara blush as she remembered what happened the last time they'd been alone in his book-lined study. Then just as quickly, she pushed the memory out of her mind. Damned if she'd act like some pimple-faced schoolgirl mooning over the latest rock star, she thought, pride firming her chin. He seemed cool enough despite what had passed between them, and she would take her cue from him. If he wanted to act as if the kiss had never happened, that was fine by her.

The rest of the meal passed in casual conversation, and by the time Stephen guided her into his study Cara felt she had herself well under control. When he closed the door and turned to face her, she was ready for whatever he might throw at her.

"Now, Cousin," he began, his voice mocking as he regarded her, "I want to know the real reason you're suddenly so anxious to see Covent Garden. And don't think to fob me off with that Banbury tale you spun for Aunt Minn; I know you don't give a tinker's damn about cabbages."

His aggressive manner made her grin. "You're right," she confessed without so much as a hint of remorse, "I can't abide the wretched things. But I had to think of something, didn't I?"

"Cara . . ."

"Oh, all right," she huffed, wondering how he was able to put a wealth of warning in a single word, "since you're going to be that way about it. I want to go to Covent Garden so I can view the latest crime scene. I know if I tried going on my own, a woman alone, civilization as you know it would probably come grinding to a halt. But I thought if I had you with me, a macho English lord, I could—"

"Absolutely not."

The interruption was so calm, so lacking in emotion, that at first Cara wasn't even certain he had spoken. Then she saw the deadly look in his blue eyes and knew she wasn't mistaken.

"I see," she said, taking a deep breath to calm herself. "Any particular reason, or are you just being bloody overbearing as usual?"

The muscle ticking in his cheek was mute evidence to the fact she wasn't the only one working on control. "I can think of several reasons," he replied in a cold voice, "but at the moment those reasons are immaterial. You are not going to Covent Garden, and that's the end of it. I forbid it."

"Forbid?" Cara repeated, any thought of managing her temper forgotten. "You *forbid* me to go to Covent Garden?"

Stephen gave her a wary look, obviously realizing he'd overplayed his hand. "Perhaps forbid is too strong a word," he conceded. "What I meant to say is that it would be best if you kept out of this unpleasant business and allowed the proper authorities to deal with it, That is their duty, after all."

Cara remained silent for several seconds, her hands curling into fists as she resisted the urge to toss Stephen out the nearest window. "For your information, you condescending pig, I *am* the proper authorities!" she exclaimed, furious with herself for thinking she could ever expect him to understand what she was about. "And as for doing one's duty, I took an oath to serve and protect the citizens of London, and the fact I'm trapped in the past doesn't change a bloody thing! You've a crazed killer on the prowl, and the only thing standing between him and his next victim is me!"

"That is precisely my point!" he snapped, clearly abandoning any attempts to reason with her. "What you are proposing is dangerous, and I refuse to let you take such foolish risks. You are not going to Covent Garden, Cara. That is final."

Cara glared at him for several seconds, words she had learned working two terms in Narcotics burning on her tongue. It was sweetly tempting to utter them, but she managed to control the impulse. Stephen's paternalistic attitude wasn't anything she hadn't encountered before, and she knew there was but one thing she could do. She raised her head and met his watchful gaze.

"Are you quite finished, your lordship?" she asked, her sweet tone at odds with the anger she could feel burning in her eyes.

"I am," he replied, his attitude markedly distrustful.

"Good." She turned and walked to the door. She pushed i

pen, her palm resting against the cool wood as she turned to face him.

"Lord Harrington?"

"Yes?" His tone was even more wary.

She gave him a beatific smile. "Sod off," she said, and then slammed the door closed behind her.

Stephen stared at the closed door, torn between the urge to storm after her, and the equally strong urge to laugh. Impertinent wench! he thought, deciding it was safest to give in to the last impulse. Just when he was certain she couldn't do anything else to astonish him, she pulled something like this. Visiting a crime scene, indeed. He shook his head. *Whatever would she think of next to torment him?*

And yet, his conscience urged quietly, wasn't her unpredictability one of the things he admired most about her? That and her blasted sense of independence that made it possible for her to defy him with such appalling regularity? Certainly she was nothing like the women of his day, and he realized now how wrong he had been to attempt to hold her to those same standards. If their situations were reversed, he wondered, would he fare any better in the incredible world she came from?

While he was being so brutally honest with himself, he also admitted his reasons for wanting to keep her well away from the scene of the bloody crime weren't all due entirely to his concern for her safety. That was his greatest worry, certainly, but that wasn't what made his heart race with sick fear at the thought of what she would find did he give in to her wheedling. He allowed himself to consider that for a moment, and then went over to the wall and give the rope pull a tug.

"Yes, my lord?" Hargraves himself responded to Stephen's summons, one dark eyebrow arched in polite inquiry.

"I wish you to inform Mrs. Marsdale that I've changed my mind," he said, ignoring the speculative gleam in the butler's dark eyes. "Tell her if she wishes to visit Covent Garden, I should be happy to take her."

"Very well, my lord," Hargraves replied with a low bow. "Will there be anything else?"

He thought about that for a moment and nodded. "Tell her I am leaving in a quarter hour," he said. "If she's not down here and waiting, I shall leave without her."

She was down in ten minutes, her crooked bonnet and half-buttoned pelisse testimony to the fact she'd taken him at his word. Her golden-brown eyes were filled with curiosity, but there was no faulting her manners as she offered him a smile.

"It is very kind of you to alter your plans to accommodate me, my lord," she said, as much for the benefit of the hovering servants as for his. "I am most grateful."

"I am sure you are," he replied, sliding his hand beneath her elbow and guiding her out of the door. "Only mind that you do not give me cause to regret my decision."

A footman flagged down a passing hack, and they were soon en route to Covent Garden. When they'd travelled for several blocks in stony silence, Stephen gave her a measuring look.

"You'll be wanting an explanation, I suppose," he said, leaning back against the leather cushions and holding her gaze.

Her expression was grave as she considered his words. "Only if you feel like giving one," she said at last. "You have to admit you were rather adamant about my not going."

He inclined his head, granting her the point. "I am still concerned about your safety," he admitted. "And even though in your time you are a police officer, I do feel you shouldn't be subjected to such horrific sights as we are about to see. However those aren't the only reasons I forbade you to go."

When she remained silent, he sighed heavily, struggling to put his confusing tangle of emotions into words. "After . . . after Proctor identified that drowned girl as Miranda and I was charged with her murder, gawkers came pouring into my home from every part of London," he said rawly, wincing as he remembered the horror. "The servants tried keeping them out, but they were overwhelmed. The house was ransacked, by people wanting mementos, and there wasn't a bloody thing I could do to stop them. I felt . . ." his voice cracked, and he gestured helplessly, "violated," he concluded, telling her what he had never told another living soul.

"I know you aren't going to this house out of any prurient interest," he added, leaning forward to take her gloved hands and willing her to understand. "But I can not help but wonder how this poor woman would feel having strangers poking about and speculating. She has already been murdered, having her home invaded as well seems to me the final degradation."

The shimmer of tears he saw in her eyes stunned him almost as much as the gentleness with which she touched his face. "I'm sorry, Stephen," she said, her gloved finger stroking down his cheek. "I was so intent on the case I never stopped to think . . . I never realized how upsetting it might be for you."

"I know," he said, revelling in her gentle touch. "I only realized it myself after you'd stormed off. I also realized something else," he added, meeting her gaze with determination.

She hesitated briefly before speaking. "What is that?"

He reached out and brushed a dark curl from her cheek. "That I had no right expecting you to be anything other than what you are," he said bluntly, a feeling of relief flowing through him as he confessed what was to him his greatest transgression. "And I certainly had no right forbidding you to do your duty. I understand duty, more than you may realize, and I would never want to come between you and what your honor demands of you."

Her eyes grew even brighter, and her bottom lip trembled before she pulled it between her teeth. She gazed at him for several seconds, and then leaned forward to press a light kiss on her mouth. "Thank you," she said softly, her breath feathering over his lips before she drew back. "I can't tell you what that means to me. I . . . oh, bloody hell," she broke off, fumbling in her reticule for a handkerchief.

The sight of her tears touched something in Stephen; something deep and primal that left him shaking. After surviving last

year's debacle he'd set a course he was certain would restore his
lost honor and good name. At the time that course seemed the
most important thing in this world, and he committed himself
totally to achieving the objectives he'd set. Those objectives were
still important, but for the first time he wondered if they would
be enough. The thought terrified him, and he maintained an edgy
silence as the hack wound its way through the heavy traffic.

Finding the crime scene proved ridiculously easy. A huge
crowd had gathered around a squalid house, and what passed for
law enforcement had its hands filled keeping the mob under
control. Stephen used his walking stick and his own intimidating
presence to part the crowds, easily shoving his way to the head
of the line. Once there he employed a more direct method of
persuasion, casually handing the constable guarding the door a
gold sovereign along with a request to view the murder room.

"Reckon 'twouldn't hurt none," the man said, sliding Cara a
nervous look. "But I'd not be taking yer lass in there, sir. It ain't
a fit sight fer a lady."

"My cousin is more resilient than you may suppose," Stephen
said, giving Cara's hand a pat. "She'll be fine."

Cara was flattered at his faith in her, although the way he was
patting her hand made her want to kick him. She stole a glance
over the constable's beefy shoulder, her brows gathering in a
frown when she saw several men already in the room. Terrific,
she thought sourly. God only knew the evidence that had already
been destroyed or thoroughly compromised. Oh well, she forced
herself to let the matter go. Beggars couldn't be choosers, and
she'd have to be satisfied with what she had.

She felt Stephen watching her, and worried he was afraid she
wouldn't be able to handle what was inside the small room. She
was about to assure him she'd be fine when she saw him dig
another coin out of his pocket and hand it to the constable.

"I'm sure it might be possible to insure my cousin a bit of
privacy, would it not, my good man?" he asked with a cultured

smile. "In the event she should be overcome, I would not wish her to be ogled by strangers."

"No problem, me lord," the man said cheerfully, slipping the coin into his pocket. "Only give me a moment while I chase this riff-raff out, and then you may look all you please."

He slipped into the room, taking care to close the door behind him. Even through the thick wood Cara could hear the indignant voices of the men being ousted, and she flashed Stephen a wry grin.

"How much do you think they paid him?" she asked, thinking how aristocratic he looked in his many-caped Artois cloak, his beaver hat set at a rakish angle. She imagined the constable's eagerness to please him had as much to do with Stephen's quiet aura of power as it did the gold he'd slipped into his palm.

"Not as much as I did, apparently," Stephen drawled, pulling her to one side as the door flew open and three men stalked past them, casting them withering looks as they departed.

Cara gave herself a moment to gloat, and then sobered, turning her mind to doing the one thing she knew best; being a cop. She drew a deep breath, reaching deep inside for the composure she knew she would need before stepping into the room and closing the door behind her and Stephen.

Twelve

"Dear God!" The exclamation burst from Stephen's lips as he glanced slowly around the disheveled room. "The place looks like a slaughter house!"

"That's what it was," Cara replied, her stomach rolling as it always did at the smell of blood. "Watch where you step, I don't want the scene mucked up any more than it's already been."

She felt his incredulous gaze on her as she walked around the room. "How can you look at this and be so calm?" he demanded, sounding furious. "Have you ice in your veins, instead of blood? How can you feel nothing?"

His words hurt, but she put them down to shock. "I feel plenty," she said, thinking she'd kill for a tape recorder. "But I can't let it get to me. If I did I couldn't do what has to be done, and so I concentrate on other things instead."

"What sort of things?" The anger in his tone had faded, but she could still hear the horror he couldn't quite disguise.

She let her protective shield drop enough to feel anger. "Catching the bastard who did this and putting him in a cage so dark and deep he'll never again see the light of day," she said flatly, and then closed down again. "Now be quiet, I need to think."

She walked over to the wall that was awash with blood, forcing herself to think about the reddish-brown splatters only in terms of their importance as evidence. "The victim was apparently struck from behind," she began, knowing it would help organize her thoughts if she spoke them aloud.

"The spray of blood on the wall indicates she was standing

approximately two feet from the wall when the suspect slashed her throat. She was either similar in height to the suspect, or he may have partially lifted her off the ground. From the location of the first blood splatter I would place her height at 5'5", which means her assailant was at least three to four inches taller. I would place his height as between 5'8" and 6'1". Oh, he was left-handed."

Stephen moved closer, regarding her skeptically. "How can you tell all that?" he asked, swallowing as if fighting nausea.

"If he'd been right-handed, it would have changed the direction of the spray," she said, indicating the wall with a wave of her hand. "It would have landed here, instead of where it did. And if he'd been much taller than the victim, his arm would have crossed over her throat, partially blocking the blood. His coat or shirtsleeve would have absorbed most of it."

Stephen turned a delicate shade of green. "I see," he said faintly, and then remained silent as she continued her careful examination of the crime scene.

"The mattress has been removed from the scene; hopefully by the authorities, but from the stains pooling on the floor I'd say that's where the killer finished the attack. Was the body mutilated? If so, was the mutilation sexual? I'd say it was; this scene reeks of it."

She walked around, bending to touch some things, always taking care to put them back where she'd found them. As the papers indicated their were several words scrawled on the wall, and their crude nature added to her certainty the crime had been motivated out of some sort of twisted sexual fantasy. She muttered a disgusted curse under her breath at the realization. Sexual serial killers were among the most vicious and prolific of murderers, and she knew catching them was usually due more to luck than skill.

"Are you quite finished?" Stephen asked when she'd finally stopped pacing. "You'll be costing me another sovereign if you linger much longer."

"I'm almost done," Cara replied distractedly, studying one of the words painted on the rough wall. "Did you notice the way he wrote whore?" she asked, frowning as she contemplated the implications. "The 'r' and the 'e' are backward. I wonder if he's dyslexic."

"Dis . . . what?" Stephen stumbled over the word.

"Dyslexic," she repeated, her heart beginning to hammer with excitement. "It's a learning disorder that makes people see letters and numbers backward. People who suffer from it often have difficulty reading. And," she grinned as she suddenly remembered something, "they're usually left-handed."

"You consider that significant?" he asked, tilting his head to study her.

She nodded. "It eliminates a good portion of the population. Dyslexia's not that common, and it was unheard of in this time, so I needn't worry about the suspect planting false clues." She cast a final glance about the room, her expression wistful.

"I wish I could get a forensic team in here," she said, as he guided her from the room. "But that's impossible. The science won't exist for another one hundred and seventy years."

Stephen didn't reply until they were out on the street and walking away from the shabby rooming house. "Did you get what you came for?" he asked, his hand resting on her arm as they crossed the cobblestoned street leading toward Bow Street. "You seem rather satisfied, if you don't mind my saying so."

There was an edge of bitterness in his voice, but she decided to ignore it. "It's a start," she said, her mind whirling with facts she'd filed neatly away. "I know more about my killer now than I did a few hours ago, and I'm ready to begin my profile."

"Your profile?" he stopped, casting her a startled glance. "Do you mean to draw a picture of this fellow? How can you if you don't know what he looks like?"

"Not that kind of profile," she corrected, understanding his confusion. "It's a psychiatric profile . . . a description not of how he looks, but how he *thinks*. In my day we've learned that if we can learn how a suspect thinks, what his motivations might be, we can sometimes predict his next move, and that puts us one step closer to catching him."

Stephen look unconvinced. "I am sure that is all very helpful, but what good will it do you if you don't know what the . . . what did you call him? . . . the suspect look like?"

"Actually," she smiled smugly," I do have a fair idea what our boy looks like. He's medium height, probably medium build, he's left-handed, and suffers from a learning disorder. We can also safely assume he's caucasian . . . white," she added when he gave her a questioning glance, "and somewhere in his late twenties or early thirties. I'd also guess he was impotent with women," she added, remembering the vicious words scrawled in the victim's own blood, "although I'd need to see a copy of the autopsy report to be certain. But it fits."

"You can tell all of that just from what you've seen?"

"And from experience. I got on the homicide squad by solving a string of serial murders when I was working sex crimes," she said, and then stopped walking, tilting her head to one side as a sudden thought occurred to her. "It's fascinating, now that I come to think of it, that a serial killer should be operating in this time. Jack the Ripper was always considered the first real serial killer."

Stephen's face grew ashen. "Jack the Ripper?"

"He's one of the most famous killers in history," Cara replied, hoping she wasn't endangering the future by speaking of the horrific crimes. "In the late 1880s an unknown man stabbed several women to death, but was never caught. I studied the case while I was in university, and—"

"Harrington! Mrs. Marsdale! Hold up there!"

Both Stephen and Cara turned as they heard their names being called, and Cara suppressed a grimace when she saw Gilbert Holloway hurrying toward them. She'd met Stephen's friend some weeks ago, and she couldn't say she cared for him. He reminded her of one of the neighbor kids when she was growing up. The spoiled little rodent was forever getting other people in trouble, and then sitting back to watch the results with that self-satisfied smirk on his face. She supposed it was wrong of her to hang Holloway for Cedric's crimes, but she couldn't help herself. She simply didn't trust the man.

"What brings you to Bow Street on such a fine morning?" Holloway asked, greeting them with one of his mocking smiles. "Come to surrender to the authorities, have you?"

Stephen returned the other man's smile. "Not that I am aware of," he replied sardonically. "I was showing my cousin Covent Garden, and she expressed a desire to see The Royal Opera House. One thing led to another, and here we are."

"And what brings *you* to Bow Street, Mr. Holloway?" Cara asked sweetly, unable to resist paying the man back with a little of his own coin. "Come to turn yourself in?"

"Me?" Mr. Holloway exclaimed, clapping a hand over his heart and affecting a hurt expression. "You wound me, Mrs. Marsdale, truly you do. You must know I live the most exemplary of lives. I'm all but a monk in my habits, aren't I, Harrington?" And he turned to Stephen for support.

Stephen's eyes twinkled in amusement at his friend's antics. "Perhaps I shouldn't go so far as that," he drawled, turning to face Cara, "but Gil is an all right fellow, Cousin," he assured her, "else I should never have introduced the pair of you."

"I believe that is called being damned with faint praise," Holloway observed with a laugh. "But speaking of monks, I am glad to have run into you. I have been hearing the most extraordinary gossip about our friend Sir Q, and I want to know if you've heard anything."

Sir Q! Cara jerked in reaction. In the future, she'd read a book describing the trial that had originally ended with Stephen's execution, and in that book a Lord Q had given the most damning testimony against Stephen. Had the author been implying Sir Aidan Quarry had been the one to hang his friend?

"Aidan?" Stephen appeared genuinely astonished by Holloway's question. "What are they saying?"

Holloway's brown gaze flicked in Cara's direction. "I know what an ogre of propriety, you are, Harrington," he cautioned, "and I fear that the gossip may not be suitable for your cousin's delicate ears."

The sexist remark side-tracked Cara. "Oh for heavens sake!" she snapped angrily. "I'm a widow, remember? I'm hardly a green girl who'll swoon if you talk about a man's love life!"

Holloway's lips twitched in one of those smirks that set Cara's teeth on edge. "So you're not," he agreed smoothly. "But as it happens it is not Aidan's . . . er . . . love life that is the topic of speculation. No, indeed. Gossip links our illustrious baronet with a group of magicians, as it happens."

"Magicians!" Cara and Stephen echoed the word together.

"Or wizards, or whatever the devil they are calling themselves," Holloway gave an elegant shrug. "There's a club of sorts, it seems, and Quarry is said to be of them. Is that not the most astonishing thing?"

"It's nonsense!" Stephen insisted, his jaw getting that set look. "Aidan would never be involved in anything so half-witted. What has he to say about all of this?"

"Quarry defend himself against idle gossip?" Holloway asked, arching an admonishing eyebrow. "Perish the thought, old boy. He's even more stiff-necked than you are. He is maintaining an icy silence, as always, and should one be so ill-bred as to mention the matter, he favors him with one of those killing glances he learned from you."

That sounded like the enigmatic man she had encountered several times in the past weeks, and Cara was deeply troubled.

If Quarry was the Lord Q mentioned in the book, then he was Stephen's most deadly enemy. Even if it meant jeopardizing the future, she decided she had no other choice but to warn him. And yet, she brooded, thinking of Quarry's aristocratic features and cool, remote manner, and yet something about it just didn't feel right.

She'd seen him and Stephen together any number of times, and the relationship between them reminded her of Alec's friendship with Ryerson Keller. Rye had been her brother's old commander when Alec was a member of the elite SAS, and the two had remained fast friends. Rye would lay down his life for Alec in a heartbeat, and she got the same impression from Aidan Quarry. She was certain the man would die sooner than betray Stephen, but what if she was wrong?

Another thought occurred to her as well, jolting her. The killings she'd been involved with in the future had been carried out by a half-crazed Satanist wannabe. His victims had all been slashed as well, satanic symbols carved into their bodies. Had the victims in this time been similarly mutilated? she wondered. And this club Holloway spoke of, what if it was a coven? It made a horrible sort of sense, when she thought of it, and awful as she knew it sounded, a coven would be easier to deal with than a sexual serial killer.

She mentally shook her head, wishing she knew what to do. Common sense told her to warn Stephen about Quarry, but instinct argued it might be better to wait. If she was right and Aidan was innocent of harboring any animosity toward Stephen, then remaining silent would be the best for all concerned. And if she was wrong, waiting would give her the opportunity to gather evidence against the handsome baron. She knew without considering the matter that Stephen would require a great deal of evidence before believing Aidan had betrayed him.

Yes, she concluded, breathing a mental sigh of relief, that's what she'd do. She'd keep silent and watch Quarry like a hawk, and the moment she even suspected him of moving against Stephen, she'd tell him everything. It wasn't an ideal solution, but it was the only way she could think of to protect Stephen without hurting him.

In the days following the visit to the murder room Stephen struggled to come to terms with what he'd seen in that miserable little room. The memory of the blood-drenched walls and floor would not leave him, and he'd awakened several nights in a cold sweat; tormented by the most horrifying of dreams. It also brought back images of the murdered girl he'd seen shortly after

Miranda had disappeared. At first he'd thought the poor child was his missing wife, and he'd felt a sick sense of relief when he learned she was not. Then as now his relief shamed him, and he wondered what sort of monster must he be to rejoice another had died so horrible a death.

He was also deeply concerned about Cara. Since returning from Covent Garden she seemed unnaturally quiet and distracted, and several times he'd caught her watching him with the oddest expression in her eyes. At first he attributed her behavior to an understandable fit of the vapors, but when she began pestering him to obtain a copy of the coroner's inquiry so she could see if the victim had been disemboweled, he quickly put that explanation aside. No, it wasn't her feminine sensibilities that were troubling her, he decided. But something *was,* and his guts warned him that something was him.

The matter was uppermost in his mind some three days later as he sat in his club brooding over a glass of excellent claret. He had been in Parliament all morning, and the ponderous speeches he'd been subjected to left his mind feeling heavy and full of cotton. He was debating whether to endure another session of endless bickering or take the coward's way out and go home, when the sound of arguing drew his attention to the door. He had no sooner glanced up than he saw Elias Proctor shove his way past the determined footman. His former father-in-law spied him at almost the same time, and from the furious look on his face Stephen knew an unpleasant scene was imminent.

"Murdering whoreson!" Proctor's was thick with drink as he made his way to where Stephen was sitting. "You think yourself a proper gentleman, don't you? You think your fine title and grand manners gives you the right to steal the pennies from an honest man's pockets! Well, you're no better than a thief, do you hear me? A god-damned thief!"

There was a shocked silence, and Stephen could see several club members whispering behind their hands. He rose slowly to his feet, struggling to keep his expression blank as he faced his nemesis. "I have already warned you to mind your tongue," he said, his stomach churning with fury. "Watch well what you say, sir, my patience is not boundless."

If Proctor gave Stephen's warning any credence he gave no indication. "Thief!" he shouted, his eyes glittering with a burning hatred as he hurled the accusation. "And the bit of muslin you're passing off as your cousin is no better than a whore! All of London knows what she is, and—" his words ended in a choking gasp as Stephen's hands closed around his throat.

"One more word, you miserable little worm, and I shall snap your fat neck in half," he said, his lips peeled back in a vicious snarl. "Say what you want about me, I don't care, but keep your filthy mouth off my family or you're a dead man. Do you hear me?" He shook Proctor once for emphasis.

A gurgling sound emitted from Proctor's mouth, and his hands flew up to bat ineffectually at Stephen's hands. The footman, accompanied by four stout-looking lads, came dashing up, and Stephen flung Proctor in their waiting arms.

"Get this piece of dung out of my sight," he snarled, his chest rising and falling as he fought to regain control of himself. "I'll kill him if he crosses my path again!"

The footmen took him at his words and dragged Proctor away, ignoring his vociferous complaints. Stephen remained standing for several seconds, stunned by the intense savagery shimmering inside him. He'd never considered himself a violent man, but when he heard Proctor slandering Cara he wanted to kill him. When he felt the older man's throat beneath his fingers, he'd wanted to squeeze and squeeze until the bastard was dead.

"Sit down, Harrington, don't give the scavengers anything else to pick over," Aidan's voice sounded in Stephen's ear, and he felt a hand pressing urgently on his shoulder. "That's it, sit down, old fellow."

Stephen did as ordered, his knees giving way as he resumed his seat. He picked up his glass, studying the blood-red contents with intense concentration. "I wanted to kill him, Aidan," he said, his voice raw with emotion. "I wanted him dead."

"I do not blame you," Aidan's grim tone matched his expression. "I heard what he said about Mrs. Marsdale, and I was tempted to take a whip to him myself. It is a pity the fellow is so common. If he was a gentleman, you would have been well within your rights to challenge him."

"It's not true, is it?" Stephen asked, his fingers tightening around the fragile stem of his glass. "Are people gossiping about Cara as he says?"

Aidan didn't reply at first, and Stephen repeated the question. "There have been . . . whispers," he admitted, his gray eyes meeting Stephen's. "They started about a week ago, and I've had little success in tracking them down."

Stephen raised his glass to his lips, choking down a mouthful before speaking. "What are they saying?"

"Only that her appearance seems rather sudden, and her past somewhat mysterious," Aidan said, keeping his voice pitched in a low, soothing tone. "But upon my life, Stephen, I've not heard a single doubt being cast upon her honor. If I had, I should have called the man out at once."

Stephen gave a distracted nod, wondering how much pressure he could apply on the glass before it shattered into a hundred shards. "And where did you hear these whispers?"

"At a club, here and there," Aidan gave an uneasy shrug. "I have been paying closer mind to such tattle since I discovered someone is spreading tales about me as well. I trust you know the ones I am referring to?"

"The ones about your being a member of a society of wizards?" Stephen asked, allowing himself to be temporarily diverted. "Yes, I have, Gilbert mentioned it to me a few days past. I meant to warn you of it, but this is the first time I've seen you in over a week. Been off perfecting your spells, have you?" He spoke the words teasingly, and was amazed how good it felt to make a joke of something. Already he could feel the tension easing out of his shoulders, and he breathed out a heavy sigh of relief.

A half-smile touched Aidan's mouth. "What would you do if I said that is precisely what I was doing?"

"Remind you that it is Gil who is the prankster, not you," Stephen answered, leaning back in his chair. "Have you any idea who is spreading these tales, or why they should do so?"

"The who I can not say," Aidan said with a sigh, "but the why is a little easier to understand. It is well-known I have an interest in preternatural phenomenon, and I belong to any number of societies which study such things. I suppose it is not unrealistic to assume some person, knowing of my interest, could chose to extrapolate on the matter and infer the worse."

Aidan's words made Stephen think of the mysterious items hidden in the secret room. Cara had told him they were Satanic devices, and tied somehow to the power that controlled the time spell. Perhaps if he were to show them to Aidan he might be able to make some sense of them. Perhaps he might even help Cara find a way back to her time, he mused, and was amazed at the pain that jolted through him at the very thought.

"Yes, I'd forgotten you were cursed with a rather Gothic turn of mind," he said slowly, giving Aidan a measuring look. "I believe I may have some items which may be of interest to you."

"Oh?" Aidan looked intrigued. "What are they?"

"Just a few things I found hidden in the wall," Stephen said, deciding he'd seek Cara's advice before showing Aidan the ancient objects. "I'll show them to you later, but first I think we should concentrate on discovering the sources of these rumors. Do you think they are related?"

Aidan appeared to consider the matter, and then shook his head. "They could be," he said, "but I doubt it. As I told you, most of the talk being spread about Mrs. Marsdale is vulgar curiosity, while the gossip concerning me is more in the nature of embellishment. And in both cases the talk is relatively benign . . . for the moment."

Stephen contemplated his friend's face for several moments before speaking. "What do you think I should do?"

"What you suggested," Aidan replied with alacrity. "We shall look into the matter, discretely, mind, and when we determine the source of the rumors we can decide what next to do."

"I know what I shall do if I find Proctor is the one who has been spreading his filthy lies about Cara," Stephen said, his mouth thinning in a fresh anger. "I'll slit his damned throat."

"A tempting thought," Aidan agreed, casting a warning glance about him. "However, might I suggest that you keep such blood-thirsty sentiments private? After last year I do not think you would care to have your remarks misinterpreted."

Stephen grimaced at the thought. "You're right," he said, suppressing a shudder. "I shouldn't care for that at all. How much damage do you think I did to my reputation today? Be honest now," he added when he saw Aidan hesitating.

"Some, perhaps, but not as much as you seem to fear," Aidan said at last. "Proctor was being damned provocative, and once he slandered your cousin, there was precious little you could do. As a gentleman, you were honor-bound to defend her name by whatever means necessary. The men here know and understand that, and if they should speak of it, I am sure it can only reflect well on your character."

"I wish I shared your optimism," Stephen said, frowning at the painful memories washing over him. "But unfortunately I do not. I have bitter experience of the power of society's tattle, and I can not like the notion of Cara being the newest *on-dit.*"

"I can not say that I blame you," Aidan sympathized, albeit with a twinkle in his eyes, "but you forget this is the height of the Season. Some fine lord or lady is certain to do something scandalous in the next week or so, and once a juicier morsel of gossip appears this will all be dismissed as a seven days wonder. You've nothing to worry about, I promise you."

Stephen thought about that for a moment and then decided Aidan was right. If there was one thing society could be counted upon to provide, it was a new scandal. "Very well, Aidan," he said with a low chuckle, "I bow to your superior knowledge of the *ton*. In the meanwhile, I am most curious about something."

"Oh?" Aidan's gaze became wary. "And what might that be?"

"This society of warlocks you belong to," Stephen began, his lips curving in a wry smile, "are they interested in admitting new members? I've had a few preternatural experiences of my own, and I would know of such things. Tell me what you can."

"Excuse me, Mrs. Marsdale." The young maid standing before Cara bobbed a nervous curtsey. "But there is a gentleman downstairs asking to see you. Are you in?"

Cara glanced up from the map she was studying, her brows meeting in an impatient scowl. "What is the gentleman's name?" she asked, thinking that if her visitor was another of the idiotic men who had been plaguing her, she'd tell the maid to send him packing.

"A Mr. Thomas McNeil, ma'am," the maid provided dutifully. "Mr. Hargraves has put him in the drawing room, and wants to know if you'll be wishing tea."

Belatedly Cara remembered the proposed drive through the park, and fought the urge to swear. She supposed she could plead indisposition, but she hated women who hid behind illnesses as an excuse to get out of things. She glanced down at her map, remembering Mr. McNeil hadn't responded to her request to be allowed to assist. The possibility he was here with an answer was all it took to make up her mind.

"Tell Hargraves tea would be greatly appreciated," she said, rising swiftly to her feet. "And please inform Mr. McNeil I'll be with him shortly."

While the maid was off delivering her messages, Cara rang for her own maid and began changing out of her simple day dress. She'd become accustomed to wearing a half-dozen different gowns in the course of a day, and no longer gave her immense wardrobe a single thought.

Twenty minutes later she was hurrying down the stairs in a new walking dress of green and gold striped velvet topped with a spencer of darker gold velvet. She'd rebelled at wearing the accompanying bonnet, but as usual her maid would not be swayed, and in the end Cara had donned the gold chip straw bonnet with its enormous green satin ribbon in sullen resignation. Thank God none of her old mates from the Sex Crimes Unit were about, she mused, scowling as she tugged on her matching kid gloves. They'd laugh themselves silly if they should see her looking like something from a bloody film.

Mr. McNeil was standing by the window, and at the sound of the door opening he turned to greet her. "Mrs. Marsdale, how good of you to see me," he said, stepping forward with a hesitant smile. "I was afraid you'd forgotten our little outing."

"Of course not, Mr. McNeil," she lied sweetly, offering him her hand. "I've been most anxious to see you again, there's something I want to discuss with you."

He raised an eyebrow, but offered no response. Soon they were climbing on top of the black and silver phaeton being drawn by a set of matching black geldings. Cara had been back in time long enough to know rigs like this cost the earth, and she wondered if Mr. McNeil was perhaps richer than she'd been led to believe. Not even Stephen had a coach like this, and he was an earl. Like a good cop she filed the little discrepancy away, thinking she'd mull the matter over when she had more time. At the moment she had more pressing matters troubling her.

"Have you had time to consider what we discussed at Almack's?" she asked, after they'd driven several blocks in silence. "I really do want to help you."

"I am sure you do," Mr. McNeil said gently, sparing her a sidelong glance as he maneuvered his rig through the heavy traffic on Park Lane. "And I must tell you I admire your desire to help those so far beneath your social class. I can think of no other lady willing to act with such magnanimity."

Cara thought of a commonplace four letter word that succinctly expressed her feelings, but quickly amended it. "Stuff!" she said, folding her arms across her chest and flashing him an indignant glare. "I keep telling you I'm no Society miss who has to be protected from every ill wind. I can catch the bas—the blackguard responsible for these homicides, and I mean to do it; with or without your approval!"

Her vehemence startled him, and he waited until they had

wheeled into Hyde Park and were approaching Rotten Row before responding. "You sound rather vociferous on the matter,
ma'am," he said, in the slow, careful manner she was learning to
associate with him. "May I ask why?"

Now it was Cara's turn to be silent as she struggled to think
of a plausible explanation. Since he seemed to accept her story
about being trained by Indians she decided to expand on the
story, and gave him a cool look.

"The Indians near my farm may never have heard of Donne,"
she began, "but they would have no problem understanding what
he meant by "No man is an island." In their society every person
is connected with every other person, and an attack on one is an
attack on all. I believe that, Mr. McNeil," she added, her voice
steady with conviction as she met his gaze, "and I can no more
sit by doing nothing about these women's deaths than I could if
a member of my own family was killed. I have to act. Doing
nothing is not an option for me."

He gazed at her for several moments, his dark eyes filled with
an emotion she could not name. "Your eloquence is most affecting, Mrs. Marsdale," he said with visible reluctance, "but I fear
it will not serve. The area of London where these dreadful crimes
are being committed is perilous even for a man, and your cousin
would have my head were I to expose you to their dangers. I am
sorry, but I can not accept your help. Much as I might need it."
he added with a self-deprecatory laugh.

Cara swallowed her furious response, forcing herself to be
calm. "As it happens you wrong my cousin to say he would not
approve of your taking me into the area," she said, deciding to
attack the heart of his argument. "He took me there himself right
after the last murder."

"What?" Under any other circumstances Cara would have
found his slack-jawed look of astonishment diverting, but there
was too much at stake for her to find any amusement in the
situation.

"Another prostitute was murdered the night we met at Almack's," she explained, swallowing at the memory of the carnage

evident in that small room. "When I learned of it, I badgered his lordship until he took me there."

"You and his lordship went to a-a murder scene?" Mr. McNeil looked ready to swoon. "Surely he did not allow you inside!"

"It wouldn't have done me much good to go there and stand out in the hall, now would it?" she snapped, and then hastily softened her tone. "I mean, I was able to convince my cousin that I wouldn't faint, and he agreed with me that if I could be of assistance to the authorities I should try. You must know my cousin has a very stern sense of duty," she tacked this last bit on with a prim look.

"Indeed," he seemed taken aback by her revelation. "Well, if Lord Harrington supports you in this, then I suppose it would be all right. I shall have to seek the magistrates' approval first, but it shouldn't be a problem; especially if I inform them your actions have his lordship's approval. I am sure they must still be feeling badly after that dreadful business of a year or so ago. You know of that, don't you?" He cast her an anxious look.

"Yes, Aunt Minn wrote me of it," Cara said, trying not to think how furious Stephen would be when he learned what she'd done. Even though he'd promised not to stand between her and her duty, she doubted this was what he had in mind. Oh well, she pushed the thought of his displeasure from her mind. He'd just have to live with it, wouldn't he? He'd known she was a cop from the moment they'd met, and if they were ever to have a serious relationship, it was time he learned precisely what that meant. She squared her shoulders and turned to Mr. McNeil who was watching her with an enigmatic glow in his velvet-brown eyes.

"Then you will let me assist you?" she asked bluntly, and then held her breath as he hesitated.

"I suppose it would do no harm," he said at last, offering her a slow smile. "And in the end, who knows? It might prove to be for the best. Very well," he gave a decisive nod. "I shall welcome your assistance, Mrs. Marsdale. You may begin by telling me what you observed at the scene of the last murder. I am most eager to hear your impressions."

Thirteen

"No! Absolutely not! I will not hear of it!"

Stephen took the news she would be assisting Mr. McNeil better than Cara had hoped, and she congratulated herself for following her instincts and confessing what she'd done. She'd considered letting him find out on his own, but knowing how imperious he could be she decided telling him the truth straight away was the best way to avoid a full-scale battle. A wise decision, it would seem, she thought, hiding a triumphant grin.

"You've lost your mind, that's what," Stephen continued, his eyes flashing blue fire as he raged up and down the room. "All this racketing about in time has disordered the few wits you do possess, and this is the result."

"Hey!" Cara's complacency vanished at the insult. "I thought you said you wouldn't come between me and my sense of honor!"

He whirled around at her indignant protest. "Not coming between you and your honor and allowing you to run tame through the worst stews in London is hardly the same thing!" he snapped, jabbing his finger at her. "And you damned well know it!"

She cast him a fulminating glare, furious because the stupid sot was right. "I won't be running tame, whatever that means," she grumbled, scrambling to defend her position. "I've told you Mr. McNeil will be with me every second, and since he's even more priggish and protective than you are, I couldn't be any safer if you locked me in the bleeding Tower with the bleeding Crown Jewels!"

His head snapped back, his eyes narrowing as he cast her a

look that could have frozen fire. "I have observed your already lamentable language tends to suffer when you are in one of your tempers," he observed, his tone coldly brittle. "However, do you think you might lower your voice? I do not care to expose the members of my staff to your colorful vocabulary."

"My—!" Rage choked off Cara's reply, leaving her sputtering incoherently. For two pence she'd treat him to some *really* colorful vocabulary, but the knowledge he'd probably wash out her mouth for it kept her from cutting loose. Instead she rose from her chair, her back ram-rod straight as she stalked over to where he was standing.

"Listen," she began, tilting her head back until her gaze met his, "I've told you what being a cop means to me, and you said you understood. I'm not playing games, Stephen, nor am I defying you for lack of something better to do. I'm doing what I feel I must, and either you accept that, or you don't. Which is it?"

The hard cast of his jaw told her that like her he was making an effort to reign in his temper, and the wild glitter in his eyes warned her the outcome was not at all certain. Finally he expelled his breath in a gusty sigh, lifting his hands to cradle her chin between his palms.

"You're so alive," he murmured, his voice raw as he gazed down into her eyes. "I couldn't bear it if you were hurt."

His words were like taking a karate chop to the chest, and for a painful moment Cara couldn't catch her breath. His fingertips were brushing her ears, while his thumbs bracketed either side of her lips. Those lips were trembling, she realized dazedly, and did her best to firm them.

"I can't make promises," she said, hardly recognizing the tremulous sound of her own voice. "What I'm proposing is dangerous, and there's no sense denying otherwise. But," she added when she felt his fingers tightening, "I will tell you I wouldn't take this on if I didn't honestly think I could do the job. What good would that do the next victim?"

He closed his eyes. "Cara . . ."

"Can't you see she's the one who matters here?" she implored, covering his hand with hers and pressing his flesh to her own. "Not you, not me. Seven women have already been slaughtered; I can't let there be another."

Stephen's eyes opened, and the pain and desire she saw warring sent her heart rate soaring. "I can't stop you?" he asked, his fingers sliding deeper in her hair.

She shook her head, her mouth suddenly dry as dust. "I . . ." she moistened her lips with the tip of her tongue and tried again. "I don't want to hurt you, Stephen, but I will do what I must. I'm hoping you'll understand that."

He was quiet a long moment the intensity of his gaze all but searing her. "I understand," he said thickly, using his hold on her to draw her nearer. "God help me, but I understand precisely what you mean." And then he was taking her mouth in a kiss that was a stunning combination of naked need and frustration.

The moment his lips found hers Stephen lost himself in a whirlwind of emotion. Desire, terror, tenderness, it was all there, tendrils of feeling snatching at him as he surrendered to the glory of it. Her mouth parted beneath the onslaught of his, her tongue joining his in a scintillating game of thrust and parry. The taste of her, the feel of her, was every sweet and wild dream he had ever had come to life, and he could no more resist it than he could the screaming needs of his own body.

"Cara," he whispered her name hungrily, savoring the sound of it. He kissed her again, harder, hungrier, and moaned in delight when she responded with a passion that more than matched his own.

He moved his mouth down her neck, dipping lower to brush kisses across the swell of breasts revealed by the décolletage of her gown. His hands followed eagerly, caressing and teasing until he was aching with need and she was writhing in his arms. At some point she'd tugged his cravat off, and she was trying to pull his shirt from his breeches when reality intruded.

"Stephen, I was wondering if you could speak to Cook, I—"

The words ended in a shocked gasp, followed quickly by the sound of running feet and the slamming of the door.

Stephen jerked back, his body trembling as he fought to regain control of his rioting senses. His heart and blood were thundering in a pagan rhythm, and his hands were shaking as he brushed back a lock of hair that had fallen across his forehead. He tried to think, but his mind was a bog and every thought he had was sucked down almost before he could form it.

"Damn, damn, double damn, triple damn, *hell!*" Cara muttered furiously, her face flushed as she frantically rearranged the bodice of her gown. "We're in the soup now, aren't we?"

The soup. Stephen considered the words with a dazed sense of fatalism. He supposed it was as good a word as any to describe the ruin he had made of his life. He glanced down at her, sanity returning in slow, reassuring waves. There was so much he knew he should say, but instead he uttered the first words to pop into his mind.

"We have to get married."

Her head popped up so fast the top of her skull connected with his jaw and for a moment, they both saw stars.

"Bloody hell!" She was the first to recover, swearing succinctly, and glaring at him as she rubbed her aching head. "Watch it, won't you? You all but knocked me senseless!"

Stephen could barely feel the pain for the roaring in his head. He stared down at her, forcing his frozen tongue to function. "Cara, didn't you hear me?" he demanded hoarsely. "We have to get married."

"Of course I heard you, you dolt!" She'd rearranged her gown to her satisfaction, and was now attempting to repair the damage done her elegant coiffure. "But you're out of your mind to think I'd marry you just because we got caught with our hands in each other's cookie jars."

"Cookie jars?" Stephen wanted to howl with frustration at her incomprehensible response.

"An American expression," Cara replied, meeting his gaze with cool defiance. "It's considered more polite than *in flagrante delicto,* but it means the same thing. We've been caught doing something we shouldn't have, and now according to you, we have to pay the piper. Do I have the right of it?"

He should have known she would be as obstreperous about this as she was everything else. "Cara . . ."

"If you're going to say we've been compromised," she interrupted, her quiet tone making him more nervous than her shouting had ever done, "then I'm warning you, I'll drop you where you stand if you even try."

He actually took a step back before his pride brought him to a halt. "I'm only trying to be sensible," he began, trying to think of a way to say the words without actually saying them. "We've talked about honor often enough for you to know it is not a matter I take lightly. My actions here have put both our honors in peril, and I'll do what I must to set them right again."

If he thought his stiff explanation would satisfy her, he was quickly dissuaded. "Your actions?" she snapped, planting both hands on her hips in indignation. "Why, you egotistical pig! You weren't operating on your own in here, you know! I was kissing you every bit as you were kissing me, and if you're at fault then so am I! I'm not some Victorian miss whose reputation has been sullied beyond any hopes of redemption, and even if I were, it would be my concern, not yours. So we were kissing, big deal! It doesn't mean a bloody thing."

He opened his mouth to protest, then closed it again at the shimmer of panic he could see in her eyes. Clearly a rational discussion was impossible at this point, he decided it might be best to beat a strategic retreat. "As you wish," he said, pleased he could sound so reasonable despite the riot in his head. "Now if you will pardon me, I need to go upstairs and change. We are promised at the Berkshams, if you will recall."

He saw the confusion cloud her face. "Of course I remember," she said crossly. "But what about—"

"My mother had a lovely set of rubies that managed to survive my father's gaming," he interrupted, determined to keep her off her feet. "It would please me if you would wear them along with that lovely gown Aunt Minn described to me this morning at breakfast. The red silk with the cream underskirt. Would you do that for me?"

"I suppose so," her cross expression made it plain she was beginning to suspect what he was about. "But first don't you think one of us should go check on Aunt Minn? The poor thing's probably up in her room having a fit of the vapors."

"I'll see to it," Stephen promised, edging around her and toward the door. She shifted her body in response, and he decided a diversionary tactic might prove beneficial. It didn't take him long to think of the perfect topic.

"If you've time, you might wish to write your Mr. McNeil and inform him I have granted you permission to assist him in his inquiry," he said, purposefully injecting a note of cool condescension into his voice. "But warn him I shall hold him personally accountable for your safety, and I will expect to be kept abreast of all your movements."

"What do you mean you've granted me permission?" she demanded. "I never asked for permission!"

"Didn't you?" He reached the door and sent her a cool bow. "My mistake. Good bye, Cara. I shall see you tonight." And he closed the door, shutting off her indignant protests.

Cara was simmering over the matter as she dressed for dinner that night. She was annoyed enough with Stephen to be tempted to don the ugliest gown in her wardrobe, but she'd walked the razor's edge already this afternoon and she wasn't up to risking more. Lucky for him, she thought, her brows meeting in a scowl.

"Is that not to your liking, ma'am?" The maid halted in her ministrations and was regarding her anxiously. "I can use the curling tongs, if you would rather."

"What?" Cara blinked, staring at her reflection in confusion. "Oh, no Anne, it's fine."

"You have such lovely hair," Mrs. Marsdale," the pert maid continued, sighing as she began arranging Cara's hair in a so-

phisticated chignon. "So soft and shiny, and dark as night. Not
at all green and pointy like they said it was."

It took a few moments before the maid's words to make sense,
and when they did, Cara had to force herself not to leap out of
her chair. "Someone said my hair was green?" she asked, feigning amused interest. "Good heavens, what an appalling thought."

"Oh, none of the upper servants believed a word of Tom's
ranting, madam," Anne assured her earnestly. "Just a silly boy,
that's all he were. Saying how you was dressed in garments no
decent lady would wear, your face painted all colors . . . ! Mr.
Hargraves finally had to threaten to turn him off without a character if he didn't stop spreading such tales."

"So I should hope," Cara replied, her mind racing at the implications. From what Stephen had told her she thought they'd
managed to scotch any rumors about her other-worldly appearance, but perhaps they hadn't been as fortunate as they'd supposed. She'd been in this time long enough to know that
household gossip seldom remained private very long. If this Tom
had been blabbing to Stephen's servants, then chances were the
story was making the rounds to every household in London.

"Here are the jewels his lordship wished you to wear," Anne
said, opening a velvet-covered box and handing it to Cara. "Shall
I help you put them on?"

At first Cara couldn't speak, her mind wiped of thought by
the sight of the stunning necklace nestled in a bed of white satin.
The rubies were a dark red, the fire in them burning black from
the heart of the stone. The dazzling white glitter of diamonds
provided a stunning contrast to the brilliant-colored stones, and
a single ruby hung from the center like a precious drop of blood.
It was the most spectacular thing she had ever seen.

"Wow." The modern expression slipped from her lips, but Cara
was too dazzled to care. "Oh wow."

"A sight, isn't it?" Anne agreed, lifting the necklace from the
case and draping it about Cara's throat. "And it's just the thing
to set off your lovely gown, don't you think?"

Cara gazed at her reflection, and her mind went blank again.

That couldn't be her, she thought, raising a trembling hand to caress the exquisite necklace. That couldn't be her.

The woman in the mirror was like something out of one of those grand old Hollywood movies her mother so adored. The ones with so much color everything and everyone in them seemed unreal, and where lush music dramatically underscored every scene. In the flickering candle light her hair was ebony, and her face was as pale and smooth as the richest cream. Even her eyes seemed different, glittering with a topaz fire that made her look as exotic as some princess from a fabled land. She was beautiful, she realized, her heart swelling with pride. In that gown, with rubies dripping from her throat, she was beautiful.

"There's earbobs as well," Anne said, bending down to slip them on Cara's ears. "And a fine ring for your hand, if it fits." She picked up Cara's hand, and gave a startled cry. "Heavens, your hand is like a block of ice! Are you cold?"

Cara stared down at the magnificent ruby solitaire, glittering on her finger. "No," she said, her voice unnaturally calm. "I'm fine." She raised her head and gave her reflection a final gaze. "Are you finished?"

"Yes, madam." Anne stepped back, beaming at Cara like a proud mama. "And if you don't mind my saying so, Mrs. Marsdale, you do the Harrington rubies and the Harrington name proud."

Cara pulled out of her fog long enough to reach for her beaded reticule. She extracted a coin and handed it to the delighted maid along with a smile. "You're a regular miracle worker, Anne," she said warmly. "Thank you for everything."

The sight of the gold coin had Anne's brown eyes popping in amazement and she bobbed a hasty curtsy, stuttering her thanks in an incoherent tone. Cara gently brushed the effusive gratitude aside, and it was only as she was making her way down the staircase to where Stephen and Aunt Minn were waiting that the maid's odd words occurred to her. Do the Harrington name proud? she wondered, her brows wrinkling in thought. What the bloody hell did that mean?

* * *

She was the most beautiful woman he had ever seen. Stephen sat opposite Cara, his jaw clenched as he kept his head turned toward the window of the coach. When he'd seen her descending the staircase it had taken every ounce of willpower he possessed to keep from gaping at her like an addle-pated clod, and he had yet to recover his *sang-froid*. He'd wanted to show her proudly to the world, and then lock her away so no other man could gaze upon her beauty. The warring impulses confused and irritated him, although he supposed he should be used to the sensation by now. The wretched creature had been having the same affect upon him since the moment he first clapped eyes upon her.

It didn't help his exacerbated nerves that the silence between Cara and his aunt was so thick it could have been cut with a knife. He'd already had a private conversation with Minn, assuring her of his intentions, but she'd yet to discuss the matter with Cara. He was trying to think of some polite way to broach the topic to break when Cara turned to Aunt Minn.

"I've always believed that trying to ignore an embarrassing situation is rather like trying to ignore an elephant in the parlor," she said in her appallingly blunt manner. "You can only walk around the bloody thing so long, then it trumpets and the secret's out. Now, let's talk about this afternoon when you walked in and caught me kissing Stephen."

Minn shifted uncomfortably on the leather seat, her gaze flicking first to Stephen and then to Cara. "I do not feel this the time or the place to speak of this," she said at last, her usually warm voice reserved. "His lordship has already spoken with me, and I am content to let the matter rest. For now," she added, pinning Stephen with a stern look.

He accepted her censorious glare as his due and said nothing, reliving again the dreadful scene when he'd walked into her sitting room and found his aunt collapsed on the settee, sobbing into her handkerchief.

"Oh, Stephen how *could* you!" she'd wailed, her blue eyes

awash with tears. "Your reputations . . . hers . . . ! Whatever could you have been thinking of?"

Since there was no way to defend himself without defaming Cara he'd said nothing, waiting until the storm of weeping had passed before quietly informing Minn that he and Cara would be marrying as soon as it could be discreetly arranged. Then he confounded her by insisting she tell no one, not even Cara of their discussion until he gave her leave.

"Don't be absurd, Stephen," she had scolded, shaking her head at him in maternal disapproval. "The gel has to be told some time! She's as sharp as anything, and she's bound to suspect something is afoot when the pair of you stand before a curate and begin exchanging vows!"

He hadn't argued but had merely repeated his request, earning Minn's grudging promise to hold her tongue. Now all that remained was convincing Cara; a task he was certain would prove even more arduous than had proving his innocence when he had stood before Parliament charged with Miranda's murder.

As if guessing his thoughts, Cara launched into an indignant protest. "Let me guess," she said, folding her arms across her chest, "he offered to make an honest woman out of me. Didn't he?" And she fixed Minn with an intimidating scowl.

The older woman's hands flew to the broach on her cloak. "I . . . that is something best discussed with your cousin," she said, tossing him to the wolves without the slightest compunction. "But again, this is neither the time nor the place for such a discussion. You must wait, dearest."

Cara's scowl grew more pronounced. "But Aunt—"

"We have arrived," Minn interrupted, making no attempt to hide her relief. "My, look at the line of carriages, will you? It looks as if the countess has invited every person of consequence in the city! This is certain to be a fashionable crush."

And a crush it was. Stephen had to keep a steady hand on both Cara and his aunt to keep them from being swept away in the teeming crowd of well-dressed men and women streaming into the Berkshams' elegant home on Cavendish Square. While his aunt accepted his escort, Cara kept tugging in an attempt to free herself. When one of her efforts almost sent them all tumbling down the steps, he tightened his hold in warning.

"Watch yourself, hell-cat," he warned, keeping his voice low-pitched so as to avoid being overheard. "That last maneuver of yours could have made me lose my balance."

"Good," she snapped, although he noted she was careful to keep her voice low. "It's no more than you deserve, you bugger!"

"Perhaps," he agreed, nodding at an old friend, "but don't forget about Aunt Minn. Or are you so hipped with her you wouldn't mind causing her a serious injury as well?" When she ceased her struggles he permitted himself a small smile.

"I thought not. Now behave. I promise when we are alone you may rail at me as you please. You may even strike me, if you would like," he offered, sliding her a teasing glance from the corner of his eye.

"Oh, I'd like," she said, her full lips curving in an evil smile. "I would like very much."

The next several minutes were taken up with greeting their hosts and lovely daughter, and in the midst of the melee Cara managed to give him the slip. Since he'd been intending to release her once they reached the formal drawing room, Stephen decided to let her enjoy her brief victory. Still he was careful to keep a sharp eye on her, a task made more difficult by the fact she was surrounded by a crowd of admirers from the moment she entered the ball room. He was watching her, trying to decide what to do when Lady Felicity walked up to join him, her duties as hostess apparently over for the moment.

"Mrs. Marsdale is looking lovely tonight," she commented, unfurling her fan and smiling. "That is an exquisite gown."

Stephen gazed down at her, wishing there was some way to avoid the next few minutes. Unfortunately his honor would not permit such cowardice, and he knew what he had to do.

"Yes, it is," he said quietly, laying his hand on her arm and holding her gaze with his own. "I should like to speak with you, my lady, privately, if I may."

Her hazel eyes widened, and a delicate blush stole across her cheeks. "Very well, my lord," she murmured, and he could sense her discomfiture. "My father's study is just across the hall. I am sure he would not mind if we were to make use of it. Or," she paused, studying him through her thick lashes, "or if you prefer, there is a small parlor where my mother interviews potential servants. We could go there, if you like."

The second offer startled Stephen. He knew she was expecting him to propose, and it was natural to assume he would wish to do so in her father's study. By mentioning the second room, she was giving him a graceful way to bow out of the situation with both their reputations more or less in tact, and her generosity left him feeling even lower than he already felt.

"Your mother's parlor sounds fine, my lady," he said, his voice slightly gruff. "Will you be so good as to take me there?"

An odd look flashed in her eyes and was gone, and she turned and guided him from the crowded ball room. The Berkshams' home was twice the size of his house, and he was marvelling at its vast elegance as she led him into a modest room located at the back of the house. She had retrieved a candelabra from the hallway and she set it on the small desk before turning to face him; her expression carefully guarded.

"Very well, Lord Harrington," she said in a soft tone. "What is it you wish to say?"

Suddenly his cravat seemed unbearably tight, but he allowed none of his discomfort to show as he faced her. "Lady Felicity, before I say anything else, I should like to apologize to you," he began resolutely. "I feel as if I have done you a great disservice, and I wish you to know I am very sorry for it."

She looked momentarily startled, and then her expression smoothed out again. "I see," she said, her tone revealing nothing of her emotions. "And precisely what disservice have you done me, Lord Harrington?"

God, this was even harder than he'd feared, Stephen thought, fighting the impulse to run his finger under his starched collar. "I allowed you and your parents to believe I was contemplating making an offer for you," he admitted at last, knowing only the blunt truth would serve. "Worse, I allowed Society to believe it as well, and did little to quell the speculation."

She studied him for several moments before responding. "Am I to take it no such offer will be forthcoming?"

Maybe he just should have taken the gentleman's way out and put a bullet through his head, Stephen mused, before giving a jerky nod. "Yes, my lady," he said stonily, "you may."

Again she gave him an enigmatic look. "Then there is nothing left to say," she said, turning to pick up the flickering candles. "Shall we return to the ballroom?" she asked coolly. "I am sure the others must be wondering where we are."

Even as Stephen was telling himself he should be grateful Lady Felicity was accepting his unprincipled behavior with such grace, he was reaching out to take her arm. "Is that all you have to say?" he demanded, his pride stung at her indifference.

"What would your lordship have me say?" she asked, gazing up at him with steady hazel eyes. "There was never a formal agreement between us; nor even an informal one, if it comes to that. You are quite free to marry where you please, I assure you."

He released her arm and stepped back. "Who said I was marrying?" he demanded, feeling oddly defensive.

Her lips curved in a half-smile. "Isn't that why you wished to speak with me? Because you have offered for another woman?"

"I haven't offered for another woman," he replied, wondering if all women were possessed of preternatural abilities.

Lady Felicity's smile grew beatific. "But you are contemplating it," she said, nodding her head as if in approval. "Your cousin, I presume?"

Stephen didn't even try to hide his astonishment. "How do you know that?" he asked, his tone as incredulous as his expression.

She gave a pretty shrug. "Your responses to her always struck me as being rather too intense for mere cousinly fondness," she said, not seeming the slightest bit perturbed at the knowledge. "I take it this is to be a love match, then?"

Stephen was about to issue a vociferous denial when he suddenly paused. Was the tangle of desire and exasperation he felt toward Cara love? Certainly he felt more for her than he had any other woman, even Miranda, and God knew he couldn't even think of marrying another while she held sway in his emotions. Perhaps it was love, he told himself, and if not, it was the closest to that tenuous emotion that he was ever likely to come.

It also occurred to him that if Lady Felicity thought he was marrying Cara out of love, it would render the blow to her pride easier to absorb. It might also help ease Cara's acceptance into the *ton;* for despite their show of cynicism, he knew there was nothing Society liked more than a blissful romance.

"Yes, my lady," he said, assuring himself he was only saying what was necessary to save Cara and spare Lady Felicity's pride. "It is to be a love match."

Fourteen

"Good evening, Mrs. Marsdale," Gilbert Holloway's voice was as smooth as the bow he offered Cara. "May I say how enchanting you look in that gown? Harrington is to be envied for having such a beauteous relation."

From her seat beside the dowagers' bench, Cara fought the urge to scream in frustration. She'd deliberately parked herself on the sidelines to avoid the idiotic men swarming around her; a ploy that had worked with everyone except Holloway. She was strongly tempted to tell him to shove off, but since he was Stephen's friend, she forced herself to answer politely.

"You are too kind, sir," she said, trying to decide if he was being obnoxious or was merely dense. "But your compliments would better be directed to my modiste rather than my cousin. His lordship had little to do with my gown."

"True," his smirk made it obvious he wasn't dense. "But I daresay he had a great deal to do with that lovely sparkler adorning your equally lovely neck. The Harrington rubies, if I am not mistaken."

That was the second time her necklace had been referred to in such a manner, and Cara's hand crept up to stroke the glittering stones. "He said they were his mother's," she said, frowning as she recalled the casual way he'd requested she wear them. At the time she'd thought their importance lay only in their monetary value, but now she was beginning to have her suspicions.

"And so they were, in a manner of speaking," Holloway said, taking the seat beside Cara without seeking permission. "They are given to the Lady Harrington upon her marriage, and they remain her private property for the remainder of her life. Upon her death they pass to the next Lady Harrington, a tradition which has more to do with economics than sentiment. Since they are entailed, you see, they cannot be sold. More's the pity," he added with an exaggerated sigh. "They're worth a fortune."

Cara was hard-pressed not to shudder in revulsion. She supposed his mocking, caustic wit would be considered clever by most people, but he was beginning to get on her last nerve. More and more he reminded her of the nasty little brat who'd been the bane of her existence when she'd been twelve, and with that thought in mind she turned her head and gave him a sweet smile.

"I meant to ask, Mr. Holloway, but are you perhaps related to a Mr. Cedric Montgomery of Braxton Court?"

"Montgomery?" His brows met in confusion. "I can not say that I am, ma'am. Why do you ask?"

"Oh, no reason," she smiled again, taking refuge behind her fan. She was starting to like the affectation of a fan, she decided, waving hers with indolent grace. So much could be implied with a mere flutter or a snap.

She could tell by the way he hesitated that he suspected she was having him on, but he quickly recovered. "Speaking of Harrington, do you know where he is?" he asked, glancing about them in studied innocence. "I was hoping for a word with him, but I haven't seen him since he and Lady Felicity slipped out of the room shortly after your arrival."

Bloody snake, she thought, her smile never wavering. "No, I've not seen him, either, Mr. Holloway," she said, her light tone letting him know his ploy to rattle her hadn't succeeded. "But if I do, I'll be sure to tell him you're looking for him."

He looked at her for a moment, and then gave a low chuckle. "Which is your discreet way of telling me to go to the devil," he said, flashing her a wry grin. "And 'tis no less than I deserve, I'll admit. I was being rather an insufferable ass, wasn't I?"

The candid admission took Cara by surprise, and when she cast him a suspicious look he chuckled even louder. "Yes, Mrs.

Marsdale, you heard me correctly. I admit I was obnoxious; deliberately so, but I pray you do not take lasting offense. It is the way of our world, you see. It is widely accepted that Lord Harrington is a noble man of impeccable honor and integrity, while his racketing friend Mr. Holloway is a cynical, care-for-nothing dandy with a wit more cutting than his tongue."

Cara didn't quite know how to take the rueful admission. "You sound fairly content with the status quo," she said, wondering how far to trust his open humility. As a cop, she'd learned to mistrust such seeming frankness.

"Not so much content as resigned," he corrected, his brown eyes thoughtful. "I haven't Harrington's birth and now fortune to grease my way in Society, and must rely upon my wit to insure the flow of invitations. The *ton* dotes upon we malicious raconteurs, when it's not them we're sharpening our tongues upon, and they will keep inviting me so long as I prove amusing."

"Maybe," she said, deciding to accept his show of penitence for the moment. "Just remember I'm not a member of the *ton*, and I don't like it when someone thinks I'm too stupid to know when I'm being made sport of. Or that I don't know how to tell a genuine compliment from a false one," she added with a pointed glare.

He actually flushed. "I am sorry you feel that way, for the compliment was sincere, if the way I offered it was not. It is just I am so used to playing the gadfly that sometimes I find it impossible to separate myself from the pose. I-I suppose that sounds nonsensical," he added, sending her a contrite smile.

"No," Cara managed weakly, thinking of her days undercover when she feared losing herself in the lie she was forced to live, "it makes a great deal of sense, actually."

"Does it?" He studied her intently. "I am glad. As to the first part of my apology, ma'am, I wouldn't want you to think I am not without some virtues to recommend me. I may not be so wealthy as Harrington, but I am in line for a title, and I'm not nearly so devoted to politics as his lordship so I shouldn't prove

nearly as tiresome. Not that I suppose all that matters now," and
he gave a mournful sigh.

Cara felt a cold frisson of alarm. "What do you mean?"

"The rubies," he waved his hand at her throat. "I've told you
they're given to all Harrington brides. Naturally when I saw you
wearing them I assumed you and Stephen were about to announce
your coming nuptials."

As this was what Cara was beginning to suspect she managed
not to screech a denial and rip the necklace from her throat. She'd
have it out with Stephen later, but in the meanwhile something
Holloway had said piqued her curiosity.

"Did Miranda—Lord Harrington's first wife, wear the rubies?" she asked, wondering why Miranda hadn't mentioned the
necklace to her or Alec when talking of her brief marriage.

"I am sure I do not know," he replied with a sniff. "I was at
my uncle's estate when the wedding took place, and heaven
knows the troublesome creature didn't remain countess long
enough to have her portrait painted in them as is the custom."

An image of a woman in Restoration dress, a necklace of rubies resting on her starched ruff, flashed in Cara's head. How
many other portraits were there? she wondered. *And what the
bloody hell had happened to them? Had any of them survived
into the future?* That damned house was like the Bermuda Triangle, she thought, scowling in frustration. Things were forever
appearing and disappearing. She jolted at the thought.

Maybe that was the clue to the Triangle, she mused, her mind
racing off on another tangent. Maybe it wasn't aliens or electro-
magnetic fields like the tabloids claimed. Maybe it was a time
portal; a portal that, having been created, was both accessible
and controllable. Like the time portal in the house could be if
she could just figure out a way to access it . . .

"Mrs. Marsdale?" Holloway laid a gentle hand on her arm and
was regarding her with genuine alarm. "Is everything all right?
You've the oddest expression on your face."

"What?" She gave him a blank look, her mind whirling with
fantastic possibilities.

"I believe I saw your aunt in the next room," he continued, his manner surprisingly firm. "If you think you'll be all right, I should be happy to go and fetch her for you."

Cara managed to pull herself together and gave him a reassuring smile. "I'm fine, Mr. Holloway," she said, closing her fan with a snap. "There's no need to disturb Aunt Minn, I promise you. However, there is something I should like you to do for me, if you would be so kind."

"Certainly, ma'am," he inclined his head with the grace worthy of a Spanish courtier. "You have but to name it and it shall be done."

"The task I have in mind isn't quite so strenuous as that," Cara replied, deciding perhaps he wasn't such a bad sort after all. "Has Sir Aidan arrived as yet?"

"Our learned baron?" Holloway looked thoughtful. "I believe I saw him in the conservatory while I was seeking out Harrington."

Cara rose to her feet, leaving him no choice but to follow suit. "I'd like to speak with him," she said, too focused on what she meant to say to the baron to note the edge of command that had stolen into her voice. "Take me to him, please."

"Certainly, ma'am," he offered her his arm along with another bow. "It would be my pleasure."

It took several minutes of shoving their way through what seemed like half of London, but they were finally able to run Quarry down to earth. He was just coming out of one of the rooms set aside for card play, and Holloway turned her over to him with what seemed to Cara immodest haste. Nor was she the only one to take notice of his relief. Sir Aidan watched him serpentine his way through the crush of people, and then turned to Cara.

"What have you done to overset poor Holloway?" he asked, a glimmer of amusement in his silver-colored eyes. "I've not seen him move so dexterously since we were lads together at Eton, and he saw the doctor coming at him with a jar of leeches."

"Now there's a fine compliment," Cara muttered, annoyed

with the analogy. "I've been compared with a great many things, but certainly never a jar of parasites."

"I'm sure I should never be so ungentlemanly as to say such a hen-witted thing," he said, lifting her hand to his lips for a teasing kiss. "I merely meant to say that Gil seemed in an uncommon hurry to be elsewhere. Not that I am complaining, mind. I had been hoping we might have a chance to talk privately."

"Oh?" She asked coolly, something in his voice setting alarms ringing in her head. "What was it you wished to discuss, sir?"

He gave her a calculated smile. "Canada," he said, his gaze sharp as he studied her. "It is interesting, don't you think, that in our grandfathers' day a journey there took many months. Now the same trip can be made in a matter of weeks."

Cara moved her shoulders in a casual shrug, affecting indifference even as she was wondering what he was after. "If you say so," she replied in a bored tone. "But that is progress, is it not? Who knows," she added challengingly, "perhaps one day the voyage might be even shorter."

"Perhaps," he agreed, his gaze never wavering. "But my point was that now that the journey to Canada is so easy, there are ships arriving at our docks each month. And of the ships docking in the past year, none of them has record of a Mrs. Cara Marsdale having booked passage. As I said, I find it interesting."

Cara froze, her blood draining from her face at the skill of his attack. She remembered thinking he had a cop's eyes, but now it seemed he had a cop's instinct for sniffing out facts as well. She was silent for a moment, weighing, deciding, and then she tossed back her head and gave him a cool smile.

"I am glad you find it so, my lord," she said, and was grimly pleased when he seemed taken aback by her glibness. "But it is hardly surprising, since I didn't arrive by packet ship."

The look in his eyes became menacing. "Then perhaps you'd be so good as to tell me how you did arrive," he said, making no attempt to disguise the chilling anger radiating from him.

Cara stood her ground defiantly. "And perhaps I would not."

He took her arm, leading her through the card room and out on to the balcony overlooking the Berkshams' garden.

"You seem an intelligent female, Mrs. Marsdale," he began, releasing her arm and discarding any pretense of cordiality. "I am sure you can see the folly of displeasing a man who commands the power I can should I choose to do so. Stephen is one of my oldest friends, and I wouldn't take kindly to his being hurt. I would take even less kindly to his being used by a scheming baggage who has her eye on the main chance. I trust you take my meaning?" he added when she didn't speak.

Cara studied his remote, dangerous expression for a long moment, and then surprised them both by smiling. "Actually, I do," she said, the suspicions she'd been harboring fading in light of his fierce defense of Stephen. "And I'm glad Stephen has such a friend as you. I care for him very much, and I give you my word I would never do anything to harm him."

He returned her intense scrutiny before giving a slow nod. "Do you know, Mrs. Marsdale," he said, a note of wry disbelief creeping into his voice, "I believe you are telling the truth."

"I am," she assured him. "And I now believe that you'd never harm him as well."

His head jerked back as if she'd slapped him. "Why should you think that I would?" he demanded, clearly incensed.

Cara wrestled with her conscience before deciding that so long as she wasn't *too* specific, she could reveal a part of what she knew. "Someone did," she said bluntly, wishing the light wasn't so bad so she could better gage his reaction. "Someone did their damnedest to put a noose around his neck and they almost succeeded. I thought it was you."

His eyes flashed in furious denial. "Never!" he exclaimed, his hands curling into fists. "I would die sooner than betray him! I insist you tell me why you should think such a thing!"

Again Cara hesitated. She was fairly sure he wasn't involved in the plot against Stephen, but until she was certain she thought it wisest to play her cards close to her chest. It wasn't just that she was afraid of revealing information to a man who might still be a suspect, she admitted, chewing on her lip. There was the whole time-travel thing to consider. If Aidan was mucking about with a bunch of wizards, the last thing she wanted to do was let him know that time-travel worked.

"Mrs. Marsdale?" He was scowling down at her with obvious impatience. "I am waiting. Why do you think I would hurt one of my oldest friends?"

"Because you're always watching people," she blurted out, seeking refuge in the truth. "You're always standing back and watching. It's as if you're studying us, like we're toys you find mildly amusing. When I began hearing stories that Stephen had been framed—made to look guilty in his wife's disappearance," she amended, "it occurred to me you may have done it to see what would happen."

"That's utter rot!" he declared so fiercely that she had to believe him. "Stephen is like a brother to me, and I moved earth and heaven to have him freed! I would have done anything to secure his release. How dare you accuse me of plotting against him out of idle curiosity!"

"And what about Miranda?" he added before she could respond. "Or do you think I hurt her, a woman I admired for her gentleness and beauty, out of this same macabre curiosity?"

Cara's eyes widened in shock. "You knew Miranda?" she asked, recalling how her sister-in-law had insisted she hadn't known the identity of the man in Stephen's room on the night she had been swept forward in time.

"We were acquainted, yes," he said, still looking offended. "I was delighted when she and Stephen became engaged, and I was sickened when she disappeared and we thought she'd been murdered. When she returned in time to have Stephen acquitted, I didn't know whether to kiss her feet in gratitude or have her stoned."

Oddly it was this rather brutal declaration that convinced Cara of his innocence. If someone had put Alec in the docket, that was precisely how she would have reacted. Without thinking she reached up and pressed a kiss to his cheek.

"I'm sorry, my lord," she said quietly, gazing up into his eyes. "It seems I've misjudged you. I hope you'll forgive me."

His brows met in confusion as he returned her somber gaze. "I do not understand," he began, and was interrupted by the sound of approaching footsteps. He turned just as Stephen stepped out on to the balcony.

"Here you are," Stephen's voice was rigidly proper as he gazed at Cara. "I have been looking for you. It is time for the dance you promised me."

To Cara's surprise Aidan interposed himself between her and Stephen. "You may relax, Harrington," he said coolly. "Nothing untoward was happening between your cousin and myself; I give you my word."

Stephen reached around Aidan and grabbed Cara's hand, pulling her to his side. "I am aware of that," he said, tightening his grip when she tried tugging free. "And for your information, Cara is not my cousin. She will be my bride. Good night, Quarry." And with that he turned and drug a stunned Cara back into the crowded house.

The next few hours were amongst the longest in Stephen's life. He divided his time between keeping a wary eye on Cara and fending off increasingly pointed questions. As he expected Cara's wearing his family's rubies hadn't gone unremarked, and he knew that by the following morning rumors of his engagement would be all over town. He supposed he should feel guilty for playing such a shabby trick, but Cara's fiercely independent nature had left him no other option. Unless he presented her with a *fait accompli*, she'd argue all the way to the altar.

Finally the tension-filled evening was at an end, and he was able to collect his aunt and Cara for the journey back to Curzon Street. Minn kept up a lively monologue during the short ride, doing her best to fill the brittle silence that grew more pronounced with each passing second. But soon even her bright chatter faded, and when they arrived home she picked up her skirts and fled up the stairs without so much as a backward glance. Stephen couldn't fault her for her desertion. God knew he'd have fled as well had he any say in the matter. Unfortunately he did not, and his expression was somber as he turned to Cara.

"We need to talk," he said, taking her by the arm and staying her when she would have fled.

She shot him a quelling look and jerked her arm free. "I'll say we do," she muttered and stalked off, leaving him no choice but to trail after her.

Stephen wasn't overly surprised when she led him into the drawing room rather than his study. The study was his bailiwick, and he knew she'd never give him such an advantage over her. Without offering comment he took his stand in front of the fireplace, his back to the dying embers as he waited for Cara to begin speaking. It didn't take very long.

"Have you lost your bloody mind?" She erupted, her eyes shimmering with temper. "How could you have told the baron I was your fiancee? I thought he was your friend."

Knowing she'd ride rough-shod over him if he showed the slightest weakness, Stephen concentrated on appearing coolly in command. "He is," he replied, his voice as imperturbable as his manner. "I told Aidan you were my fiancee, because you *are* my fiancee. We are getting married the moment I can secure a Special License."

Her jaw dropped and then snapped shut again. "Like hell we are!" she retorted furiously. "I've tried marriage, thank you very much, and I'd rather be lined up against a wall and shot!"

"I've also tried marriage," he reminded her, amused by her blunt declaration. "And I was almost executed for my pains. If I'm willing to give the married state another go, I don't see where you have room to quibble."

"And that's another thing," she shot back, looking decidedly harassed. "Let's say we do marry, and either I decide to attempt the return to my time or the bloody room malfunctions and zaps me God only knows where? How do you think you'll explain another missing wife to understandably skeptical authorities, hm?"

Although he'd already taken such a possibility into account, Stephen couldn't help but feel a superstitious jolt at her taunting words. "I am not sure what I would do should such a thing happen," he admitted, his heart racing with emotion. "But I refuse to live my life worrying about a future I have no hopes of controlling. I want you as my wife, Cara, and that is all that matters."

"But—"

"Cara," he walked over to where she was standing and laid his hands on her shoulders, drawing her inexorably against him. "I'm not asking you to marry me because I feel I must. I'm asking you to marry me because I want to."

Her eyes grew impossibly wide, and he felt a fine tremor shake her slender body. Nonetheless her voice was steady as her gaze met his. "Are you saying that you love me?"

For a moment he considered declaring his eternal devotion, but when he saw the courage and honesty in her eyes he knew he couldn't lie. "No," he admitted, aware of a small pang of regret. "I desire you very much, but I cannot say I love you."

She gave a half-nod. "Good. If you'd said yes, I'd have kicked your bloody teeth in. But if you don't love me, why do you want to get married?"

Blunt for blunt, he decided. "Because although I want you until I ache with it, I won't make love to you until we are husband and wife," he said, refusing to let her glance away. "I'm not saying I haven't had mistresses in the past, but what we shared was nothing more than a simple exchange of money for physical pleasure. What I feel for you is stronger, deeper than anything I've ever felt for another woman; including Miranda, and I refuse to dishonor those feelings by offering you no more than I offered those other women. I don't want you as my whore, Cara. I want you as my wife."

To his distress her eyes filled with tears. "But I was miserable as a wife," she said, her voice shaking with sorrow. "You've only to ask my husband, and he'd tell you how hopeless I was in the kitchen and . . . and in the bedroom as well." A single tear wended its way down her cheek as she gazed up at him.

"He's not half the man you are," she added brokenly, "and I could never satisfy him. How could I ever hope to satisfy you?"

Of all the arguments he had steeled himself to resist, it had never occurred to him that she should have the slightest doubt as to her ability to please him. He wanted to laugh in disbelief, but the misery in her eyes quickly killed the impulse. Instead he leaned forward and pressed a gentle kiss to her forehead.

"You do satisfy me, my angel," he said gently, holding her against him in a comforting embrace. "More so than any woman has ever done. We've scarce exchanged more than a kiss, but the pleasure we've shared has convinced me that in bed we shall deal very well together. As to the other," he drew back, tilting her head up with his finger, "as to the other, I already have a perfectly adequate cook in my kitchen. I scarce need to go to all the trouble of marrying in order to secure another."

As he'd hoped a smile trembled on her lips, but it faded almost as quickly as it appeared. "But how would I ever know?" she asked miserably. "I want you so much, Stephen, but I don't want you tied to me for the rest of our lives unless—unless I could be certain it's what you want."

"But I do want you, my love," he exclaimed, growing alarmed at the desolation in her voice. "What more can I do to convince you of that fact?"

She hesitated a moment before rising on tip-toe to press a kiss to his mouth. "You can make love to me," she said simply.

Stephen squeezed his eyes shut, his body shuddering with desire. "Cara," he groaned, feeling as if he was being broken on the rack, "don't do this to me, my love. I've already told you—"

"That you want a wife, not a mistress," she interrupted, brushing her mouth across his throat. "I know. But don't you see I can't be either until I know I can please you?"

As if possessed of wills of their own his hands slid up her back, stroking the warm flesh barred by the cut of her gown. She felt like sweet heaven in his arms, and he wanted her with a need that bordered on desperation.

"Are you certain?" he asked, making one last grab at self-control. "I couldn't bear it if you should ever regret anything we shared together."

She stepped back, taking his hands and placing them boldly on her breasts. "I'm positive," she said softly, her eyes lambent as she met his gaze. "If *you're* certain you want to marry me, come to my room tonight. I'll be waiting for you."

He could feel her nipples hardening beneath his fingertips, and his own body responded with a surge of passion. "Cara . . ."

"Come to me," she repeated. "And—and tomorrow, if you still want to be married, ask me again. I promise I'll answer." She gave him one last somber look and then quietly walked away, her head held high with pride.

Fifteen

She'd lost her bleeding mind, Cara decided, studying her reflection somberly. Either that, or she'd had one glass of champagne too many. Certainly she had to be drunk or crazy or both to have offered herself to Stephen the way she had. Offered hell, she admitted, wincing as she turned away from the cheval glass. She'd all but *ordered* the man to make love to her! She supposed she'd be lucky if he didn't bar his door against her and have her charged with indecent liberties. God knew it was no less than she deserved.

What could she have been thinking of? she castigated herself angrily. Hadn't her marriage to Paul shown how inadequate she was as a bed partner? She was too aggressive, or not aggressive enough. She didn't know how to move, how to touch, how to please; Paul's litany of complaints had been endless, until she was quite frankly grateful when he began seeking his pleasure elsewhere. Oh, she knew the failure of that side of their marriage was as much his fault as it was hers, but she couldn't quite bring herself to forget his jibes at her femininity . . . or rather, at her lack thereof. What if he was right?

"Are you all right?" Stephen's voice sounded behind her, and she turned to find him leaning in the doorway. He was wearing a dressing gown of dark blue satin carelessly knotted at his lean waist, and she decided he must have had a quick bath. His hair was brushed damply back from his forehead, and she could see the droplets of water glistening on the cloud of golden hair dusting the planes of his broad chest. When she saw her watching him he pushed himself away from the doorframe, and started toward her with a slow saunter that made her mouth go dry.

"I have been thinking," he said, his tanned fingers undoing his belt, "and I've decided you have the wrong of it."

"I . . . I have?" Cara's voice quavered when the robe fell open, revealing the hard perfection of his body.

"Yes," he shed the robe with a grace any stripper in Soho would have envied. "I think rather than your doubting your ability to please me, you are doubting my ability to please you." He came to a halt in front of her. "I've decided to remedy the situation."

As a cop she'd have sworn she'd seen it all and that she was virtually unshockable, but the sight of Stephen's body so gloriously aroused, made her blush as furiously as the greenest virgin. Only she wasn't a virgin, and when she thought about what that splendid body was about to do to hers, she literally went weak in the knees.

"I . . . I don't think that will be a p-problem," she managed, stuttering as he bent his head and pressed a sizzling kiss against her neck.

"You don't?" His mouth slid up her neck as his fingers began tugging at the ribbon holding her peignoir closed.

"No." Her hands fluttered up to his broad shoulders and she tilted back her head, her senses swimming with desire.

The silk of her gown parted, and his hands cupped her breasts possessively. "Good," he said softly and she could feel his lips curving in a smile. "Neither do I."

Cara didn't bother replying, she simply moaned; her eyes drifting shut as she gave herself over to the mastery of his touch. His hands were warm and sure, caressing her with a skill that drove all thought from her dazed mind. His thumbs teased her nipples until they were exquisitely sensitive, and then he bent his head and drew them into his mouth. She gave a low cry, burying her fingers in his hair and holding him against her.

"Stephen!" His name was all she could utter, but it seemed to be enough for him. He swept her up into his arms and carried her over to the bed, his eyes never leaving hers as he lay her gently on the coverlet.

"You are so beautiful," he whispered, his voice shaking with passion. "Your husband must have been a half-blind eunuch not to see you are woman enough for a dozen men. I adore you."

His words filled her with fierce pride, driving the last, lingering doubt from her mind. Smiling with sweet anticipation she held out her arms to him, welcoming as he joined her on the wide bed.

They kissed and touched each other hungrily while Stephen's hands stroked the gown from her body. His lips and fingers skimmed over every inch of her, tasting and teasing until she was writhing beneath him. She tried reciprocating, but he always shifted just out of reach tempting her with his body but not letting her touch. Even as she was shuddering in near-climax, she was moaning in frustration.

"Let me touch you," she begged, struggling to free her hands from his grip. "I need to touch you, damn it!"

"And so you shall, my angel," he promised, turning his head to playfully nip her inner thigh. "Later." And then he sent her crashing into madness with the most intimate of caresses.

She was still trembling from the force of her pleasure when he moved over her, his hands cupping her buttocks and lifting her as he thrust deeply into her. Her legs locked around his surging hips, holding him in a lover's embrace as he moved in a powerful rhythm. A second climax soon had her crying out but he seemed as indefatigable as ever, thrusting harder and deeper until they were both gasping and drenched in sweat. Just as she was certain the pleasure would surely kill her he gave a harsh cry, his back bowing in a perfect arch as his body shook with completion.

"Cara!" His face was contorted in a grimace of raw pleasure, and incredibly she felt another orgasm shake her.

"Stephen!" She called out his name in a thin, high voice, her eyes wet with tears as she struggled to come to terms with the enormity of the pleasure she had just experienced. Nothing in her life could have prepared her for such a thing, and so she lay in silence, her legs and arms locked around Stephen's body.

He began moving again, his thrusts even more powerful as he rocked them in a hard cadence that had them both crying out with pleasure. But this time he let her touch him as she would, and she revelled in the freedom he granted her. She touched as much of him as she could reach, stroking and scratching until he abruptly reversed their position; his strong hands grasping her hips as he held her in place.

"Ride me," he urged, his face dark with pleasure. "Make me your lover in every way there is."

She obliged him happily, her eyes half-closed as she watched him writhing beneath her. When he gave a final surge, throwing back his head and moaning like a soul in torment, she climaxed again, and it was the most glorious feeling of her life.

She collapsed on his chest, her head pillowed by his sweat-dampened chest. They were both breathing as if they were about to die, and several minutes passed before Stephen spoke.

"I pray that proves my point, madam," he said breathlessly, stroking a shaking hand down her back. "Any further attempts to convince you of your desirability will doubtlessly kill me."

"Is it morning yet?" Stephen asked drowsily, his hand drawing lazy circles on her bare shoulder.

Cara turned her head, peering at the thin line of sunlight peeking through the shuttered windows. "Probably," she said, lowering her mouth to drop a damp kiss on his chest. "Why? Got a pressing appointment?"

"You might say that," he said, rolling over and tucking her beneath him. "You said that if I still wanted to be married in the morning, I should ask you again and you'd answer me. Well, I am asking."

Cara's warm feeling of contentment vanished like a soap bubble, and she glanced nervously away. "Stephen, I . . ."

"You can't have the slightest doubt as to your ability to please me?" he demanded, a lock of brownish-blond hair falling across his forehead as he scowled down at her. "Good God, woman, are you insatiable? We almost killed each other! Surely you must know how well-suited we are for each other?"

Cara was irritated to feel herself blushing at the memory of the wild loving they had shared during all the long hours of the night. "Of course I know that . . . now," she said, refusing to meet his gaze. "That's not what I was about to say."

His hands slid into her tousled hair, turning her face until he was once more gazing deeply into her eyes. "Then what were you about to say?" he asked, his tone abruptly somber. "You can tell me anything, Cara. Don't you know that by now?"

Damn, now she was about to cry! Cara thought crossly, blinking rapidly to clear her eyes. "I was about to say that I still don't think we need to be married," she said, trying not to weaken at his stern expression. "If-if we're discreet no one would ever need to know, and—"

"Cara, do you honestly think I could offer my name to another woman while I am making love to you?" he asked gently. "Do you think so little of my honor as that?"

"No!" she exclaimed, grasping his shoulders with trembling hands. "You're the most honorable man I've ever known!"

"Then why should you think I would do anything so lacking in integrity?" he chided, ducking his head and placing a tender kiss on her lips. "And there's another possibility we need to consider as well." His large hand rested on her stomach. "I may have made you pregnant."

Cara's eyes flew wide. She'd already thought about that, of course, what sensible woman wouldn't? But she was almost certain she was safe. It was the wrong time of the month, and she and Paul hadn't conceived even when she'd tried. Still . . . she felt a dreamy smile settle on her face. "A baby?"

His lips quirked in an answering smile. "Our baby," he corrected. "My son, perhaps. And if you think I would allow him to be born on the wrong side of the blanket, you have sadly mistaken my nature. I would never allow such a thing."

She scarce heard him, her thoughts centered on the image of what their child would look like. He would have Stephen's hair, she mused, and his deep blue eyes and slow, sexy smile. Marcus had inherited her father's nose so perhaps her child would be spared that indignation, but she thought it might be nice if he or she did inherit her family's strong chin. The Bramwell curse, her mother had once called it, lightly cuffing her on the same stubborn chin. Her eyes grew misty at the thought of the family she would likely never see again.

"Cara?" Stephen was frowning at her. "What is it?"

She shook her head, a new and wondrous thought taking form in her mind. Her old family was lost to her, but that didn't mean she couldn't create a new one. If she and Stephen married, any children they might have would be her family. Even Aunt Minn could become her real aunt. It wouldn't make up for what she'd lost, but it was better than ending her days alone and lonely in a time that was not her own. She glanced up to find Stephen's worried gaze resting on her face.

"If we did marry," she began, her heart hammering as she realized she was actually considering accepting his proposal, "I'd need to know that you accepted my work as a vital part of who and what I am."

"Oh, I know we've already had this discussion and that I can't do *real* police work," she added at his puzzled look, "not here, not now. But perhaps I could help others as I am helping Mr. McNeil. It seems a small thing to me, but I know what it would be asking of you. It would be asking you to accept me as an equal. Can you do that?"

The fact he hesitated before answering touched her deeply. "I would try," he said at last, his eyes dark as he met her gaze. "I cannot say I would always succeed, but I would try."

She closed her eyes, believing his guarded reply sooner than if he had offered heart-felt assurances. Her entire future seemed poised on the razor's edge but when she searched her heart for advice as to what she should do, the answer was amazingly simple. She gave a contented sigh and opened her eyes.

"Very well, my lord," she said quietly, granting him the title she had always avoided using. "I should be happy to be your wife."

"Oh my dears, I am so happy!" Aunt Minn announced, bursting into tears and sobbing into her handkerchief when Stephen announced his and Cara's engagement over breakfast that morning. He'd already told his aunt he would be marrying his erstwhile cousin, but evidently the sight of the family's betrothal ring on Cara's slender finger had proven more reassuring to his aunt's shocked sensibilities.

"It shall have to be a small wedding, of course," Minn had stopped crying and was applying her energies to more prosaic matters. "St. James, I think, small but imminently respectable for a . . . er . . . second wedding. And naturally we shall have no less than a Bishop officiating. The Bishop of Bath and Wells is an old friend of my late husband, and I am sure if I were to write him he should be happy to oblige us. We would not wish this thing to smack of haste, you know."

Cara and Stephen exchanged bemused looks. "Actually, Aunt Minn, I was thinking of a simple ceremony here in the house," Cara said, her manner firm but gentle. "I've only been out of official mourning for my husband for a few weeks, and I feel it would be most improper to indulge in even a small ceremony."

"That is so," Minn frowned and hastily reshuffled her plans. "Well, in that case, perhaps it might be best if you were to postpone your nuptials until the end of the Season. That would give the *ton* time to accept the situation, and—"

"Aunt," Stephen laid his hands over Minn's, halting her flow of words, "Cara and I are being married by Special License as soon as it can be arranged. The *ton* may go hang for all I care."

Minn's eyes popped from her head at such blasphemy. "But-but Stephen, you can not mean that," she stammered weakly. "Think of the gossip, and the damage that might be done to your reputation should you do such a thing! It would be whispered that your marriage was a-a runaway match!"

For some reason that appealed to Stephen's sense of the ridiculous and he threw back his head and laughed. "A little over a year ago I stood accused of murdering my wife," he reminded Minn, his eyes dancing with black humor. "Surely being accused of anticipating my vows could prove no less injurious to my reputation than that."

"Stephen!" Minn paled dramatically, her gaze flicking toward Cara. "How can you speak so lightly of such things?"

"Because it is better than weeping over them," he answered, somewhat amazed to realize he was speaking the truth. After living the past year in terror of what others might think or say of him, it was rather liberating to discover he no longer cared.

"Hmph, well I am glad you can find the matter so amusing," Minn grumbled, folding her arms across her breasts and glowering at Stephen. "But may I remind you that until quite recently it was assumed by everyone that your interest lay in quite a different direction? Have you stopped to think how all of this will affect her? You have all but publically jilted the gel!"

That did get Stephen's notice, and he drew himself up proudly. "I've already spoken with Lady Felicity," he said, his voice cool, "and she agrees with me that there was never anything approaching a formal agreement between us. She even wished me happy," he added, as if daring Minn to disagree.

"You spoke with Lady Felicity before you spoke to me?" Cara looked annoyed. "What would you have done if I'd said no?"

He recalled the incredible night they had shared, and gave her a thoroughly knowing grin. "Oh, I would have thought of some way of changing your mind," he drawled, his grin widening when she began blushing.

"Lady Felicity may have wished you happy, but I can not say others will share her forgiving nature," Aunt Minn opined, clearly referring to Lord and Lady Berksham. "Have you thought of what you shall say to them?"

In truth he had not, but now that he considered the matter

Stephen supposed he did owe the earl and his haughty countess the courtesy of a personal call. "Again, there was never a formal offer either made or accepted," he said in answer to his aunt's question. "But if you wish, I'll call upon them this very morning and inform them of my plans. Does that satisfy you?"

It did, and Minn gradually allowed the conversation to turn to the more practical concerns such as notices to the journals. It was decided this was another matter Stephen would tend to, and he pushed himself away from the table with a put-upon sigh.

"If I'm to get all this accomplished by nightfall, then I suppose I had best get started," he said, holding out his hand to Cara as he rose to his feet. "Cara, I should appreciate it if you would accompany me to the front hall. There is something I should like to discuss with you."

"Certainly, my lord," she demurred, her eyes sparkling with excitement as she placed her hand in his and allowed him to guide her out of the small dining room. He led her into the drawing room, and the moment they were alone he was pulling her into his arms and kissing her with scarcely-contained passion.

"Well," she drawled, twining her arms about his neck and smiling, "I can see where being engaged has its advantages. Now did you really want to discuss something with me, or did you just drag me in here to cop a feel?"

"Cop a feel?" He repeated, delighting in the unfamiliar cant. "Is that like getting caught with our fingers in each other's cookie jars?"

"That's hands," she corrected, grabbing his and removing it from her buttocks, "and if you don't keep yours to yourself, you pig, I may have to get nasty."

"Really?" He gave her a hopeful look. "Does that mean you'll toss me on the floor and have your wicked way with me?"

She shook her hair back from her face and laughed. "In your dreams, my lord," she said mischievously. "Now answer my question. Was there something you wanted?"

Stephen stole another teasing kiss before answering. "I've already informed Mr. Hargraves of your change in position, and he'll doubtlessly inform the rest of the staff. I want you to meet with Mrs. Finch and arrange to take over the running of the house from Aunt Minn. If that is acceptable to you?" he added, wondering if he should ask his aunt to remain with them until Cara had more time to adjust to her new role.

Cara titled her head to one side as if considering the matter. "Does this mean Hargraves will be taking his orders from me?" she wanted to know.

"Of course," he assured her. "You shall be the Countess of Harrington, and he the butler. It will be his duty to obey you."

She stood on tip-toe to return his kiss. "Cool," she said, leaning back and grinning up at him. "When do I start?"

The news of Stephen and Cara's pending marriage struck the *ton* with the impact of a bomb. The house was quickly filled with callers, and Cara was growing increasingly pressed to put up with their pointed questions and sneering innuendos. If it hadn't been for Stephen she would have told the lot of them to go to hell, but the knowledge she would soon be the Countess of Harrington kept her sharp tongue in check . . . most of the time.

"Really, Cara, I can not think what you meant by making that unkind remark about Lady Gilford's neck," Aunt Minn reproved after they'd chased off the third round of callers in as many days. "Whatever did it mean, by the by?"

"Rubber neck?" Cara smirked as she recalled the plump marchioness's response to her question if she rubber-necked at carriage accidents. "It's an American expression, Aunt. It means to gawk at something that is of no concern to one."

"Well, if something is of no concern to one, then why should one wish to gawk at it?" Minn wanted to know crossly. "But I suppose that's the Americans for you. I vow, they have the most curious methods of speech. I find it hard to credit we started out speaking the same tongue."

"Yes, we're two nations divided by the same language," Cara quipped, paraphrasing one of her favorite quotes.

"Cara! How clever of you!" Aunt Minn gave a delighted laugh. "You must be sure to write that down so you shan't forget it."

Considering the quote wouldn't be made for another hundred or so years, Cara didn't think there would be much danger of that. "Is that the last of our illustrious guests?" she asked, leaning back against the stripped club chair and closing her eyes. "I hope so. If I have to be polite to one more self-important prig, I swear I'll scream my bloody head off."

"Such language, my dear," Minn reproved, albeit in a tired voice. "It ill-becomes a peeress to speak so commonly."

Cara peeled open one eye and shot Minn a rueful look. "Stuff," she responded, borrowing one of Miranda's favorite phrases. "One thing I've already learned is that a countess has far more freedom than a poor widow from the colonies. A countess can say or do whatever she pleases, and no one dares say a word against her. It's ridiculous when you think about it."

Since it was more or the less the truth Minn didn't debate the point, although it was obvious by her loud sniff that she disagreed. Cara hid a smile, a feeling of tenderness for the older woman welling up inside her. Last night while she and Stephen had been talking he made cautious mention of his country estate, and she meant to ask him if he'd invite Minn to stay with them while they were there. She was debating whether she should ask Minn now or wait to discuss it with Stephen when there was a tap on the door and Hargraves bowed his way into the room.

"I beg your pardon, Mrs. Marsdale, Mrs. Greenborough," he said, his tone as bleak as it had been since learning Cara was to be his new mistress. "But Mr. McNeil has called to see you, Mrs. Marsdale, and is requesting to speak with you. Privately," he added the last word with a twitch of his magnificent nose.

Mr. McNeil! Cara popped out of her chair, her interest caught at once. "Show him in, Hargraves," she said, her mind racing. He must have more news on the murders, she thought, trying not to feel guilty because she'd been too caught up in her own happiness to give the gruesome murders their proper attention.

"Really, Cara, do you think that wise?" Minn had risen to her feet and was regarding her speculatively. "Granted you are an engaged woman, but that doesn't mean you may turn your back on all maidenly propriety! Mr. McNeil is scarce more than an acquaintance to you. It is hardly proper for you to admit him to your presence without someone being present to chaperon you."

"It's all right, Aunt," Cara bent to kiss Minn's cheek, brushing her complaints aside with a gentle smile. "Stephen knows I have personal matters to discuss with Mr. McNeil, and he has said I may receive him in private."

Much to Cara's disgust hearing Stephen had given the matter his approval was all it took to win Minn's cooperation. "Well, if Lord Harrington has said it is all right, I am sure it must be fine," she said in satisfaction. "Just mind you don't allow Mr. McNeil to keep you overly long, dearest. Tomorrow is an important day you know," she added, giggling like an excited schoolgirl as she hurried away.

Cara could have told her aunt she needed no further reminding. Tomorrow was her wedding day, and the thought filled her with a curious mixture of anticipation and terror. She hadn't been anywhere near this afraid before her first wedding, but then she supposed that was because she hadn't known then how disastrously it was all going to end. At least in this time she needn't worry about the pain and humiliation of a divorce, she decided, taking an odd comfort in the fact.

She'd just poured a fresh cup of tea when Mr. McNeil was ushered into the room by a stone-faced Hargraves. The butler's disapproval was so palpable that Cara decided to take pity on the man, and requested that he remain nearby should she have need of him. The older man brightened at once, bowing with more warmth than he usually showed.

"I shall be without, madam," he intoned, fixing Mr. McNeil with a fish-eyed stare. "Should you have need of me, you have but to call." And he took his dignified leave, taking care to leave the door open a slight crack behind him.

Cara hid a smirk before turning to her guest. "I hope I haven't offended you, Mr. McNeil," she said, offering him her hand. "But

I've learned it's sometimes easier to go along with the servants than to upset them."

"That is quite all right, Mrs. Marsdale," he assured her, his brown eyes shy as he met her gaze. "And-and pray allow me to offer you my felicitations on your coming nuptials. You will make an admirable countess, I am sure."

"Thank you," Cara replied, hoping he'd come to do more than offer his best wishes. She'd had a bellyful of playing the gracious hostess, and she wanted to concentrate on something a little more substantial than the social niceties. Taking care to hide such thoughts she waved Mr. McNeil on to one of the chairs, pouring him a cup of tea before settling back with her own.

"Now, what is it I can do for you, sir?" she asked, deciding to bring the matter up herself rather than leaving it to him. "How is the inquiry coming? Are there any new leads?"

"Leads?"

"Developments," she corrected hastily. "Was the material I gave you of any use to the officials handling the investigation?"

"Oh, indeed, Mrs. Marsdale, they have proven most helpful!" he exclaimed, his confusion giving way to pleasure. "The magistrates were most impressed with your acuity, and they wish me to offer you their personal thanks. The help you have provided has been invaluable, and we are grateful for all you have done. I only wish—"

"Wish what?" she pressed when he came to an abrupt halt.

"That you might continue doing so," he concluded, shooting her a wistful look. "I truly feel that we are within days of catching the man responsible for these murders, and I had hoped you would continue helping us. But I understand you cannot."

"Because I'm getting married, you mean?" Cara asked, congratulating herself for having anticipated the problem.

"I . . . well, yes," McNeil stammered, looking uncertain. "Lord Harrington is an important man. Naturally he wouldn't wish his wife to be exposed to anything so unsavory as murdered whores."

She stiffened in dislike of the demeaning reference to the victims, but reminded herself it was the fault of the times, not the man. Still her voice was edged with coolness as she said,

"My husband's views on the murdered women may surprise you, Mr. McNeil. He feels that no woman, regardless of her profession, deserves to die, and he is as concerned about apprehending their killer as we are."

He flushed dark red and ducked his head at her unspoken censure. "I am sorry, Mrs. Marsdale," he said quietly. "I had no right to use such language in the presence of a lady."

He looked so much like a beaten puppy that Cara's first impulse was to soften, but she battened it down with determination. She wouldn't have let one of her mates in the future get away with such a flagrantly sexist remark, and she was damned if she'd allow it now.

"What you had no right doing was referring to those women as whores," she said bluntly. "They were victims, Mr. McNeil, innocent victims of a madman. Be as angry as you want to about that, but keep that anger focused where it rightfully belongs; on the killer and on catching him."

His flush deepened, but his gaze was resolute as it met hers. "You are quite right, ma'am. Pray accept my apologies. Now," his manner became briskly efficient, "if I understood you correctly, you say your husband has no objections to your continuing to aid us. Is that correct?"

She nodded, relieved he hadn't taken offense. "He has given me permission to lend you whatever assistance I can, so long as it doesn't interfere with my duties as countess, and so long as it is safe." This last stuck in her craw, but she knew it was what McNeil would expect to hear.

"You may assure his lordship I will protect you with my life," he said so ardently that Cara was taken aback. "I would never allow any harm come to you!"

"Thank you," she mumbled, not certain what else to say. "I'm sure the earl will find your assurances uh . . . reassuring." She busied herself with pouring another cup of tea for them both before speaking.

"I haven't seen mention of another murder in the papers," she said, calmly handing him his cup. "Is that because there hasn't been one, or is the Home Office keeping a lid on everything?"

"No, there hasn't been another murder," he replied, fumbling with his cup. "Or at least, not one that matches the . . . what did you call it? the profile of the others." He took a noisy sip of tea. "If you do not mind my saying so, Mrs. Marsdale, you do have a rather interesting turn of phrase. Profiles, serial killers, keeping lids on things, psyc-psyc—"

"Psychological," she provided, smiling as he stumbled awkwardly over the unfamiliar word.

"Yes," he gave a relieved nod. "What does it mean, if I may ask? You used it several times when referring to the suspect."

Cara juggled several explanations in her head before coming up with one she thought he would understand. "It's a way of explaining how a person thinks, and why he does what he does," she said, pleased with her concise outline. "Psychologists believe serial killers are driven to kill, and if you can understand their motivations, you can catch the killer."

"Psychologists?"

"A tribe of Indians who live near my old home," she invented without so much as blinking, unable to remember when the word came into vogue. "They believe it's possible to predict a man's next move by studying what he's done in the past. Do you remember the paper I gave you describing the last murder scene?"

McNeil turned a delicate shade of green. "Indeed," he said weakly, setting his cup down and reaching for his handkerchief. "It was most . . . er . . . vivid."

"If we look at that scene and compare it to the other crime scenes we can extrapolate on his next move," Cara said, her fear of upsetting the future forgotten in her excitement of the case. "We know he prefers blonds, usually young, and that he's fixated on prostitutes, although that might have more to do with their availability as victims rather than any sort of preference."

"But how can knowing such things help us catch the man?"

Mr. McNeil asked, his expression confused as he struggled to make sense of her increasingly technical explanation.

"Because it's another piece of the puzzle," Cara said, leaning forward in her chair. It was something most women in this time never did, but she hadn't quite been able to break herself of the habit. "A small piece, I grant you, but that's how you put a puzzle together; piece by piece."

Mr. McNeil remained silent for several seconds, and then gave her a slow smile. "Another lesson you learned from your Indian friends?" he asked, his voice gently teasing.

She returned the smile, thinking of Alec. "From my brother, actually," she said softly. "He was always fond of solving puzzles, the more complex, the better."

"Regarding our killer, what other pieces of the puzzle have we?" he asked, folding his hands and sitting back in his chair like a diligent pupil awaiting instruction.

Cara took a moment to sift through her mental notes before responding. "We know he's left-handed, of medium height and build, and educated. I'd take it a step further and say he's either a member of the upper class, or associated with it in some capacity; an upper servant, perhaps, although I doubt it."

"Why is that?"

She considered his question thoughtfully. "There's a certain arrogance to these killings," she said slowly, "an arrogance that makes me think our prime suspect considers himself to be superior to his victims. Most serial killers feel this way, but with our boy I have a feeling it's the way he's been taught to believe. That indicates we're dealing with the master, not the servant."

Mr. McNeil opened his mouth to say more, but the door opened without warning and Stephen walked in, his blue eyes speculative as they moved from Cara to Mr. McNeil.

"I trust I'm not disturbing you?" he asked coolly, his eyebrows arching in haughty inquiry.

"Indeed not, my lord," Mr. McNeil rose and bobbed a hasty bow. "I was just offering my felicitations to your fiancee, and— and to you too, of course. Good day," and he turned and fled from the room. The moment the door closed behind him Cara whirled to face Stephen.

"What the devil was that all about?" she demanded indignantly. "You all but chased the poor boy out of here!

Stephen didn't bother with a reply but pulled her into his arms, silencing her with a sizzling kiss. By the time he lifted his mouth from hers, she'd forgotten all about McNeil. She looped her arms about his neck and gave him a slow smile.

"Good answer," she murmured, and then returned the kiss, her heart racing as she lost herself in the moment and the man.

Sixteen

It was his wedding night. Stephen stood in front of the fireplace in his sitting room, gazing down at the flames with unseeing eyes. It had also been his wedding night almost two years ago, and the aftermath of that momentous night still dominated his life.

It was odd, he mused, but if he'd gone directly to Miranda she would never have hidden in the secret room and been swept into the future. And if she hadn't been swept into the future, he would never have been put on trial for her murder. And if that hadn't happened she would never have come back to exonerate him, and he would never have learned of the room's power; a power responsible for bringing Cara into his life. He shook his head, amazed at the chain of events linking past, present and future.

What would have happened if he'd gone to Miranda? he wondered, not for the first time. They would still be married, perhaps might even have a child, and he supposed he would be as happy in his marriage as the rest of the *ton* was in theirs. It was a truly appalling thought.

The sound of rustling cloth drew his attention to the door and he glanced up to find Cara hovering there, her slender body encased in a peignoir of rich gold silk. Her hair had grown out in the weeks she'd been in the past, and it cascaded to her shoulders in thick, ebony waves. When he saw him watching her, her lips curved in an uncertain smile.

"I thought that since you came to me that first time, it was only fair that I come to you," she said, although she remained rooted in place. "In my day, there's even an expression for it. Your place or mine?"

Stephen turned his back on the fire, his philosophical musings forgotten. He walked over to where she was waiting, his body responding to the sight of her. There was a slight flush on her otherwise pale cheeks, and her magnificent eyes were wide with emotion. He remembered seeing those same eyes fluttering shut as ecstasy sent her soaring over the edge, and felt his own gaze narrow with hunger.

"I think I should prefer my place," he said, coming to a halt in front of her. He reached out and drew her slowly against him, taking pleasure in the natural way she slipped into his arms.

Their first kiss was light, almost friendly; a direct contrast to the passion burning inside him. The second kiss was harder, more demanding, as his mouth moved on hers in urgent demand. She responded eagerly, her lips parting as she accepted the sensual intimacy of his tongue seeking hers. He tightened his arms around her, lifting her off the ground and carrying her toward the bed. Halfway there he changed his mind, and set her gently down in front of the fireplace.

"What's wrong?" she asked, her breath coming fast and shaky. "You haven't forgotten something, have you?"

His answer was another kiss and if the way she returned it was any indication, it was obvious he had more than made his point. Or most of it, he decided, drawing back to smile down at her.

"I forgot to tell you how beautiful you are," he said, his hands caressing her through the silk. "I look at you and think of a goddess from some exotic land. You make me tremble, Cara."

He saw her swallow, and her eyes grew even more luminous. In the firelight she glowed like a statue carved from purest gold, and he gave a low groan. "I dream of you, do you know that?" he whispered, moving his mouth over her throat. "I dream of touching you," he bared her breast, "kissing you," his tongue flicked over her nipple, "and of making love to you until neither of us can even think of moving."

She responded by burying her fingers in his hair, holding him to her and letting her body go limp. He lowered her to the carpet, stripping off his own robe with rough, impatient hands before lowering himself on to the floor beside her. Holding her gaze with his own he slowly removed her gown, driving them both insane with his deliberate caresses. The first time with her had been a wild ride into ecstasy, and he was determined that this time should be a prolonged slide into euphoria. He wanted to please her in every way a man could please his woman, and closing his mind to the screaming demands of his own body, he set out to do just that.

The night slid away as he kissed her again and again, learning her body with every inch of his own. When she was screaming his name he slid into her, moving furiously until they were both shuddering in climax. Then he rolled over and pulled her on top of him, letting her touch and kiss him in return. After they'd made love a second time he rose on legs that weren't quite steady and weaved his way to the bed where a bottle of champagne and a pair of glasses were waiting. He retrieved the tray and returned to Cara.

"You look thirsty, my lady," he murmured, pouring a glass of the golden wine and offering it to her with an approving smile. "Allow me to remedy that for you."

She accepted the glass with a slow smile of her own, her slumberous gaze moving possessively over his body. "Thanks," she drawled, taking a grateful sip. "Can't think of what I might have done to have worked up such a thirst."

He merely grinned, drinking his own wine as he settled beside her. He supposed it should have felt odd and slightly decadent to lay naked with his bride in front of the dying fire, but instead it felt . . . he searched his mind for the correct word. Right. It felt wonderfully right to lay like this with Cara, and he had no intention of moving for some time. Although he would take care to see she was snugly tucked into his bed before the servants blundered in and found them, he decided, dropping a proprietary kiss on the top of her head.

As if sensing his thoughts she leaned against him, crossing

her arms over his. "This is nice," she said, sighing as she gazed into the red and yellow embers. "But I guess we should be getting into bed before the maid finds us. She'd probably scream and faint, and then Hargraves would look down that beak of his and make me feel like an abandoned woman."

Stephen gave a low chuckle, envisioning the contretemps she described. "What rot," he chided teasingly. You're the Countess of Harrington now, and you may behave however abandonedly you please; so long as you do so with me. Hargraves is free to give notice, if he can't accept that."

"Nah," she snuggled closer. "I like the idea of keeping the old fish-face about. He reminds me of Ketterick, one of my first chief inspectors. The annoying little slug was always making my life hell, but it kept me on my toes; made me a better inspector. You know I can't resist a challenge," she added, grinning at him over her shoulder.

He pressed a kiss to her mouth, and they both settled back in companionable silence to enjoy the dying heat and light of the fire. After a few minutes Stephen said,

"I wish I might see your world some day. You seldom speak of it, and yet I know you must miss it."

She remained silent for several seconds before answering. "I do miss it," she said, her tone pensive. "Sometimes I miss it so much I feel like screaming."

The staggering sense of loss in her quiet voice tore at him like the talons of an eagle, but he wouldn't back away. "What do you miss most?" he asked, determined to learn all he could. They'd never discussed the past, or rather, the future, and he knew it was something he needed to understand if they were to build a life together.

"The people," she admitted after another pause. "My family and friends, especially. Marcus is growing so, I probably won't even recognize him should I ever find my way home. And my work. I miss being a cop most of all."

"What else?" He pressed, eager for more information.

This time there was no hesitation. "The modern conveniences

I always took for granted until I met Miranda," she said decisively. "If I had a computer with the proper data base, I could solve these damned murders in about half an hour's time. And a proper forensic kit," she added with a wistful sigh. "Although that probably wouldn't do much good since I couldn't use any of the results to press for an arrest decree."

Another silence fell between them and then she said, "I miss cheese pizza with extra sauce, watching television, listening to rock and roll, and Diet Pepsi. God," she tipped her head, her eyes closing, "I'd kill for a Diet Pepsi."

A particularly sharp stab of guilt sliced through him at her mournful expression. "What is Diet Pepsi?" he asked, deciding it must be something important to have caused Cara such distress.

"Heaven," she said, and then gave a small shake. "Oh well, no use crying over spilled milk, as my gram used to say." She turned in his arms, pressing a warm kiss to his mouth and giving him an inviting smile that sent his pulses racing. "Besides, this time has some advantages of its own to recommend it."

His body was already stirring to life when he picked her up and carried her over to the waiting bed. "Enough to make you forget Diet Pepsi?" he asked, laying her on the counterpane.

Her eyes fluttered shut as she drew him down to her. "Almost," she said, and then gave a soft moan as he took her once again to the very heights of glory.

The next two weeks passed quickly for Cara. In between adjusting to her new duties as Countess of Harrington and making love to Stephen whenever the opportunity presented itself, she worked diligently helping McNeil with the murders. There hadn't been a murder in almost a month; a definite break in the pattern that had her holding her breath with hope. In the future she would have assumed the killer had either changed locations or was laying low, but as in this time he could have no hint they were on to him, she decided to take it as a hopeful sign.

"Not that I think he's simply stopped," she told Mr. McNeil over tea one afternoon. "He can't. It won't let him."

"What won't let him?" He asked, blinking in confusion.

"The compulsion to kill," Cara said, recalling the classes the Yard had taught on the subject. "One serial killer called it The Beast Within. Oh, the feeling might go underground for a few months, maybe even a few years, but it's always there; like a hungry lion crouched in a cave. That's why serial killers are so dangerous. The only way they stop is if they get caught, go mad, or end up killing themselves. Many do," she added, not bothering to admit she considered their suicides a fitting sort of justice.

"But you've said most of these men are quite intelligent," Mr. McNeil protested, his brows meeting in a frown. "An intelligent man would never allow himself to be at the mercy of his baser passions. He would master them."

"Very good," Cara said, applauding his objection. "You're starting to think like our boy. Control is a common theme amongst sociopaths. They kill to demonstrate their power over their victims, but in the end they're the ones who are powerless to resist the very urges that drive them to kill. It's rather pathetic when you think about it."

He set his cup down with an angry clatter. "I do not consider this man in the least pathetic," he said stoutly, his brown eyes surprisingly cold. "He is a killer, and I mean to catch him."

Cara decided to take pity on the poor man. Even cops in her day had trouble understanding Forensic Psychology, so she supposed she could see why he'd have a hard time accepting why it was so important. She mentally shrugged the matter off and turned her mind to more pressing concerns.

"Have you thought about the matter we discussed the last time you were here?" she asked, setting her cup aside and giving him a hopeful look.

"Yes," he said, not sounding very pleased with the fact. "I've also discussed it with the Bow Street magistrates, and they have decided it wouldn't do any harm to let you see where the first few murders occurred. Although I'm not sure why you wish to bother," he added with a shake of his head. "I doubt if even the skills your Indian friends taught you will do you much good."

"You'd be surprised," she said softly, knowing that unlike most killers, serial killers often did return to the scene of what they viewed as their greatest triumph. It gave them a sadistic kick. Sometimes they'd even try worming themselves into the inquiry; not so much to keep tabs on the investigation, as to get their jollies watching the police busting their guts trying to catch them. She said as much to McNeil, and he gave a slow nod.

"Yes, I can see where that would prove rewarding," he said in his thoughtful manner. "He'd think himself a clever fellow, wouldn't he, having so many people dashing about trying to apprehend him but never quite succeeding. I daresay he would find it the ultimate challenge."

They left the house soon after, travelling by in a less-than-new looking hack. She wore a plain gown of blue bombazine and a prim bonnet and cape she'd borrowed from one of the maids. Considering some of the areas of London they'd be visiting, the last thing she wanted to do was make an ostentatious display of wealth.

She also had her tazer stuck in her reticule; just in case. She'd been carrying it with her for some time, although she prayed she'd never have to use it. Not because she was afraid of using dangerous force, but because she didn't relish the notion of explaining a stun gun to people who were just now beginning to experiment with electricity. Somehow she doubted she'd be able to pass the late twentieth century weapon off as an interesting trinket she'd acquired from her Indian chums.

The site of the first homicide was in a filthy little alley just off Butten Court, close enough to Beaufort Docks so that Cara could smell the stench from the Thames. After so many months all traces of physical evidence had long since vanished, but Cara still took her time, pouring over the ground as if it was a perfectly-preserved crime scene.

The second site was a few streets away on Bedford Street in a dimly-lit passageway between two buildings. This victim had also been brutally slashed, and for the first time the killer had written his obscene opinion of the victim on the wall. Cara stared at some fading black stains, and even though she knew it wasn't the victim's blood, she still shuddered with horror.

"Are you all right?" Mr. McNeil was studying her worriedly. "His lordship would never forgive me if I allowed you to become overset."

"No, I'm fine," Cara answered, annoyed with herself for letting her emotions show. She'd never lost it at a crime scene before, and she wasn't about to start now. "I was just thinking this was a wretched place to die." she added, giving her surroundings a derisive glance. "Let's get out of here."

The third scene was a mews on Martlet Court; almost within earshot of the Bow Street Magistrates Court. Like the first two sites this one was also out-of-doors, although just barely. This time the victim had been savaged, and as Cara surveyed the small, enclosed space a sudden realization occurred to her, and she wondered why she hadn't thought of it before.

"The more isolated each murder site became, the more violent the killer became," she said slowly, intrigued at the revelation. "Why? Was it because he felt safer and let himself experiment, or was it because the killings were becoming more personal and he was less willing to share them?" She turned to McNeil and found him regarding her with a look of fascinated horror.

"Were any of the victims sexually mutilated?" she demanded.

He went from pasty white to bilious green. "My lady!"

"Were they?" she pressed, not giving a damn about his delicate sensibilities. "This is important, blast it!"

"I-I am not certain what you mean," he replied, his voice stiff as he fixed his gaze at a point over her shoulder.

Cara forced herself to back off, trying to phrase her questions in terms a man of his period would understand. "Did any of the victims suffer knife wounds to their womanly organs?" she asked, and was privately pleased with her cleverness.

Mr. McNeil removed his handkerchief from his pocket and

dabbed the beads of sweat from his forehead. "Yes. Th-this one, and the last four all had wounds such as you describe."

Cara nodded, debating whether to continue backing off, or press for the information she needed. What the hell, she decided. If McNeil swooned she could always bring him around with a whiff from the vial of smelling salts Minn had given her.

"Were the wounds external or internal?"

This time he didn't bother pretending not to take her meaning. "Internal," he said, breathing in slow, shaky breaths.

Time to go for broke, Cara thought, and asked one last question. "Did he take any trophies?" He gave her a blank look. "Were any body parts removed?"

"Good God!" The words burst from Mr. McNeil's lips and he dashed around the corner, becoming thoroughly and noisily sick.

"Really, sir, there is no reason to keep apologizing," Cara assured Mr. McNeil some ten minutes later as he guided her through the crowds filling the large market square. "I told you I don't think less of you for having such an understandable reaction. It's nothing to be ashamed of."

"I didn't notice you suffering a similar reaction," Mr. McNeil grumbled, his grip remaining firm as they stepped around a large woman selling her fresh produce from a dusty basket. "You behaved as if you were discussing nothing more interesting than the latest fashions from Bond Street."

"That's because I was raised on the frontier," Cara invented, still hoping to soothe his wounded male vanity. "We must be hardy to survive there, you know."

"Perhaps," she could tell by the way he pursed his lips that he was allowing himself to be persuaded, "but I am still—"

"Well, well, what have we here," a florid-faced man with gray hair blocked their path, his blue eyes cold with contempt as they swept over Cara. "If it's not the Harrington whore."

Mr. McNeil thrust Cara behind him, his chin coming up as he faced the furious man. "Mind your language, sir," he warned, his voice taking on a surprisingly dangerous edge. "I shall call you out if you dare say another word against Lady Harrington."

The man's eyes narrowed. "Do you think Elias Proctor is afraid of a little dog like you?" he jeered. "I could snap you like a twig if I was of a mind to."

Cara jerked at the man's words. So this was Miranda's stepfather, she thought, her gaze narrowing in fury. She'd once told Miranda the man was a greedy bastard, and it would seem she was right. It was equally obvious he was a braying bully as well, and she was about to tell him to sod off when he turned around and stormed off, pushing his way through the crowds that had gathered to gawk.

"Of all the insolent, ill-bred Cits!" Mr. McNeil's brown eyes were flashing with outrage. "I vow, I shall chase after him and take a horsewhip to him! The man deserves to be flogged!"

His vehemence alarmed Cara, and she laid a restraining hand on his arm. "It's all right, Mr. McNeil," she said, aware of their audience. "The man is obviously beneath our notice. We shan't pay him any mind."

"But he called you a . . . a . . . harlot!" Mr. McNeil continued furiously. "He dared compare you to those despicable creatures!"

Cara was too upset to bother correcting his demeaning reference to the victims. She recognized one pinch-faced woman who was an intimate of Lady Berksham standing off to one side, and knew her hopes of keeping this little encounter quiet had just evaporated. The important thing now was to get the bloody hell out of here before the situation got any worse. Thinking quickly she lay her hand on her forehead and swayed dramatically.

"Mr. McNeil, I am feeling faint," she announced in what she hoped was a convincingly weak voice. "Kindly take me home."

He was at her side in a moment, instantly solicitous as he led her out of the market and out on to the wide square where a queue of hacks were lined up awaiting passengers. He helped her into the first one and would have hopped in after her, when she held out a restraining hand.

"No, Mr. McNeil, I-I should prefer to be alone, if you do not mind," she stammered, blinking her eyes as if fighting tears. "My nerves are quite overset."

He gazed up at her, clearly torn between honoring a lady's request and his desire to do the proper thing. "Are you certain, my lady?" he asked frowning. "I think it might be better if I were to see you home. And naturally I should like to speak with your husband; to explain to him what happened."

Panic welled up at her at the thought of how Stephen would likely respond to Proctor's actions. "No!" she said quickly. "That is . . . I feel this is a private matter between my husband and myself, sir, and I should prefer apprizing him of what occurred in my own way. Although I shall be certain to inform him of your gallant defense," she assured him with a fatuous smile. "I am sure his lordship will be as grateful to you as I am."

He preened at her effusive praise. "It was an honor, my lady," he replied with a bow. "I only wish the vile coward hadn't fled. Nothing would have given me greater pleasure than teaching him the lesson in manners he so obviously needs."

Cara muttered something appropriate, wanting nothing more than to get away. McNeil must have sensed her desperation because he stepped back from the carriage, giving the coachman her address. The door was slammed shut by a waiting link boy, and she was on her way to Curzon Street.

She arrived home to find Aunt Minn and Stephen still out, and breathed a sigh of relief. Inspecting the murder scenes and encountering Miranda's stepfather had left her drained, and she wanted nothing more than to lock herself in her room and collapse. Just thinking how Stephen would react when she told him about Proctor made her head ache, but she knew it would have to be done. God help her if he learned of it on his own, she thought, starting for the stairs. She almost made it.

"My lady! My lady!" Mrs. Finch bustled toward her, a thick leather book tucked beneath her arm. "I hope I haven't kept you waiting, but there was a problem with one of the kitchen staff. I am ready now, however, if you wish to start."

Cara's hand clenched around the newel post. "Start?" she echoed, trying to think what the housekeeper was talking about.

"The ledgers, my lady," Mrs. Finch said, her pale blue eyes growing apprehensive. "You-you did say you wished to go over them this afternoon. But naturally if you are tired, we can always examine them some other time.

Cara paused, wildly tempted to take the graceful out she had just been offered. She was feeling filthy and exhausted, but the demands of duty were something she could never turn her back on. Shaking off her fatigue she gave the housekeeper a polite smile.

"No, this afternoon would be fine, Mrs. Finch," she said, turning away from the stairs. "Shall we go into my study?"

The first quarter-hour was given to reviewing staff salary, and Cara was appalled by the pittance they received. She suggested doubling them but Mrs. Finch seemed so outraged, she allowed the matter to drop. When she had time she'd look in to how much servants were paid in this time, and rectify the situation if need be.

They also went over menus and plans for the ball she and Stephen would be hosting at the end of the Season, and the amount of work entailed made the headache Cara had been fighting become a throbbing reality. She was about to suggest they wrap things up for the moment when Mrs. Finch said, "And while I am thinking of it, my lady, what do you wish done with those things from that dreadful room? We have been keeping them in the attic, but I do think it is past time we were disposing of them."

Instantly Cara thought of the missing items she'd been searching for since discovering they were missing. "What things?" she demanded, thinking that if the journals had been stuck away in the attic this entire time, she'd kick herself. She'd spent hours searching for the bleeding things.

"Let's see, there was a carpet, very old and quite beyond any hopes of repair, if you want my opinion," the housekeeper began, frowning thoughtfully. "There's also an oddish mirror fashioned out of black glass, some chairs, and a tapestry covered with all sorts of heathenish symbols. Not at all the sort of thing one would wish to hang in a *proper* household." She emphasized the word with a twitch of her nose.

A sharp pang of disappointment tore through Cara. "Was there anything else? she asked, mentally crossing her fingers.

"Just some tables and a ghastly desk," the housekeeper said, shrugging. "We cleaned the tables as best we could and placed them about the house. Mr. Mansfield, he was the butler before Mr. Hargraves, took a liking to the desk and had it put in the study off the kitchen. I believe it is still there."

Cara did a mental jig, vowing to search the desk the moment she and the housekeeper finished talking. Then something the other woman said struck her. "What heathenish symbols?" she asked, giving her a puzzled look.

"My lady?" Mrs. Finch glanced up from her book.

"The tapestry," Cara reminded her. "You said it was covered with heathenish symbols. I want to know what kind."

Mrs. Finch's brows wrinkled in thought. "I really cannot say, my lady," she confessed at last. "I only saw it the one time, you know, and then I was so taken aback, I vow I did not know quite what to think. I was all for burning the thing, but Mr. Mansfield reminded me it was his lordship's property to dispose of as he saw fit, and so I had it bundled up and put away. Would you like to see it?"

"Yes, please," Cara answered, fighting to hide her excitement. To the best of her memory the tapestry hadn't been there when Alec rediscovered the room in the future, and she hoped studying it now might eventually lead her to the journals.

Mrs. Finch excused herself, returning almost twenty minutes later accompanied by two footmen carrying a muslin wrapped bundle. Mindful of the need for secrecy, Cara dismissed the curious servants before slowly unrolling the tapestry.

The colors were amazingly bright, and were an intriguing blend of silver, black, and a symphony of blues from a pale shimmering hue to darkest midnight-blue. She easily identified the pentacle and several other satanic devices, as well as some insignias she thought might be Druid in origin. Her flatmate at university had been mad for anything connected to Druidism, and she'd educated herself in their meaning in self-defense.

The symbols were arranged in neat columns, like Japanese, and she was certain they were a code of some sort. But a code for what? she wondered, running her finger down one column and up another. *Were the symbols merely decorative, or were they an incantation of some kind?* She was trying to decide if there was any way she could hope to decipher the code when she saw a symbol set off to one side by itself.

It was woven in black and silver, and something about it was vaguely familiar. A device that looked like a cross between the letter 'I' and the numeral '1,' with a backward 'c' in the center. She'd seen it before, of that she was certain. *But where, and more importantly, when?* Her brows met in a frown as she tried to remember. She was about to give up in frustration when a mental image of a silver watch fob dangling from a waistcoat flashed in her mind.

Damn! she cursed beneath her breath. In the future she and Miranda had debated why the unknown man she'd overheard in Stephen's room that night might have wanted to betray him to the hangman. It couldn't have been for money or for position, Miranda had insisted, because those had evaporated with Stephen's death. But now Cara realized there had been another motive for causing Stephen's death; one of the oldest motives in history. Greed. But not for money. Not for revenge. For power.

Someone had known of the secret room and the time spell it contained, and had schemed and lied to get it. Someone who wore the curious emblem on his watch fob. Someone whom gossip had recently linked to a group of magicians. Someone who was one of Stephen's oldest friends; Sir Aidan Quarry.

Seventeen

"Good afternoon, my lord." Hargraves greeted Stephen with a low bow as he relieved him of his hat and gloves.

"Good afternoon, Hargraves," Stephen returned, running a tired hand through his disheveled hair. He'd spent a long, exhausting afternoon in session, and he was so weary and disgruntled he felt like collapsing on the doorstep. Unfortunately he had a mound of paper waiting in his study, and he wasn't the kind of man to put aside his duties merely because he was tired. He was about to start in that direction when he suddenly thought of Cara.

"Has her ladyship returned?" he asked, trying not to think about how his wife had spent her day. She'd told him last night that she and McNeil would be touring the scenes of the first few murders, and although he hated the thought of her being exposed to such ugliness, he admired her too much to try and stop her.

"Indeed, my lord." The butler replied, his mouth thinning with disapproval. "She arrived home approximately two hours ago. She is in her bedchamber, and left word that she wishes to speak with you at your earliest convenience."

An image of Cara waiting for him in their bed flashed in Stephen's mind, and in a heartbeat his exhaustion vanished.

"Did she?" he asked, his lips curving in a wolfish smile. "In that case, I had best see what she wants." He started toward the stairs, pausing on the first step before turning back to face the hovering butler. "Oh, and Hargraves," he said, his gaze meeting the older man's in silent command, "should we have any callers, they are to be told we are not at home. Is that clear?"

Hargraves proffered another bow. "Quite clear, Lord Harrington," he said, his cultured tones stiffly proper.

Stephen turned back toward the steps, dismissing the butler's priggish attitude from his mind. He supposed he'd have to do something about the situation sooner or later, but at the moment he had more interesting matters to occupy his thoughts. He made his way to the bedchamber he shared with Cara, his pulse picking up when he saw her standing by the window. She was wearing a peignoir of russet silk, and his mouth went dry at the thought of the sweet, creamy flesh covered by the shimmering material. He must have made a noise because she glanced up, a smile of delight lighting her face when she saw him standing there.

"Stephen!" She hurried toward him with outstretched arms. He caught her up easily, taking her mouth in a warm kiss of welcome before drawing back.

"Hargraves said you'd left orders that you wished to see me," he said, grinning as he wrapped his arms around her slender body, "and I was to come up at once with no dawdling."

As he'd expected, her elegant black brows slammed together in a scowl. "He said *what?*" she growled, her eyes flashing with fire. "Why, that lying, pompous twit! I said nothing of the sort! I only said I wished to speak with you!"

He laughed at her aggrieved expression, catching her in another hug and stealing her breath with a lingering kiss. "Perhaps that's what he said, after all, and I interpreted the rest," he said, untying the ribbons on her silk robe with deft fingers. "I rather like the notion of your laying in our bed eagerly awaiting my arrival."

She tipped back her head, giving his searching hands and mouth freer access. "Do you?" she asked, her own hands moving up and down his back with an increasing boldness that delighted him.

"Mmm," he stroked her robe from her shoulders, leaving her body clad in the diaphanous silk. He could see her nipples beneath the soft material, and bent to take one in his mouth.

"Stephen!" she called out his name in a low, urgent voice, her fingers burying themselves in his hair.

He swept her up in his arms, carrying her over to the bed, and joining her in a quick, desperate coupling that left them gasping and sweating in each other's arms. Stephen recovered first, rolling over to pin her against the tousled bedsheets.

"You are so beautiful," he murmured, his gaze moving over her face as he brushed back a strand of hair from her cheeks. "I have only to look at you, and I want you until I am mad with it."

A look he couldn't describe stole into her eyes and was gone. "I know," she said softly, tracing her fingers over the curve of his mouth. "I used to think sex was the most over-rated thing on the face of the planet." Her amber eyes took on a smug sparkle. "Guess I know better now, hm?"

Her words were meant to flatter, instead they inflicted an odd hurt. His feelings for her went far deeper than the physical, and the thought that her own did not was suddenly terrifying. So terrifying, in fact, that he inadvertently tightened his hold on her hair causing her to cry out in protest.

"Ow! Watch it, you poncy sod!" she said, giving his hand a playful slap. "That's my hair, not a bleeding wig!"

He released her at once. "Did I hurt you?" he demanded, his gaze scorching over her as he searched for any sign of injury.

She shook her head with a light laugh. "Of course not," she said, her expression softening. "I was only teasing you."

He laid his head on her breasts, his shoulders slumping as he breathed out a ragged sigh. "I can't bear the thought of anything hurting you," he muttered, turning his head to press a kiss against her throat. "The very possibility makes me insane."

The hands that had been tenderly combing through his hair stilled. There was a long silence, and then she was tilting his head up. Their gazes met, and her somber expression made his heart beat slow and then accelerate with fear.

"Stephen," she began, her voice more hesitant than he'd ever heard it, "there's something I have to tell you . . . two somethings, actually, and I'm not certain how to start."

Telling himself not to panic just yet, Stephen forced himself to speak coolly. "Start with the truth," he advised, steeling himself as if for a blow, "that's always best."

She nibbled on her bottom lip before speaking. "I found something today," she said at last, and some of his fear eased because her gaze met his. If she'd been about to tell him she was returning to her own time, his instincts told him she'd have looked anywhere but at him. "Something very troubling."

"Has it to do with the killer you have been seeking?" he asked, praying that was what had upset her.

"No," she killed his fragile hopes with a shake of her head. "It has to do with Quarry."

Whatever Stephen had been expecting, it wasn't that. "Aidan?" he repeated in disbelief. "What about him?"

"I've reason to believe he's a warlock."

He gaped at her in astonishment. "What?"

"A warlock," she repeated, her expression as resolute as ever. "It's a male witch."

"I understand the term," he interrupted, levering himself off her and glowering down into her face. "I simply cannot believe you would think a man as intelligent as Aidan could possibly involve himself in something so sordid. Has this to do with that silly rumor making the rounds?" he demanded suspiciously. "Good lord, Cara, you know better than to believe such fustian!"

She shoved at his bare shoulder until he shifted off of her, freeing her to roll to her feet. "You're right," she said, as gloriously unaware of her nakedness as a pagan goddess. "I don't believe in listening to rumors. What I believe in is evidence, and I've enough of it to convince me your precious Aidan is into this occult business up to his sweet neck!"

Stephen tried to ignore the affect her nudity was having upon his body. "What evidence are you talking about?" he demanded, his eyes never leaving her as she plucked her robe off the floor and jerked it on.

She froze in the process of tying her ribbons, and then resumed the task, albeit with fingers that weren't quite steady, "Do you recall the day you took me riding in the park and we met Aidan?" she asked, her gaze fastened on her hands.

It took him a few moments to dredge up the memory, and he gave a reluctant nod. "Certainly," he said, wondering what was going through that fertile mind of hers or why she wouldn't look at him.

"Do you also remember I mentioned one of his fobs, a fob that had an emblem on it? I asked him if it was a family emblem and he said no?"

That image was a little longer in coming, but eventually he was able to recall the incident. "Vaguely," he admitted, uneasiness turning to irritation. "But why do you care about that? Quarry's family crest has a hawk with a lion rampant on it."

Her head popped up at that, and she sent him an impatient glare. "I don't give a tinker's damn what his crest looks like," she said bluntly. "That's not the point. The point is, he made the emblem seem meaningless, something made up, even. Then today I found a tapestry that had been discovered in the hidden room; a tapestry covered with satanic symbols. Including," she added meaningfully, "the insignia your friend wears on his fob."

Despite his irritation Stephen felt a decided stirring of unease. He remembered Aidan's interest in the arcane sciences, his admission to belonging to a society that studied the mysterious forces of nature. What if . . . he halted the thought before it could form, angry with himself and angrier still with Cara for making him doubt his oldest friend.

"That proves nothing," he said brusquely, balling up the pillow and stuffing it behind his head. "It is a coincidence, that's all."

She gave him a look that could best be described as pitying. "Is it?" she asked quietly. "There's more. I never told you this because I didn't want to hurt you, but in the past—the past that would have happened if Miranda hadn't come back—it was the testimony of a friend that led to your being convicted. A friend who said he'd seen you with Miranda's blood on your hands."

He was out of the bed like a shot, his nakedness forgotten as he confronted her. "And you think Aidan is capable of this?" he demanded furiously. "Aidan, whom I have known over half my life? You're mad!"

She took a hesitant step toward him. "I know this is difficult for you to accept," she began gently, "but you—"

"Aidan is the closest thing I have to a brother," he interjected, his hands rough as he grabbed her and pulled her against him. "I know him as I know no other man on this earth, and for all his aloofness he is the greatest friend a man could ever want. I refuse to believe him guilty of such a betrayal."

"Besides," he added before she could protest, "what possible motive could he have? He already has a title, and he is far richer than I am even now. Why would he do such a thing?"

"I don't know," she admitted, facing him with quiet bravery. "Perhaps he's not the friend you think him to be, or—or perhaps he wants something you have but won't give him."

"The house." The words slipped out before Stephen could stop them, and Cara gave him a sharp look.

"He wanted to buy this house?"

Stephen did his best to look haughty, although he was badly shaken. "What has that to do with anything?" he demanded crossly.

"Has he?" she pressed.

"Yes, blast it, he has!" he admitted, a greasy feeling of sickness settling in his stomach. Don't let it be true, he prayed silently. Dear God, don't let it be true. He couldn't bear it if he learned his betrayal had been at Aidan's hands.

Cara's hands gently cupped his face, her fingers stroking soothingly over his jaw as she met his gaze. "When?"

Stephen closed his eyes, wearily accepting the comfort of her caress. "Shortly after I inherited it," he admitted, a bitter pain welling up from his very soul. "Then again after . . . after Miranda disappeared."

She considered his answer a long time before replying. "Has he tried to buy it since then?

Stephen remembered their conversation in the club the night he had first met Cara. "The day you arrived he made an offer," he said, and then flashed her a fierce look. "But I rejected it as I had all the others, and he hasn't mentioned it since."

She gave a vague nod, obviously still preoccupied. "Does he know about the secret room?"

He stepped back from her, as if trying to distance himself from the conversation. "No!" he snapped, them prayed it was so. "How could he? I didn't even know of it myself until we discovered it quite by chance."

"I don't know," she conceded, looking thoughtful. "But if it turns out he *does* know that would certainly supply us with motive. And we'll have opportunity as well if he was the one in your bedchamber the night Miranda dis—"

Stephen couldn't bear any more. Cara's relentless questions were slowly tearing him to pieces, and he wanted the inquisition to end. "Stop it!" he snarled, his hands clenching into fists as he glared at her. "I won't stand for any more of this, do you hear me? Aidan is an honorable man. He is my friend. He would never, ever betray me."

"Stephen,"

"No!" he interrupted coldly, stalking over to the large wardrobe and retrieving his dressing gown from inside. "I have already said I won't discuss this any further, and I meant it! Now," he donned the robe before turning to confront her with a look that could have frozen an inferno, "what else is there you wish to discuss? You did say there were two things."

She hesitated again, her eyes wary as she studied him. "I'm not certain I should say anything now," she muttered in an aggrieved tone. "You're upset enough as it is, and the last thing I need is for you to go tearing after Proctor with murder in your eye."

"Proctor?" He stiffened at the mention of his nemesis. "What has that black-hearted whoreson to do with anything?"

She gave a heavy sigh, accepting the inevitable. "You'll probably be hearing about it by tomorrow," she said reluctantly, "but I want you to know it wasn't as bad as it sounds."

A muscle began ticking in his cheek. "What wasn't as bad as it sounds?" he asked, his voice ominously even.

She gave a nervous half-shrug that told him more concisely than words might have done how unpleasant the encounter had really been. "Mr. McNeil and I ran into the bleater at Covent Garden, and he got a bit mouthy."

An anger colder and more powerful than anything he had ever experienced filled Stephen's heart. "Define mouthy," he requested quietly. "Did he insult you?"

Another shrug. "In a way," she admitted, "but it's all right. Mr. McNeil rose gallantly to my defense, and the bloody weasel went slinking off. I doubt if the whole episode took more than ten seconds, so there's no need for you to—"

"What did he call you?" he asked, his mind filled with the image of Proctor's throat beneath his hands.

She sighed, raising her gaze to heaven in a mute plea before meeting his gaze. "The Harrington whore," she said calmly, "but as I said, Mr. McNeil handled the situation. Very few people witnessed the exchange, so there's nothing left to be done."

He gave her a frozen look. "Isn't there?"

"No, there's not," she insisted, grabbing his arm and staying him. "Listen to me. We've avoided scandal so far, but if you go after Proctor then this whole thing will be all over London in a matter of hours. So he called me a whore," she added, impatiently brushing the hair from her eyes. "So what? I've been called far worse, believe me."

He shook her off. "You fail to comprehend the situation, Cara," he said coldly. "You are my wife, *my wife,* and no man insults you with impunity. I warned Proctor to keep a lock on that vicious tongue of his, but he would not listen. That was his mistake, and it will cost him dearly." With that he turned and stalked out of the room, shouting for his valet.

It took two hours of searching, but Stephen was finally able to run Proctor down to earth. Having been denied *entree* to the highest echelon of Society the older man had been forced to make do with far less exalted surroundings, and Stephen discov-

ered him in the taproom of an inn catering to the merchant trade.
He wasted little time with the formalities, striding up to his prey
and knocking the tankard of ale from his hand.

"Harrington! What the devil—" Proctor began indignantly,
only to be silenced by a stinging blow to his face.

"Name your seconds, you bastard!" Stephen snarled, towering
over him. At that moment nothing would have given greater
pleasure than to give Proctor the beating he so richly deserved,
but he managed to control the impulse. The fracas drew the attention of the innkeeper, who came bustling over with a look of
outrage on his swarthy face.

"Here, now, what's all this about?" He demanded, wiping his
hands on his less-than-clean apron. "What right have you to
come in here makin' trouble for this gent, eh?"

Stephen ignored him with lordly indifference, concentrating
the full force of his attention on Proctor. "I have done all that is
possible to avoid a quarrel with you," he said heavily, making
no attempt to hide his contempt, "but you seem determined to
provoke a fight. Very well, you shall have it."

Proctor scrambled to his feet, his actions made ungainly by
drink and temper. His chair clattered to the floor behind him as
he faced Stephen, his face twisted with bitter hatred.

"So, the little strumpet came crying to you, did she?" he
sneered, his eyes narrowing to glittering slits. "And did she tell
you she was with another man when we met? I'll wager not."

Stephen drew a deep breath, trying to think through the red
mists filling his head. "You will not talk of my wife," he warned
in a deadly tone. "You are not fit to speak her name."

Proctor's smile grew even more hateful. "And what will you
do to stop me, my fine lord? Challenge me to a duel?" He threw
back his head with an evil laugh. "That will only work if I accept,
and I'd have to be mad to do that, wouldn't I? You'd put a bullet
through Elias Proctor, and never lose a night's sleep."

Stephen didn't bother denying the obvious. "Are you saying
you refuse to meet my challenge?" he asked, his hands clenching
into impotent fists. This was a possibility he'd been too furious

to consider, but he supposed he shouldn't be surprised. He'd long known the other man was a blustering, bullying coward.

Proctor's eyes gleamed with triumph. "By the rules of your precious world only a *gentleman* may accept a challenge on the field of honor, and you've always made it plain you don't consider me a gentleman. I'm a Cit to you, nothing more, so to the devil with you and your whore of a wife. I'll say as I please, and there's nothing you can do to stop me!"

Stephen didn't stop to think. He reached for Proctor, his fingers closing around the other man's throat. He could feel other hands snatching at him, feel Proctor's struggle and see the panic in his eyes, but he kept squeezing. It took the combined efforts of three men, but they finally succeeding in pulling him from Proctor. The older man collapsed to his knees, his face purpling as he gasped for breath.

"You'll pay for this, you bastard," he said, his eyes wild as he glared up at Stephen. "I'll see you in hell!"

Stephen fought off the hands restraining him, straightening his jacket with an impatient shrug. Anger had faded, leaving him oddly flat. He stared down at the man at his feet, and felt nothing save a cold, pure hatred.

"I will see you there first, Proctor," he said, the threat all the more meaningful as it was delivered with dead calm. "You have provoked me for the last time. If it costs me everything, I will destroy you."

"I beg your pardon, my lady," the footman hovered in the doorway of the study, his expression anxious as he danced from one foot to the other. "But are you at home to callers?"

Cara glanced up from the tapestry she had been studying, irritated at the interruption but not wanting to take it out on the hapless servant. Besides, it could be something important. It had been over three hours since Stephen had stormed out of the house on his macho mission of revenge, and for all she knew this caller could be bringing news of him. Hopefully the obstinate fool hadn't got himself arrested, she thought sourly, laying the magnifying glass she'd been using on to the table beside her.

"Does the caller have a name?" she asked, deciding that unless it was someone with news of Stephen, she'd send them packing.

" 'Tis Sir Aidan, my lady," the footman provided eagerly. "He has asked to speak with his lordship, and says 'tis urgent!"

Quarry! Cara was careful to keep her face expressionless. "I should be delighted to speak with him," she said calmly, wondering what that lying, traitorous son-of-a-bitch could want with Stephen. "Please show him in at once."

The servant withdrew with a grateful bow, and while he was gone she quickly rolled up the tapestry and hid it, not wanting Quarry to see it just yet. She'd barely secured it when he walked in, a look of caution on his handsome face.

"Sir Aidan, how delightful to see you," she drawled, affecting a languid smile as she held out a hand to him. "I am afraid Stephen isn't at home at the moment, but perhaps I might be of assistance to you?"

He stepped forward to accept her hand, his icy gray eyes glittering with that watchful look that reminded her of her brother's intimidating stare. "I am afraid I am rather pressed for time, my lady," he said in tones of cool regret. "I had hoped to speak with Lord Harrington, but as he is not here I am afraid I must be taking my leave."

"What nonsense!" she forced herself to give a pretty laugh. "If Stephen were here the pair of you would be closeted away for hours in his study, and well you know it! Surely you can spare a few minutes for his wife." And she indicated the chair across from her, knowing the conventions of the time would leave him no choice but to accept. "Please will you not be seated?"

As she knew he would, Quarry settled on to the chair. "I have had little opportunity to congratulate you on your marriage to Stephen," he began, his manner as stiff as his posture. "Pray allow me to wish the both of you happy."

"You are too kind, my lord," she replied, feeling the surge of adrenaline she always experienced before beginning an interrogation she knew would end in an arrest. It was a pitting of her skills against those of her opponent's, and she let herself revel in the sensation before ruthlessly tamping it down.

"I am so glad you have called," she continued, purposefully adopting an air of indifference. "I found something rather intriguing tucked away in the attic, and it reminded me of you."

He stiffened imperceptibly. "Indeed?" he asked, but she could see the uneasiness darkening his silver-colored eyes.

"Yes," she said, wishing she'd thought to order some tea. She could have used the ritual of pouring tea to draw out the time between questions, and watch him squirm. It was a procedure she'd learned from one of her inspectors; the more information you wanted, the fewer questions you asked. It drove the suspect balmy, and he'd end telling you far more than you might ever have learned other wise.

He shifted in his chair, crossing one leg over the other as he feigned apathy. "And what is this rather intriguing something you have found? he asked, his bored tones at odds with the intense glitter of his eyes.

In answer she retrieved the tapestry from behind the settee, spreading it out on the Pembroke table as she made idle conversation. "The colors are rather lovely, don't you think?" she asked, when he stood and came over to examine the tapestry. "I was thinking I might hang it in the front hall when it is cleaned. It is very striking."

"It is lovely," he conceded in a tight voice, "but I fail to see why it should remind you of me."

"Oh?" She feigned surprise. "Then you mustn't have seen this," she tapped the emblem with her finger. "Don't you recognize it? It's the same symbol that you wear on your watch fob. A rather interesting coincidence, do you not agree?"

She saw his jaw tighten. "I fail to see why it should be so," he replied in a clipped tone. "The symbol is meaningless."

"Is it? Perhaps that's because you don't recognize the other symbols," she said smoothly, moving in for the kill with practiced skill. "Do you see this oddly-shaped star? It is a pentacle; a sign associated with the worship of the devil. And these other designs, the goat's head and inverted crosses are also Satanic devices. This tapestry was designed for practitioners of the Black Arts," she paused, nailing him with a look that dared him to deny the truth when it was spread out before him. "But you already know that, don't you? You're a warlock."

Eighteen

A charged silence followed Cara's heated accusation, then Aidan's lips curved in a slow smile. "That would depend upon your definition of the term," he drawled. "Am I a disciple of the powers of darkness, no. Am I a believer in the powers of the unknown, yes; decidedly so. Whether that makes me devil or angel is up to you, I would suppose."

His cocky complacency infuriated Cara, but she'd gone toe-to-toe with too many criminals to let her emotions show. Instead she continued regarding him steadily, feigning a coolness she was far from feeling. "What it makes you, sir, is a traitor. A traitor to a decent man foolish enough to call you a friend."

Her goading words had the desired affect. The smug look vanished, and Aidan's eyes narrowed in fury. "I believe we have already had this conversation," he said in freezing accents. "And I refuse to keep defending myself to you."

"Then why don't you trying defending yourself to me instead?"

Both Cara and Aidan turned at the sound of Stephen's voice, and saw him standing in the doorway. For a moment Cara was frozen with shock, but the hollow pain she saw in his eyes broke her paralysis and she hurried to his side.

"Are you all right?" she demanded, laying her hand on his chest and scanning his face for any sign of harm. "You've been gone so long, I was beginning to worry."

He laid a comforting arm about her waist. "No, I am fine,"

he said quietly, his gaze never leaving Aidan. "I did not mean to cause you alarm."

Cara heard the distant note in his voice, and knew he must be hurting. Her gaze strayed to Aidan, and the strained look on his face made it obvious he was similarly affected. She hesitated; torn between her need to keep digging and her desire to spare Stephen any further pain. In the end her instinct to protect Stephen won out, and she turned back to face him.

"I am sure you and Sir Aidan will want to be private," she said quietly, swallowing her pride with considerable difficulty. "I shall be waiting for you upstairs." And she took her leave, hurrying out of the room before she could change her mind.

Stephen watched her close the door behind her. Knowing her pride and fierce tenacity he could only imagine how it must have vexed her to go, and yet she had departed without a murmur of complaint. That she had done so had been for him, of that he was certain, and her unselfish actions touched him deeply. He was trying to think of some appropriate way to show his gratitude when Aidan finally spoke.

"Stephen, before this goes any further I want you to know I have never done anything to cause you harm," he said, his gaze unwavering as it met his. "I don't know why your wife should think otherwise, but she is wrong."

Stephen gazed at the man he knew and loved as a brother, and felt the bitter sting of doubt. Hearing Aidan admit to being a witch shook him, and he wondered that if Aidan could have hidden that from him, what else had he kept secret as well?

"So you are a warlock, as rumor claims," he said, trying for the cool air he had seen Cara displaying. "Why did you deny it when I first asked?"

"Because I am not a warlock," Aidan answered quietly. "A warlock is one who mocks God by worshipping Satan, and who uses the Craft to evil ends. I believe still in God, and I would never misuse the powers I control. I am . . . a wizard, I suppose you would call me. A member of The Brotherhood of Watchers."

Stephen couldn't have been more stunned had Aidan confessed to being a by-blow of the king's and a French agent in the bargain. He stared at the other man for several seconds before managing to find his tongue.

"And what is that?" he asked, wondering how many more shocks he would have to endure before the day was ended.

Aidan was silent a long time before answering. "It is a very ancient, very powerful society whose roots date back to the time of the Templars, and beyond, some say. We regard ourselves as explorers in the truest sense of the word; only the worlds we explore are the unseen realms of the natural and the supernatural."

To buy time Stephen splashed a generous portion of brandy into a glass. While he sipped the potent wine he recalled that Aidan's insatiable curiosity had been one of the things he had most admired about him. He supposed he could understand why he would be drawn to such a group, and the fact he belonged to one didn't necessarily mean he was guilty of conspiring against him, as Cara insisted. Unless he knew of the room and the time spell, he added silently, passing the snifter from one hand to another as he struggled to accept the possibility of Aidan's duplicity.

"Tell me more of this Brotherhood," he said, his gaze holding Aidan's as he took a sip of brandy. "What is their purpose?"

"To gain knowledge," Aidan said, his voice intent. "To us, knowledge is power, and power is sacred. There are forces in the universe that would boggle the pedestrian minds of ordinary men; forces we have controlled for centuries. Heaven and hell, Stephen," he added, his eyes taking on a silver gleam, "and all the wonders in between. They are there to be commanded if one knows how."

Again Stephen's thoughts drifted to the secret room, and his fingers clenched around the fragile glass. "Why did you want to buy this house?" he asked suddenly. "Is it because of the room concealed behind the wall?"

Any hopes he might have held died at the closed look that stole over Aidan's face. "I know of no such room," he said carefully. "There have been rumors, of course, but no proof. And I admit it was the possibility of discovering the room that was most responsible for my offer, but that is all."

Stephen set the glass down, unable to drink another drop. He still had no true evidence Aidan was his enemy, but he knew he could no longer trust him. For the first time since they'd met as lads of ten, Aidan had lied to him.

"I had another encounter with Proctor," he said, deliberately changing the subject. "I fear I may be forced to take action against him."

Aidan looked momentarily non-plussed, but he was quick to follow Stephen's lead. "What sort of action?" he asked, his expression solemn.

Stephen waited a moment before replying. "I have information he has been sailing rather deeply into dun territory," he said, inventing the tale as he continued. "He is, in fact, almost penniless. It would be a simple matter to buy up his debts and use them to force him out of the country . . . or into prison. A rather fitting revenge, don't you agree? It was due to his lies that I was thrown into prison and almost executed. It seems only proper I should repay him in the same coin."

"Most proper, I agree," Aidan said, frowning slightly. "But are you certain of your intelligence? I know the man's pockets are to let, but I had no idea the situation was so serious."

"I've had my man of business investigating the matter since Proctor returned to the city," the ease with which he spun the tale stung Stephen's sense of honor, but he clung to his story. "I am, however, rather puzzled to learn that you should know of it," he added, folding his arms across his chest and regarding Aidan coolly. "I had no idea the matter was common knowledge. Or did you use some of those preternatural powers you mentioned to learn of it?" He was unable to hold back the bitter taunt.

Aidan rose to his feet. "No," he said quietly, "like you I set my man of business to it after Proctor began making a nuisance of himself. That was the reason I stopped to see you. Proctor's position is becoming precarious, and that makes him twice as dangerous as he was before. I thought you should know."

Stephen felt a sharp twinge of guilt at the pain he sensed in the other man's words. The possibility he was making a grave mistake gnawed at him, and for a moment he almost weakened. Then he thought of Cara. If it was just him he would gladly take the chance Aidan was his true and honest friend; but it wasn't just him. He had a wife to think of now, and he would do whatever it took to keep her safe. Even if it meant cutting dead his oldest friend, he concluded with a bleak sigh.

A painful silence descended between them. Aidan took a hesitant step forward, then stopped, a look of resignation on his face. "I will go now," he said, his tone making it obvious he was saying goodbye. "But if you should ever have need of me, Stephen, you have but to send word. I swear by all that I am, I will use all the powers I possess to help you. You have only to ask. Then perhaps you will remember I am your friend."

"What if I was wrong, Cara?" Stephen's voice was filled with anguish as he lay in Cara's arms. "What if we were both wrong?"

Cara's fingers moved gently through his hair, soothing him as best she could. He'd returned from his confrontation with Aidan strained and silent, and after one glance at his taut face she'd canceled the plans they'd made for the evening. She next bullied him into the bath and then into bed, holding him close as he made love to her with an intensity that boarded on desperation. That had been hours ago, and they had lain in the darkness ever since, each wrestling with the painful consequences of their emotion-filled day.

"I don't know," she confessed softly, wishing there was some way she could take his bitter pain on to herself. "I suppose there's no way we can ever really know. But you have to admit the evidence points to his involvement. And he did lie to you about the room," she reminded him reluctantly.

"I know," he said, his hands moving slowly down her bare

arm. "It is just I find it difficult to imagine Aidan conspiring with Proctor. And for what? The house?" He shook his head in disbelief. "Would any man cause the death of another merely to possess a pile of brick and timber? It is almost obscene."

Cara remained silent, lost in memories from the world she'd left behind so many weeks ago. "I'd been a constable for less than four months when I responded to the scene of a knifing," she began in a quiet voice. "It was a homeless woman . . . you'd call her a tramp. She'd been accosted by a mugger, and she wouldn't give up her suitcase. He stabbed her to death. Later when we caught the bastard we recovered the suitcase, and do you know what was inside? A baby doll. A bloody plastic baby doll with a broken head," she blinked back tears similar to those she'd shed that day in the privacy of her room. "I gave up then trying to understand why people do what they do. They just do it."

He pressed a kiss on her forehead before tucking her beneath him. "How harsh a world you sometimes make this future of yours sound," he said, his voice reflective. "And yet . . ."

"And yet?" She pressed, alarmed at the tension she could feel stealing into his body.

"And yet I sometimes cannot help but think you would be safer there than you are here," he concluded quietly. "You have done remarkably well adapting to this time; far better than I should have done were our positions reversed, and I am lost in admiration for you. But you are still a stranger here, a stranger who could be in the most deadly of dangers if anything were to happen to me."

His words filled Cara with terror, and she shifted away from him long enough to light a candle. In its flickering light Stephen looked grimmer than she had ever seen him, and the terror she was feeling doubled as the truth she had been avoiding since long before their marriage slammed into her. She loved him, she realized in disbelief. God help her, she loved him.

"Cara?" Stephen looked alarmed, the sheets pooling to his waist as he sat up. "What is it? You look as if you've seen a ghost!"

She opened her mouth, the words of love she longed to utter trembling on her lips. She even reached for him, her arms sliding easily about his neck, but at the last moment she found she couldn't speak. He'd been through so much today, she decided, pressing her mouth to the pulse beating in his throat; how could she burden him with a love he did not return?

"You've frightened me, that's all," she said, knowing he would press her until she answered. "What do you mean 'should anything happen to you?' You've not challenged that ponce Proctor to a duel, have you?" she drew back and gave him a fierce scowl.

He smiled and ran a finger down the length of her nose. "I have, but the . . . er . . . ponce declined to meet me," he said. "What is a ponce, if I may ask? It is an epithet you use with a great deal of relish, I've noticed."

She bent her head and nipped his chin. "It's the same thing as a pimp," she said, doing her best to hide her love. She wanted the chance to come to terms with her feelings in her own way before deciding what next to do. But in the meanwhile she was determined to learn what he'd meant by that enigmatic remark.

"Well, if it's not fear Proctor will put a bullet through you that's worrying you, then what is?" she asked, striving to appear coolly in control.

His lips twisted in a bitter smile. "The fact he refuses to meet me doesn't mean Proctor won't try to kill me. In fact, it makes it far more likely." His eyes met hers with a sudden seriousness. "I want you to promise me something."

His expression froze her. "What?"

"If I do die, I want you to give me your word you will do your best to return to your own time."

She stared at him in astonishment. "But that's impossible!" she protested weakly. "The journals are gone, and without them there's no way I can access the room."

"I know," he agreed softly, "but something Aidan said about this Brotherhood of Watchers he belongs to leads me to believe he may be able to help you. If anything happens to me, you are to go to him and tell him the truth of what you are."

The mention of the Brotherhood of Watchers stirred a memory, but she brushed it impatiently aside. "Why should I go to Aidan?" she demanded hotly. "He is your enemy!"

He dipped his head in acknowledgment of her protest. "Allow me to rephrase," he replied wryly. "If I'm killed and Aidan is *not* implicated, I want your word you will go to him and tell him who you are. If it is at all possible, I know he will do all that he can to see you safely returned to your own time. And if he cannot, I know he can be counted upon to keep you safe."

His continuing faith in Aidan both touched and angered her. And yet if push did come to shove, she admitted with a grudging sigh, she respected Quarry more than any other man she'd met in this time; with the possible exception of Mr. McNeil. If he was innocent of betraying Stephen, she could think of no one else she would trust with the truth.

"Cara?" Stephen was gazing down at her with worry. "Will you do as I ask? Will you go to Aidan?"

She glanced up at him, her heart so filled with love it literally ached. In that moment she would have done anything he asked of her, and if promising him she would go to Quarry brought him peace, then it was a promise she would gladly make. She reached up a hand to stroke his face.

"I will go to Aidan," she promised, her gaze following the path her fingers took as they moved over his cheeks and down to his jaw. "Now there is something I would ask of you."

He turned his head to nip at her fingers. "What is it, my love?"

"Make love to me," she said, sliding into his arms and giving herself up to the wonder of his touch.

They were up early the following morning. Stephen had urgent business at Parliament, and after refusing Aunt Minn's offer to join her shopping, Cara decided to resume her meeting with Mrs. Finch. She'd ended the interview rather abruptly yesterday, and she was anxious to make amends.

To her relief the housekeeper appeared not to bear any

grudges, and they soon dispensed with the household business. They were sharing a companionable cup of tea when Mrs. Finch gave a startled cry.

"Mercy, my lady! I nearly forgot!" She exclaimed, scrambling to her feet. "One moment, and I shall be back straightaway!" She dashed out of the room, returning a few minutes later with a wooden box held gingerly in her arms.

"Your asking me to fetch you that dreadful tapestry made me remember this, and I thought mayhap you should like to see it," she said, placing the box on the table in front of Cara. "Mind what you touch, that dagger is sharp."

Cara sat her tea cup down carefully, her hands shaking as she reached for the items tossed helter-skelter into the silk-lined box. The obsidian dagger was there, its wavy blade flashing with menace in the pale sunlight streaming through the opened drapes. A small mirror, also of obsidian, and a bag of goatskin lay inside with several other items Cara recognized as having been in the hidden compartment when Alec opened it in the future, and her heart began to pound with hope.

"Where did you find these?" she asked, her voice filled with awe as she picked up the mirror, tracing a finger over the mysterious symbol carved deeply into its handle.

"It's interesting you should ask, my lady," the housekeeper said, looking smug. "They was in that room upstairs, if you can credit such a thing! We should never have known they was ever there, if it hadn't been for Sir Aidan finding them."

Cara dropped the mirror as if it had become super-heated. "Sir Aidan?" she asked carefully. "Do you mean to say he has been in the secret room?"

"Oh my yes, my lady," Mrs. Finch gave an eager nod. "Any number of times. After Lord Harrington was clapped into the Old Bailey, the gentleman came here to search for evidence his lordship was innocent of killing his bride."

"What sort of evidence was he seeking?" Cara asked, hiding her rising fury behind an air of polite interest.

The older woman looked uneasy. "A secret passage, I believe

is what he said," she said, nervously fingering her chatelaine keys. She bit her lip, obviously torn between the desire to protect Stephen and the desire to answer Cara's question. In the end the desire to answer the questions proved stronger, and she leaned forward in a confiding manner.

"You see," she began cautiously, "his lordship came to believe his wife must have gone into the room for something, and was somehow carried off. I'll own at the time I had my doubts. Her ladyship was terrified of the place, and she wouldn't go near it for all the gold in the king's purse. Yet what else could it have been? All the doors were locked and barred from within when we began searching for her. Later one of the footmen mentioned the hidden door was open, but I thought it had been opened by one of the others and thought no more of it."

Cara, who had helped organize numerous searches for missing people, couldn't believe such an obvious clue had been overlooked. "And someone mentioned this to the Quarry?" she asked, forcing herself to concentrate on the matter at hand.

"Yes, my lady," Mrs. Finch said quickly. "That was when he said there must be a secret passage, and that was how her ladyship was carried off."

"And was such a passage found?" Cara asked, even though she already knew the answer.

"No, it was not. Sir Aidan came by several times, God bless him, but he never found a thing. Then one day he called me into the room and showed me those beastly things he'd found hidden in the wall."

"Did you tell his lordship Quarry had been here while he was away?" Cara asked, her heart weeping when she thought of how devastated Stephen would be when she told him.

"No, my lady," Mrs. Finch began, then frowned. "At least, I do not believe I did. After her ladyship returned things were in such a proper tangle, I can't recall what was said and what was not." She bit her lip and gave Cara an uncertain look. "Do-do you think I should mention it now?"

Cara shook her head with a dispirited sigh. "No, I will tell him myself," she said, then paused as she thought once more of the journals. "But tell me, Mrs. Finch, do you recall Quarry saying anything about some books he might have found with these items? Perhaps he may have asked to borrow them?"

"No, your ladyship, he did not," the housekeeper answered with alacrity, and then hesitated. "Although now that you mention it, he did borrow some other books. Greek books, he told me they was, and I remember thinking that was what they must be for they had these queer little scribbles on the covers."

"I see," Cara's shoulders slumped in defeat. "Thank you, Mrs. Finch. You have been most helpful."

Stephen knew something was wrong the moment he walked into his club. He had barely crossed the threshold when a suffocating silence descended upon the room, and everyone in the library turned *en masse* to stare at him. Then just as quickly everyone glanced away, and the conversation level in the normally quiet room rose several octaves. The sensation was so like what he had experienced before and after being charged with Miranda's murder, that he felt a superstitious jolt of fear. He was considering beating a strategic retreat when he saw Gilbert Holloway sitting in front of the fireplace. Gil saw him at the same time and gestured him over, and after a moment's hesitation Stephen started forward; resolutely ignoring the whispers and pointed glances that followed him.

"Well done, old boy," Gil toasted him mockingly. "Now I know how Daniel must have looked being led to the lion's den. You were the very image of British *savoir-faire,* I assure you."

"I am delighted you approve," Stephen muttered, still feeling very much like a specimen in the Royal Menagerie as he settled in one of the club's red leather chairs. "The way everyone was gaping at me, I was beginning to wonder if my valet had put my smallclothes on over my trousers. What the devil is going on?"

"Proctor, of course," Gil answered, draining his snifter of brandy. "Dashed rum business, that."

Although it was more or less what he had been expecting to hear, Stephen was still angry. "Do you mean to say it is already common knowledge?" he demanded in a frustrated tone. "It only happened yesterday!"

Gil gave an indifferent shrug. "You know how Society loves to tattle, and for all he was an encroaching Cit, Proctor was not without his influence. I fear the next few days are going to be rather dicey; especially once the papers get wind of it. You might consider taking your lovely bride and retiring to the country for the next month or so."

Stephen gave him a confused glare. "Why the devil should I be the one to flee like a thief in the night?" he demanded indignantly. "Proctor is the one who insulted Cara, and then refused to meet me when I challenged him. Let him leave."

Gil's eyes widened in shock. "Do you mean you do not know?"

The unease Stephen had felt earlier returned ten-fold. "Know what?" he asked, his senses prickling in alarm.

"Proctor is dead," Gil said quietly, his expression abruptly serious. "He was found murdered last night."

"What?"

"I thought you knew," Gil said, looking apologetic. "The story is all over town. I assumed you would have heard."

Stephen shook his head. "This is the first I have heard of it," he said, a sick feeling of shock stealing over him. He'd hated Proctor with all his might and would have gladly killed him himself for the way he had slandered Cara, but that didn't mean he was pleased to hear of the other man's death. Then he thought of the silence and the whispers that had greeted him upon his arrival, and he sent Gil a horrified look.

"My God," he whispered hoarsely, "do you think *I* had something to do with it?"

"Of course not!" Gil denied, and then added, "But you must own it looks rather odd. You've publicly quarreled with him any number of times, and yesterday you physically attacked him."

"He'd just insulted my wife!" Stephen snapped, tamping down

the cold panic rising in him. "What the hell was I supposed to do? Buy him a tankard of ale?"

"No one blames you," Gil assured him anxiously, his brown eyes earnest. "The man's conduct was beyond the pale! Of course you had to defend your countess, no one disputes that fact."

Stephen began to shake as a horrifying sense of unreality stole over him. It was precisely as it was two years ago, he realized bleakly. The pointed stares, the whispered accusations that became shouted indictments, and the charge of murder that had landed him in the docket fighting for his life. "I didn't do it," he whispered, raising empty eyes to meet Gil's gaze. "Upon my honor, I didn't kill Proctor. I don't even know how he died!"

"His throat was slit," Gil said, looking slightly green. "And there are rumors that he was . . . er . . . mutilated as well."

An image of a blood-soaked room flashed in Stephen's mind, and he shook his head in an effort to drive it out. "How?" he asked rawly, his hands clenching into fists.

"They're saying his tongue was cut out."

"God." Stephen ducked his head, fearing he was about to disgrace himself. He tried to think, but he was unable to move past the horror and fear that was threatening to overwhelm him. He'd barely survived with his honor and his sanity intact last time, and if he was to be accused again . . . He couldn't bear it, he admitted savagely. He simply couldn't bear it.

"Stephen," Gil bent forward and laid a comforting hand on his arm, "I know you didn't kill Proctor; it is too ludicrous to contemplate! But I think you should be prepared to be charged. The authorities have already been nosing about."

Cara! Stephen stumbled to his feet, his panic vanishing as he thought of her. He turned and dashed out of the club, ignoring Gil's cries to come back. St. James Street was crowded with hacks to let, and he was soon in one and headed home through the thick flow of traffic. He used the journey to compose himself, not wishing to alarm Cara by appearing like a Bedlamite. He also decided to put aside his mistrust of Aidan. His friend had promised to use all his powers to help him, and he was determined to take him at his word.

To his relief Cara was at home, and after dismissing Hargraves he went in search of her; discovering her in his study, her dark head bent over a book. He paused in the doorway, drinking in the sight of her with a heart that was overflowing with emotion. As if sensing his presence she suddenly glanced up, her topaz-colored eyes growing wide at the sight of him.

"Stephen!" she cried, setting the book aside and rising gracefully to her feet. "What are you doing home? I thought you would be in session all day."

Stephen stared at her, facing the full depth of his love for her even as he made the silent vow not to speak of it until he was certain he wouldn't be charged with murder. If she even suspected how he felt, he knew she would defy hell itself to remain with him.

"Proctor's been murdered," he said bluntly, deciding it was best to deal the shocking blow as quickly as possible. "The authorities think I did it."

"What?" She paled, and then rushed over to join him. "Stephen, are you certain?"

He touched his hand to her cheek. "Of what?" he asked softly. "That Proctor is dead, or that I stand a good chance of being charged with his murder?"

"Both," she replied, returning his caress while examining his face with worried eyes. "Tell me everything that's happened."

He did his best to oblige her, telling her what he had learned from Gilbert a quarter-hour earlier. She remained silent for several moments, her expression growing thoughtful.

"His tongue was cut out?" she asked at last, sounding more intrigued than sickened. "That's rather odd."

"I thought it was horrifying," he answered, still shuddering at the notion. "Having one's throat slit is a common enough problem in our city but that . . ." He gave her a sharp look as a sudden thought occurred to him. "These murders you are investigating," he began carefully, "did any of the victims . . ."

"Have their tongues cut out?" she interrupted, shaking her head. "No. At least, not that I've been able to learn. But even if they had, I doubt we're talking about the same perpetrator. Proctor doesn't fit the profile of the other victims. He's not female or a prostitute, and I can't see our lad changing targets; he's too fixated."

That she could discuss such things so dispassionately was surprisingly soothing, and he decided to follow suit. "I fear the authorities will not share your certainty," he said, striving to appear calm, "and that bodes ill for me. On the face of it I am the most likely suspect, and I will in all probability be charged. If I am, I want you to do as I ask."

She gave him a suspicious look. "What is that?"

He pressed a kiss against her forehead before answering. "Yesterday you gave me your word to go to Aidan if anything were to happen to me. I am asking you to honor that promise."

"But Stephen . . ."

"No," he drew back to meet her gaze, "hear me out. If I am arrested, I want you to return to your time. Aidan will see to it, if it is at all possible. He has given me his word."

"Aidan!" Her eyes flashed with contempt. "That thieving sneak was the one who took the journals in the first place!" And she proceeded to tell him of Aidan's clandestine search of the house in his absence.

"I'll not deny I would have preferred he asked me rather than simply taking them," he said when she was finished, feeling sadly disappointed at Aidan's treacherous conduct, "but it changes nothing. Aidan is still your best chance for getting home, and I want you to go to him and tell him who you are. Explain to him that the journals and the other artifacts must be returned to the room and then tell him the room is to be walled up. I know he will do it."

She jerked out of his arms, tears showing in her eyes as she confronted him. "You're giving up, aren't you!" she accused furiously. You're going to act the martyr and sacrifice yourself to your noble sense of duty! Well, you can forget it, Harrington, do

you hear me? Because I'm damned if I'll let you trot meekly off
to Tyburn Hill!"

"I'm not giving up," he corrected firmly, "nor do I intend
going meekly to my fate. If I'm charged with Proctor's murder,
I shall fight those charges any way I can. But in order to do that
I want to know," he stopped and drew a deep breath, "I *need* to
know that you'll be safe. I won't be able to cope otherwise."

"But—"

"Cara," he interrupted, silencing her with a gentle kiss, "do
you want to help me?"

"Of course I do, you idiot!" she snapped, dashing at the tears
staining her cheeks. "You must know that I do!"

"Then do this for me," he said, his hands tightening on her
slender shoulders as he met her gaze. "Swear to me you'll go to
Aidan, and have him send you home. Swear it to me, Cara!"

Her eyes closed briefly, and when they opened again he was
stunned at the desolation he saw reflected in their jeweled depths.
"Very well, Stephen," she said, her voice devoid of its usual heat.
"I'll do as you wish."

Nineteen

Despite her pleas that she be allowed to accompany him, Stephen set off alone for Bow Street the following morning. Cara stood at their bedroom window, tears blurring her vision as she watched him climbing into a hack. She loved him so desperately. If anything happened to him, she didn't give a tinker's damn if she made it back to her time or not. What difference would it make? she wondered bleakly, her fingers closing about the velvet drapes as she watched the hack rumble away. Without him, she was just as dead in this time as she was in any other.

She remained at the window until the carriage was out of sight, and then she turned back to begin dressing for the day. With her promise to Stephen uppermost in her mind she had decided to pay Aidan a visit; a prospect she viewed with a decided lack of enthusiasm. Stephen might think the wizard was trustworthy, but she wasn't about to take any chances. Since she was going to tell Aidan the truth about herself, she also decided to tell him everything she knew about the first trial. Let's see him wriggle out of his lies once he was hit with a few hard facts, she mused, her mouth set in determination as she rang for her maid.

Less than an hour later she was standing on the doorsteps of Aidan's house, preparing to do battle with a suspicious manservant who could have given Hargraves lessons in how to be a pompous pain in the arse.

"Perhaps you did not hear me, my good man," she said, her manner imperious as a queen's as she gave the butler a frosty look. "I am the Countess of Harrington, and if you wish to keep the position for which you are so obviously ill-suited, you will inform your employer of my arrival."

The butler's round face turned a dull red, but he remained as unmovable as ever. "I am sorry, my lady, but as I have already informed *you,* Sir Aidan is in his study and he has left strict orders he is not to be disturbed on any account." His dark eyes flicked over her in obvious satisfaction. "However, I will be happy to give him a message, should you care to leave one."

Cara thought of the tazer in her reticule, and was giving serious consideration to using it on him when she suddenly remembered the other item tucked in the purse. She weighed the dangers of losing control of the pentagram against the dangers of returning to the house without achieving her mission, and then shrugged. *What other choice did she have?* She dug into the reticule, extracting the necklace and handing it to the butler.

"This is my message," she said calmly, her gaze commanding as it met his. "Give this to Sir Aidan now, and I promise not to tell him you've kept me cooling my heels on the doorstep for the past quarter-hour."

Whether it was because he recognized the necklace or because her cool confidence had rattled him, the butler relented. "As you wish, your ladyship," he said, bowing as he took a step back from the door. "If you would care to wait in the drawing room, I will see if Sir Aidan is available to callers."

Cara hadn't waited above five minutes when the door to the drawing room opened, and she wasn't in the least surprised when Aidan himself came striding inside. He stopped when he saw her, a muscle in his lean jaw ticking as he held out the pentagram.

"Where did you get this?" he asked in a stilted voice.

Cara gave one last thought to the havoc she could be creating with the delicate fabric of time, and then gave him the answer she had silently rehearsed on the brief carriage ride from Curzon Street. "From Miranda. She was wearing it when she appeared in the secret room in my brother's house."

The mention of a secret room made him jerk, but his manner

remained wary. "Your brother's house?" he repeated, his silver eyes narrowing in speculation. "Which house might that be?"

Cara leaned back in her chair as she delivered the *coupe de grace*. "The house on Curzon Street," she said calmly, smiling when he paled in understanding. "I'm from the future."

He gave her a stunned look, his legs folding up beneath him as he collapsed on the chair facing hers. "My God!" he said weakly, staring at her with a mixture of wonder and delight. "Then it is true! I'll own I was beginning to suspect, but I never . . ." His voice trailed off in obvious amazement.

For a moment Cara wasn't sure what to make of his response. She'd been hoping her confession would throw him into such a state of confusion she'd be able to shock him into admitting his guilt. He was shocked, yes, but he was also surprisingly matter-of-fact. Not certain what she should make of his reaction, she decided to stall for time. "Since you suspected I've travelled through time, am I to take it you've made the same journey?" she asked, striving for a show of polite interest.

He gave a weak nod. "Yes. Travelling through time is a common thing for members of the Brotherhood, but it was always a conveyance we thought reserved for our kind. Unless . . . unless you are a witch?" he asked, casting her a speculative look. "It has long been suspected they have mastered a similar spell."

Cara managed to hide her shock that in Aidan's world, witches were as commonplace as time-travel. She had enough on her plate as it was without going into that, she decided, fiddling with the strings of her reticule. "I'm no witch," she assured him with alacrity. "The blasted time spell sent me back in the same manner it brought Miranda forward to nineteen ninety-five."

Aidan's eyes almost popped from his head. "You are from the year 1995?" he exclaimed. "But that is impossible! No one has ever travelled further in time than eighty years! It is considered too dangerous to break the boundaries of centuries."

Cara thought about the horrifying pain both she and Miranda had suffered, and wondered if breaking the barrier of the century might account for it. According to the journals translated in her time, the passage was supposed to be relatively benign. The journals! She sat forward and glowered at Aidan.

"You've taken the journals, you thieving sot!" she charged furiously, not wasting any more time with pretense. "I want them back at once, do you hear me?"

He absorbed her demand with a look of horror. "You know of the journals?" he asked, his tone scandalized.

"Of course I know of them!" she snapped irritably, not about to back down so much as an inch. "And we have to put them back straightaway, because they have to be there when Alec discovers the room in *1995*. They're what makes it possible for Miranda to travel back again and save Stephen from being hung, which ought to come as quite a disappointment to you . . . Lord Q!" And she hurled the name at him as if it was a dagger.

He looked even more confused. *"Lord* Q? I am Sir Aidan Quarry."

Cara leapt to her feet, refusing to waste any more time listening to his show of innocence. "Don't lie to me, you bloody bastard!" she snarled, her hands clenching into fists. "I know all about how you lied to the authorities, telling them how you'd seen Stephen with Miranda's blood on his hands! You—"

"What the devil are you talking about?" Aidan was also on his feet, glaring at her. "I never said any such thing!"

"Oh yeah, right!" she sneered. "And I suppose you never stopped by Stephen's house on his wedding night to wish him happy, either!"

"As a matter of fact, I did not," Aidan said between clenched teeth. "I left for my country house in Hertfordshire directly after the ceremony, and didn't see Stephen again until after I returned to London upon learning of Miranda's disappearance. I did all that I could to help prove Stephen's innocence. I stood beside him when the world condemned him as a foul murderer."

Cara gave a scornful laugh. "Sure you did. Well, for your information, I read the book about Stephen's trial and execution, and there was no mention of your doing a bloody thing to—" she stopped, remembering Stephen had told her almost the exact same thing; how he would never have survived if it hadn't been for Aidan's faith in him. What the hell . . . she wondered, her brows knitting in mounting confusion.

"What book?" Aidan was still furious. "Upon my word, did I not know you to be a time-traveller, I would take you for a Bedlamite! Your conversation makes less sense than the ravings of the king! I tell you I know nothing of this book, or this Lord Q in Stephen's bedchamber. Why will you not believe me?"

Cara couldn't answer, her brain whirling with possibilities. Miranda's return to the past had canceled out the book's very existence; she knew, because when she went to find it some months later, it had disappeared without a trace. If it could do that, she reasoned, then couldn't everything, including Aidan's involvement, have been altered by Miranda's actions? It made sense, she realized bleakly. It made damned more sense than Aidan's having betrayed a man he professed to admire and respect.

"Lady Harrington?" Aidan was glaring at her. "Did you not hear me? Why do you insist upon believing I would harm Stephen?"

"Because you lied about knowing about the secret room," Cara blurted out the first excuse she could think of. "And because you took the journals without telling Stephen about them."

Aidan had the good grace to flush with shame. "I had to lie," he admitted reluctantly. "To the Brotherhood the time portals are sacred, and never to be discussed with outsiders. To do so can earn the sentence of death; not just for the one who speaks of such things, but to the one who learns of them. Our sect all but perished in the witch hunts, and we learned at a terrible cost the need for secrecy."

Cara nodded, relieved at his explanation. "Is that why you wanted to buy the house?" she asked curiously.

Aidan nodded again. "The original owner of the house, Aylwyn Murrdoc, was a powerful warlock who was lost in the Great Fire. It was suspected he had built a portal, but it could never be proved. When Stephen came into possession of the house it seemed the perfect opportunity to learn the truth of the matter I offered to buy it several times, but Stephen wouldn't hear of selling. After Miranda disappeared I stumbled upon the room and the truth of what had happened to her. Unfortunately, I could tell no one, lest I risk death from my own people or incarceration in an asylum by the rest of society."

His anguished words and the tortured expression on his face convinced Cara of his innocence as nothing else could have done. How awful, she thought, to know the truth that could free an innocent man, but not being able to utter it for fear it would never be believed. Now she understood his fierce devotion to Stephen, and the reason he had found her accusations so painful. Not because they offended his sense of honor, but because he believed them. He blamed himself for not doing more to help Stephen the first time he had stood accused of murder.

"I was making plans to activate the time spell when she returned," he said quietly. "That was why I took the journals; I needed them to access the portal. Naturally I shall return them and the other tokens I . . . er . . . borrowed. All must be as it will be when the room is discovered in your time."

"That's why I came to see you," Cara told him, remembering the reason for her visit. "In case you haven't heard, Proctor's been murdered, and Stephen's the prime suspect."

"What?" He seemed genuinely shocked.

Cara quickly related everything that had happened, including her own encounter with Proctor. He seemed just as furious as Stephen had been, muttering dark imprecations beneath his breath at Proctor's insulting behavior.

"I know without giving the matter further thought that Stephen had naught to do with Proctor's death," he said, his mouth thin with anger. "But I would not blame him for having done so. By God! I should have held the knife for him myself!"

"That seems to be the consensus of opinion," Cara said with a sigh. "Unfortunately that won't do Stephen much good at the moment; he's at Bow Street being questioned. We decided it would be better if he went to them rather than waiting for them to come after him. Luckily for us, this time he has an alibi for the time frame when the murder occurred. Me."

"You were with him?" Aidan looked relieved.

"We were in bed," she said, deciding she could be blunt with Aidan. "I doubt Stephen will tell them that, exactly, but I'm sure they'll get the gist of it. I was with Stephen all night, and I can vouch for the fact he never left the room. I would have noticed; believe me."

To her amusement Aidan did blush when he took her meaning, but he was soon frowning again. "Is Stephen worried he will be arrested? Is that why he sent you here? So that I might look after you in . . . in the event history should repeat itself?"

Cara raised her eyes heavenward. "What is it with you men?" she asked rhetorically. "But yes, that's why I'm here. Stephen wants you to zap me home in case things turn sour."

"Zap you home?" Aidan repeated the unfamiliar phrase. "Do you mean he wishes me to access the portal?"

Cara nodded, repeating her conversation with Stephen. She was telling him about the events leading up to her own journey through time when a sudden realization burst into her mind.

"Wait a minute," she said, mentally calling herself every name she could think of for not having thought of this sooner, "what are we thinking of? *I'm* not the one you ought to be sending back, it's Stephen!"

"Stephen?"

"Yes," Cara gave an excited nod, her mind racing as she made her plans. "In the event he's charged, we can push him into the room and zap him into the future! It's the perfect answer!"

Aidan frowned as he considered the possibility. "But if he fled, that would make it appear as if he was guilty. Stephen would never agree to such a thing."

Cara gave him an annoyed scowl. "Who says we'd give him the chance?" she demanded querulously. "He might not like the idea, but it beats the bloody hell out of hanging for murder!"

"I don't know . . ."

"You could do it, couldn't you?" she leaned forward, her eyes meeting his. "You could send us both back to the future?"

"I suppose it could be done," he agreed slowly, his expression reflective. "Sending two people through a portal at the same time is usually not done as the risk is so great, but if you have come back beyond a century, something considered impossible until now, it is conceivable it could be attempted without danger."

The thought of exposing Stephen to any danger had Cara hastily modifying her plans. "Then just send Stephen," she said, determined not to cry at the thought of never seeing him again. "If you can only send one of us, send him."

Aidan gave her a long look. "You must love him very much," he said quietly, his deep voice filled with respect.

Tears burned her eyes. "I do," she admitted, feeling an incredible sense of relief at speaking the words. "I love him more than I've ever loved anyone or anything."

His expression remained solemn. "Have you told him?"

She shook her head. "I . . . no," she confessed, angry with the tears she seemed helpless to control. "I only admitted it to myself a day or so ago, and then all of this happened. He has so much to worry about just now, I didn't want to burden him."

A soft smile touched Aidan's lips. "Love is never a burden," he informed her gently. "And it might be just the thing Stephen needs to hear at the moment. He loves you too, you know."

Cara paused in wiping her cheeks. "He does?"

"Why do you think he is so determined to send you away?" he asked, his tone making it plain he considered her a blithering idiot for not having guessed this for herself.

She gave a loud sniff, wanting to believe Aidan was right, and yet afraid of what would happen if he was wrong. She'd once believed Paul loved her, only to have that belief shattered along with all of her secret dreams. If she allowed herself to believe Stephen loved her and then learned she was mistaken the pain of it would make the searing pain of passing through time pale in comparison. But if he was right . . . she leapt to her feet.

"Come on," she said, reaching down to grab Aidan's hand. "Let's go."

"Go where?" he asked, although he followed docilely enough.

"To our house, of course," she said, leading him toward the door. "You've a time spell to cast. And after that, we're going to Bow Street. I want to tell my husband I love him."

"And you say you never left your house the whole of last night?" The magistrate drawled, his expression skeptical as he surveyed Stephen. "You can verify this, I trust?"

Stephen's jaw clenched as he fought down his irritation. Since presenting himself at Bow Street some two hours earlier he'd been subjected to an endless round of questions, and his patience was beginning to thin. "I can," he said, keeping his voice even with considerable effort. "My wife was with me the entire night."

"I see," the magistrate's expression didn't alter by so much as a flicker. "And will she swear an oath to this effect?"

"She will," Stephen agreed, hating the necessity of dragging Cara into this mess. He'd have preferred keeping her out of it altogether, but as she had pointed out, she was his only alibi.

"A wife's duty is to her husband," a second justice opined, his attitude just this side of respectful. "Would not your good lady say whatever was required to insure your safety?"

His hint that Cara would lower herself to committing perjury made Stephen's eyes narrow in fury, but he managed to keep his temper in check. "My wife is a lady," he informed the magistrate in a clipped voice, "she does not lie. But even if she was willing to do so, it changes nothing. I did not leave the house the entire night, and that is the truth."

The two men bent their heads together for a whispered conversation, then drew back again. "Let us say you are correct and that you did not leave your house," the first magistrate allowed, inclining his head gravely. "It does not change the fact you were heard threatening the victim on several occasions, and that on the day of his death you challenged him to a duel and then attempted to choke him. How do you explain that?"

"Proctor insulted my wife and my honor on too many occasions to count," Stephen replied coolly, grateful Cara had anticipated the question and instructed him on the best way to answer. "I attempted to handle the matter as a gentleman would, but Proctor refused my challenge. I admit I lost my temper, but were you in my position, would you have acted any differently?"

Another whispered conference. "If you challenged the victim to a duel, then you must have been prepared to kill him," the first magistrate continued, his eyes not quite so cold as before. "Or was it your intention to try for a less mortal shot?"

Stephen debated the wisdom of owning to the truth or lying, and then decided to stick with the truth. "No," he said quietly, "had Proctor accepted I would have done my best to kill him. But," he added before either man could speak, "killing a man in an honest duel is one thing, slitting his throat like he was a cattle at slaughter is another."

"Not to the law," the second magistrate said, his mouth pursed with disapproval. "Duelling is illegal as well you know, and had you shot Proctor you would still have risked being charged."

"I know."

His blunt reply seemed to take both men aback, and they exchanged speaking glances before the first one gave a reluctant sigh. "It does seem unlikely a gentleman such as yourself would have stooped to so despicable an act," he said heavily, "but at the moment you are our strongest suspect. If you did not kill Proctor, then who did? Do you know if the man had other enemies who might have wished him harm?"

Before Stephen could reply the door to the small room was pushed open and Cara walked in, a protesting beadle trailing at her heels.

"I am Lady Harrington," Cara announced, her chin held high as she swept an icy gaze over the two magistrates who stumbled belatedly to their feet. "And unless it is your intention to charge my husband, I demand you release him at once."

"We have no intention of charging your husband, my lady," the first magistrate assured her with a bow. "At least not at this time. However, there are still several questions we need to ask him. If you would care to wait outside—"

"He was with me last night, did he tell you that?" she interrupted, her expression fierce. "We were together the entire time, so there's no way he could have killed Proctor."

"So he has informed us, ma'am," the second magistrate answered, looking less than pleased. "Now, I must insist that you leave. This is an official inquiry."

Cara ignored him. "Is Mr. McNeil about?" she asked," concentrating her attention on the first magistrate. "I know he is not a Runner, but I am sure he will be happy to vouchsafe my husband's character. He was with me when Proctor insulted me."

"Who?" Both men looked puzzled.

"Mr. Thomas McNeil, the member for Dorking," Stephen supplied, fearing Cara's protective instincts would land them both in the gaol. "He is helping in the investigation of those murdered prostitutes, I believe."

"Ah yes," the first magistrate nodded his head in recognition, "I know the gentleman. But I was unaware he was assisting us in that particular inquiry. Perkins?" He turned to his associate.

The other man gave a negligent shrug. "Heard he was poking about," he said indifferently. "Can't say as I've seen him for the past fortnight or so."

Cara looked momentarily non-plussed, and Stephen took advantage of her confusion to beat a hasty retreat. "I believe I have answered all of the questions that I can," he said, giving both magistrates a frosty bow. "If you are not intending to charge me, then I wish to go."

"See here, my lord, you can not just walk out of here—"

"Yes, I can," Stephen cut off the second magistrate's sputtering protest with a cool look, remembering how Cara had instructed him on what she called his civil rights. "However, if it will relieve you, I give you my word not to leave the city until you have cleared me of any suspicion. Is that acceptable?"

It clearly was not, but it was equally clear that neither magistrate was willing to risk jailing a rich and powerful lord with no more than the paltry evidence they possessed. They grudgingly gave Stephen leave to go and he rose to his feet, his expression proud as he regarded them.

"You asked me if I knew if Proctor had any enemies who might wish him ill," he said coolly. "The answer is that almost everyone who knew Proctor wished him ill. The man collected enemies the way other men collect friends, and I very much doubt I'm the only one to have threatened him. However, if I were you, I would start first with the men to whom Proctor owed money. It is my understanding that those who lend money can be most unpleasant if they are not repaid when they desire it. Good day," and he led Cara from the room before they could stop him.

Once out on the street he wasted little time in bundling Cara into the first available hack. When they were safely inside he turned to face her, fully prepared to lecture her for her disobedience. He barely got his mouth open when she threw herself into his arms.

"I love you, Stephen," she announced fervently, her arms twining about his neck. "And if you think I'm going to leave you and go back home, you can bloody well go to hell!"

At first Stephen was too astounded to speak, then he was too busy returning his wife's kisses to care. Every dream he had ever had was coming true, and he willing surrendered himself to the miracle of it.

"Cara, my angel, I love you," he whispered passionately, his mouth taking hers in a kiss of burning passion. All sense of time and place dissolved under the twin suns of love given and love accepted, and it was only when he began brushing kisses across her breasts that Cara pulled out of his embrace.

"Not now, you oaf!" she exclaimed, half-laughing, half-crying as she straightened her gown. "Aidan's waiting at the house to speak with you. I can't arrive looking as if I've been necking in the back seat of a mini!"

For once Stephen had no trouble comprehending her speech,

and his mouth curved in a wolfish smile. "Aidan is a man of the world," he drawled, eyeing her mussed appearance with satisfaction. "I am certain such a sight would not overset his sensibilities for very long."

"What Aidan is is a time-traveller," she replied, rearranging her plumed bonnet with unsteady fingers. "And he has a few things he needs to discuss with us."

Stephen would have sworn that after all he had experienced this day nothing could have stunned him, but the news his life-long friend had passed through time rocked him back on his heels. "But that is impossible!" he protested, struggling to accept the truth. "I have known him since we were lads! He couldn't have come from the future!"

"He didn't," Cara said, abandoning her toilette to press a gentle kiss to his mouth. "He's from your time."

"But—" he began only to be silenced by another kiss.

"Bugger Aidan," Cara said, moving on to his lap with a boldness that delighted him. "I love you! Tell me again that you love me."

He complied gladly, whispering words of love as he kissed and caressed her during the brief ride to Curzon Street.

Aidan was indeed waiting for them, and while Cara dashed upstairs to repair the damage done to her gown during the blissful ride home, Stephen went into the parlor to confront his old friend. The moment he walked in the room, Aidan rose to greet him.

"Stephen, you do not believe I had anything to do with your being arrested last year, do you?" he demanded, cutting to the heart of the matter in his usual blunt manner.

Stephen stared at him a long moment before shutting the door quietly behind him. "To be honest, I have been too busy trying to keep myself from being arrested this year to give the subject much thought," he said, crossing the room to pour three glasses of brandy. "But now that you mention it, no, I do not believe such a thing, and the fact that you are here leads me to believe my wife now feels the same. You have made your peace with her, I take it?" And he offered Aidan a glass with a wry smile.

Aidan accepted the drink, seeming to understand that Stephen was offering him more than a mere glass of spirits. "After a fashion," he drawled, lifting the glass in a mock-salute. "She swore at me and then proceeded to insult my honor in every way you could think of. But once she learned I had travelled through time, she seemed ready enough to give me the benefit of the doubt. A circumstance for which I am most grateful, by the by. Your wife is a most formidable lady."

"I love her," Stephen said, and was amazed to discover he didn't feel the slightest bit foolish at having shared such a private thing with the other man.

"I gathered that much when you sent her to me," Aidan replied quietly. "Although I must own to being a trifle confused. Why would you have done such a thing if you doubted my loyalty?"

Stephen took a thoughtful swallow before answering. "Perhaps because I never truly believed you guilty of such betrayal," he said reflectively. "I will own that on the surface there was a great deal to doubt, but as I have learned, appearances are not always the same thing as guilt."

"You are referring to this business with Proctor?"

"And to Miranda's disappearance," Stephen agreed with a weary sigh. "In both cases I was the most likely suspect, and the first time I nearly swung for it."

Aidan nodded, his silver eyes grim. "I suppose it is too much to hope that devil Proctor passed through time as Miranda did," he commented, and then at Stephen's confused look he added, "Cara explained it to me on our ride over here. She says Miranda is happily married to her brother now. How do you feel about that?"

"Relieved, confused, perhaps a bit angry," Stephen admitted with a shrug. "I did not love Miranda, but I will admit it hurt to learn she was another man's wife."

Aidan accepted his explanation with a nod. "I can see where

such a thing could prove most painful," he said. "All the more so, considering the price you nearly paid."

"Cara told me the reason I was found guilty was because a friend of mine lied at the bar," Stephen said, gazing down into the contents of his snifter. "When Miranda came back she showed me a book from the future detailing the trial. I glanced at it, but at the time I was too stunned to understand a word of what I was reading." His lips twisted bitterly. "I wish I'd read the thing from cover to cover. If I had, I wouldn't be wondering if the man who betrayed me then has betrayed me now."

Aidan stiffened warily. "Are you saying Proctor's death may not have been a simple murder?"

Stephen gave another shrug. The thought had come to him while he had sat in that stuffy little room being interrogated by the two men who looked as if they'd just as lief hang him and be done with it. Cara was vociferous in her insistence he had been "framed," as she called it, and he reasoned that if it had happened once, it could easily have happened again. But the problem was who? And why should they do such a thing to him?

He shared his disturbing doubts with Aidan, and they were discussing possibilities when Cara returned. She went directly to Stephen, kissing him with enough warmth to make the brandy seem tepid in comparison.

"Hi," she said, gazing up at him with luminous eyes.

"Hi," he returned, winding his arms around her narrow waist.

"Shall I take my leave?" Aidan asked, looking amused. "I am beginning to feel sadly *de trop* at the moment."

"No, that's all right," Cara gave Stephen another kiss before stepping back and glancing toward Aidan. "Have you asked him about who was in his room that night?"

"What night?" Stephen's question was all the answer she required, and she turned her attention to him.

"Your wedding night," she said, giving him a reproving look. "Miranda said she heard you speaking with someone, and he was congratulating you for making a good marriage of convenience. Naturally it upset her, and that's why she went into the secret room and ended being sent into the future."

"She heard us?" Stephen was genuinely amazed. "But how could that have been? Gilbert wasn't in my room longer than—" He stopped, a look of anguish twisting his face. "Not Gilbert," he whispered in a guttural voice. "Oh God, not Gilbert."

"Holloway?" Aidan was on his feet at once, his hands clenched in fury. "He is the one who was with you that night?"

Stephen gave a miserable nod, his shoulders slumping as he met Aidan's gaze. "He'd missed the wedding because he'd been in the country dancing attendance on his uncle, remember?" he said, feeling as shattered and hurt as if had been Aidan who had betrayed him so cruelly.

"I was preparing to go to Miranda's room when the footman brought me a note saying Gilbert was below asking to see me. He was one of my oldest friends, and I was touched he'd gone to such trouble. Naturally I invited him up. He even brought us a bottle of wine; a present to celebrate my wedding night, he said," and he closed his eyes as the full weight of Gilbert's perfidy washed over him.

He felt Cara's comforting arms slip about him, holding him in a gentle but protective embrace. "I can't say I'm surprised," she said, stroking his hair with a loving hand. "He always struck me as being a smug little ass. But the book referred to the man who betrayed you as Lord Q. That's why I was so convinced it was you," she added, addressing Aidan.

"I fear you have yet to master the proper way of addressing peers," Stephen replied, managing a bitter laugh. "As a baronet, Aidan would never be referred to as Lord anything."

"Well, yes, but he still has a title," Cara defended herself with a scowl. "I thought Mr. Holloway was a plain old nobody; like me. He's not even an Honorable; is he?"

"No," Aidan said grimly, "but he was in line for his uncle's title; Viscount Quigley. Lord Q. In the past that was altered he must have inherited the old man's title."

A black silence descended on the room, and then Cara turned

her head to give Aidan an apologetic smile. "It looks as if I owe you another apology."

They spent the next half hour in desultory conversation before deciding that Stephen and Aidan would go to Holloway's house the following afternoon and confront him with what they knew. Aidan suggested informing the magistrates of his involvement in the first trial, but Cara quickly squashed the idea.

"Since the past was changed and Holloway was never called to testify we don't have proof he would have perjured himself, and whether or not it would have been done at Proctor's behest," she pointed out, her expression stern. "And in any case, the last thing we want to do is provide the authorities with another motive."

"What do you mean?" Aidan asked, frowning thoughtfully.

"She means that if I tell the magistrates I think Holloway killed Proctor because the two were responsible for having me charged with Miranda's death, they'll decide I had an even greater reason for wanting him dead," Stephen concluded, meeting Cara's gaze. "Is that right?"

Cara nodded. "Motive is usually the most compelling piece of evidence in any murder inquiry, and right now yours is compelling enough. Muddying the waters by bringing in the last trial could work against you. And again, we've no proof Holloway was acting on Proctor's behest."

"Then we'll get the proof," Aidan announced, rising to his feet to take his leave. "Even if we have to beat it out of him."

"Perhaps we needn't go quite that far," Stephen said, a grim coldness settling in his heart. "But one way or another, I will have the truth of what happened."

As it was already fairly late in the day Stephen and Aidan decided to continue the discussion the next morning, and Aidan took his leave a few minutes later. The door had scarce closed behind him before Stephen was sweeping Cara into his arms, carrying her past the gawking servants and up the stairs to their room. By the time he reached his destination she was roaring with laughter; a reaction he found most disconcerting.

He dropped onto the bed with her still in his arms, pinning her beneath him with an expert shift of his body. "You find something amusing, madam?" he growled, looming over her in mock anger.

"Did you see the expression on Hargraves's face?" she chortled, her eyes dancing with delight as she grinned up at him. "He looked like he was about to swoon!"

"Let him," he announced, his nimble fingers making short work of her elegant muslin gown. "He'd best accustom himself to such sights if he wishes to keep his position."

"Do you mean to make a habit of carrying me up stairs?" she asked, her own hands equally agile as she divested him of his neck cloth.

"Only if I can wait that long," he muttered, rearing up to tear off his tight-fitting jacket and elegant shirt. "Otherwise Hargraves may have to tolerate even more licentious behavior."

Her eyes grew lambent with desire. "Will he?" she purred, running her hands across his bared chest. "Good."

The rest of their clothing was dispatched with similar haste, as Stephen gave himself over to the pure joy of making love to his wife. Loving her and knowing that love was returned made each kiss, each caress that much sweeter, and when he slid into her welcoming softness he was unable to keep from crying out.

"I love you!" he exclaimed, his head thrown back as he moved against her with frantic need. "I love you!"

"Stephen!" she gasped, wrapping her slender legs about his hips and moving with him in urgent rhythm. "I love you!"

Her breathless declaration sent him soaring over the edge and he gave one last, harsh cry, shuddering in pleasure as he lost himself in the arms of the woman he loved beyond all time.

Twenty

When she woke late the following morning, Cara was alone. Fighting off the sting of disappointment she gave a jaw-popping yawn, lost in the sweet, hot memories of the previous evening. God, what a night, she thought, her lips curving in a decadent smile as she stretched lazily. Stephen had been an incredible lover. Sensitive and demanding by turns, he'd overpowered her with the words of love he kept whispering as he drove them both to the point of madness and then beyond. Even when they were both too exhausted to move he'd held her close, his lips brushing through her hair in a kiss made all the more powerful for its exquisite gentleness. She was loved, she thought dazedly, she was really loved, and the knowledge made her heart sing.

While enjoying a leisurely breakfast in bed she found herself remembering her life before being zapped back in time. Her work had been everything to her, leaving little room for anything approaching an intimate relationship. She remembered telling herself that it didn't matter, that like sex, love was a greatly over-rated commodity that never quite lived up to the hype. Certainly that had proven to be the case with her and Paul, and she'd assumed that was the way it would always be. How odd, she mused, that it had taken a spin through time to show her how very wrong she could be.

After dressing Cara paused to peek into the secret room. Aidan had recast the time spell while she'd been fetching Stephen, and she was curious to see if it had taken. She'd barely ventured across the threshold before receiving her answer.

"Bloody hell!" she exclaimed, scrambling back from the jolt of raw power. Her skin was tingling as if she'd been sunburned, and her heart was thudding with a healthy dose of fear. This tangible proof the spell was working was both reassuring and frightening, as she realized it meant she now had a way home. She closed the door quietly, wondering how she felt about that.

Downstairs she buried herself in her ledgers, taking quiet satisfaction in the one chore she was allowed to do. She'd always loathed housework of any sort, but since being back in time with a household filled with servants she found herself missing such prosaic tasks as vacuuming and even dusting. She supposed it only proved her mother was right, she thought with a grin. There simply wasn't any pleasing *some* people.

She'd just finished approving the week's menu when one of the maids brought word Mr. McNeil had arrived and was asking to speak with her. The announcement came as welcome news to Cara. She'd been toying with sending him a note on the off-chance he might have information on Proctor's murder, when she realized she didn't know where he lived. This time she'd be careful to get his address, she decided, rising smoothly to her feet and following the maid out of the room.

Mr. McNeil was perched nervously on the edge of the settee, and at Cara's entrance he hopped to his feet. "My lady," he exclaimed, brown eyes anxious as he rushed to her side. "I came as quickly as I heard the news!"

Cara's thoughts flew at once to Stephen and the murder charges hanging over his head. "What news?" she demanded, deciding that if those oafs at Bow Street had charged him she'd sue them within an inch of their miserable lives.

"There's been another prostitute murdered."

The murders! Cara breathed an unconscious sigh of relief, and then was immediately ashamed of her reaction. "When and where?" she asked, shoving her emotions aside and concentrating on the matter at hand.

"The body was only just discovered," he said, his eyes glittering with an excitement Cara hadn't noticed before. It reminded her of the gleam she'd caught in her own eyes when a case was about to explode open, and she felt a flash of empathy.

"Have the authorities been notified?" she asked, wondering what her chances of examining the body would be once Bow Street arrived. Not very good, she'd wager. The two magistrates she'd met yesterday struck her as being as territorial and difficult as any Chief Inspector.

"No!" Mr. McNeil shook his head in answer to her question. "No one else knows! We shall be the first to view the victim!"

No wonder he was so pleased, Cara thought, tamping down her own excitement. An untouched crime scene was a boon every inspector prayed for, and yet . . .

"What do you mean we shall be the first to view the victim?" she asked, frowning as the realization struck her. "If the murder's not yet been reported, how do you know of it?"

He blushed with distress and glanced away. "I bribed the owners of certain . . . er . . . establishments to inform me the moment any of their tenants met an unfortunate end," he confessed. "I suppose it was wrong of me, but I kept remembering how you said we should learn so much more if we were the first upon the scene, rather than last. But if you would prefer, I can have a message sent to Bow Street." He sent her a penitent look.

Bloody hell, now what am I supposed to do? she wondered sourly. As an inspector she knew she'd scream her head off if she learned a civilian—even a talented one—had been the first on a crime scene. It would blow a case clear out of the water, and any evidence discovered would be subsequently declared tainted and dismissed by the magistrates. Or at least, she frowned, that would be the case in the future. Here there were no other inspectors to fuss, and the laws regarding the chain of evidence had yet to be written.

"No, don't," she said, reaching a painful decision. "At least not yet. I want to examine the body first."

"That is what I thought you'd say," he replied, looking relieved. "Shall we go, then? Each second we delay increases the chances the body will be discovered by someone else."

Cara cast a glance down at her elegant gown and decided it would have to do. "Just let me fetch a few things," she told him, starting toward the door. "I'll be right back."

She dashed up the stairs, disregarding the proprieties and the censorious look Hargraves gave her as she flew past him. She grabbed her cloak and bonnet from the wardrobe, pausing long enough to make sure her stun gun was hidden inside her reticule before hurrying out again. She also took a pad of paper and a piece of artist's charcoal from her desk, deciding they were the closest things to a notebook and pen she was likely to find in this benighted time. Hargraves was waiting at the bottom of the stairs when she returned, and when she tried moving past him he stepped directly into her path.

"My lord left strict instructions that my lady was not to leave the house," he intoned, dark eyes frosty as he regarded her down the length of his nose.

"My lord is my husband, not my owner, and so I intend telling him when I return," Cara shot back, too irritated to be politic. "Now get out of my way before I lose my temper."

The long-suffering sigh the butler emitted made it plain he'd expected no other answer. "As you wish, Lady Harrington," he said, bowing coolly. "But might I request that you leave word of your destination? I am sure his lordship would be gratified."

Cara was tempted to tell him to stuff it, but after a moment's consideration she decided the request was not without reason. "Oh, all right," she said crossly, and then returned to the room where Mr. McNeil was waiting.

"My husband wishes me to leave word of where I am going whenever I leave the house," she said, making her way to the small writing desk tucked against the wall. "Where did the murder occur?"

"Number Six Cecil Street," he supplied, albeit with a frown. "But I am sure you must understand the need for complete secrecy. If the authorities should learn of this matter while we are still with the victim . . ." his voice trailed off meaningfully.

"They won't," Cara promised, scratching down the information on a piece of foolscap. "And you may rely on Stephen's complete discretion, I promise you. It's just he tends to worry about me when he doesn't know where I am," she added, hoping her simpering smile would reassure him.

To her surprise he cast her an ardent look. "I understand perfectly, my lady," he said, rising to his feet. "If you were my wife, I should never let you out of my sight!"

His fervent reply caught Cara by surprise, and she realized he had developed a crush on her. The knowledge made her vastly uncomfortable, for while she didn't return his feelings she was rather fond of him, and she hated the idea of hurting him.

After handing the note to Hargraves they hurried outside, and Cara was taken aback to find an elegant coach-and-four waiting for them. It was the same rig he'd used once before, and this time her curiosity was piqued enough for her to comment on it.

"This is a lovely coach, Mr. McNeil," she observed, running her hand across the plush velvet seat. "But isn't it a trifle dear to keep a coach and team in the city?"

"To be sure," he agreed, looking pleased with her interest. "But fortunately I am in the enviable position of not having to worry about such matters. I am, in fact, rather well-heeled."

"Indeed?" Cara replied, hiding her confusion behind a show of interest. Prior to her and Stephen marrying, Aunt Minn had showed her a list composed of England's most eligible bachelors, and she was certain she hadn't seen his name set down.

"It is not something I wish to be common knowledge," he continued with a sneering touch of arrogance. "I've no wish for a bunch of painted trollops to fawn over me for my fortune."

Cara managed a polite response, although she was shocked to the toes of her delicate slippers. She was sorry now she'd even mentioned the bleeding coach, and she made a mental note not to do it again. It was evidently a sore spot with McNeil, bringing out aspects of his character she'd just as soon not see.

The rest of the journey passed in silence, and while McNeil gazed out the window at the passing traffic, Cara silently steeled herself for what awaited her at Number Six Cecil Street. She'd been at the scene of dozens of homicides, and she survived the horror by pretending that the victims were nothing more than a big doll or a tailor's dummy. No matter how pitiful the victim looked or how brutally they'd been slain, she wouldn't let herself believe they'd once been someone's little boy or little girl. If she'd allowed herself to accept that she would have gone quietly mad, and so she played her little game; keeping her emotions locked tightly inside and doing what had to be done.

Thinking of controlling her own reactions made her remember how McNeil had thrown up at the last scene when she'd mentioned the possibility of the killer taking trophies. The memory made her hesitate, and she raised her head to study him.

"Perhaps I should be the first through the door," she began, trying to phrase her suggestion so as not to ruffle his ego. "I'm used to such sights, and—"

"Oh, you needn't worry on my account!" he interrupted with a quick smile. "I have myself well in hand, I promise you."

Cara wasn't sure what to make of his jaunty reply. He was acting very strangely, although she supposed it was probably just for show. She'd seen officers cracking off-colored jokes over the bodies they'd pulled from the Thames, and then go back to HQ and toss their biscuits at the sight of a bit of underdone lamb. Braggadocio was an odd thing, she mused, and she'd given up trying to make any sense of it a long time ago.

Cecil Street was located near the docks in a part of London that even in her day was a bleak and depressing place. She stepped down from the coach, swallowing her nausea as she gazed up at the dilapidated structure that barely passed as a house.

"Front or rear?" she asked, donning her role of a police officer.

"In the rear, on the ground floor," he answered, whistling as he extracted a rusty key from his pocket and holding it up for her inspection. "I made certain to tell the landlord the room was to be completely secured, and so he sent me the key along with the news," he said, in the manner of one bestowing a rare treat. "Aren't you pleased?"

Cara shivered, feeling a cold trickle of unease. Maybe McNeil was becoming hysterical, she worried. Certainly he wasn't behaving in anything approaching a rational manner. One would think he was about to take her to the Pier at Brighton for a spin on the rides rather than getting ready to unlock a murder scene, she thought in mounting agitation.

"Are you certain you wouldn't rather wait here?" she asked, deciding to hell with diplomacy. "It's bound to be a bloody mess, and if you screech or swoon they might send for the watch."

"I shan't screech," he promised, starting up the crumbling brick steps. "And as for sending for the watch, I shouldn't think they would dare. I own the building, you know. In we go," and he pushed open the front door, leaving Cara no choice but to follow.

"Money. You sold me out for money," Stephen said, staring down at Gilbert with weary disgust. Up until the moment he and Aidan had confronted him he'd wanted to believe his friend was innocent, but Gilbert hadn't even bothered denying the charges. Indeed, he revelled in owning to them.

"You needn't act like I'm Judas, old boy," Gilbert said, his brown eyes sparkling with malicious pleasure. "He sold our Lord for a mere handful of silver. You'll be gratified to know you fetched a much higher price; ten thousand pounds, to be exact."

"But if you were so desperate for money why the devil didn't you come to me?" Stephen demanded, his hands clenching into fists as the pain in his chest threatened to explode. "You were my friend, Gilbert. How could you have lied to see me hang?"

Gilbert shrugged indolently, a faintly bored expression touching his boyish features. "You were becoming tiresome," he said in a petulant tone. "Always prattling on about your honor and your duty even while you were three steps from debtor's prison. I used to laugh at you, you know, for being so pathetically gullible and noble. I couldn't wait to see you humiliated the way I was humiliated because I was poor and untitled, but then Proctor made you his devil's bargain and it seemed as if you would triumph at last.

"You ought not have tried to cheat the bastard, Stephen," he added, his lips curving in a hateful sneer. "Only look at the trouble you might have saved yourself."

"I never tried cheating him," Stephen denied quietly, his feelings of anger and betrayal giving way to a blessed numbness. "I merely objected to signing the papers on the church steps. If he'd come 'round to the house a few days later as I suggested, I would have signed whatever papers he wished."

"Do you know that is what I told him," Gilbert informed him with a mocking drawl. "But the tiresome fellow was so certain you had cozened him, there was no convincing him. Then when your bride turned up missing so providently, he saw his main chance and took it."

"But how did you become involved?" Aidan asked, his cold voice making his disgust plain. "Had Proctor discovered you had been in Stephen's room that night?"

"No, although he couldn't have been more delighted when I told him," Gilbert told him. "He came to visit me at Quigley Hall with a portmanteau stuffed with bank notes; all mine, he said in return for a *small* consideration. As my uncle was taking an unconscionable time dying and my cousin's health was uncertain, I was at my wit's end. I had several debts that were becoming pressing, I fear I had no other choice, but to agree to assist him. Sorry, old fellow," and he cast Stephen a taunting smile.

In response Stephen gave him a contemptuous look. "I suppose I should call you out," he said coldly. "But the plain truth is you're not worth the price of the bullet."

Rather than being cowed Gilbert appeared amused by Stephen's cutting words. "Were I you, my lord, I should be careful in uttering such threats. The last man you challenged turned up dead, and I should hate to see you charged with two murders."

His hateful words broke the cage of ice Stephen had built around his emotions, and he reached down and grabbed the other man by the lapels; hauling him to his feet and shaking him soundly. "What the devil is that supposed to mean?" he demanded, his eyes narrowing as his fingers tightened about the elegant cloth. "What do you know of Proctor's death? Did you kill him?"

"Me?" Gilbert gave a wry laugh, not even attempting to free himself from Stephen's hold. "Don't be absurd, Harrington. I should never do anything so strenuous; especially as there was to profit in it for me. Like as not the fool angered the wrong person and got his throat slit for his impudence. However, if it is any consolation, I am convinced you had nothing to do with his death, and so I told Bow Street when they came sniffing about."

"You have been interviewed by Bow Street?" This from Aidan, who looked as if he'd like nothing more than to help Stephen choke the very life from him.

"Several times," Gilbert replied, prying Stephen's fingers from his coat and stepping back. "And then this morning that tiresome Thomas McNeil called to see me. He claimed to be working for the Runners, but I take leave to doubt it. I mentioned his name to one of the magistrates, and they said they knew naught of him."

A cold droplet of unease trickled down Stephen's spine at the artless confession. Yesterday the magistrate's questioning him had said much the same thing when Cara had asked about McNeil. "Why should McNeil trouble himself with you?" he asked, an odd feeling of dread settling in his stomach.

"I am sure I do not know," Gilbert answered with an affected sigh. "You must know he is madly in love with your beauteous wife, and was doubtlessly hoping to gage his chances of winning her should you be hung for Proctor's murder. But if you are so curious as to his motives, why not ask the gentleman himself? He was bound for your house when he left here."

Stephen jerked his head back in shock. "He was going to my house?" he repeated, wondering why the disclosure should fill him with such disquiet. "Are you certain?"

"I am certain that is what he said," Gilbert answered negli-
gently. "Whether he keeps his word is something I can not vouchsafe; although it seems likely. He said he had a present for her,
and seemed as eager as a schoolboy to give it to her."

Stephen turned toward the door, an overwhelming need to be
with his wife taking precedent over dealing with Gilbert. Halfway there he stopped, his heart heavy as he knew it was better
to end everything here and now. Stifling his impatience he turned
back to face Gilbert.

"You no longer exist," he told him, a cold finality in his voice.
"If you approach me in public I shall cut you dead, and if you
make the mistake of attempting to take revenge against me or
my wife, I shall put a bullet through you. Is that clear?"

Gilbert affected a low bow. "Perfectly clear, my lord," he said,
and when he raised his head Stephen thought he detected a glimmer of regret in his eyes. "And may I say you need have no fear
of me? Vengeance is a commodity only the wealthy can afford,
and since my uncle has decided to bestow his fortune on another
cousin, I fear I haven't a feather left to fly with. Though I shall
have hopes of becoming Lord Q. You caught me as I was packing
to flee the country; a rather trite but necessary response if I'm
to escape my creditors."

Stephen felt a sharp pang, knowing this was probably the last
time he would see his one-time friend in this life. There was so
much he wanted to say, but the words would not come. Instead
he turned his back and walked out. He expected Aidan to follow,
but the other man held back.

"I will be but a moment," he said, his eyes not quite meeting
Stephen's gaze. "I would appreciate it if you would hold the
coach for me."

Stephen gave him a sharp look and then nodded, deciding that
whatever transpired between the two men was none of his affair.
He did spare a moment to hope Aidan didn't kill Gilbert, and
then hurried down to the waiting coach. True to his word, Aidan
joined him within a few minutes.

"I've wanted to do that for more years than I can count," he said, shaking his hand to settle the bones. "God, it felt good."

Stephen smiled, empathizing with Aidan's need to take a more physical revenge against Gilbert. If he hadn't been so concerned about Cara, it would have given him the greatest pleasure to thrash his treacherous friend within an inch of his life.

"I was tempted to cast a spell and give him a case of the pox," Aidan continued, his mouth thinning "But unfortunately the Brotherhood doesn't permit us to use our powers to harm. More's the pity. It is only justice that he should suffer as he has caused you to suffer."

The fact he could accept that his friend possessed such abilities amazed Stephen, but there was no time to dwell on such preternatural matters. Concern for his wife was uppermost in his mind, and after giving his address to the driver he settled back against the squabs to brood over Mr. McNeil and his involvement with Bow Street.

After careful consideration he proceeded to tell Aidan everything he knew of the man's involvement with the horrifying murders, and how Cara had been helping him with her unique knowledge of crime detection. "I wish I knew what the fellow was up to," he concluded with an unhappy sigh. "I've never been comfortable with Cara's being exposed to such danger, but I allowed it because I was certain McNeil would keep her safe. Now I do not know what to think." His raised his eyes and met his friend's gaze. "I'm afraid, Aidan," he confessed rawly. "Something is wrong. I can feel it."

They arrived at Curzon Street a quarter of an hour later, only to learn Cara and McNeil had already left the house. Stephen was about to rip into Hargraves for not following his orders when the butler handed him the note Cara had left. A quick scan of it had Stephen's jaw clenching in anger.

"She's gone to Cecil Court with him," he said, handing the note to Aidan. "There's been another murder."

"I haven't heard anything," Aidan replied, looking equally as troubled. "But perhaps it has only just been discovered."

Deciding he was wasting valuable time Stephen returned to
the street, flagging down a passing hack and ordering the driver
to take Aidan and him to Cecil Court. Whether it was the urgency
in his voice or the gold coin he tossed him, the driver gave no
argument; cracking his whip over his horses's heads and sending
the coach lurching into the thick stream of carriages and wagons
clogging the streets. Stephen tried desperately to relax, but he
could not. A fear stronger than anything he'd ever felt was driving
him on, making him sweat as the carriage made its torturous way
through traffic. *Hurry,* he thought desperately, his hands clenching into fists as he gazed out the window. *Hurry.*

Although she'd been raised an Anglican, Cara had never really
bought into in the concept of hell. Even as a child she'd believed
only in the here and now, and she'd decided somewhat cynically
that like Father Christmas and the Bogeyman, hell was an adult
invention and didn't exist. Glancing about her, Cara hastily re-
vised that long-held conviction. There was a hell, all right, she
realized weakly, and it was obvious she was standing right in the
middle of it.

The walls were so covered with blood it was impossible to
discern their original color, and adding to the horror were the
crude words scrawled above the bed. The distinct backward 'R'
was there, and as Cara had told no one save Stephen, not even
McNeil of its significance, she knew it meant they weren't dealing with a copy cat. A quick glance at the victim also made it
appallingly obvious the killer was a sexual psychopath, and Cara
knew that one glance would remain with her until her dying day.
"What do you think?" McNeil asked, his voice as eager as a
young boy's seeking approval. "Is it what you wanted?"

Cara, who had been busy copying the obscenities written on
the wall on to her sketching paper, glanced up at his question.
"What do you mean is this what I wanted?" she demanded, appalled. "How on earth could you think anyone could possibly

want this?" She waved a hand toward the pathetic remains of the sagging bed.

He paled, his brown eyes going wide. "I . . . I only meant I was hoping you would be pleased," he said, sounding more like a child than a man. "You were so upset you couldn't see the bodies when they were fresh, I thought this would make you happy."

Cara repressed a shudder, and turned back to the wall. "Well, it doesn't," she grumbled, unable to ignore the frantic warning her instincts were screaming at her. It was something he'd said just as they were starting in the building, she remembered, copying down the other words. Something about the other tenants wouldn't call the Watch because the landlord was . . . the piece of chalk snapped between her fingers. She raised her head, her heart hammering in fear as she turned around and found herself staring into the eyes of a monster.

"It's supposed to be like your notes," Mr. McNeil continued, his lips thrusting out in a childish pout. "I worked very, very hard to get everything just the way you wanted."

Oh God! Cara swallowed in horror, fear and a cold feeling of sickness welling up inside her. She beat both back, forcing herself to think like a cop. "You're right," she agreed, shifting away from him. "I didn't see it before, but you're right; it's exactly like my notes. You did a very good job, Mr. McNeil."

He beamed at her stilted praise. "I wanted it perfect," he told her, and she began sweating as she recognized the awful note of reason in his voice. "It's for you. Just as that man was for you. To show you how much I love you."

"That man?" she repeated, and then turned cold as she understood. "Proctor? You killed Proctor?"

The pout became more pronounced. "He called you a whore," he said, folding his arms across his chest and looking mulish. "He dared compare you with one of *them!* I had to kill him; it would have been wrong to let him live. And so I snuck up behind him and slit his throat, just as I did to all the others. Then I cut out his filthy, lying tongue. All for you, my darling mother."

The desire to run was powerful, but her cop's instincts honed by her years on the street were more powerful. She knew if she turned and ran it would break his fantasy, and if that happened she was as good as dead. She had to keep him talking, keep him calm until she could think of a way out.

"Tell me about your mother," she said, setting down the pad and chalk with exaggerated care. "You loved her, didn't you?"

"Mama?" His eyes grew wild. "Why should I love her? She was the whore of Babylon. I told her what my tutor, Mr. Wilscomb, was doing to me, and the nasty, hateful things he made me do to him, and she laughed. She said it was no more than I deserved and to shut up. Then when I threatened to tell Papa, she had me sent away to school where those other boys hurt me, too. I know she told them to do it, because I was a whore's son and that's what happens to whores' sons."

Cara heard the faint note of hysteria edging into his voice and slowly opened her reticule, inching out her tazer with exquisite care. She didn't want to use it, but she didn't want to die, either. She felt it's familiar weight in her hand, and thumbed the switch to the highest setting. The movement caught his interest, and he gave it a panicked glance.

"What is that?"

"It is a vial of smelling salts," she said, thinking quickly. "I am beginning to feel rather ill."

"You are?" he blinked, his brows gathering in a disapproving frown. "But you haven't even looked at my present to you." He gestured toward the bed. "Don't you want to see?"

Cara's control slipped as his meaning became all too clear. "For me?" she repeated, nausea rising in her throat. "You killed that poor woman for *me?*"

He nodded. "You're the only one who saw, the only one who understood my genius," he whispered, his lips curving in a dreamy smile. "I was growing bored before, but you made it exciting. You were so clever, but never clever enough to see the truth. I kept waiting for you to see, but you never did."

"You bastard!" Cara sprang forward, her tazer in her hand.

McNeil gave a scream of pain and terror as the electrical charge tore through him. The jolt downed him and Cara fought the urge to keep pressing the wires against him; sending shock after shock through his body. For the first time in her life she wanted to kill a man, and the realization sickened her almost as much as had McNeil's insane declaration. She stumbled to her feet, and was halfway to the door when it flew open and Stephen and Sir Aidan came running into the room.

"Cara!" Stephen caught her in his arms, holding her close as Aidan rushed for Mr. McNeil. "Are you all right?"

"It was him," she mumbled, clinging to Stephen's coat as reaction set in. "It was him all along."

Stephen's arms tightened about her, and she heard his shocked gasp as he saw the pitiful form on the bed. "Oh my God!"

Cara opened her mouth to suggest they send for the authorities when she heard Aidan give a sharp cry. She and Stephen turned in tandem and saw Aidan stumbling back from McNeil, bright red blood spurting from his arm. McNeil stumbled to his feet, a dripping knife in his hands and utter madness in his eyes.

"You lied," he accused in that high, childish voice she was beginning to recognize. "You said you understood, but you never did. You lied!"

Terror for Stephen almost swamped Cara's senses, especially since he seemed determined to keep himself between her and the madman. She wouldn't lose him, she thought determinedly, even if it meant her own life, she wouldn't let Stephen die.

"Put down the knife, McNeil," Stephen ordered, his voice was as cool and deadly as the pistol he produced from his pocket and leveled at the other man's chest. "You can't hope to get out of this room alive."

McNeil turned his head until his gaze caught Cara's, and in that moment she saw the toll his insanity had taken on him. "For you," he whispered in a broken voice, raising the knife high and starting forward. "All for you."

"Stop!" Stephen shouted, but even as he was cocking his pistol Aidan managed to draw and fire his weapon. Blood blossomed on McNeil's chest as he staggered, but he kept coming leaving Stephen but one option. He took it, ending a madman's life and a city's nightmare with a single shot.

The next few weeks were filled with scandal and its aftermath. The news that McNeil was the brutal murderer of eight women sent waves of horror rippling through the *ton,* all but overshadowing the whispers of Gil's flight to the continent to avoid his creditors. With Cara's testimony that McNeil had also admitted to killing Proctor, Stephen was completely cleared by the authorities of having any involvement in the case; a circumstance that relieved him more than he cared to admit. With the threat of gaol no longer hanging over his head he was able to turn his energies to helping Cara deal with the horror of what she had seen in that dank little room.

Three weeks after rescuing Cara Stephen awoke with the disquieting sense of something being terribly wrong. Cara was sleeping soundly in his arms, and after making certain she was safe he rose from their bed and tip-toed quietly out into the hall. He decided he must have heard a housebreaker, and he was starting down the stairs to investigate when an eerie glow caught his eye. He turned his head, terror washing over him at the sight of the glowing light spilling out of the hidden room.

He stared at the opened door, his one thought to take Cara as far from the room and its power as possible. But even as he began formulating desperate plans he realized he couldn't do it. If the room was glowing it meant the time portal was accessible, and if he took her away he could be denying her her only chance to return to her own time. He loved her more than life itself, he admitted, his eyes burning with pain, and given that love, what other choice did he have? He returned to their room, lighting a candle before bending over her.

"Cara?" He gave her a gentle shake. "Wake up, my darling."

"Go 'way," she grumbled, batting grumpily at his hand. "I'm tired."

He hid a smile at her sharp words, loving her more than ever. "Cara! You have to get up, sweetest, the room is glowing."

As he expected her eyes flew open at the news, and she came instantly awake. "What? Are you sure?"

He nodded miserably, his gaze devouring her face as he committed each beloved feature to memory. "It is time for you to go," he said, and unable to help himself, leaned forward to press a soft kiss on her lips.

She returned it automatically then pushed him back, her brows gathering in an impatient glare. "Go where?" she demanded, and then her glare deepened. "Do you mean go back?"

He gave another nod, his gaze holding hers as he cupped her face between his palms. "You told me you loved me," he said quietly, forcing himself to speak rationally. "But you did not come to this time of your own volition, and knowing that, how can I ever be certain this is really what you would want had you any choice in the matter? I don't know why the portal is working or if it will ever work again, but I don't believe we should risk it. This may well be your only chance to return to your home, Cara, and I want you to take it."

She gazed up at him, her eyes softening as understanding dawned. "Is that what this is all about?" she asked, looping her arms about his neck. "Don't be an ass, Stephen. Aidan recast that spell weeks ago; I could have left any time I wanted to."

"What?" He pulled back in shock.

She hesitated for a moment before responding. "I wanted the bleeding thing ready in case those idiots at Bow Street tried arresting you," she confessed gruffly. "It's glowed twice before this, but I didn't tell you."

Stephen felt as if he'd been stunned by the amazing device she'd used on McNeil back in that chamber of horrors. The weapon was now in Aidan's possession, and he'd promised Stephen and Cara he would dispose of it when it was safe. "What do you mean you didn't tell me?" he asked, dismissing the gun with an angry shake of his head. "Why should you do such a thing?"

She blinked back tears, her hands burying themselves in his hair as she met his troubled gaze. "Because I knew you'd react like this," she said quietly. "I knew you'd want me to go back, if there was any chance I could do so safely."

"I'm not going to say I wasn't tempted," she added before he could speak, "because I was, more than I can tell you. I kept thinking about my world and what was waiting for me, and knew that if I really wanted it, all I had to do was put on the pentagram and walk across that threshold. But then I thought of you," she said, tears shimmering in her magnificent eyes, "and I knew I couldn't go. I love you, Stephen, and there's no way I'd willingly leave you. Unless . . ." her voice trembled with emotion, "unless you want me to."

In answer he buried his face against her throat, pressing frantic kisses against the scented flesh. "Never!" he vowed fervently, his arms closing about her and holding her against him. "I love you, and I would sooner die then send you from me!"

"Then bugger the room!" she exclaimed, half-laughing and half-crying as she returned his kisses. "Let's wall it up like we'd planned, and forget the damned thing! We don't need it."

He kissed her again, his own eyes smarting with tears. "Are you certain?" he implored, scarce believing that the one thing he feared most had happened and he was still holding his wife in his arms. "I could never live with myself if I ever thought you regretted your decision."

"I'm certain," she promised softly. "I'll always grieve for my family, and I'll probably grouse about all the modern conveniences I'm giving up by remaining here, but I'm certain." She took his hand and placed it on her belly. *"We're* certain."

"We . . ." he swallowed uncomfortably, his gaze dropping to her stomach. "You are with child?"

She nodded, her gaze so brilliant it made the breath catch in his throat. He bent his head and pressed a kiss to her still-flat stomach, loving her so much his heart threatened to burst with the force of his happiness.

"You spoke of your family," he said after a few minutes, holding her close. "Wouldn't you like to go back just long enough to tell them what happened to you?"

She gave a decisive shake of her head. "I don't want to risk the baby," she said. "And in any case, I thought I'd let Aidan do it for me. He's been asking me all sorts of questions about the latter part of the twentieth century, so I shouldn't be surprised if he doesn't decide to pop back there to say hallo. I shall have to give him a note for Alec, though," she added with a frown. "Knowing that bloody-minded brother of mine he's likely to hit first and ask questions later."

Stephen thought of the hard-faced man he'd seen in the images of the future, and gave a quiet laugh. "I think he should find himself evenly matched when it comes to Aidan." Then he sobered again. "Are you positive this is where you want to be?" he asked, desperate for reassurance.

She kissed him. "Do you love me?"

"With all my soul," he assured her ardently, his hands moving over her body as he sought to show her his love.

"There. I'm positive," she replied, slipping his robe from his shoulders. "Now stop talking, you bloody damn man, and make love to me!"

Stephen threw back his head and laughed, the last of his doubts fading. "As you wish, my lady," he said, moving over her and pressing her against the bedsheets. He began kissing her, sealing their marriage with his body and his heart as the door to the secret room swung shut; the power of time vanquished by the more potent force of love.

ZEBRA REGENCIES
ARE
THE TALK OF THE TON!

A REFORMED RAKE (4499, $3.99)
by Jeanne Savery

After governess Harriet Cole helped her young charge flee to France—and the designs of a despicable suitor, more trouble soon arrived in the person of a London rake. Sir Frederick Carrington insisted on providing safe escort back to England. Harriet deemed Carrington more dangerous than any band of brigands, but secretly relished matching wits with him. But after being taken in his arms for a tender kiss, she found herself wondering—*could* a lady find love with an irresistible rogue?

A SCANDALOUS PROPOSAL (4504, $4.99)
by Teresa DesJardien

After only two weeks into the London season, Lady Pamela Premington has already received her first offer of marriage. If only it hadn't come from the *ton's* most notorious rake, Lord Marchmont. Pamela had already set her sights on the distinguished Lieutenant Penford, who had the heroism and honor that made him the ideal match. Now she had to keep from falling under the spell of the seductive Lord so she could pursue the man more worthy of her love. Or was he?

A LADY'S CHAMPION (4535, $3.99)
by Janice Bennett

Miss Daphne, art mistress of the Selwood Academy for Young Ladies, greeted the notion of ghosts haunting the academy with skepticism. However, to avoid rumors frightening off students, she found herself turning to Mr. Adrian Carstairs, sent by her uncle to be her "protector" against the "ghosts." Although, Daphne would accept no interference in her life, she *would* accept aid in exposing any spectral spirits. What she never expected was for Adrian to expose the secret wishes of her hidden heart . . .

CHARITY'S GAMBIT (4537, $3.99)
by Marcy Stewart

Charity Abercrombie reluctantly embarks on a London season in hopes of making a suitable match. However she cannot forget the mysterious Dominic Castille—and the kiss they shared—when he fell from a tree as she strolled through the woods. Charity does not know that the dark and dashing captain harbors a dangerous secret that will ensnare them both in its web—leaving Charity to risk certain ruin and losing the man she so passionately loves . . .

Available wherever paperbacks are sold, or order direct from the Publisher. Send cover price plus 50¢ per copy for mailing and handling to Penguin USA, P.O. Box 999, c/o Dept. 17109, Bergenfield, NJ 07621. Residents of New York and Tennessee must include sales tax. DO NOT SEND CASH.

ZEBRA'S REGENCY ROMANCES
DAZZLE AND DELIGHT

A BEGUILING INTRIGUE   (4441, $3.99)
by Olivia Sumner

Pretty as a picture Justine Riggs cared nothing for propriety. She dressed as a boy, sat on her horse like a jockey, and pondered the stars like a scientist. But when she tried to best the handsome Quenton Fletcher, Marquess of Devon, by proving that she was the better equestrian, he would try to prove Justine's antics were pure folly. The game he had in mind was seduction — never imagining that he might lose his heart in the process!

AN INCONVENIENT ENGAGEMENT   (4442, $3.99)
by Joy Reed

Rebecca Wentworth was furious when she saw her betrothed waltzing with another. So she decides to make him jealous by flirting with the handsomest man at the ball, John Collinwood, Earl of Stanford. The "wicked" nobleman knew exactly what the enticing miss was up to — and he was only too happy to play along. But as Rebecca gazed into his magnificent eyes, her errant fiancé was soon utterly forgotten!

SCANDAL'S LADY   (4472, $3.99)
by Mary Kingsley

Cassandra was shocked to learn that the new Earl of Lynton was her childhood friend, Nicholas St. John. After years at sea and mixed feelings Nicholas had come home to take the family title. And although Cassandra knew her place as a governess, she could not help the thrill that went through her each time he was near. Nicholas was pleased to find that his old friend Cassandra was his new next door neighbor, but after being near her, he wondered if mere friendship would be enough . . .

HIS LORDSHIP'S REWARD   (4473, $3.99)
by Carola Dunn

As the daughter of a seasoned soldier, Fanny Ingram was accustomed to the vagaries of military life and cared not a whit about matters of rank and social standing. So she certainly never foresaw her *tendre* for handsome Viscount Roworth of Kent with whom she was forced to share lodgings, while he carried out his clandestine activities on behalf of the British Army. And though good sense told Roworth to keep his distance, he couldn't stop from taking Fanny in his arms for a kiss that made all hearts equal!

Available wherever paperbacks are sold, or order direct from the Publisher. Send cover price plus 50¢ per copy for mailing and handling to Penguin USA, P.O. Box 999, c/o Dept. 17109, Bergenfield, NJ 07621. Residents of New York and Tennessee must include sales tax. DO NOT SEND CASH.

ELEGANT LOVE STILL FLOURISHES —
Wrap yourself in a Zebra Regency Romance.

A MATCHMAKER'S MATCH   (3783, $3.50/$4.50)
by Nina Porter
To save herself from a loveless marriage, Lady Psyche Veringham pretends to be a bluestocking. Resigned to spinsterhood at twenty-three, Psyche sets her keen mind to snaring a husband for her young charge, Amanda. She sets her cap for long-time bachelor, Justin St. James. This man of the world has had his fill of frothy-headed debutantes and turns the tables on Psyche. Can a bluestocking and a man about town find true love?

FIRES IN THE SNOW   (3809, $3.99/$4.99)
by Janis Laden
Because of an unhappy occurrence, Diana Ruskin knew that a secure marriage was not in her future. She was content to assist her physician father and follow in his footsteps . . . until now. After meeting Adam, Duke of Marchmaine, Diana's precise world is shattered. She would simply have to avoid the temptation of his gentle touch and stunning physique — and by doing so break her own heart!

FIRST SEASON   (3810, $3.50/$4.50)
by Anne Baldwin
When country heiress Laetitia Biddle arrives in London for the Season, she harbors dreams of triumph and applause. Instead, she becomes the laughingstock of drawing rooms and ballrooms, alike. This headstrong miss blames the rakish Lord Wakeford for her miserable debut, and she vows to rise above her many faux pas. Vowing to become an Original, Letty proves that she's more than a match for this eligible, seasoned Lord.

AN UNCOMMON INTRIGUE   (3701, $3.99/$4.99)
by Georgina Devon
Miss Mary Elizabeth Sinclair was rather startled when the British Home Office employed her as a spy. Posing as "Tasha," an exotic fortune-teller, she expected to encounter unforeseen dangers. However, nothing could have prepared her for Lord Eric Stewart, her dashing and infuriating partner. Giving her heart to this haughty rogue would be the most reckless hazard of all.

A MADDENING MINX   (3702, $3.50/$4.50)
by Mary Kingsley
After a curricle accident, Miss Sarah Chadwick is literally thrust into the arms of Philip Thornton. While other women shy away from Thornton's eyepatch and aloof exterior, Sarah finds herself drawn to discover why this man is physically and emotionally scarred.

Available wherever paperbacks are sold, or order direct from the Publisher. Send cover price plus 50¢ per copy for mailing and handling to Penguin USA, P.O. Box 999, c/o Dept. 17109, Bergenfield, NJ 07621. Residents of New York and Tennessee must include sales tax. DO NOT SEND CASH.